AGGIE IN ORBIT

R. C. Thom

Aggie In Orbit
Library of Congress registration number, effective February 4th, 2018
TXu 2-085-206
ISBN for Print 978-1-7321459-7-9
ISBN for E-book 978-7321459-6-2

R.C. Thom
Email: RC@RCThom.com
Web: RCThom.com

Cover art: Rachel C. Thompson
Book Design: Gayle F Hendricks
Line editing and proof reading: Pattie Giordani
For editing services contact Pattie Giordani
at pattiegiordani@gmail.com

E-book price is $3.99 Print book is $12.95

Other books by R.C.Thom:

SOUL HARVEST
print ISBN 978-1-7321459-1-7
e-book ISBN 978-1-7321459-0-0

DRAGON FIRE
print ISBN 978-1-7321459-2-4
e-book ISBN 978-1-7321459-3-1

STALKING KILGORE TROUT
print ISBN 978-1-7321459-4-8
e-book ISBN 978-1-7321459-5-5

INTRODUCTION

This volume is a stand alone follow up to my novel SOUL HARVEST.

In *Soul Harvest* our hero Aggie Piper is a high school senior nerd and outcast living with her hippie parents who are squatting on Aggie's grandfather's abandoned marina near Key West, Florida. Aggie's estranged grandfather, Al Branford, is a defense contractor who back-engineers alien technology for the U.S. government's deep state. Because of Branford's connection with the deep state and the nefarious organization MJ-12, an alien pirate named Karnack kidnaps Aggie's parents in order to force Grandpa Branford into helping Karnack steal the world's life force, which will kill all life on planet Earth. Aggie overcomes her fears, grows up a bit but not all the way, and ventures out to rescue her parents. Aggie saves the day when she sneaks onto the enemy's space shuttle after a difficult adventure and ejects Karnack from his spaceship in the nick of time. In doing so, Aggie saves the world and becomes master of the pirate's fleet. Aggie then goes on to land her new alien mothership on Key West's Sunset Pier, which exposes the alien presence on Earth to the entire world. The deep state, whose motives and activities are back stories integrated into Aggie's tale are enraged, their plans were ruined. Alien disclosure was never meant to happen. Aggie saves the world to find herself in trouble with the powers behind the curtains of secrecy, but she doesn't know it ... yet.

At the end of *Soul Harvest*, the world is on fire with the news of aliens and Aggie is a celebrity in the crosshairs of the deep state. President Jane Albright is doing what she can to protect Aggie form the military industrial complex who will stop at nothing to take Aggie's ships. Aggie won't play ball, but she doesn't yet know the true nature of the game. Here in *Aggie In Orbit* our hero experiences how far the deep state will go to get what it wants.

PRELUDE
August Third 1945 South Pacific

Navy Air Corps Lieutenant Benjamin Franklyn Sanderson was the old man at this Navy Airmen's flight club and he was only twenty-seven. Not many lived long enough to fly as many missions as him. He flew Hellcats from flat tops and later was given a P-38 to fly bomber escort out of forward Navy Air Corps fields. Why they pulled him back to the Marianna Islands had to be for discharge.

This wasn't much of a flight club, just an old faded tent, a bar, tables and bench seats that were made out of empty bomb crates. A variety of worn out girlie calendars with pages missing hung off the three center poles. The floor was sand and the tent's canvas smelled like piss. The place was ass-ugly but recovered booze flowed free. He drank his share yesterday.

There wasn't much chance of getting called out. The Japs were on the run, and the U.S. had taken the entire string of enemy islands. Even where he was now, at the back of the pack on Tinian and out of harm's way, he was in bomber range of the Japanese mainland. The radio played the usual Tokyo Rose propaganda between big band tunes but young Rose wasn't cheerful lately. Ned switched the radio to an Army channel and the press was saying the war could go on and on and millions of lives were at stake but Ben thought that was bull. He was there, he flew over Okinawa and saw the aftermath of the world's greatest fighting force. It was the same island by island. There wasn't much left of the enemy. On his last mission he splashed a kid flying a beat-to-hell Zero. That Nip was just a pimple-faced boy on a suicide run. If that's all they have left, they're finished. The look of fear on that kid's face when Ben strafed him still haunted. He tried drinking it out of his mind last night but gave up, realizing it would never work.

Someone set a glass before him and he almost sucked the Sake down just to get past that kid's face and onto a stiff Scotch. Ned always had some good stuff stashed somewhere. He could get drunk again, he wanted it, but he had a feeling he shouldn't—such feelings kept him alive. He looked at his drink and pushed it away.

"Sanderson, you drinking that, or just reading tea leaves?" Kowalski, that guy never shut up.

He considered his aluminum canteen cup; the wine somebody liberated out of a Jap bunker was cloudy but passable. "Naw, I'm still hung over, here take it." Sanderson handed Kowalski the cup and the younger man downed it. The rest of the short-timers in for liquid breakfast also drained their cups; all for one and one for all.

Someone handed Sanderson an old jelly jar half filled with hot, flat Japanese beer. "That'll take the edge off, LT. It ain't Rheingold, but it's free."

Sitting in here was better than anywhere outside. The entire island smelled of dead bodies; the pits had burned dead Japs day and night for weeks and the stench remained. The war was closing out and everyone knew it even if equipment still poured in. Eleven new B-52s were just delivered with one veteran airplane called the Enola Gay. *What kind of name is that?* Security at the airfield was tighter than a buzzard's ass in a power dive, but nobody stopped the old man when he staggered out onto the flight line yesterday. His P-38 was back from refitting and he wanted to check on it. They put on two new drop tanks and patched the bullet holes and that's about all he saw before an MP chased him out.

His kill rate was high, but he had orders, he was going home. He just had to wait it out. He considered staying in but that depended on a few things. After the South Pacific, life down on the farm wasn't going to cut it. Mary was on the big island and she liked it just fine. If he re-upped maybe they'd let them stay in Honolulu. He had to think about it, ask around and check on the possibilities.

If he stayed in, he was afraid they'd want him back in the states. Command called him a hero, but he wasn't, he just did his job. Brass liked to parade vets around but he didn't want that either, what do they need parades for now? How many war bonds do they have to sell?

The Japs were in retreat. He had six weeks to think about it and by then, he was sure, it'd be over. Stay or leave, he wasn't committing yet. No, Ben figured he'd ride it out, stay low and go home in one piece. His wife wasn't the public display type. All he had to do was not volunteer and not do anything stupid for the next six weeks.

When an Army Air Corps general marched into the officer's club with a stick up his ass, Ben wanted to dive under a table. The bastard walked right up to him like he and the general were old pals.

"Sanderson, they told me I'd find you here." He thrust out a bear paw hand. Ben took it with reservations. Someone should tell the general to cut his fingernails, but Ben wasn't volunteering.

"I need you for a special mission, nothing dangerous, escort duty, special weapon deployment over Japan, it's hush-hush, only the best are invited. This is history, son. One or two big missions and ToJo is finished."

"Sir, I'm scheduled to out process, I'm going home." Ben said. He felt his resolve for leaving the military building steam all morning but patriotism was snapping at his heels all the while. It was hard to say no to big brass even if it was Army.

"Son," The general pulled his shades down, "I've asked your command for the best they got and they are on board. I could pull your discharge, come along voluntarily and you'll go home on time, better yet, after this one mission, I'll push the discharge myself...if that's what you want. You refuse and..." The general splayed his hands out as if to say, oh well. "...stop-loss still stands. The PX is short on officers. One more time son, that's all I'm asking. What'da ya say we win this thing?"

"This'll be my last flight, you're sure?" Ben asked, not convinced. Washington's stop-loss order gave rank the privilege of overriding anyone's timed out hitch. If he refused he'd be have to peel potatoes for the next six weeks and maybe for years to come. *If I go I get home early.* "No more flights?"

"I give you my word."

"Count me in," Sanderson called to the barman, "Ned, break out that Scotch, the general here is thirsty."

At the pre-flight meeting Sanderson learned a few things that were disturbing. First, whatever the bomber group had was mean, real mean—kill one hundred thousand people per unit mean, but they didn't say what the ordinance was, some kind of new cluster bombs? Everything was top secret. They wouldn't say what was what and when he asked he got the same answer every time. "You don't have a need to know."

His P-38 was stripped to the skin, only one 30cal remained. His other guns were gone to save weight, and to gain even more range they added two of the biggest drop tanks he had seen. They added interior tanks where his ordinance should have been. That too was secret. None were to know they tripled the P-38's range, but so what? What good was it with hardly any ammunition on board? The plan was after the drop run like hell, fly out to sea and ditch. There wasn't enough gas to fly home. PT boats were supposed to pick up the escorts.

His cockpit smelled like an ESSO station. One spark and it's all over. He barely made it off the ground when it was time to go and a downdraft made his P-38 wallow in the air like a drunken goose. Nobody was allowed to know how many planes where on the mission, what they carried, and that the bombers had escorts. It was all, as the general said, hush-hush. However, those B-52s weren't warming their engines for nothing.

His bomber group was smaller than usual. The flying formation was spread wider, too. His escort group was less than able—only two fighters for each bomber. Later the press reported only the Enola Gay flew the mission and without escorts. But he understood after the fact why the truth would never be told. Nobody would believe it. Only the Enola Gay returned while the other bombers and escorts were never seen again, as far as anyone knew, his P-38 included.

As the group got closer to the coast the order was given to disperse, thirteen bombers all with secret orders went their separate ways. He was tagged with the bomber Fair Maiden, the other veteran bomber in the group. From his position he saw the Enola Gay's drop results from fifty miles down range.

The Enola Gay was the first to let go and what came up from the ground shocked him to his core: The whole damn city blew up. One bomb, he heard the bombardier say on radio, "One away."

But Sanderson didn't have time to think about it. Out of nowhere and everywhere balls of light came at his team. He thought they were taking flack, but he didn't see any gun flash below, in fact the sky was clear, no flack and no fighters, it was strange. The Japs were helpless until those light balls showed up.

The balls ran right at him and broke off but they weren't shooting. It was chaos; the damn things were all around. He tried to engage as he was lighter with his fuel spent. He dove after one looking for a dog fight. He fired his 30CA. and swore he hit it but it didn't go down. Instead it stopped and went reverse, next thing he knew, it was right next to him. Sanderson reacted and turned out and ran right into another one he didn't even see. Sanderson's wing tip got smashed but Mary's Hope still flew. He worked like a madman to keep her level. Even so occupied he could not help but watch the light-ball show around Fair Maiden intensify.

In a panic, Fair Maiden dropped and turned out. Sanderson watched it fall, it was huge, but it didn't get far. A light ball swooped in with a tight flashlight beam and the bomb broke up into dust.

He jacked his stick to follow the bomber and the Maiden should have been there, but it wasn't. Head on a swivel, he didn't see her anywhere but light balls were swarming like hornets where she should have been.

"You bastards, you killed the Maiden!"

War lust was on him. Reaction told him what to do. All he could see was red. He wanted revenge for the Maiden. A much bigger ball—the size of his airplane—suddenly appeared. He aimed for it. It just hung in the air, maybe it was a dirigible. He couldn't miss. He'd blow his canopy and eject just before hitting, ramming was the plan, but the canopy wasn't charged. It did not blow off. The last thing he saw was his P-38's nose crumpling up like a beer can.

***

Two alien students were cruising around in their private magnetic aircraft. One child was from the planet Moby, the other was of the Tall Gray race who occupied many planets. The students were watching the war. It was class work and not a fun trip. When the anti-nuclear probe alarm went red they decided to go in for a closer look. The Earth people managed to get one off. The Earth wasn't going to get another one to explode that day. MAC probes were busy mopping up the bomb-carrying Earth aircraft and rescuing their crews, so the two students weren't paying close attention to minor details like flying. They had a good overview of the activities, however. They didn't notice the little Earth ship until it crashed into them. Auto defense took care of it.

"Maybe we should go," The Gray kid said.

"We can't, look at that. We have an Earth man caught in our quantum net."

"What do you suggest?" The Gray asked. Moby people were always worried about equipment.

"He is injured, sensors say life threatening. He is unconscious."

"We aren't permitted to do harm, or contact him, this is a quandary." The Gray said.

"We better lose him before he wakes. Then, we'll go home. They'll never know."

"Agreed," The Gray checked his holo feed, "But first, we better put him in re-gen or he'll die. The probes have the rest of them. The Earth crewmen will have their memory wiped and be set down somewhere safe."

"We don't have memory mod, what if he remembers?"

"Give me a break, gosh! How will they know? You don't want demerits, do you?"

There was nothing more to say and they proceeded in such a way that they hoped would not get them into trouble.

***

Sanderson was lying in a hospital bed and he was getting tired of it. He felt fine and it was weeks past his discharge date but they pulled a stop-loss order on him. They said it was because he was still injured but that was bull, they wanted something he didn't have.

The Office of Strategic Services agent sitting next to his bed taking notes was more out of place than the topless local girls repairing fishing nets outside his window. The OSS man with no name wore a black suit and fedora. Sanderson wasn't sure where he was, they would not tell him. It had to be Tahiti, he guessed that's where he had washed up and that was a hell of a long way from Japan.

"So, tell me again," The OSS man said, "What do you remember after the collision?"

What happened in between was a blank, Sanderson didn't have a clue what happened. He'd have lied just to get released but he didn't know what they wanted, they didn't give any hints of what they were after. A dozen different men from suits to uniform asked him the same damn questions every time.

"I was on the beach, white sands, sun on my face when I opened my eyes. I thought I was dreaming. But my legs and feet were wet. My feet were in the water and the bottom of my flight suit was wicking. I sat up and saw the ocean, I wasn't dreaming. But I was weak you know, felt like I got hit by a truck, I figured it had to be a dream so I laid back. As you know I was all bruised up, everything hurt. I must have nodded off. Half awake, I felt like somebody was near so I opened my eyes again and this half-naked Polynesian girl was hanging over me, looking me over. She ran off when I sat up..."

"How did you know her race?" The man pushed back his fedora.

"You think I'm stupid." Sanderson snapped. "Man, I've been around, I know a Southeast Native when I see one."

"I see," the man in black didn't react to Sanderson's outburst. The OSS man flipped a couple of pages in his note book. He had a notebook like a schoolkid's composition book. A copy of a medical report was in his lap, he spent some time reading that and examining a medical chart.

"When are you going to release me?" Sanderson said. "There's nothing wrong with me."

"That's the problem sailor. You don't recall having surgery? How's your back feel?"

About then the phone rang. It was an army green-drab rotary phone and brand-spanking new. It had just been brought in. Sanderson was told not to touch it. The man looked at his watch and said, "Pick it up, Sanderson."

Ben pulled the phone out of its cradle. Some secretary was on the line and said, "Please hold for the President." Before Sanderson could think of a question the President came on. He had heard the man on the radio so it sounded right, but Sanderson could hardly believe it was him. He missed half of what Truman said but he got the gist of it. The President wanted him for special duty, all hush-hush, promises were made, and rank and money were offered. Sanderson got the message: It was…take the offer and get rich or don't take the job and suffer the consequences. Sanderson had a baby on the way and due any day, he'd have to ask Mary, but Mary wasn't in the loop, she couldn't know what he'd sign on for either way. Ben was a patriotic man and Truman put it in terms of service, service with special benefits.

The President hung up and Sanderson dropped the phone back into its cradle. "They want me for something called Majestic Twelve."

"I know," the OSS man said standing. "You are never to utter those words again, understand?" For the first time this calm individual was mad as hell but he relaxed quickly and retook his chair. "If you accept the position then next stop is Honolulu. Mary is waiting there; you in or not?"

"I'm in," Sanderson said.

The OSS man picked up his papers and stood. "Stay here a few minutes. I'll see to your medical discharge. Gather your things, we're leaving. When the phone rings, pick it up." He walked out.

Ten minutes later the phone rang and he expected orders but what he got came out of the blue…it was Mary.

"Ben, Ben I was so worried. They said you were shot down! They said you were missing in action." She cried and cried.

He cried too. When he finally got his emotions under control he asked her. "Why so emotional, I told you I'd make it, didn't I?"

"I'm sorry; I am so much out of sorts. It must be postpartum blues. They told me about hormones."

"What's that?" Ben asked.

"Oh, they didn't tell you? It's feelings you get after having a baby, that's all."

"Who had a baby…wait a minute, you had the baby!"

Sanderson whooped and hollered so much the Doc rushed in. Ben waved him out with a hand. He and Mary talked an hour and they decided to call her Sarah. After the call and his excitement had worn thin, he had to stop and think:

He could not believe his good luck. He ignored that deep gut warning, the god-damned war was over, wasn't it?

A new job, a new baby, Mary was doing fine; all seemed right in the world. Hitler and ToJo faded like bad memories and he'd get to help keep it that way. Special duty was his ticket to happiness. Had he known what was in store, in the end, he would have preferred peeling potatoes.

The medic came in and said his flight was ready. Sanderson had next to nothing in the new duffle bag they gave him, just a couple of spare uniforms and underwear. So, on a whim, and feeling like he could do no wrong, he snatched the new olive-drab phone off the nightstand and stuffed it into his bag. It was a great souvenir. The best news of his life came by way of that ugly green object. That phone would remain in his possession for the next eighty-seven years.

ONE

Video blog

Aggie and Mel had this idea. She sat down at the computer and began the test. She and Mel had been video blogging for a while and half of them never saw light. That pissed Aggie off. The butt-head Feds removed her blogs at will. They said it was secret information. What about free speech! It didn't help her mood that the wild roosters woke her up so early again. She wished she knew how to make one into fried chicken. Everybody in the Keys treats stupid wild chickens like an endangered species.

"OK, so let's try this." Aggie said to Buddy.

She talked to Buddy the way people talk to dogs; like dogs can actually understand. Yeah, Buddy had the personality of a Labrador. He acted like one, but he was really an alien robot so he did understand a lot of junk. It was weird how Aggie sensed when he was close by. Buddy felt like a real live dog to her, but he wasn't that at all. He was really just a semi-intelligent, flying, metallic, oversized, beach ball.

"Let's see if you can put this out for me, right Buddy."

The two-foot-high ball behind Aggie's computer desk rolled back and forth a certain way, which meant yes. Aggie started the camera and ducked her head so the desktop computer's camera could see Buddy back there next to the old converted bait shack's bedroom door.

"Hey everyone, Buddy's in the house, show the people. Roll over, good boy."

He rolled back and forth with a little spin and lit white, but not too bright. Aggie got back into the camera's view. She had a postage stamp window on screen so she knew where the shot was.

"The Man doesn't want me online. I'm a public relations problem, what a bunch of crap. Some of my blogs didn't take because the Man had a problem with it so they cut my junk off." She looked down at her lap. "OK not that junk, god, what are you thinking. So that's censorship and that's crappy, I'm a free citizen, right. Right Buddy?" She turned to him.

Her probe rocked in a way that made Aggie think of a dog getting tickled. Aggie got up, went to Buddy and pretended to scratch him behind the ear. Of course, he didn't have any.

Everyone knew about Buddy from her press interviews. Her little robot was an internet favorite. Tons of UFO videos past and current were attributed to him. Some might have been Buddy, Buddy used to have to work for that butt-hole pirate Karnack, but most sightings weren't aliens. Some sightings that were aliens were mostly just kids from the moon out joy riding. When Karnack was going around stealing junk he did it quietly. She didn't say it to anyone, but she suspected the Feds let the Galactic Trade Organization aliens milk people for Life Force. No way all those abductions could be from just one raider. Aggie paused the recording.

Aggie was technically free. The President forgave her and Mel for any accidental wrongdoing, like knowing top secret junk like somehow that's a crime while saving the world. All kinds of government goons threatened her but she wouldn't sign the oath they shoved into her face. Also, they didn't believe she told them everything, and she didn't, if she had to do that, she'd tell everyone. But a little at a time, there was a lot of shock to absorb here. Slow and easy wasn't always her policy but now it made sense. She returned to her chair. *This'll get me in deep.* She took in a lungful of air and restarted the recording.

"So, anyway, Praytis said Buddy is a communications probe, OK weird it can't talk, but what he did for Karnack was go around sucking up information like spies tapping phone lines. He'd beam it out to Mother's on-board stores. Info's a commodity for trade, see. Aliens love anthropology."

Aggie clicked and put up a picture of her in Haiti standing next to Mother. Aggie was like a tiny white girl speck standing next to giant beached oil tanker. Mother's skin was kind of snarly, all pitted and discolored. Base ship, or Mother as the ship's AI preferred, was ten stories tall and three-plus football fields long. Aggie had her land on top of a dead coral bank. She was about fifty yards wide on her flat bottom before she arched up round so Mother bridged the coral bank lying on an offshore sandbar and the beach. As she was flat on the top and bottom, Mother didn't roll. Aggie picked the spot that she thought would do the least environmental damage.

"Information is a commodity to aliens. OK, but the big value thing is life force. See how all of you are valuable? Every person's life is meaningful. Anyway, aliens use metals, they need food. They're all human, like us but different. Karnack's shuttle was stuffed with canned food, they have to have people stuff like anyone, but information and ideas are really big. When you know everything about your planet, you'd look at others, right, so social studies are a big deal: Different human races are wired so they like different kinds of stuff for entertainment but Earth TV isn't a big seller although Praytis likes Earth movies, but that's just him."

Aggie put up a picture of her standing next to Praytis on Mother's ramp when they parked hovering above Sunset Pier in Key West at the cruise ship docks. Similar photos were famous the world over. That one was taken by a drunken tourist who was there for the Hemmingway look–alike weekend getaway.

"A lot of people asked what about abductions? Karnack was doing them, stealing LF without asking. But were others doing it? I really don't know. I'll ask and let you know. My guess is yeah, the Man and the GTO aliens probably made some kind of deal, I don't know, but if you look at the history of government and the horrible crap they do, I would not be surprised."

Buddy was back there rocking like a beach ball with attitude. The old pine plank floor squeaked like crazy. Aggie moved her head so the people could see.

"Gosh, he's excitable. One thing I know for sure, the government was talking with aliens for a long, long time and some agencies were shooting them down to recover technology, but I'm not supposed to say that. I got that crap right from Karnack's mouth and he would know."

Buddy's rocking intensified. "Maybe Buddy's got to go out, you want out boy?" Buddy glowed and began to pulse.

"OK, I'll end it here. I'm hoping to get this blog out right past the Man. If y'all get this let me know on tomorrow's live subscribers' chat. See you on Faceplant."

Aggie leaned in and shuttered the camera. She never left it uncovered. The stupid federal cops were always watching her. The NSA can watch you from any phone or TV. Aggie knew too much about the Man from mom and dad's constant reminders, backed with facts, to ever trust the Feds. She wasn't too sure about the President, either.

Buddy rolled outside and flew off. He did that once in a while. She knew he needed to go back to Mother and get charged although she didn't know how she knew it. Maybe he had to get airborne to transmit. Praytis didn't know much about how that works, he's not a techie. She'd pick his brain some more on that later. Praytis wasn't allowed to tell Earth people a lot of stuff, but, a little at a time, Aggie picked alien chestnuts out of Praytis. What good are chestnuts if you don't share them? The aliens have their rules and she's got hers.

Mel's chat window popped up on Aggie's computer. They had to be careful not to give it away, that they communicate regularly. They talked in hints and whispers when they were out together, if the stupid security guy wasn't too close, that's how they mostly made their plans. That's how they also worked out some code words.

"Dude, that telescope my dad gave me is way rad, I'm going to set it up on the widow's peak tonight. I don't have lights so I'll do it like just before sundown." Mel said. "I got that blog, by the way."

"Way cool, I meditate at sundown, so see if you can see me."

Mel laughed, "Dude, that's not what it does and you'd be upside down anyway."

"Great, everybody will see up my dress…Maybe I should put on underwear."

They chatted a while, just normal junk. The message was out. Aliens recorded all Earth communications and Karnack's satellite system was high-end stuff. Of course, that system now belonged to Aggie and she had Praytis program it to zero in on her and alert him when she was online. He knew the code words. Mel would get picked up off her roof, same as before.

Karnack's spy stuff was the kind of junk the Feds wanted from her, but she wasn't about to tell them she had access to all that trick hardware. No way. This was the only way Aggie and Mel could get out at night without a bunch of government butt-holes following them around.

Aggie pulled the computer's cord out of the wall and waited while its internal power died.

"Tibet, here we come." *Unless I change my mind.*

She had the ability to go anywhere in the world and get back before morning bed check. The biggest problem was where to go next.

TWO

Sanderson in D.C.

Admiral Sanderson flew out right after reviewing Piper's latest squelched blog. The Powers weren't happy about Piper's loose lips. Once they got a load of this one, shit's going to fly south. That girl was a little too smart for her britches. She made people think and that was dangerous.

The President had put him in charge of the Piper girl, so he had direct access to whatever he needed, including a supersonic transport. Two hours later he was in Washington sitting in a cafe; it was a nice little place, not a corporate place but more like a hippie place. His flannel shirt and blue jeans fit in nicely. He needed a little time to sit and think with his phone turned off, not that it would make much of a difference. He was called to report in person. The Joint Chiefs weren't about to let him out of their sight.

One thing he would say about the Chiefs, if it wasn't classified, was that none of them trusted the other. In fact, some hated each other. But even in that club Sanderson himself was the least trusted, the most suspect and for good reason. He had zero respect for them and they knew it. It was the flag representing the Constitution he respected and they walked all over it when it suited them and that was too often.

None of them were his senior, not in years, and Sanderson didn't think any of this newer group knew that. To them, he was just a high-ranking freelance. They didn't know he was plucked up out of the Pacific by an alien medevac. Ike knew, the original Majestic working group knew it, but they were all long dead and he'd soon join them if he didn't get a new heart from the aliens.

One hundred and ten years was too long on one lightly modified human heart. Maybe the aliens didn't know regenerating him would slow his aging or give him such a long life or that he would need replacement parts. Maybe they planned it that way just to keep an Earth man on their puppet string. Maybe they played America like a wired mannequin all this time. He flipped the page of his newspaper with a little too much force.

"That bitch is slick." He said, thinking of Pharaoh, the GTO negotiator, or whatever her real role was.

The lady on the sofa across from him said, "Yeah that Albright is a piece of work."

Sanderson lowered his paper and peeked over the top edge and past the lady opposite him. That black limo was still circling the block. His metro dodge couldn't work for long. The tubes are wired of course, so they picked up his trail again pretty fast.

"Fuck 'em, they can wait."

"Yeah I don't get it. What's her hurry anyway? Do you believe she wants to fire so many directors, what if we need them?" The lady said. "It's a witch hunt to dump the Republicans."

Sanderson glared at the women. Middle-aged, Brooks Brothers business suit, flag pin, must be a Republican staffer. Most of the directors were Repugnut hold-overs from the last puppet of power. The Demoscripts were no better. The lady must be responding to the headline on his paper. 'The President Announces Big Shake-Up.'

Sanderson gulped down his black coffee and stood. "They all stink on ice, lady." He wanted to say it but thought better of it; *don't worry lady, if Albright pushes too hard she'll be the next one to go down in flames.*

He walked outside and didn't get three yards when that limo pulled up and stopped in the street. The CIA man in the front passenger seat hurried out and opened the back door. Sanderson had a mind to walk to the Pentagon, knock on the front door like a beggar, it seemed right. He took a few steps past the car, but traffic was stopped, cars were beeping and the CIA man's head was swerving around like he expected a sniper's bullet.

"This way Admiral Sanderson, please." The CIA man said.

"Goddamn it," Sanderson said as he got into the car.

On arriving, Sanderson was led to a conference room and ushered right in. The Chiefs were waiting and the secretary, Brinks, was there. No doubt whatever was said would go straight back to MJ-12.

Without preamble, Sanderson reported on Piper: Still a petulant child, still uncooperative. He was told her parents weren't budging on giving the U.S. access to the big spaceship. In fact, Branford was making waves too—he liked that R&D money and he'd keep it flowing. That ship down in Haiti was a huge space development shortcut and the Pentagon's national defense contractors wanted it bad. Sanderson smelled so many opportunistic rats in the wind it permeated through the room's cigar smoke. Protecting the Constitution was getting harder all the time. The revolving door was spun up like a centrifuge.

"We should just take it," The Army was saying, "Just move in now. We've done it before and worse. We got away with Iraq, why not Haiti?"

"Don't be stupid Bill, the goddamn President's all over this." The Corps said. "Can't go direct; we'll wait until we annex it."

"We can't annex it unless it's approved." Navy shot back.

"We own them, congress will annex Haiti." The Corps said.

"They'll never get Albright to sign off; it'll take months to bypass her." Army said. "What if the aliens move? We need that ship pronto."

"What if we crack that Piper girl open?"

"What about Branford?"

"We can't afford to piss off Space Fleet."

The conversation moved into the usual debates and Sanderson drifted into his own thoughts. The Chiefs had a people problem: Branford is Piper's grandfather and also one of the U.S.'s top reverse engineering firms. He developed the Earth-human MAC control systems from shot down alien crafts and without it, no human could fly one. Now, it's the star drive they want out of Branford. What good is light speed without weapons? *Hell, I don't even know what MJ is working on. They'll never get past the aliens' force fields.* We don't have gravity pocket or anti-gravity technology either. This problem isn't a nail and they want to swing a hammer at a goddamn anvil. We need a soft approach; Piper's a goddamn kid for Christ's sake. All she cares about is going to college. U.S. space hegemony isn't even on her plate. If the people knew what the Chiefs were after there'd be blood in the streets and Piper would clamp down like an oyster at the Sea Food Mall.

"What about it Sanderson?" Army was saying. "You see any kinks in that girl's armor?"

OK so it's back around to the soft target. If Piper's grandfather wasn't a defense contractor she'd be floating face down in a lagoon before now.

"College, she wants to go to college, there's one on the moon." Sanderson said. "Let her go, the longer she's away from her ship, the less interest she'll have."

"How's that helping us?"

"I'll get the GTO to do their mind control trick, change her mind. That ship is a big pie. They're bucking for a slice; I'll trade off Piper's no star drive ships. We can't fly them anyway. They'll sign a promissory note."

"What about Albright?" Army said.

"Why tell her?" Navy said.

"She is the Commander-in- Chief," Air Force said.

At that everyone laughed. As far as the Chiefs were concerned, Presidents were just ass-end figureheads. When war dogs wagged, the tail followed. Albright wasn't playing nice, but they'd get their way—they always do. He'd seen it before. This disturbed Sanderson. This wasn't how the Constitution was written, not the way it was supposed to be. Worse, the Chiefs weren't even leading; they were all just a bunch of lobbyists for defense billionaires when you got right down to it. He needed to see Branford and find out what the Powers really had up their sleeves.

"I'm going over to see Branford," Sanderson said just before leaving, just to cover his ass. "Let me see if he can't get his granddaughter under control."

There were no objections. The left hand didn't know what the right was doing, and Sanderson never showed his hand anyway.

THREE

General Mayhem and the Joint Chiefs

After the Sanderson meeting Brinks went to the capital building for his first stop. General Mayhem is what they called him behind his back. No one had the balls to say it to his face. In Iraq he had shown his ruthlessness and earned the moniker. He was able to intimidate enough silence to avoid a war crimes court martial. His peers feared him and the Senate Arms Committee respected him— they'd eat any arms industry bullshit cotton candy he spun. He didn't care what the senators thought of him as long as they did what they were told.

He only spent a few minutes with them and left the Arms Committee sure they'd keep grazing on his hand-fed fear; it's why MJ-12 let them get elected and they knew it. Nothing like a good propaganda eater, he thought. You don't fuck with puppet masters. That congress of stooges he just reported to didn't matter. The ones that mattered hired him, or better put, they made him a partner.

It wasn't his bloodthirsty appetite that earned MJ-12's notice, it was his ability to do the impossible and deflect official inquiries while doing it. The U.S. Government didn't have the guts to do what is necessary, but he and his partners did. The people would call it treason. The Government's eggheads might say he was selling out the human race, but he knew better. American hegemony in space justifies any Earthly crime. Why be content as king of the hill when an entire universe full of mountains was ripe for the taking? But first he had to secure the hill.

General Tommy Brinks rounded a corner and found the Representatives' private keyed elevator on this floor, the one that was inactive. The Department of Homeland Security guard standing there didn't salute, it wasn't required.

"Hey Stacks, busy over this way," he asked the DHS man.

"No Sir, everything's right as rain." Stacks said with a southern drawl.

"Good man, keep it that way." Brinks shoved a hundred-dollar bill into Stacks' hand. Stacks was good at looking the other way in Iraq. Brinks got him hired and placed in the capital building for that reason.

Brinks looked down the hall, no one was around. He used his key and got on the out-of-order elevator. He shoved his special key into the lock for the elevator's control access panel and removed it. The elevator went straight to a sub-basement that no one had access too.

This is where MJ operated from in Washington. The space was mostly surveillance equipment. The few workers there thought they were working for the NSA and even they didn't know about the hidden tunnel system. They took an underground tram to the location so they didn't know where they actually were. *Nice of the GTO to build it for us.* No workers were there now. MJ didn't take any chances. Many of the group came in person this morning and that was outside of their agreed protocol, but these times required quick and direct actions. The gloves were coming off.

Brinks entered the conference room, only a few of the twelve didn't come. Each man was dressed casually; they could be any man anywhere. The Saudi Prince passed for a taxi driver and maybe that's his mode of operation while in town. If the people knew that this guy and his family owned or controlled every major oil concern, there would be riots. Only the English banker looked like a businessman. He would be more noticeable in casual attire; his arrogance couldn't be disguised. Sometimes you roll with what you got.

"Very good, Seven, shall we get on with business?" One said. He was a Greek shipping baron.

"Here, here," everyone said. They didn't stand on formalities.

"Eleven, please proceed." One said. Nobody took notes.

Brinks cleared his throat. "Branford says the remainder of our MAC fleet should be online in two weeks, but we have enough operational craft to take a run at the moon. With all the insanity going on in the world, ready-made distractions all, we should launch ASAP. Clandestinely of course, but UFO reports are flying, they won't know it's us. The moon won't know what hit them."

The Chinese industrialist stood. He was number three, worth more money than a third of the world. He fumbled with his alien translator and pressed it to his neck. He didn't speak English. "The fleet is operational, but we still have not protection cloaking, and we only have Earth born weapons. I do not think we are ready, this social unrest is good opportunity, yes, but we can always make new distraction as before, perhaps the Eiffel Tower this time?"

"Time is of the essence," Seven said, "But we do need the LF weapon first, and our Israel man assures me a prototype is days away. If this works…"

"That is a big if," Brinks said. He loved war but he wasn't stupid. Going after the GTO they'd use all the help they could get. "We need to test it on a real alien craft, one that won't piss off the GTO. What about Piper's mother ship."

"We should put Branford with Zelly."

"No, military is my area," Brinks said. "Branford is too close; it's his granddaughter's ship for Christ's sake. No, we keep Branford on the string for now, he's useful, but we don't get him involved yet. I don't trust the bastard."

"Eleven, you don't trust anyone."

Everyone around the table chuckled on that one. Brinks was the newest member, Branford would have been Twelve had he the personality type to accept the invitation. He would never be asked.

The banker harrumphed. "Quite so, should the attempt fail, the GTO will not think well of us. Should Eleven convince the Joint Chiefs a test is in order, the heat, as they say, won't be on us. Meanwhile, we'll continue our trade deal with the GTO, they'll not suspect us. We have contracts after all, why would we greed-ridden Earth people forgo a lucrative arrangement?"

"How do we make this happen?" One said.

"I'll send troops to crack that ship open," Brinks said. "When it defends itself we'll have just cause to attack it. I'll sell it to the media. Meanwhile you people work on the GTO, send out red herrings. We don't want them seeing the double-cross coming. We don't know what they're capable of."

"What of this girl Piper, is she not a problem?" The Arab said.

"Not at all," Brinks said glad the people here didn't micro manage. Piper's internet presence was creating a lot of controversy and social unrest but it was manageable. The CIA was chomping at its bit to go after her. *I'll shut her down soon enough*, "I have her where I want her; she won't get near that ship. That girl can very well be used to good effect. If she won't play..." Brinks spread his hand as to say, oh well. "That ship is a sitting duck and I'll make sure it stays that way."

"Why not kill her?"

"When it's necessary, right now she's a great tool, dumb and young. We'll use her. Hold her hostage; drug her for info, whatever it takes. But if we piss off Branford, we'll be up shit's creek, we still need him. We still don't have star drive and he's the only one close to figuring it out."

"Have you a contingency should your President overstep us? How will you control her?" One asked. "She is making life difficult."

"The usual, same way we got the rest of them. If she won't take the money, play ball...accidents do happen." Brinks made a gun with his hand and flicked his thumb indicating shots fired.

"Aye at least this time it's not a Kennedy," The Irish banker said. He and JFK were distant relatives.

The Irishmen's father was there. Kennedy should never have tried to close the Federal Reserve Bank which would have killed MJ-12's space fleet project. *You don't fuck with puppet masters.*

"Isn't there a better way?" The UK banker said. This President is popular. Many of us are engaged in trade deals we cannot allow to falter. Such turmoil, such as an assassination may well be overdoing it."

General Mayhem loved a good kill, seeing Albright's head explode would tickle him no end, but the banker was right. Things were getting out of control and more chaos wasn't the answer, not this time. Now wasn't ripe for the coup, soon, very soon, but not yet. There were ways to keep the game going, a new controversy would do. A discredited President giving congress cause to focus in other areas such as an impeachment would do the trick. He eyed the media mogul, funny how the man who controlled 70% of the world's media had nothing to say. However, the Aussie's wheels were already turning, Brinks thought.

"Once Albright is out of the way we can attack the Piper problem head on." One said. "If she won't sell out…one way or another that mothership is ours."

"Or, if not, it will be no one's." Brinks said. "Of course, it is better for us to acquire it whole. Our plan to force a sale is on track."

Brinks left the meeting thinking of how Piper was digging her own grave. The little bitch had a mouth on her and he was just the man to nail it shut.

FOUR

Sanderson and Branford

Branford was a wealthy man; he had a house right there in D.C. spitting distance from the action. The driver got Sanderson there in a snap. Sanderson had the man stay in the car and he rang the door himself. A butler opened the door.

"Mr. Branford is expecting you, right this way sir."

"No shit. Every goddamn spook in town knows I'm here, lead on." Sanderson said with as much vitriol as he could muster against an innocent bystander. No doubt someone was listening, he wouldn't drop the act. NSA and god knows who else had to have ears on this place twenty-four-seven, every defense contractor got that same treatment weather they knew it or not. Branford was smarter than most of them.

"Follow me please," the butler said.

It was a big house, three stories, maybe 5000 sq. feet, fancy trim and decorated like an old Victorian. But, the place was new and its walls had to be loaded with countermeasures. It was one of the few safe places to talk in D.C. The butler knocked once and swung open a big oak door. Branford was sitting in an overstuffed chair near the fireplace—good place for a man that was built like a fire plug. The room was setup like an old English library except for the alien artifacts, illegal as hell, placed between book spaces. It'd pass for a 19th century gentleman's club otherwise.

"Ben, it's been a while, glad to see you." Branford stuck out his hand.

The man still had an iron grip, apt for a guy with Popeye the Sailor forearms. Was Al pulling sails in his spare time? Sanderson's own grip was getting weaker by the day.

"Good to see you, too, Al wish it was under better circumstances."

"You lost a lot of weight," Branford said looking Sanderson over.

"Doc says I have to lose more."

"Any luck getting that new heart?"

Sanderson caught himself in the mirror. The room was dim, which made his pale complexion stand out. More than stress ate his health away. "With Aggie changing the game, it might not happen."

"Don't count her out. The aliens might be tight with their resources, but she's generous as hell."

"That's just one of my problems; you might say it's a National Security problem."

"That's a crock of shit. Sit, sit, brandy?"

No need to open that topic. The phrase National Security was just a license to print money anymore, America wasn't in any danger, not from anyone on Earth or the moon and they both knew it. Al poured two while Sanderson got settled in his chair. It used to take time, his bulk and size made furniture cry but this chair fit better than the last time he parked his ass in it. What, three years and a hundred pounds ago?

"Aggie's a whip," Al said handing the drink over, "Get with her and you'll be better off."

"I'd rather not talk politics. But I have to tell you, they need her to back down."

"You tell them bastards, if they want star drive, they'll leave her alone. I'm closing in on it."

It was contract law between them. Branford and he each had their own boat to row, sometimes they pulled together, and sometimes it was a tug of war, but they remained friends. They respected each other's distance. *I hope so for her sake.*

"I need to know," Sanderson said. "Does MJ have anything that'll splash aliens? I don't mean MAC killers, anything to take out a big spaceship?" Al was the man building America's Space Fleet. Fleet status Ben didn't know and he wasn't supposed to know about it nor would he ask for the official figures.

"If I was working on space weapons," Al Branford said, "I couldn't say, but since I'm not." Al took a gulp of his brandy. "I hear they got Lock Industries working on something. It's not ready, but they think they'll pull it off pretty soon. They think they'll use LF to make a bomb. Trust me, it'll never work."

Sanderson knew better than to ask why, or how Branford knows what he knows. Al was the tech man and most of this stuff was way over Sanderson's head anyway. The concept is all he really needed. If Al said it doesn't work, it doesn't work. Sanderson filed that in the back of his mind.

"Tell me something Ben, is Aggie safe? If they fuck with my family they can kiss star drive goodbye. Hands off Aggie's ship, see, you pass that down the pipeline."

MJ knew better than to screw with Branford, but then again, after they got what they wanted, all bets are off. Branford wasn't stupid, he knew that. Maybe he wanted access that only his own blood might give. That's the unsaid trump card. But Branford's men were nowhere near Haiti. The push was on for the Space Fleet and the old man had his hands full.

"I'm doing what I can, the President is the main thing, but the Chiefs will work around Albright, you know that. She's safe for now, but how long, I can't say. MJ will work around you, too, to get what they want. I'm not betting on Albright's survival." Sanderson downed his drink. "Or mine either."

Branford reached down alongside his chair and brought up a slim, long gift-wrapped box and handed it to Sanderson. "It's a phone-watch for Aggie; her 18th birthday's coming up. I hoped to go down there myself, but I'm up to my ass in alligators."

Sanderson examined the wrap, turned it over. It looked normal. "Is it something from Van Ness?"

"Better, it cleared checks; my scanners only see a watch phone."

"What does it do?"

"Wish I knew. It came from Praytis, not the GTO. One of them damn probes dropped them off."

"Them?"

"It gave me two. Pick one and keep it if you don't trust it, your choice. I'm telling you it's clean, just a gift."

How Branford got in touch with Praytis didn't matter. The aliens had tractor beams and matter distortion. The bug man could beam himself straight into Al's bedroom if he had a mind to. What was true here or not, Sanderson couldn't say.

"You trust Praytis?" Sanderson asked. He never trusted the alien man.

"I don't have too, Aggie trusts him. She made him First Mate, told me when they were up here for the Fourth of July. Anything happens to Aggie, it's his fleet. They'll get nothing, just goes back to the GTO."

"I'll see she gets this."

Sanderson stood and slipped the boxes into his jacket's inside pocket. They shook hands. Maybe it was treason to pass this along. It had to be less illegal than whatever MJ was up to. Screwing with aliens was pissing up a rope but MJ liked wet shoes and they had no qualms about pissing away the people's money.

Praytis was MIA since the President put Aggie into high-security status. No sign of her space shuttle seen anywhere since then. The ship she had parked under the National Monument had up and left one night without warning. The GTO still had Praytis tied up on contract so the bug man wasn't free to act alone, or was he?

Sanderson never told the Chiefs everything and he would not share this new information either. The deep state wasn't trustworthy and the shadow government was worse. Branford was smart to keep a lid on certain things he knew. Need-to-know works both ways. He and Branford had other things in common, they were both patriots. The men of MJ, whoever they were, they were not beholden to the United States.

The rest of the conversation was the usual stuff. Branford ratted on about how his daughter Charlotte, calls herself Sky Flower, took up the family mantle and went back to being a lawyer. Pretty damn good lawyer too from what was in the news. Branford actually called her Sky Flower and that was new. He was proud as hell of her. She's fighting for Aggie and Haiti like a bear protecting cubs and that son-in-law Al never liked was given quarters as well. Po-boy was staying there in fact, writing a damn UFO book. Sky was down south now setting up a human shield around that damn ship. It seemed like after twenty years of estrangement Branford's clan was becoming a family.

All this talk of family made Sanderson nostalgic. When was the last time he saw Sarah?

FIVE

Joy Ride

It was pretty late when Aggie and Mel finished pre-recording blogs. That live one they did was sure to piss off the Man. *Just wait until tomorrow's blog goes out.* That was her intent. Aggie was sick of it, sick of government guys following her around since the President said on TV, "Agatha Piper is a national treasure." That's why she quit high school. OK Jimmy got his wish and got Aggie's scholarship, but she bugged out more to get away from all the embarrassment. Bad enough everyone hated her anyway before. But, government goons driving her to school was worse than Mom riding her there on a bicycle built for two. At least things have slowed down since she stopped doing press interviews. Her place wasn't crawling with military as bad, just Dave and a few other MPs and they kept a respectful distance. The President told the military to give her space. That's how she got out at night—bitching to high places paid off.

Her probe Buddy rolled up the porch steps. Aggie heard him but knew he was coming anyway. Before, they didn't have air conditioning, so the regular door was always left open to let air in through the screen door. Buddy's way of knocking was to roll up and back a few times, bumping the door. He can't reach the knob; he was only the size of an extra-large beach ball. That little mechanical arm he had was only like twelve inches long and wasn't good for much. He could hold her new I-Know phone in flight, but not while rolling on the ground. She made some cool drone videos that way, and it helped her figure out ways around security.

Buddy was getting insistent. Aggie laughed, "OK Buddy, I'm coming, gosh." Aggie had Mom on the face-phone app. She checked the time, it was almost dark. "Mom I got to go."

"Before I forget," Mom said. "I'm on TV tomorrow, Senate hearings; it'll be on public access. I'm leaving Haiti in a few minutes."

"Mom, God, your hair looks like crap." Mom was on the computer screen and Aggie hated that Mom had cut her hair just like Aggie's hair. Mom's dreadlocks were dumb, but that spiky punk cut with six colors wasn't cool at all. "Why don't you dye it, looks better for TV? Why you got to have my hair cut?"

"We've had this conversation before." Mom said. "Moving on…"

Mom went over some of the stuff she was up too, mostly trying to convince congress to leave Mother alone and get off Haiti's neck. The buzz was, the Feds wanted to annex Haiti. Mom thought it was just to get Aggie's ship. Crap was flying in Washington. Mom always ended on a high positive note so the last thing she said was, "Don't forget to thank the Goddess."

The face-phone app screen went blank. Aggie shut off the computer. "All the time, Mom." More knocking, Buddy was getting really impatient.

"OK Buddy, I'm coming."

Aggie stepped out on the porch and her robot got excited, it rolled up and back and nudged her, and spun around on his access like the Earth's processional wobble. It was weird how a metallic object could feel so soft. Maybe Buddy's dog-like intelligence and that fuzzy-wuzzy charm just made his metal skin feel soft.

"OK, OK Buddy, gosh relax."

Aggie made for the back beach; it was just a little strip of white sand fifty feet behind the shack on the Gulf side. Beyond was a shallow cove, too shallow for boats. Bixby's boat storage was across the mucky waterway about a mile. Mangrove swamps on either side made it a very small but private beach.

Aggie stopped at the path which went to the water and looked down the lane. Dave was there at his post just past dad's old van. The 1970 Econoline still had bullet holes in it. She waved at Dave and proceeded to pull off her sundress. Of course, he turned around. Naked, she went down the short path.

Sky Flower and Po-boy had this family ritual, every night they'd all go to the beach, stand in knee–deep water and thank Gaia. Sometimes Sky would make an offering of some pot leaves, or Dad would toss some fish guts out for the crabs. Aggie usually just meditated on the shore because before recently, she was afraid of the water.

Aggie was over her fear of water so she recently took up wading in just to make sure she didn't regain such fear. That first toe in the water always shot panic into her chest but she stepped in anyway. All this ritual junk was on record so the government goons had to back off at prayer-time. "Religious freedom, you know it's our right." Mom had hammered that phrase into everyone, she forced them to listen. The press ate it up and the authorities did their usual reaction dance.

Buddy was on shore, for a robot with the mind of Labrador, he sure hated water. He was rocking like crazy when Aggie looked back. He started to light; he had to put his glow on before he could fly.

"No Buddy, stay here, keep an eye on things OK, I'll be back soon, God. Keep the guards away till I get home."

The MPs won't bother her until morning. They did a check every day at seven a.m. With that stupid cock rooster crowing every morning, she was normally up before they knocked. No big deal. She wondered what would happen if she didn't get back before dawn.

The shuttle was near, she felt it. She thought it was kind of strange how she always knew when Buddy or her other alien ship stuff was around. She never felt so connected to a machine before, but she didn't really want to think about it too hard. Aggie didn't even like computers. She was more into primitive technology. She loved old stuff, anything before 1900 was cool. All this high-tech crap was too far away from the source of life. The past interested her way more than the future.

In her mind, there wasn't much hope for a future with climate change and pollution, and all the crazy crap governments were up to. Everybody was chewing everybody's tail. It was all so stupid, now was the time for people to pull together. But do they? No way.

She was thirty yards off shore and her ship was right in front of her in stealth mode hovering above the water, but Praytis couldn't open the door or the light would alert the MPs. She moved out further still so the shuttle could turn around and put its back to the land making the light less obvious.

"OK Buddy." Aggie called in a hissing whisper, "Keep Dave busy, go boy."

Buddy lit up, took to the air and raced off toward Dave about three feet off the ground. Aggie wasn't sure but Buddy might have had a stick in his grabber.

"Play fetches, really?"

The gangway dropped. It was really just the side of the hull splitting, one way up the other down. Aggie hurried up the ramp. It shut quickly behind her.

Mel was looking at a screen. She was learning how to work the communications junk. "Dude that was close, Dave almost saw."

"Did you get the dead man switch done?" Aggie asked as she lifted her sundress over her head and let it fall into place.

"That is a familiar term," Praytis said, "You Earth people are warlike, is that a reference to the electric chair?"

"All set." Mel said.

Aggie had to explain it while the ship climbed into a low orbit. Aggie kept forgetting he wasn't from around here. Weird that she felt that way. Praytis was human but he had a body like a praying mantis with a long torso like appendage and four legs. From his chest to his face he looked normal that is, for a ninetieth century man wearing a corset. His waist was tiny like a thorax. Male corsets were a big thing in the1870s.

"Oh, so I see. It is rather inefficient how Earth English has so many ambiguous meanings. I fear I will never master it."

"You're better than half the people in America." Mel said.

"You should hear my dad when he gets going with his French, Creole and English blend," Aggie said. "So where do you guys want to go? I was thinking about Fungi, or Tibet, it'll be daytime there."

"No way dude, let's go the moon. Let's land this time. That first time was poop, we didn't see shit."

"Of course not, we process waste discreetly." Praytis said.

Both girls did a double take and laughed. Aggie slapped her forehead.

"No, no silly, the space port. I need ideas for Haiti. You said the port is neutral, they can't block us access especially since my ships are getting re-fits there."

Praytis had avoided it before. He talked them out of it each time. He said he didn't trust the GTO, like why she didn't trust the government. Yeah, they had rules and junk, but the top guys don't seem to follow them much. Praytis was all about rules. He says that's how it is in space, its survival stuff, and so you can't mess around in space. But what about the moon kids joy riding for the past hundred years, how's that happen?

Praytis started going down his list of reasons why it wasn't a good idea to land on the moon. Aggie let it go in one ear and out the other.

"But there's a college there, right? I'm a student, I got the money. We should check it out, you said we could."

"Oh dear, I misspoke, one needs an invitation to attend and the GTO is not issuing any at this time."

"Dude, this is our last chance. When our blog hits the net they'll lose their shit. We'll have a harder time getting out. I'm still grounded you know."

"I don't know I, well, oh bother…"

Praytis kept moving from one suction cup foot to the other making a weird sucking sound. He was way easy to read. Something was eating him, for sure.

"Perhaps if we stay inside the port, it is true that section is open to fleet owners."

"It's settled," Aggie said. "I'm the captain; I'm paying for all this ship work. I have a right to see what's going on. This ship needs junk, right? They want the business, what can they do?"

"I really do not believe—."

"You're outnumbered, majority rule," Mel said.

"Shit," Praytis said.

Aggie and Mel turned heads toward him. He never said that before. Praytis touched his belt and the gray bio-bots entered their flight destination. Aggie's rationale worked. That blog wasn't a big deal, but Praytis didn't know that. Who cares what teen girls have to say online? Aggie was pretty sure it would be OK, pretty sure.

SIX

Nursing Home Visit

Sanderson left D.C. in the early afternoon and drove up to New Jersey. The pressure was on, he really didn't have the time but sometimes you just have to say screw it. But that wasn't it, Sanderson knew deep down he didn't have a lot of time left on this Earth and, at this moment, family felt more important to him than national security. She'd never forgive him if he didn't say goodbye. Still Sanderson took the long way. He used back roads through the Pine Barrens sucking on gumdrops and memories as he drove. He camped and hunted there as a kid and it was remarkably untouched. The Pine Lands Act stopped man's attack on this nature back in the 60s. Only the remaining cranberry bogs told the story that this real estate was once in the gun sights of fruit juice producers.

He took the ferry, landed in Cape May and came through New Gretna, across the Warden Track State Forest and up to Chatsworth passing what was left of old bog-iron mining and blueberry towns. From Chatsworth he took an unnamed road and landed in the back of Pinewall, or that's what it used to be called. Now it was part of Berkley Township. He was happy to see that not much changed since his days. The high school was bigger, not his old school, he went to Toms River, but he knew the place well. A few more houses sprang up every year but at least it felt familiar. The old gangster's golf course was now a county park.

He arrived at the nursing home near sundown but he didn't have the guts to go in. He pulled out and drove around Crystal Lake. He wanted to see the old swimming hole from when he was a kid. He liked this place. Al Capone liked it too. The gangster built a luxury hotel there that made his childhood swimming hole into a lake. Now that once famous building served as a nursing home. He pulled over south of the place on the far side of that artificial waterway and watched from across the lake. It still looked like a hotel.

He remembered seeing men in fancy suits on the portico when he was a kid… one man had a tommy gun. He was scared then. Today he felt the same, he was afraid of what he'd find inside. The portico had long been closed-in and converted into a sunny dayroom. Sarah loved it in there, she might be there now.

He started the engine of the rented Caddy and went back the way he had come. This time, he got out and walked up to the entrance. He had to pass security, everything is about security.

He went to the section where Sarah lived to check in with the head nurse. She was busy and he had to wait. The head nurse was a black woman, and in his day that was never the case. It used to be before the war when a white man showed up the blacks paid attention. He didn't miss those times; he'd seen too many black men serve with distinction to think they were inferior. He felt a little uncomfortable, it wasn't that he didn't respect blacks; he didn't experience minorities in his upbringing. He never met a black person until he was in the war. Your childhood sticks with you.

In Toms River, at his three-room schoolhouse, there were no blacks, just a few quiet Indians. Leftovers from when Indians were slaves. His folks told him to stay away from the Indians. This little kid he recalled, and Indian boy named Albert Thompson, stuck out in his memories. Leo, Albert's father, was famous locally. The kid's old man was a stunt driver in the silent movies back when they were made in Hoboken, New Jersey, and the old man ran rum out of Barnegat inlet during probation. That crazy red man did all kinds of other shenanigans. Old Leo might have been New Jersey's last wild Indian. It was rumored that Leo and his band had burned the KKK meeting hall down too, but that was never proven true. All this history and more were lost on the people that lived in Berkley now. Sanderson's sadness deepened. Nobody had any roots and maybe that was good, might be easier to explore the universe that way.

"Mr. Sanderson, please sign in."

Sanderson snapped out of it on the word Mr. He had to check himself, he was in civilian clothing. He had forgotten.

"Nurse, how's Sarah doing?"

He slid an envelope over to her and she quickly pocketed it. His insurance was good, the best, but Sanderson long knew if you wanted special treatment forget the brass and make deals with the sergeant. The stack was thick; she'd share it with her enlisted. That was the deal. It usually got there by messenger and it was hand delivered early this time.

"Physically she is doing very well, for one in her late eighties, looking at her chart, you'd think she was closer to sixty…except for her heart."

"That's genetics, for you. What about her mind?"

"The new medication is working very well. She's doing crossword puzzles again and reading a lot. I'd say she is doing remarkably well, but there is still that little issue with cognition. She still thinks you're her daddy."

"That's fine. If she wants to think that let her. What's the harm?"

"She should be dressed now; she was being washed when you came in. She just had her meds so she should be lucid. I'll walk you down."

Sanderson followed the nurse to Sarah's private room. It took a lot of muscle to pull that off. New Jersey has a bed shortage: Too many baby boomers. He could move her to D.C., but this was better, this was home. She could look out on the lake where she played as a child.

The nurse walked in first, "Someone to see you Sarah."

She was sitting by the window and jumped a little in her easy chair on the announcement. "Daddy, Daddy!"

Sanderson walked right up to her. "How's my girl?" He bent down and held her carefully. When they parted from a long hug the nurse was gone.

"Dad...you look awful," Sarah said, "You've lost weight, and you're so pale."

"I know honey; I'm not getting any younger." Sanderson took a seat and they chatted a while. Of course, Sanderson couldn't say much about the aliens, but he did anyway. She was interested and no one here took anything she said seriously. Hell, the staff didn't even know he was military.

"So, what gives, things are hot now and you ought to be elsewhere."

"Remember when I used to...I used to come and see you and mom whenever I was going on a new mission, missions I might not come back from...I just wanted to see you."

"That's silly, you can't die. You told me that."

"Honey, this is just in case, that's all. I don't go on long trips without saying goodbye."

Sarah put both hands' fingertips to her mouth and gasped. "You mean it this time, you really mean it."

Sarah began to cry. He held her and cried too. He'd give anything to get her into an alien regeneration tank. He'd give away his fortune, his life, anything they wanted so she could go on. Each one was all the other had left. He cried for her and for himself. No man should outlive his only child, but it was worse when your child died of old age before you. He tried a long time to save them both, but that wasn't to be. Now it was a death race between them. Maybe he could do some good before time ran out.

It was amazing how much Sarah had looked like that Piper girl. Maybe he'd do for Piper what he couldn't do for himself. That might wash away his accomplishments and sins alike, and what did it matter, he failed. The world was failing. The data looked bleak. Mankind was on a rail heading over a cliff, and the men that could stop it were too busy arranging first class seats on a runaway train.

The meds slowly wore off and Sarah became more childlike as the next hours passed. He should have left sooner. He wanted to remember her having intelligence. Visiting her childhood this way was too painful, he had missed most of it. Let sleeping dogs lie.

The nurse came to the door. "Mr. Sanderson, visiting hours are an hour past."

Sanderson got up and bent to kiss her. She was very sleepy now. The medications brought her back, but there was a price to pay. He pecked her cheek and she put a hand on the spot and cooed like a little girl.

Half asleep, her eyes closed, "Daddy, next time bring me a present."

"I'll do that Honey, I'll do that."

He stood up to leave when she was snoring in her chair. The nurses will put her to her bed, he knew. He watched her a few more moments in repose. She was pale, translucent skin, white hair and it was so thin, her breath barely discernible but the look on her face was pure peace. He wished to God he'd feel that sensation someday, somehow. But first, it was back to the fire. He had work to do before he could lay his weary head down and die.

He got into the car and checked his I-Know phone that he had left there. That damn Piper girl was at it again. The text said. 'Piper MIA return ASAP.' He chuckled as he pulled out of the parking lot. Damn that girl is feisty, just like Sarah used to be.

He had put on one of Branford's watches and used it to check the time, 9:30 p.m., Fort Dix wasn't far. He'd requisition a flight there. Maybe he'd get lucky and get a C-130 with a cabin so he could get some sleep. He brushed off the idea, he wasn't that lucky.

SEVEN

Space Ride

Aggie sat back in her Captain Kirk chair thinking about that first trip.

Meeting Mel and Praytis that first time they took off together had felt like a homecoming and it felt the same every time after. Mel got a little carried away with hugging that first time but Aggie liked it, they hardly got to see each other anymore except on Faceplant and that was officially inadequate. CIA goons were always on her ass, so going anywhere without them was way cool. But what really felt good that first time was that little kiss on the lips Mel planted which sent mad voltage down Aggie's vertebras. Aggie put that on the back burner, she wasn't ready to light that fuse and besides, there was way too much other crap going on, like riding in a spaceship. Like what to do next with her life. But still, that kiss stuck to the inside of her heart. But, she promised herself no romance until college: No boys or girls and that's final.

Cool how Mel and Praytis became friends so easy. On that first trip Mel was like way into it. When Earth people meet an alien for the first time they pretty much lost their minds. Not Mel, it's like she was born for weirdness.

Aggie had said, "You and Praytis OK, I hope he didn't freak you out?' Aggie asked out of concern and worry and faced Mel holding both Mel's hands. Mel's shampoo filled Aggie's nostrils with happy. She remembered thinking, wow pretty tasty. It was awkward so Aggie spit out 'I know he looks weird but—.'"

"Dude, he's the shit."

"I am? What has excrement to do with me? I assure you I am quite sanitary."

When Aggie and Mel stopped laughing she told him, "No, no it's an expression, you know, it means you're really cool. Mel likes you. OK, so we can go to the moon, right?"

They went all right, but it was just a loop, they didn't get to see anything. Praytis was pooping bricks the whole time. Not fun at all. Aggie felt bad, but now they were really doing it. And Praytis wasn't so beside himself this time, maybe he was just getting used to Earth people?

"Dude, we can't be gone too long, I'm supposed to be at the Gay Youth House sleepover, that's how I got out of grounding."

Aggie snapped out of her thoughts. "Praytis, will we make it back in time?"

"The trip will not take very long and I will have time to show you the landing facilities and return you, but nothing more."

Aggie stood and the command chair retracted into the floor. Aggie expected it, and half knew it would do that. She felt this weird connection with the ship, like it was inside her head.

"OK, cool, let's do the moon. What do I need to do, like tell the bio bots, how do I do that?"

"It is done. The ship hears you and chooses to cooperate. Base Ship Mother gives her fleet onboard AI autonomy for local travel. The command belt you previously allowed me, making me First Mate, I might add, allows me direct two-way access. If you wanted to, you could use the captain's control belt to communicate, it's the same device that forces a ship to do your bidding should it decided not to cooperate."

There was a chime and Aggie knew they left Earth's orbit. Just like before there was no sensation of movement. She had it from Mother that the magnetic drive creates its own gravity well outside of local gravity. So, it's more like they are standing still and the universe moves around them. *How do I know that?*

"I can feel the ship, we're kind of wired together but I can't reach it. But I don't want a control belt, that's creepy. This thing isn't my slave you know."

Praytis did a very Earth–like double take and tilted his head.

"Cooperation between sentient symbioses is preferable; control belts are far less than optimal, interesting that you…er feel it…Should you undergo Ram-Education, your brain will be tuned to interface with your AI symbiont…Oh dear, I've said too much. I am not authorized to divulge GTO restricted information."

"Dude, do the Vegas thing, you're the Cap."

Aggie laughed and slapped Praytis on the back. "Hey ship, what's said on board stays on board, got it? Don't tell anyone what's said on this ship, OK? Not a living soul. This is between us and Mother. Did the ship understand me Praytis?"

The alien put his hand to his ear and smiled. He had really straight teeth, like a mouth full of white breath-mint gum squares.

"Shuttle one agrees to your request. Shall we sail for the moon? She reports that she needs repairs at an estimated cost of two units of LF. We have a considerable amount of resources in onboard cargo for trade."

"Dude you can't let your kids go out like this. What will the neighbors think?"

"Yeah I get that. Praytis, have we got enough money to fix up this one, what about the others?"

"The active fleet has had upgrades as you previously requested. I did not dock this one as yet. Mother has several devices in storage that need attention, but you did not specifically address that need."

"I hope I can afford it, Mother deserves working parts."

Praytis stood up straighter, his front feet barely touching the ground.

"I am sure you have enough funds to rebuild your holdings and buy an entire fleet many times larger...oh dear. That is restricted information. You really should not ask questions that the GTO doesn't approve of. I am contractually employed there and if asked I cannot lie to them, or you for that matter."

"OK, have them all come in for upkeep, only one at a time, I don't trust theses GTO people. Let's get all of Mother's abused extensions up to awesome level. OK that's settled. Let's head over to the moon."

The ship made the trip in less than half an hour. Aggie fell into another little trance on the way.

She heard things inside her head. It was Mother, but it was just whispers. It felt like Mother was reaching out but it was just past Aggie's grasp. She wanted to ask Praytis about it, but she didn't want to get him in any more trouble than he was already in. She buttoned her lips and concentrated on the feeling. She heard Mel and Praytis in the back of her awareness but she didn't answer. The thought came to her that Mother needed rest. She was parked on Haiti and the locals were using her as a tourist trap, the hatch was open and people were in and out. That was fine but Mother didn't need all the commotion. Besides, mom said the Feds were down there. Aggie felt the shuttle just received word that it was approved for landing.

Aggie rousted herself. Mel was still playing twenty questions with Praytis.

"OK, dude, so if you're human, why do you have four legs. You said all humans come from a common DNA source, you know like the same seed stock, so why'd you get four legs?"

"It is simple evolution. My home world is largely desert. One's feet are always treading hot sand. Less contact on four feet preserves one's comfort."

Praytis lifted up one leg and spread his toes. His feet were webbed. "As you can see my feet are like what you would call a flipper. I do not easily sink in the sand. My species has evolved, as all other do, for comfort and mobility in our environment. However, we do also have large bodies of water, so we can swim, unlike Mobies."

"Comfort," the feeling of Mother's discomfort stuck to Aggie as she became fully awake. "I think Mother needs rest, I don't think she's happy right now."

"Remarkable," Praytis said, "how is it..."

"Shuttle," Aggie said. "Tell Mother to nap if she needs it. Have her shield herself, or whatever she needs to do to get some peace."

Praytis put a hand to his ear again and this time he spent a full minute in sub-vocal conversation. Aggie felt but really couldn't hear what was going on.

"Mother will go into recycle mode, that is to say she will hibernate while her interior repair bots effect much needed maintenance. She will remain in status until completed or you wake her. She has engaged auto defense; no harm will come to intruders. Only you or I can access her...we are nearing the landing garage."

"Put it on screen? Yeah?" Mel said.

"It is restricted."

"Praytis, on my boat aren't you First Mate; doesn't that mean you do what the captain asks? Are you my crew or not? Screw the rules, you're on my ship now, you don't work for the other guy while on the ship job, right? Wow, did that come from me?" *Mother put that in my head.*

"Dude, you're getting way butch, that's so hot."

Praytis face contorted, his lower jaw started to jitter. He brushed back his hair a bunch of times before the screen materialized with an outside view. The side of a crater had opened like an overhead garage door. Everything else looked like every moon picture she had ever seen.

"Oh dear, such a quandary I have."

Aggie decided she had better not press him too hard. What if he got in trouble? She needed him and it wouldn't be good if he was locked up. It was better to play things cool. She had a million questions but she'd hold them for now.

EIGHT

Moon Visit

After a long clockwise walk down a boring, gray-white hallway with hatchway doors appearing on both sides of the hall, Aggie's mind wandered.

Praytis had said a mile back, "Everything on the right is GTO spaceport including hangar space and related support."

But he didn't say what was on the left. One of the many large hieroglyphs on every door was the same. Each door for the distance had that same icon but some doors didn't have that dominate sign. At one point, only doors on the spaceport side had the GTO mark. The right-side doors were crisper and cleaner the whole way while on the left the hatches got more and more dirty and unused the further they went from their hangar access door. Moon dust, she guessed. Aggie stopped at a door that had some kind of graffiti on it, it wasn't neat and stenciled on like the other symbols she had seen but it still looked familiar, like ancient Egypt Coptic writing.

She laid a hand on the hatch wheel and said, "Hey Praytis, what's this, what's it say? I don't get it: Looks familiar."

"Oh, that is a restricted area. I'm not allowed...secure storage perhaps?"

"Is that what it says," Mel asked. "It's some kind of writing, yeah?"

"Oh yes, very observant," The Alien said but he became fidgety. "Universal station script, space stations and ports where varieties of races work use a universally agreed upon written communication system, really very simple...such knowledge is installed into every spacer."

"What's that supposed to mean?" Aggie didn't like the sound of that.

"Let us press on—our time is limited."

Something didn't set right with Aggie. Praytis was holding back, he was gulping air. He seemed jittery but he didn't hesitate to answer a question, but was it really an answer? Aggie had half a mind to rip open one of the restricted doors to see what was inside. Praytis wasn't about to break any rules The Man laid on him, the guy wasn't wired for it. The doors didn't have any locks. They were just like hatchways in old WWII submarine movies.

"Hey how come you don't have locks?"

"In space that would not do." He said. "People must respect the rules. Even pirates do that, it's for common safety. If there is a breach and a section's air is contaminated, one must be able to operate an airtight door. It is station survival protocol, the first thing every spacefarer must learn in Ram-Education…oh dear."

"Pirates, like yo-ho-ho and junk?" Mel said, "Or you mean dudes like Karnack?"

"Why doesn't the central computer do that?" Aggie said. Aggie looked around enough to know there wasn't much automation going on with doors and lights. This place wasn't supported with mad cool technology like every sci-fi movie she had ever seen.

Praytis stopped mid-floppy foot stride and balanced oddly on two opposing legs. "Oh dear, I don't know if I'm permitted to pass such information."

"How will they know?" Aggie said, but then she realized the answer. Praytis didn't look like he was about to open his mouth. "The central computer sees everything, hears everything, but she can't do everything. I'm right, right?"

Praytis let his other two feet drop. "How is it that you know? You have not yet had Ram-Ed protocols induced."

There was something weird in how he chose his words and what he didn't say that Aggie didn't like. She had a feeling she should just shut up. What was Ram-Ed anyway and did she really want to know? She had guessed right about the central AI…If the computer heard Praytis give her answer she'd bet management would too. She still didn't know how much she should trust the GTO or Praytis and what exactly is an 'induced protocol'? Ram-Ed sounded creepy! She must have got the idea from Mother. Everything depends on AI's but a little voice told her to shut up about it. She and Mother had this weird connection and Aggie still needed to figure it out. Plugging in to that spaceship filled her head with all kinds of new stuff. Maybe plugging in wasn't a good idea. But, she had to say something.

Praytis was doing his version of a little boy's I-got–to-pee dance. "This is most unusual; our organizational structure isn't for Earth human consideration, oh dear."

"Don't worry," Aggie said, "I have amazing powers of observation; Pink Floyd taught me."

"Relax bug dude," Mel said "We nerds just know stuff. It's like logical deduction my dear Watson."

Mel winked at Aggie. Aggie forced herself not to laugh.

"Oh well yes, very good." He seemed to relax a bit. "We should proceed to the landing dock, it is just ahead and it is after all rather late."

"Didn't we just walk in a giant circle" Mel said.

"Oh, dear, we are almost there."

Back on Earth Aggie was sure everyone guarding her house would freak out if they had a clue she wasn't there, well not everyone, just the Army guys and CIA and whoever else were supposed to keep her from taking off. Face it, Aggie told herself, they aren't protecting you, they're caging you. Nobody said it, but the Man had to think she was a national security risk or some other paranoid bull crap. She wasn't about to just show up back home in her spaceship and let them know she went to the moon, no way. But still, she just didn't want to go home.

Praytis opened a hatch and they stepped through one at a time. They were back in that giant hangar space, it had to be ten football fields long and four wide. Praytis led them toward a shuttle that wasn't her craft; it didn't have Mother's markings on it.

"Where's my shuttle, I'm not getting on that thing."

"This one is available and…Oh dear…I really shouldn't."

"Forget it, hey you're my First Mate right, tell me what's happening or I'll find another second in command. Mel, you won't mind filling in, right? The pay's not bad."

"I always wanted to have a spaceship command," Mel said deadpan. "Dude, I can't fit into his shoes, he doesn't have any and besides he's got too many feet, but I'll do my best."

"Oh dear, you are the fleet owner, I must answer."

Praytis hedged. He was trying to avoid the central computer's ears. He moved in close, covered his mouth and said, "Hear between the lines."

Praytis pulled himself up straight and spoke as if addressing the house computer. "The good ship Mother made a deal for repairs with Moon Central AI. Your shuttle is being fitted now. AI's have a legal right to do so. You did instruct me to gather the fleet and care for it and so I did, but the AI's work out the details between one another."

"I'm not traveling in somebody's ship I can't control…how do I know you won't make us into shrimp cocktails?"

Praytis slapped his forehead. "This is impossible."

"Dude, you're rich right, everything has a price, buy that one then they can't monitor us. You got to start thinking like a rich bitch. Dude, everything is for sale."

"How much does it cost?" Aggie asked.

"Ten thousand LF credits, you have a trillion or so on file." Praytis was obviously miserable about saying it.

"Far out, make it so Number One, do I have to sign anything?"

"Central, transfer title as spoken, disable monitoring, transfer to Fleet Mother, register when affirmative…oh dear, oh my…jeepers."

"Jeepers, really dude?"

"Transaction completed." Came out of no place and everyplace at once but it wasn't loud.

"They have good service here, but the decor is really bland, I'll give it a nine out of ten, come on let's go." Aggie took off for the ship. It was kind of cool, it was boomerang shaped but the center part was a dome. It was almost a flat bottom ball with wings.

Aggie approached the ship and the entry ramp lowered without asking. This ship was smaller and slicker than her other ones. Her other ships were oblong pie plate looking things. Aggie went up the ramp and stopped at the door and said, "All aboard, get your tickets ready."

There were already two robot pilots at the controls inside. They came with the ship. All her grays were pretty shot so Aggie didn't mind the new hardware. When Aggie spoke, they sat up and their eyes glowed indicating they were online.

On the way back to Key West Aggie tried to get more info out of Praytis, but the guy didn't give up much. She bugged him, but that Ram-Ed thing wasn't explained. She guessed it was some kind of AI forcing information into your head. The idea of it was totally uncool. How was that fun? Learning new stuff didn't suck, OK sometimes it was hard, but programming knowledge into your head like a computer was so not cool. Aggie liked learning and she found out that the hard way was the best way: If you had to work at it, it stuck better.

When they got to the Key, she had the ship cloak and hover over Duvall St. Praytis had the holograms up but with all the bright lights below nobody could see even if they weren't invisible. They weren't parked a minute when her probe Buddy came racing up from home. It streaked all around them.

"Dude he'll tip us off. Make him go home."

There was a lot of action on the ground. Lots of people were outside with cell phones pointing up after Buddy showed up with his happy dance.

"Praytis, open the bottom hatch." Aggie said, the center of the floor behind her chair spiraled open, Buddy came up into the hole.

Aggie got on her knees. "Buddy, I need you to go home, wait for me at the house, we'll play later." The probe didn't leave. Aggie let her voice become harsh, "Buddy, GO HOME!" The probe backed up but didn't leave. "BUDDY GO, git!"

Buddy rolled up to the hole slowly but he did leave. Aggie felt bad. She sensed the probe's sadness. It was really weird and it worried her. This entire thing was getting to her. Having a ship inside your head is creepy, but her feeling what that probe felt was even stranger. It felt like she had needles inside her brain that were trying to push out.

"My life is never going to be normal is it?"

"Where shall we deposit you and Melissa? I dare say, your home is in an uproar. Buddy probe reported the situation to Ship's AI."

On screens, Buddy was over the house now and his sensors were tracking a dozen military guys. They were all over the place even in the mangroves and in the drain ditch too. One guy pointed a gun at Buddy, not that it would do any harm.

"I can't go there, crap."

"Dude, tonight's the sleep-in at the Gay Youth House, let's go together. We'll sneak in through the boy's room window."

"I'm in deep crap. I'm going to get it when I get home."

"So, don't go, you don't want to out your new ship right, let's beam down behind the Unitarian Church. The rear courtyard faces the boy's room window, we'll sneak in."

"I don't know...I have responsibilities, like that junk the President said."

"Dude, stop acting like an adult, now is not the time."

"You're right, let's do it."

Praytis parked the ship over the Unitarian Church, the floor opened and Aggie stepped out into empty space without reservation. The tractor beam lowered her down no problem but Mel stayed behind looking down. It looked like a little, dull sun in the night sky with Mel's face hanging on the edge.

"Bitch" Aggie whispered a hiss, "Just step out come on!" It took some convincing but Mel finally took the plunge and landed soft.

"Man, I don't know how you didn't freak out. Dude, that scared the shit out of me."

"You get used to it," Aggie said. But it was a good question. Any normal girl would have been scared. Why wasn't she? It felt like Mother already put stuff into her head and that no fear thing was freaky. Maybe Aggie needed to rethink the whole space thing. The government was bugging her to sell her ships, at least a few, but she didn't want to bust up the family. Once Praytis and her ship was away, she felt more her old self.

Aggie and Mel made it through the window and out into the old church's hallway before one of the Gay Youth Club facilitators found them.

She came from behind. "Hold it right there girls. The gym is in the other direction."

This club event wasn't a free for all, adult volunteers always manned each sleepover to ensure nothing would happen and this facilitator, Mrs. Peterson, was pretty cool, friendly and hip for a straight woman but when Aggie turned around Peterson's smile fell away.

"Oh, Aggie Piper, I wasn't expecting you. Let me guess, you don't have a permission slip."

"My parents are away and besides, I'm almost eighteen, legal age of consent is seventeen."

"I see, very well, back to the gym girls, no more wondering around."

It was only ten p.m. and half the kids were just coming in. Many of the kids Aggie hadn't seen since quitting school. Maybe a lot of them gave her the cold shoulder because she wasn't at graduation. It wasn't Aggie's fault; the cops didn't let her go. Too big a security risk, they told her. It was a bunch of crap. But it kind of made sense too, the President wouldn't let Aggie go anywhere without an escort.

Jimmy was late as usual; he and a bunch of kids came in together. But Jimmy made a beeline right to Aggie and Mel once he saw them standing off by the bleachers.

"Where you bitches been? You missed pancake dinner; we all went to Jake's Egg House. Jake gave us student discounts."

"We had to give the cops the slip," Aggie said quietly.

She felt like crap about missing out. A few weeks after graduation and already she was forgotten. Nobody bothered to tell her about meeting at Jake's. OK the cops were on her all the time, so nobody could get close without a hassle, but what about texting, email, something. Why wasn't anyone trying to get in touch? If she didn't have a home PC she wouldn't know about anything going on.

"Jimmy, you won't believe where…"

Aggie jabbed Mel in the ribs and she shut up. OK Aggie was getting paranoid. Maybe the Feds have this place wired. Maybe she was going crazy. Maybe it was better nobody invited her to the sleepover, but something told her telling about the moon was a bad idea.

Mel covered it, she got the hint. Aggie just stood there like a stone while Mel and Jimmy jabbered and jabbered. Aggie felt like she was outside listening in. When Jimmy sailed off to a group of kids Aggie was relieved. Everybody got together and took out the padded floor mats and sleeping bags and spread them around and she felt better to have something to do.

The music blasted, kids were dancing or talking, snacks were eaten, and some kids played board games—no phones were allowed. But Aggie just couldn't get into it. She sank cross-legged into a dark corner between the retracted bleachers and leaned on the wall and faded into the dark with her thoughts alone. Everyone was avoiding her anyway and nobody seemed to notice she wasn't in on the fun. OK she was never popular, but she had friends, and many of her fellow nerds were there but they didn't want to talk, they acted more like they were afraid of her. What a sucky way to start summer vacation.

NINE

Leaving the Sleepover

Nine a.m. and the facilitators were waking everyone up, the kids that got any sleep anyway. Whoever said sleepovers were for sleeping never went to one. It took half the night, but most of the kids stopped ignoring Aggie. Nobody wanted to hear about aliens, everyone was tired of it and Aggie was glad—aliens were the last thing she wanted to think about. All night they talked of college and future plans. Many of the kids were now officially seniors although the fall session was weeks away and the postgraduation kids, Mel, Jimmy, Aggie and a handful of others were all about college talk, in between the latest gossips, of course. The night was just what Aggie needed; it was great to do what normal kids do, one last fun thing before fall and hopefully, college.

After clean up the kids filed out, parents were due to pick up at ten, but most of the kids got there on their own. Mel lived close but called her mom for a ride anyway.

"You sure your mom won't mind taking me out to Geiger Ave.?" Aggie said. She and Mel sat on the old brick wall in front of the church dangling their feet. Mel's combat boots gave a dull thud every time she hit the wall. "It is way too hot to walk; I'm baking already." If Aggie was hot Mel had to be roasting, all she ever wore was black.

"If she doesn't do it I'll take you, I have my permit."

"No way, they'll never let you drive their stuff. OK maybe the cheap car, maybe the Bentley, but forget the Rolls. For your eighteenth b-day ask for a monster-mobile, something black with big tires."

Mrs. Van Ness pulled into the loading zone and hit the auto door opener. She had the Benz SUV. Aggie slid into the back seat next to Mel. The smell of fine leather hit Aggie funny and she thought if cowhide smelled that good on living cows, they'd all be house pets instead of burgers. Bio-bots had that same smell but faint: They were made out of cow parts so it figured. Mrs. Van Ness turned to greet them with a big fashion model perfect smile but when she saw Aggie, her mouth tuned down.

"Oh, Aggie Piper, I'm afraid I can't accommodate you, not after all that trouble. You know my husband's business took a hit thanks to you. I'm afraid you are not welcome just now. Peter is very upset with you at present..."

Mrs. Van Ness rattled on with more lame excuses but Aggie tuned her out. That perfect mouth was working but the sound didn't penetrate. Aggie did notice, however, Van Ness had lines around the corners of her mouth.

"Models do age I guess."

"Excuse me young lady?"

"Nothing" Aggie said. "Can you lend me some cash for a cab?"

Van Ness took a bill from the car's visor and handed it over the seat. Aggie looked at it. It was a hundred-dollar bill. "Keep it, that's fine. Come Melissa."

"Dude, I'll call you." Mel said as Aggie slid out of the SUV.

Mrs. Van Ness drove off leaving Aggie on the curb. Aggie could swear Mel's mom had a phone on her face as she took off. Aggie started walking toward Duvall; it was only a block south, there would be cabs there. Aggie didn't want to wait for a citizen's cab. It was only a short walk but she didn't get very far.

A cop car swooped in. Two guys jumped out. They never had two guys in a car. One guy was a local cop, a real pervert named Gene Rickman; the other one was an MP.

"That's her," the MP said.

"No shit. Over here Piper, hands up."

Aggie didn't comply. She was about to tell him off but Rickman charged her, grabbed her hard, spun her around and rammed her up against the patrol car. He jerked her arms back and put the cuffs on her and too tight. Aggie was so shocked by his sudden aggressive behavior she didn't have time to think about clocking him.

He started pawing her, patting her down. All she had on was a sundress and no underwear. He cupped Aggie's ass cheek. "How'd you like that? You little bitch."

Aggie was about to back kick him right in the balls when the MP jumped in.

"Hey, asshole" The MP said, "She's a minor, knock it the fuck off."

"What're you going to do about it?" Rickman said. His voice was laced with meanness.

The MP drew his 45 like a trick shooter, cocked it and put it right into Rickman's face. "How about I arrest you? Back off. This is federal national security; under martial law, I'm in charge."

"What!?" Aggie said.

"Miss Piper, please get into the car." The MP said. He opened the door, made sure Aggie didn't bump her head, but he didn't loosen the cuffs either. "When you went missing a state of emergency was declared."

"Oh crap, oops." She realized who the MP was, one of the men that was assigned to watch her at school before she quit. She felt bad about messing with that MP guy before, he was OK. She had made fun of his rank and junk. After the two cops got in, the MP turned around. Rickman's eyes in the rearview squinted like he was pooping a brick—that guy is just way mean.

"Are you OK, Ms. Piper?"

"Let me guess," Aggie said. "Sneaking out last night was a real bad idea, right Sergeant? It wasn't that hard I just…"

"It's Captain. Please keep your mouth shut Miss Piper. Officer Rickman here doesn't have security clearance." The MP sounded kind of snippy. "This I'll say, if he treats another national treasure this poorly ever again, he'll no longer qualify as a police officer." He turned to Rickman. "You read me, asshole?"

"That's OK Cap, I'll let President Jane know he sexually harassed me." Rickman glared at Aggie in the rearview mirror. Aggie stuck out her tongue. She meant what she said. "You're toast."

Rickman didn't respond but he stomped the gas pedal a little too hard. Aggie had worked out a good story overnight to tell them. She thought she'd just show up. She never expected they'd make a big deal out of it: Getting arrested more than sucked. She did nothing wrong, wasn't she a free citizen, didn't she have rights! Dad was right about The Man. Aggie was more pissed than afraid. What a bunch of butt munches. Give small minds power and you get a crap load of Rickman types.

"Why am I arrested? I want a lawyer. I want my mom!" They didn't respond. "OK, be a butt-munch your 'er toast Rickman. I got pictures of you reading a titty book in your patrol car. I'm posting it on the Key Bulletin Board. You're so screwed. I know my rights, I have lawyers."

From the backseat Aggie could tell Richman was smiling. OK let him think he's so big. I'll have Buddy visit him. I'll show him. I'll mess up his car's electronics. Aggie worked out plans of vengeance and attack inside her head when she was mad but she'd never actually did anything. It was just a way to burn out the frustration. This time maybe she'd go further, do something mean for real. Tell Jane for sure. That guy was a total dick. Everybody knew he was the town bully.

Aggie didn't have time to plan a detailed revenge. The cop car headed straight for the Navy base, not the one near her house but the one in town. The car blasted past the main gate and parked in the security building's lot, just inside. They arrived within five minutes of leaving the Unitarian Church. The MP guy helped Aggie out of the car and he was careful about it, respectful really. He snatched Richman's key out of his hand and un-cuffed her. He didn't give that junk back to Rickman—screw that cop anyway. The MP tossed dickhead's cuffs into a ditch. Aggie prayed Goddess that Rickman would get punished for losing city property.

"Get lost Officer." The MP said. He and Aggie stood by while Rickman drove off. "I'm sorry about him Miss Piper. Let's go. Admiral Sanderson needs to speak with you."

"Oh crap, I hate that guy."

"You're not the only one."

The MP walked Aggie up to the security building, used a key card, got inside the lobby and handed her off to the guy behind a chest-high counter. She was told to take a seat, it would be a while. Aggie lowered herself into an orange plastic chair, chairs just like at the high school's office. The waiting room wasn't much different either. She felt like she did last fall, in trouble again. But this time Mrs. Preggey wasn't the one going to drill her, this time the fear she felt was serious. She had the feeling there was more at stake than suspension or a scholarship. What did he mean by 'national security matter' anyway? *God, I hate that crap; can't I just be a girl?*

TEN

Hot Water

Sanderson was up all night, which didn't help his mood. When the President found out the Piper girl was MIA, the shit hit the fan. The Pentagon wanted him back here ASAP. A couple of his men were first to arrive on site an hour after the girl was reported disappeared but he was out of communication by then. He turned off his phone on the Delaware to Jersey ferry. It was the first time he put out to sea in years and he wanted to enjoy it.

His boys told him while in flight that Piper's place was crawling with Homeland Security men—who belonged to who weren't clear. His men kept mouths shut and eyes wide. Thank God nobody from the NRO showed up.

When Sanderson left Fort Dix last night the CIA was still grilling Levine, but he knew they'd get nothing out of Levine; they didn't have a clue who they were dealing with. No point in wasting his men's time. He didn't think Levine was in on it anyway especially not with the President's special agent glued on his arm. Levine wouldn't let the Piper girl slip out. Branford was paying him to keep tabs as well. That goddamn robot was useless, alien probes don't talk. He was already at the Naval Air Station when the call came in that they found her. She went to a goddamn sleepover party like a goddamn kid. Nobody that valuable should be allowed to act like a kid. If it weren't for Albright, he'd have Piper on ice at Leavenworth breaking rocks.

He and Chief Petty Officer Hart watched from the camera room as she was brought in. Hart was a good man to know, hell any petty officer was worth five times his weight in high brass commissioned officers. NCOs are what made the Navy float.

Hart ran security under the official security commander so Sanderson had gotten to know him informally. The Admiral played it off the cuff, but like everything Sanderson did, this causal poker-game friendship was calculated to produce more than a winning pot.

After they got settled in the observation room CPO Hart said, "Admiral, good to see you again. Card game Friday at Shaffer's again. Should I let Command know we have her?"

"Not yet, I'll interview her first. No recordings, everything about her is top secret, need-to-know."

"Technically, she's not under arrest." Hart had just read the notes his MP hand wrote about the arrest. "Stupid local cop, if Albright gets wind of this...my man should have stood on that cop's neck, they'll bust me down..."

The Chief went on listing all the violations and quoting the law but Sanderson didn't care, he only had half an ear for it. He'd handle whatever came. No doubt Piper would tell all on the damn internet anyway. That girl shouldn't be allowed open communication.

Sanderson ignored the CPO and instead watched the girl intently on the HD monitor. It struck him that the Piper girl looked more like his own daughter than he first thought. That day on Sunset Pier, he saw it but didn't see it, he was too pissed, but he read the resemblance loud and clear now. This little girl was smart too, just like Sarah used to be before...Piper got away from the MPs easy enough, but how? Sanderson had a few unearthly ideas.

Hart stopped talking and blew up the picture and zoomed in. He searcher her for weapons with the computer's radar and infrared and whatever tech he had available but when he finished scanning Hart rested the camera view on her chest. The Piper girl was breathing easy. She wasn't scared, pulse was normal. Maybe she was meditating; hippies did that sort of shit.

"She's lacking in the tit department." Hart said, "She's too skinny but still doable." Hart was a well-known womanizer, or at least he talked a good game.

"She's a goddamn kid," Sanderson gave Hart the stink eye. "Go get her. I'll see her in the soundproof room."

There wasn't much to this interrogation room. Yellowed cement-block walls no doubt lined in lead, a stainless-steel table with hard chairs bolted to the floor on both sides and a big mirror next to the entry. CPO Hart would record anyway, any security CPO would. Sanderson pulled out a pen, twisted it and his alien tech jamming device went to work. The pen's clip had Branford Industries' logo on it. He laid it on the table in violation of interrogation protocol.

Sanderson stood up and put on his best smile when Piper was brought in. He stuck his hand out in greeting and said, "Admiral Sanderson, here. Good to see you again."

"I know you. No thanks dick brain, but if you want me to break your thumb, fine with me." She flopped down into a chair and crossed her arms. "You're Jon's boss, you can't be trusted. I want a lawyer."

Sanderson eased back into his chair and it didn't complain. He had lost a lot more stress-weight since Piper landed Karnack's goddamn mothership in Key West. The world was falling apart and his appetite went to shit with it. He drummed his fingers on the metal table. From what he read about her, she might well have broken his thumb. His usual intimidation dance wasn't going to work on her.

"See here Piper, you be honest with me and I'll be honest with you. You don't need a lawyer, you're not under arrest, but I can make that happen."

"Go ahead butt-hole, but you'll be nursing a busted face while I sit in jail, you locked the door right. How's your athletic ability?"

Sanderson laughed and the girl's eyes caught fire. He didn't doubt she'd put his lights out given the chance. His first impression was right; she won't fall for his bullshit. Kid or not, Levine trained her, after all.

"OK fine, but before I bring you home, answer me this, how'd you get away?"

This time Piper laughed. "Anything I say can and will be used against me. Drop dead."

Sanderson bolted to his feet and she did the same. That girl was coiled tight.

"Don't fuck with me missy, I know how you did it, goddamn aliens is how. I want to know what you know, it's national security, for America. I don't give a shit how exactly, let me guess, Praytis came and tractor beamed you out, I'm right aren't I?"

The girl flinched back like she was caught, but she leaned in quick to offset her reaction. He wasn't sure about her little reveal but she was just a kid, he had to remind himself. She's not trained for this. She was debriefed weeks ago, but apparently the warnings didn't sink in. She's tough, but he had his answer. She had outside help, had to be. Hell, the girl has a goddamn space fleet. Thank God she doesn't know what to do with it other than play hooky. It was time to double security; that fact was confirmed as the girl eased back into her chair and didn't answer.

"Praytis is behind this." He said slowly.

"How'd you know Praytis? Duh, everybody knows him. OK, so, go ask him if he helped. Go find him. I'm under the President's protection you know, I don't have to say anything; you want her to fire you? Back off Skippy."

New strategy.

"Tell you what, Aggie, I'll call you Aggie, I'll tell you some truth and you tell me some. I know Praytis firsthand and that is top secret information. I know him because I'm the Pentagon's liaison to the aliens. The U.S. Government has been in negotiations with the aliens for some time." *No doubt he told her that.* "We are working on a trade deal. This was all hush-hush, but well, you opened this can of worms. The U.S. Government needs to know all we can about the aliens. Surely you understand that? Surely you want to help your homeland."

Nothing spilled all common knowledge. Appeal to her patriotism.

"You're messing with me now." She laughed. "Oh, you mean the empire that wiped out millions of Native Americans and killed millions of innocent civilians in World War II and Iraq, no thanks."

"Don't you care about your country?"

The girl leaned back and put her hands behind her head. She took a few moments. "Country, poop, you guys are an empire, empires suck. You guys in-terviewed the crap out of me already. I told the press everything I told you guys,

OK, but OK, I'll tell you something you don't know. Praytis told me when I got Mother, there's a college on the moon. A lot of the UFOs seen are just school kids' joy riding. Bet you didn't know that. You butt munches shoot at kids, hello, just kids."

"There isn't any evidence of that." He lied.

"You're joking right? You government butt heads will kill people just to get technology that isn't even yours, not nice. What do you guys do for fun, make puppy juice? Gee this glass needs more puppy lungs, gosh." She mimed drinking from a glass. "Mmmm, could use more cat ass."

This went on for an hour and Sanderson got nothing useful, just worse and worse jokes and sharper insults. He had the sense she knew much more than she said. She surely understood the nature of the American empire. Maybe she got some stuff off him, but that didn't matter. The funnel was closing down on her and she didn't even know it. He did confirm one thing, Praytis was made First Mate of Mother—the ship has a name. That tidbit made Praytis vulnerable. Praytis can't work for two masters. The GTO wouldn't release him, not as far as Sanderson could see, so Praytis had to be off balance, divided loyalties. That was something he would use.

Praytis must have talked up a storm, the girl knew too much about the moon and the GTO. Hell, she knew more about aliens than he did after thirty years of direct contact, and she got all that while on board with Praytis. He'd let the GTO know they had a loose lips problem. She tapped the ship's artificial intelligence in what, a couple of hours? That girl was the key. Once he reported, Sanderson knew what his bosses would do next, and it wouldn't be pretty. It was fast becoming time for the Pentagon to shift gears.

"I'm done playing nice. Look missy, you had better be straight with me, you know about Gitmo, there are government operatives there you don't want to meet. It's best for you if you cooperate, or I'll arrange..."

Piper got up suddenly, jumped over the table, and before Sanderson could do shit, she had his hand and arm twisted up into some kind of karate lock. His thumb felt like it would break off. He was 6-4, she was 5-10, and he expected she couldn't take such a big man as himself down so fast, but he found out otherwise. If his goddamn heart wasn't a mess he'd flip her like a wet rag, but he just didn't have the speed anymore.

"OK Skippy, I've had enough, walk me out of here or you lose this digit, that's your thumb, in case you didn't know. I know big words corn-fuse you hard guys."

She snatched his pen off the table and pressed into his back. "Don't think I won't push this right through your spine." She let go of his arm. "Let's go."

"Fine, fine, we're leaving anyway, my pen please?"

"OK when we're out of here."

To prove a point, Sanderson did a move and reversed Piper's situation. He managed it without chest pains for a change. He twisted the pen and put it back in his top pocket. The jammer was off.

She backed away and took a fighting stance. "Lead us out of here now or I'll clobber you for real. Ever get kicked in the kidney?" The girl jumped up and flicked her foot out about 6 feet into the air and such a blow caught under one's chin would snap a man's neck. She moved faster than a snake's tongue.

Piper didn't know about his alien-made artificial back and neck bones. Bullets would bounce off it. But then again, his liver and kidneys weren't bullet proof, in fact like his heart, they were slowly failing. Damn if this girl wasn't a rip, Sarah would like Piper if she had enough of a mind left. Sanderson thought he should go see her again soon; her eighty eighth birthday was coming up. He'd go back to New Jersey for her convalescent home birthday party if they both lived long enough for him to attend.

"Fine, fine, I'll take you home, let's go."

He stopped them at the security desk and checked out. He had the desk bring up a car to take the girl home. He stayed behind.

He was done with her for now and already moving on, but the CIA and the rest were just getting started. If the President didn't have orders out to leave her alone she'd be chained up in Gitmo now.

A little pain drilled into his heart as the car rolled away with Piper in the front seat. He didn't know if it was emotion or just his pacemaker acting up. That girl had balls and he liked her for it. No wonder Al Branford was so proud of her.

"You're getting soft, Sanderson."

He felt fear for her, too. They'd torture her once they got the green light. Some of them boys would do it just to prove a point, or just for a laugh. The girl media-dumped everything she knew about aliens' weeks ago, but that wouldn't stop interrogations. If she was like his Sarah, they'd get nothing. He admired girls with guts. Sarah did duty in a Vietnam MASH unit. Too bad they'd tear Piper's mind open and make her spill her gut. That's just how empire goes, they take what they want.

His phone rang while he watched her drive off. The Chiefs wanted him back. Piper managed to get another movie out onto the net, but something else was eating them; Brinks was too nasty. The Pentagon was one step ahead and had Sanderson's flight to D.C. on the docket already. His every move was under scrutiny. What were they up to?

When did his great America become a banana republic? His internals digested that question all the way to Washington, but he got no relief, only a bitter taste in the back of his thoughts and the antacids weren't working.

ELEVEN

Jane Albright's Morning

President Jane Albright setup shop inside one of the small vintage libraries inside the White House on the insistence of her sister, Jenifer Nostrum. Jane agreed for a couple of reasons. First, Jane was warned that the Oval Office was wired, Jen would know and so did others, and secondly the President's official office wasn't conducive for work. Albright wasn't a museum docent; sitting at an empty desk while visitors waltzed in and out all-day kissing ass didn't cut it. She had accepted the election's mandate to get things done. This old obsolete in-house legal library was informal and much akin to her former law office. It was cluttered and comforting and she needed such respite in theses changing times—it felt like a solid footstone within a lake of quicksand.

Outside her open doors, in the hall, it was chaos as usual. Aides and cabinet secretaries hurried past each other, her security men were hard pressed dodging them, people were arguing in hushed tones. Everyday chaos was a given, but the Piper girl's disappearance last night added a new layer. It was bad enough that the young lady forced the alien disclosure which no one in the security state wanted, but now she was making herself even more troublesome. The new blog was a topper, too. By implication, Piper made everyone in national security look like idiots.

Brad, her assistant was milling around the double door hopping from one foot to the other. Both sides of the door were wide open so Jane had a clear view. Brad was the former house facilities staff supervisor and had been at that job with the last two Presidents. That he, a tall, skinny, flaming gay man kept his job while Republicans ran the place is why she promoted him to executive assistant. First, he was a survivor. Second, he was the only one that knew what was happening in the house.

Without Brad, her first two years in office would have been nothing but a long game of catch-up. He's the one that told her about the Olympic swimming pool in the basement that she used daily. She trusted him. She tried not to like him but that didn't work out.

Jane waved him in. There were two armed men, one on either side of the entry, but they didn't frisk him. They never did, he was in an out a hundred times a day. Jane wondered if Brad was sleeping with one of them.

"Brad, what have we got?"

"What, no good morning? I see we are tight this morning. You look like trash. Get you to the hair dresser for god's sake. You have a meeting this afternoon with royalty."

"I have a hair appointment for 8 a.m."

"Hello, that was an hours ago. I'll set you up for eleven. I cannot believe how gray you're getting; no women forty-five should be so skinny and have such bad hair. We need a national glamour girl, not Hilda the crone. Maybe they can touch you up. For god's sake eat something."

"Fine, fine, make sure you come get me so I can't forget." Jane looked past Brad; there were three people at the door waiting. More were no doubt lined up down the hallway. Her new Chief of Staff, what was his name, Paul, Paul…Clapper. "Be a dear Brad, go and get me a bagel, and tell Paul to come in."

Jane wasn't one to do politics when there was work to be done. Political favors didn't figure into her needs. She wasn't a party wonk girl and as she didn't have long standing political connections, she had HR hire the best guy they could get out of the NAO. The way things were going, politics had to take a back seat to the alien reality, and anyone that didn't understand that, like Andy who Paul replaced, wasn't going to last with her.

The door was fifteen yards away so she got a good look at Paul. She looked right past him before now. He was the typical policy wonk, she thought, soft, bald, and too ambitious for his size—he could pass for a shriveled-up Phil Silvers.

"Madam President, allow me to present…"

"Cool it Paul, we don't do formal here. I understand you were with the National Accounting Office, is that right?"

Brad poked his head inside the doorway and yelled, "Hair's on for eleven," and disappeared.

"Most unusual…"

"So as an accountant, I asked for one you know, I'm going after the military budget. I need someone with numbers chops, but of course, you'll have other duties. I understand Andy brought you up to speed."

"Yes, Madam Presi…"

"Jane, call me Jane. So, did Senator Branch confirm, he's due. Ted knows it right?"

Paul scanned his clipboard. Jane liked that, she was sick of Ultra Phones and Me-tablets or whatever they called them lately. What was so bad about pen and paper?

"Yes Madam…Jane, he is in the hallway now, and not very happy I must add."

"Fine, tell me why, that's your job, in part, is to give me the juice. What's bugging the Service Arms Committee?"

"In light of the alien presents, the Pentagon is asking for more money and..."

"They aren't getting any. What else?"

"His SAP requests are foremost on his mind, he said it's critical and..."

"Special Access Program, oh, you mean black budget money, it's off the table. If he removes SAPs I'll sign the military's basic operations budget. I want numbers; I want to know what money goes where, first. Work on that. Draft a letter to that effect. Tell them no numbers, no dice. Get cracking, I want the numbers."

Paul's complexion turned pasty. By his look, he was pretty rattled. He started stammering but pulled himself together. His voice pitched up. "You don't understand, you can't cross the Service Arms people, its political alienation...maybe worse...the Pentagon always gets what it needs."

"Need or want? That was true once, but not now, feeding more money into the military's gaping maul isn't going to make us safer; it never has and never will. We have aliens; it's crazy to think our hardware can touch them. Trade is what we must do. No more military cash cows grazing on the people's money, I'm doubling up on NASA."

Paul put his head down, shook his head and waged his droopy dog cheeks. "You don't understand...you have to play their game, you don't know...I..."

Brad again put his head into the room and yelled. "Ohhhh Jane, Mr. Branch is about to wet his panties, you better see him. I just had this carpet shampooed."

One of the guards let out a little squeaky laugh, Jane gave him the evil eye and he quickly straightened up.

"Send him in."

Jane hardly saw Paul leaving. Senator Branch entering sucked up all the light as Paul slinked away. Paul would have made a good ghost, nothing he said was material and if you didn't look right at him with intent, you'd never see him. Branch wasn't a big man, not like Sanderson, but his presence filled the room. Jane didn't buy it. The man was a shill, a salesman, a tool. After formalities, she had him sit.

"Madam President, we have a situation in Haiti, I'm sure you are aware that the Piper spaceship is hosted there and that Piper's lawyer has brought suit, and that slows our security process but let me list why that isn't..."

I know you're building steam to annex Haiti, that's what you want me to sign, not happening.

"I can't tell you how important Haiti is to American's interest..."

More to the interest of the defense industry's greed; Space girl's grandfather is a primary defense contractor, and space girl's mother is the lawyer in question and he expects me to crack that egg?

Branch went on and on spreading his political butter but Jane didn't hear much more of what he said. Same augments with different side dishes. His words always tasted sweet, just sugar floating on hot air. Like cotton candy, Branch's logic wasn't healthy, just a lot of empty calorie words sprinkled over fat lies and all so the bloated military could hog more of the people's money and worse, prevent the people from getting their fair share. This habit had to stop. America and the world had a new chance, a better path ahead, a bright future and all she had to do to make it happen was beat back the sharks. She wasn't going to blow this like Bush blew 9/11.

Brad popped into the room. "They found that alien girl; she was at a sleepover. Do you believe it?"

"Show the Senator out, please. And get my sister on the phone."

"I'm not finished." Senator Branch said.

Jane picked up her bagel and bit into it. She didn't notice that Brad had brought it until then.

"Next!"

Brad danced into the room and led the Senator out by the law maker's elbow. The Senator didn't care for a gay man handling him physically and that's why Jane instructed Brad to always give the Senator that personnel touch. Senator P.J. Branch wasn't happy, and that was fine with her. She didn't care to make even one bigot happy. She'd never convince Branch to act human; he was to politically set in his constituents' ways. His right-wing army, those who protested the aliens while calling for a holy war, those people she had a stake in; changing their minds mattered. Men such as Branch would follow suit if she won over his constituents, but how? How to turn self-deluded people, who are convinced that aliens are demons, was the challenge shaping up. She made a note to talk with the PR department about developing another public relations strategy.

"Oh Jane, the EPA is here, smoke is pouring out of her ears. Let's hope it's not methane."

"Send her in." Jane braced for the next assault. She'd call Jenifer after that.

TWELVE

Aggie Back Home

Aggie didn't say a word to the driver. She thought about going to Mel's, but Mel was up all night, too. Sanderson told the driver to take her, but he didn't say where. She told him to take her to Miami. Aggie nodded out on the ride home and she woke at her front gate. It still pissed her off that they put up gates, one on her lane and one on Geiger Ave—what was this, a police state? OK the Keys were under state of emergency laws but they still had rights, right? And what was the big emergency anyway?

As the car stopped she knew her ships weren't there, just Buddy, what's the big deal? On the thought Buddy rolled out and smacked the limo's door. Buddy flying around freaked out the guards, so she had grounded him to keep the peace. Buddy on the ground was just a big gray-white beach ball with blinking lights rolling around, but he still acted like a Labrador and followed her everywhere. Now he was bouncing off the car's door. Aggie rolled down the window.

"Buddy back up, silly I can't get out!"

As Aggie opened the door a guard she didn't know came running up, he had his rifle trained on Buddy, the guy looked pretty freaked out.

"Leave Buddy alone!"

"Kowalski, stand down, back up." Dave said running up. He was the main MP guy. Aggie thought he was OK, they had talked a bunch.

"It just took off; I thought it was a ball. It just rolled away; Jesus Christ didn't know it's a fucking alien. Thought it was a lobster pot float or something."

Buddy was close to Aggie now making little rolling motions against her leg. "I missed you too Buddy."

"Wait till you see that sucker flying." Dave said. "Stay at the gate, Aggie I'll walk you back."

"So, Dave, what's happening, what's with all the extra people? Somebody declare war on hippies?"

Buddy charged at the new guy and backed up. The guy took a few steps in reverse and Buddy followed. The guy almost fell over the gate backwards. Aggie wished the guy would wet himself, but it didn't happen. That dick head almost shot her probe.

"That's enough Buddy, chill out, come on Dave let's go." Aggie headed down the lane toward her house and Buddy rolled along behind crunching the coral gravel as he went. It was a hundred yards walk. "What's with all these men?"

"Yeah," Dave said, "When you weren't home, confirmed at morning check, day shift called in red alert. But I had to report last night, too. Nobody saw you after sunset. Sorry my shift report said that, so they started filing in overnight."

"You didn't get in trouble, right; it's not your fault I sneaked out."

"I was off duty. My eight starts at 0900. Houser sent in my shift report. I'm out of this loop."

"Thank the Goddess."

When they got to a spot where Mark said there were no ears, Dave stopped them, indicated he had a few words. She thought he'd be pissed, he was supposed to watch her. She braced for a storm.

"I don't want to know how you did it, but you're up shit's creek. You see the news?" He said quietly.

"I'm almost eighteen; I can leave if I want." Aggie said loud. She wanted the surveillance guys to know it. What were they going to do when she left for college in September? Offers came in from everywhere, maybe she'd go to Oxford which would rattle the crap out of them. Jon let the U.K. have a downed Mac, that's why he was in jail, he disobeyed direct orders—it was so unfair.

"They're putting the clamps down; they added more men to the roster. We're doubling up."

"Whatever."

"One suggestion, Kowalski isn't the only lug head in this man's Corps; I'd have that robot disappear if I were you. I know how this goes. I'd bet there are ten pencil necks lined up to dissect it now."

"He needs a recharge anyway, I'll tell him to go back to Mother, thanks Dave."

More men what did that mean? She couldn't go anywhere without a cop crawling up her ass as it was and now it'll be worse than before. What a bunch of crap. OK when she first landed Mother, they were all over her, she got that. Nobody ever hijacked and landed an alien spaceship before. Everybody wanted the story. This was getting ridiculous all over again.

But she had told them everything, why can't they just leave her alone? Well not everything. Somehow Mother impressed her with cautions. She never told anyone that Mother got inside her head. That was kind of way too freaky and scary. But Mother was on target. Aggie was brought up with certain truths, mom and dad laid them out logically and that one big idea really hit home, she saw why they said it, never trust The Man.

She made it to the porch and Dave peeled away. Buddy rolled up the stairs, how he did it, who could tell? Rolling up hill, really? It sure looked like anti-gravity. Come to think of it, Mother had Earth normal gravity in space. *I bet they'd love to know how that's done.*

Aggie booted up the PC and turned on the TV. It was weird, new furniture, new computers, big-ass Smart TV, Grandpa sent it all over. The old place seemed too modern. She felt like she didn't belong here anymore. Home was getting to be just like some kind of jail. She thought of Jon, he was in jail for real. If the TV was watching her, who was on the other side?

On TV Mom was on some news show talking about how the government was trying to annex Haiti. It was a taped interview. The reporter was saying how taking the island is good for America and junk like that—what a tool. They showed a picture of Mother parked on that dead coral beach. Army guys were standing around her. The locals were protesting the army guys.

The reporter was saying, "So then Mrs. Piper, the government is saying that the ship has acted aggressively toward American researchers, they say they feel it necessary to take punitive action."

Mom said, "First, Mother had government people on board for quite some time, it's her prerogative to eject uninvited guests. Second, this is Haiti, as you know I represent Haiti, and the U.S. doesn't have the right to do what they want here..."

Aggie heard the same arguments over and over. TV news truly sucked. Can't they come up with anything new? Same old crap over and over. Aggie clicked off the TV.

Why annex Haiti? They wanted Mother, that's why. They never gave a crap about Haiti before. That pissed her off. They had no right! Aggie lay down on the new sofa thinking she had to get lost. *First chance I get I'm outta here.* Buddy rolled over to the sofa and nudged Aggie's arm.

"Buddy," she whispered. She pressed her lips against his shell, just in case he wasn't jamming the Fed's electronic ears "Go back to Mother and get charged, when you come back stay invisible, don't let anyone see you, OK."

Buddy did his yes dance and rolled out the open door. He started glowing right on the porch and then took flight. He zipped around the compound a few times, just a puppy having fun. She heard the new guy cussing; maybe he pooped his pants, that'd be good.

Yeah, I got to go too. She had enough of this crap but she'd need a different plan. She'd escape and this time she wasn't coming back, no way. Oxford, why not check it out? Anything was better than the moon. But Dave was right, keep Buddy undercover. She had an idea how to use that. Obi Wan-Mark was always saying junk like that, like 'get an advantage and keep it secret.' Apples don't fall far from the tree and Mark's Jedi apple tree just landed a plum idea. First chance she got, Aggie was outta there.

THIRTEEN

The President Calls

Brad blew into the President's office waving a cell phone. It wasn't the official phone the CIA gave her, it wasn't her own I-Know phone; it was something special that Jen had gotten from Van Ness Industries. The CIA didn't have the backdoor codes, not yet.

"I got your sissy on the line; she's with that hunk, Mark. They're at Mark's place."

Jane took the phone and pressed it to her ear, "Jen, what the hell's…"

Brad pressed a finger to the President's lips and said, "You better take it in the can, no pun, I had them sweep the shitter." Brad pointed the way with his chin. She had forgotten about the little rest room in the back of the law library. It was a single use facility. The spy industry never wired it.

"Nixon was never back there. Maxwell Smart would have loved it."

Get Smart, 1960's TV sitcom?

"Give me a second," Jane covered the mouth piece, "Brad shut the doors on your way out."

Jane entered the rest room, closed the door, dropped the seat cover and sat down. She didn't lose the connection. Van Ness made great hardware, she wondered if it was actually secure.

***

Nostrum, her chosen name, held the phone to an ear and waited. Mark and she were in Mark's office behind his marina's cafe.

Mark had jammers going, and reflective lead linings in the walls, old-school counter measures and that's why Jen didn't trust this environment. She didn't trust anyone or anything and that was standard procedure in her and Mark's world. He got how this all works better than most agents. She didn't trust much but Mark, on the other hand, she took a chance on. She had to trust somebody. Mark proved worthy. Jennifer figured that much out about him in Span.

"I'm putting you on speaker," Nostrum said, "Mark's here." The phone had real time two-way visual. The screen was small but the picture good. Jennifer placed it on an clean eyelevel shelf.

"I need not remind you, this conversation is classified." The President said. "You both still hold clearance, but as it is, they'll pull it if they find any excuse… things are out of control, the military, press, congress; people are demanding the Piper girl's head."

"Why do they always shoot the messenger," Mark said rhetorically. They all knew the answer; it is always about maintaining power and acquiring more money.

"That's what you get when you fuck up everyone's scams." Nostrum said. "I told you up front, before you ran for office, how bad things are; Shadow Government's the real enemy."

"That messenger is important," Jane said. "She is more than just that, she has a spaceship and people, our people will kill for it. Why'd you let her get away, don't you know they'll use it?" The exasperations and stress in the President's voice was obvious. Jane's usual hard demeanor showed deep cracks on the little phone screen.

"Look Sis, you said to give the girl a break, so we did. They don't know Mark and I back her up. She was going AWOL even if we didn't help clear her way. So, don't get prickly with me."

"You did say give Aggie a break." Mark added. "Mostly, she needed to get out from under security; it's daunting for a young girl."

"I thought a day at the zoo, something escorted, secure, not this." Jane said.

"She's fine. No harm done. I'd bet the kid's even remorseful." Nostrum said.

"She's valuable, her emotional state doesn't matter." Jane said.

"You sound just like the people you're trying hard not to be. What's really going on, you're not yourself, I know you, and you've got more on your mind."

"They're isolating me," Jane said, "It's what you warned me about…I'm scheduled to do the Alien State of the Union address, if I say rainbow, you'll know…it's what we talked about…Sanderson's been called in. I'm bumping up security, hopefully real patriots. I'm afraid…I don't know how long I can keep theses war dogs chained."

"Whatever happens, Mark and I are with you."

"That's good to know. I've got to move on. I'll wink your way on TV." Jane hung up.

***

Mark saw it plain. Jennifer, that was her real name, was worried. This cool cucumber wilted before his eyes, a thing he never saw a pro do before. She paced the small room twisting a short lock of hair with a finger building a head of steam.

"She's an idiot; you can't fuck with these people, shit! Who knows maybe I really work for them, goddamn it, she needs to shut up. Why can't she just play the long game?"

"They have balls. They'd never pull a President off live TV unless...unless." Mark sat down, "Christ, a coup, or worse. Something big is busting out of the woods. I hope she knows what she's doing."

Jennifer punched a wall. "She's an idealist, how do you think this is going to play out?"

Mark took Jenifer in his arms. She fought the tears, he felt her quivering deep inside, but when he said, "It's OK, Jane will be OK." Nostrum let it out. She cried but her tears abated after a short time. He soon felt her regain control. She let go of him and stepped back.

"I can't go. I'm marked. You have to get to her, I know how. I have a way past security, I'll show you, you have to go, now, be there after the speech. Mark will you do this?"

"I'll do what I can to protect her. But what about Aggie, they want her, they'll..."

"Leave it to me. I can do more from the outside; I have avenues you don't know."

"I'll go see Aggie now, let her know I'm taking a little vacation trip."

"No, it's better that you don't, she might tip them off."

Nostrum was right, of course. One can't let the slightest clue out into the world. Mark knew better too, but his emotions got the better of him.

Mark and Nostrum exited his office like nothing was going on. Mark causally said that he's going over to the engine shop to see how his customer's boat was doing. Jen walked him over to the gate. Mark's pickup was parked there. He had a bug-out bag under the seat. He always had contingencies ready. He got into the truck and the President's field agent leaned in to kiss him. She dropped her special access badge into his lap. The new kid at the gate was a dick but he wasn't observant. Mark took off. He'd hole up a little down the road and wait until after the speech to move in.

"I'll go see how Aggie is doing," Nostrum said.

***

Her last walk down Aggie's lane was like just after the girl came home from parking Mother in the Caribbean. Camo clad special-ops people were in the brush, Seals, she thought. Two Marine guards were at the gate and a dozen more were up the road blocking Geiger Avenue. A couple of CIA SUVs were on the shoulder of the road. No cars were allowed in just like that first lock-down.

Dave, Navy's on-site Marine Corps security NCO was leaning up against the old van, same truck Karnack's boys shot full of holes.

"Aggie inside?" Jennifer asked. "Where's Buddy?"

"She'll be out in a second, watch." Dave had a shit-eating grin on his face. "Haven't seen the robot."

A second later a big black man in a black suit went flying out the door head first. He landed face-on in the coral gravel and hard, too. That had to hurt. Aggie burst out of the door swinging a frying pan.

"Butt head, you don't knock? What's wrong with you!? Just walk right in!" She swung the pan around as the man rolled over. "I told you guys, I'm done answering questions, sneaking up on a girl is, is, is, aahhhkkk!"

Aggie spun and shot back inside. Dave helped the man up. "I told you," Dave said.

Jennifer didn't even try to squelch her laugh. The big guy stormed off brushing white coral dust off his chest. Jen guessed he didn't know about the dirt and coral granules caked on his ass. Sending in a big guy to intimidate Aggie wasn't smart. That asshole should have read her file.

Jen called Aggie from outside, "I'm coming in and I'm not armed."

Aggie came to the door. "Funny Jen, like I could ever out ninja you, give me a break, come on in."

It was the same old place, still a converted bait shop but now with new furniture. She seldom came over, Po-boy's boat and Aggie's job was at Mark's place.

"I don't think his feet touched the porch deck. You seem more apt since your trip on Mother."

"Don't remind me," She said. A flash of worry lit Aggie's face. She was different, that was obvious and maybe she didn't think it good. She appeared stressed. Jennifer was always good at reading small tells.

"It looks like your training took well, but you shouldn't beat up federal agents." Jen said if for the benefit of the one's listening. She rather enjoyed Aggie kicking a CIA agent's ass. She had started there with the CIA and thought half of them deserved worse.

"OK, I'm testy, but that guy was trespassing, hello this is Florida, stand your ground and all that junk."

"They're here to protect you." Jen bit her lip so she didn't laugh.

"Protect me, give me a break, this is home room detention all over again. I've had enough grilling."

She was right; of course, they weren't there to protect her but to protect the State's interests in her. Right now, there wasn't much Jen could do to relieve the situation. Jennifer had to make tracks, but Aggie would remain safe unless Jane got unseated—it really wasn't a question of if, but when and how. Jen had to get busy setting up Mark's escape route contacts. A deep pain hit Jennifer on the thought but she covered how she felt. No need upsetting Aggie.

Looking at the media, pushing the President out was obviously in the works, but it would take time—they had nothing on her. Mark would come back after the speech, if Jane kept her mouth shut. At the moment things weren't overly hot for Aggie but that could change fast.

"So, what's going on, why are you, testy, as you say?" Jennifer asked.

"College, I can't make up my mind and everyone wants me." She pointed at her computer. "But they all want to make deals, you know, free school for access to my ship. What a bunch of crap. I have high SATs, I'm qualified. Screw them, Mark and grandpa got me the college fund, maybe I'll go to Guatemala, anywhere but here."

"You have time to figure it out. You can always start in the midterm."

"Yeah, you're right. Sorry Jen. I must have PMS. Did you see Sky Flower in the news? She's down in Haiti, or she was, I think she's back. I can't keep up. I bet she'll double that human chain, how cool is that? Mother kicked them government goons out, closed up the door. Butt-head army guys. Wish I could go. All Mother wants is some rest, you know?"

It struck Jennifer, Aggie wanted and needed to go down to the mother ship and what was stopping her? It was the State. They were intentionally keeping Aggie away from the ship. So that's the game. She saw why, separation would entice the Pipers to sell out. No point in telling Aggie, that would just aggravate her more.

Nostrum decided she'd see that she got down to Haiti after Mark got back from D.C....if he got back. Moon Dodger was still at the Sea-Tow docks, but fit and ready. It was a handy place to store her under the radar.

"I took Mark's little boat out last week." Jenifer said. "I docked it and it broke the mooring so she drifted off. No point calling Sea-Tow, we didn't know until she was long gone. She's lost at sea, lost for sure." Jennifer winked. Remote listening was good but no electronic ear saw prearranged tells. Aggie nodded, she got the message.

"Bummer man, that was a nice little boat. So, what's happening with you guys?"

"I'm taking off for a few days, leaving in the (wink) morning. I won't be gone long." That wasn't true, just half true. Jennifer had to go underground before orders changed. She mouthed the words 'Mark too.'

Aggie's eyes widened and she hunched her shoulders. Nothing like getting hit with a sudden shock; the girl had to feel panic. "I'll keep an eye on things, you may not see me but I'll be watching." Aggie seemed to relax a little. "That Dave is a good man. If you want to meditate on the east beach, like usual, he'll keep them back and give you space."

"Yeah, I need that more than ever. I always do it nude. The new guys better not be perverts."

Aggie and Jennifer shot the shit for a while, just for cover. It was a boring cordial visit for the ears that dialed in. Aggie showed her stuff on the computer, stuff related to college. Aggie was real hot on the idea. If the smoke ever cleared Aggie would be college bound in a flash. Jen didn't have the heart to tell her that the State won't let her go. They rather see the girl chained up off the grid. Aggie was too valuable to risk and campus was a security nightmare. Jane would help, but there were limits and Jane's prospects weren't good. All Jen's contacts agreed that something big was coming down.

"Don't forget to watch the President's speech tonight," Jennifer said as she left. "I'm sure you'll be mentioned."

Aggie rolled her eyes. Jen was sure the last thing that girl wanted or needed was more publicity.

Best thing Aggie could do was disappear. Mark said he thought Aggie would take the hint—take Moon Dodger and get the hell out of here. Aggie had to be left on her own until Mark got back. Until then the girl was better off missing than surrounded.

As she walked back to Mark's place Nostrum worried that Aggie might have misinterpreted the exchange and sail off to Haiti and that was a bad idea. It was too far, but more so, the place was watched hard core. The island was surrounded as well, not to keep Mother in but to keep Aggie out. Jen didn't know for sure, but that idea smelled like truth. A lot of wheels were turning and Jenifer Nostrum had a mind to jamb a few distractions into the cogs.

FOURTEEN

The President Is Served

Jane hung up the phone and hoped to God that conversation didn't get out. The press would have a field day with it, 'President Lets National Treasure Play Hooky.' She wished she never used that term. That girl was a person, not a thing. Jane had much to do the rest of the day. She had to make ready her speech. A lot of people needed her attention, and her daily planner was packed. But, there she stayed a while hiding in the bathroom like a little girl. She heard a sharp rap on the outer door, it was loud and urgent.

She exited the bathroom and went to the library door and swung it open herself, maybe a little too hard, "What now..." She expected Brad, the guards, chaos, but it was quiet and a man she didn't know wearing a general's uniform stood there. He didn't have a nametag, but he was familiar, was that Brinks?

"Madam President, I took the liberty of clearing the halls. We must have a little chat."

"I'm sorry, no. Get Brad back in here now. I'm busy."

The man pulled a gun. It was a Walther's auto just like James Bond's gun from the movies, it was surreal.

"Scream if you like, it won't matter. I only need a moment then I will go."

He backed her up with the gun until she bumped into a guest chair and sat without thinking.

"You have seen that, what shall we call it, the deep state, the deep state has a long-term agenda and it appears you are bucking the system. I would not advise it."

"The Pentagon works for me, I set the agenda!"

"No, I'm sorry that isn't true. What is true, however, is that every President plays along or, well nobody wants to be the next dead Kennedy." He tossed a folder on her desk.

"In there you'll see how we did JFK. Bobby and Dr. King were easier. We almost blew Kennedy. Oh, and I have another file on 9/11, that one was a little tricky. But as you know, it turned out well for us. We had the Patriot Act ready two years prior. The agenda must go on."

Jane was tough, and she wasn't easy to bullshit, but this man, this file, the sociopath dead look in his eyes, this rang true, this is what Jennifer was speaking of, what Jennifer said could happen. Jane felt woozy. The heights of power were beyond her sight but the effects of its weight weren't. She didn't believe it before, but now there was a smiling five-star general pointing a gun at her face.

"Inside that folder also, we wrote a nice speech for you, of course you'll rewrite and infuse it with your own personality…"

"Or what, you'll blow my head off!"

"Cooperate, you know what we want. Senator Branch and the rest will pass on to you our needs. If you play along…see how well the former Presidents are getting on? And the ones that don't assist us, last I heard Mr. Trump was losing his empire. You see, we don't need to be so crude, just direct in accomplishing our goals. Trump will never know what or who hit him…but time is short and the agenda moves forward, with or without you." The man pocketed his gun and walked out.

After things shifted back to normal she called for a house security report, no visiting generals were on it, she reviewed the security cameras later that day and he didn't appear. Nobody had anything on him. Everyone she asked only mentioned the silent fire drill.

Late that afternoon she was pacing her bedroom suite instead of changing clothes for TV. She had read the speech that the Pentagon wanted read, or better stated, the men behind the Pentagon. There was some mystical cabal she heard of but could never get any information on driving everything. Who they were, she didn't know, what they wanted was what the heights of power always want, they want everything.

They wanted Aggie Piper's ship because she will give its earning potential to the people and that wasn't mentioned. What they wanted was insidiously laced throughout that provided speech. The psychological-ops people were very good at social manipulation. The speech waxed on how the U.S. would take the lead on the Piper Space Port Project. Aggie Piper clearly said in many interviews, and her lawyer repeated, space was for everyone, she'd 'share her stuff with every nation, but the poorest first.' The young lady has guts, fortitude, and vision. The internet says of Aggie Piper what people said about Jane herself as a young lawyer fighting for human rights.

The Piper girl was just a kid trying to do what was right for humanity. In Piper's mind, so the pundits speculated, U.S. hegemony wasn't good for the world; In Jane's mind America wasn't good for the survival of mankind. The young lady was right in saying on a recent podcast, "If we don't turn things around this planet is toast." But, the mainstream media stopped interviewing Piper weeks ago—

how curious. Who pulled that plug? It wasn't the ratings hungry media. That Piper girl had saved the planet once already, we should listen, Jane thought…or, "this planet is toast."

"Out of the mouths of babes," Jane said.

President Jane Albright crumpled up the Pentagon's speech and dropped it into a waste paper basket.

FIFTEEN

Sanderson and Brinks

At least this time Sanderson got a decent ride. The military personnel transport was a converted passenger jet, but the first-class section was reserved for officers and had decent service, the chairs weren't bad, either.

He checked his watch. It was one of Branford's, he'd forgotten about it. Aggie's gift was still inside his uniform's jacket pocket. He didn't have time to get it checked out and he wasn't convinced the girl should have it either way.

"Can I get you anything?" The yeomen asked. Why'd the Navy have to make gay sailors air stewards? Too much has changed in his time. Back in his day, people ignored queers, everyone knew they were there, but nobody said nothing if the guy did his job.

"I don't want to be disturbed, I'll send up a flag if I need you."

Sanderson checked his watch again. If Branford was tracking him so what? Sanderson eased back in his chair, it was time for a little shut-eye. It's good to be well rested before your ass gets chewed to shreds.

He managed a few winks and woke on his own before landing. This time, there were no hide and seek games, he got into the waiting limo. A couple of security men were with the car. Some kind of shit was about to hit the fan and he had a few ideas about that.

The car went direct to the Pentagon and Sanderson was ushered into the meeting without preamble. They weren't waiting for him. The meeting was in progress, but he was expected; the pilot must have sent word.

The board was having a discussion about how that alien mother ship ejected their scientists, but not before it was discovered that there was no engine room inside Piper's base ship. There was no drive system that they could find. They did get a good count on its docked probes and shuttles and that Mother had far more empty cradle bays than craft. It appeared Mother was designed to shuttle smaller craft across the universe.

After they finished the business at hand, everyone looked to Brinks. He was the secretary and unofficial PR man. General Brinks was also their link to MJ. Sanderson never liked that bull-moose, Brinks was outright evil and damn proud of it.

Sanderson was expecting heat because the girl got out. The President was hot about it, but that little escapade wasn't on their agenda, which made sense, they wouldn't drag him all the way back here for anything so trivial. They didn't give a shit about the President's pet, just Piper's resources.

"Admiral Sanderson," Brinks said, "We called you in to inform you about a change of direction." He paused to fill his lungs. "As you know, the Piper ship isn't cooperating and either is the girl. We have decided to take more aggressive action. What are your thoughts?"

"The President isn't going to go for that."

"We have her handled," Army piped in. Brinks shot Army a dirty look.

"Be that as it may," Brinks said. "National security is at stake and we will proceed as required. We'll try enhanced interrogations on the Piper girl and if that fails...there are other plans in the works."

"You'll fuck up everything I've been working on for the last...many years." Sanderson had to bite his outrage back. "You want a shortcut, fine, what if I take her up to the moon and get our buddies to milk her brain? You never answered me on that."

That's better than them destroying her mind for nothing; they'll get nothing useful their way except a blabbering vegetable.

Brinks stood and visibly groused. "We don't trust the GTO. Time is short, we want that ship stat."

"I'll push her." Sanderson said.

"You've had your chance," Brinks said leaning across the table. "Stay out of the way Admiral negotiator, your efforts failed. You are off the Galaxy Project. We are decommissioning your section; the NRO will pick up your duties. You'll get official notice as soon as it is processed. We feel you should retire. The Pentagon expects your resignation as soon as you get your office's affairs in order. You may leave now."

Sanderson was escorted out like a bad employee fired from a mundane job. This wasn't over yet. He wasn't about to resign and he didn't have to. No direct orders were given, nothing is official until he got the paperwork, and he'd make sure that it got lost. Brinks had no idea how tuned into the system Sanderson was. He had tentacles in high and low places that the Joint Chiefs couldn't even dream about. Ninety years in the system had given him plenty of avenues for personnel advantages.

Sanderson was met at the door by the same driver, less the security detail, but he wasn't ready to get into the car. "Circle the lot; I need to blow off steam. I need to walk it off."

Sanderson marched across the lot feeling like a raging bull. His heart complained but walking was better than boiling his guts into pulp. "Them fuckers! The goddamned NRO, Archer said they were changing gears, Jesus Christ."

"Very bad news."

"What, who's there!"

"It's Al Branford, the watch, it's a phone watch, remember I gave you the watch."

Sanderson looked at his wrist, the oversized watch was blinking. "Christ, I forgot. Did you hear that shit Al?"

Of course, Branford wasn't supposed to hear that meeting. Sanderson wasn't supposed to carry any device inside that could be used to spy, but security didn't see anything but a big, ugly, calculator watch.

"I heard. Don't talk. I know someone next to the President. She'll sign an executive order; she'll send Aggie to the moon on an official visit. It'll be a PR thing that will delay action, I need to get Sky out of there before they get rash. Sky just left for Haiti again. Protect Aggie, trust her. They're pinging, Branford out."

Sanderson walked another lap. It was hot outside but his jets were cooling. The thought hit him; the NRO will take Piper out. He flagged down the limo. He had to get his ass back to Key West proto.

***

Brad swished into the official Oval Office with a velum folder trucked under his arm; the Presidential seal was on it. It was a presentation cover for executive orders. Jane was afraid this might happen. She had a press conference in two minutes; she was to talk about the coming state of the union address. Tradition was to give the press an advance copy of the speech so the talking heads would have something to say in commentary during commercial breaks.

Brad bent low to her. She was at her desk trying to figure out what to tell the press, no advanced copies were forthcoming.

"It's from AB," Brad whispered. "PR, we're sending space-girl to the moon for an official visit ASAP."

Jane took it, signed it without reading it. It was a delay tactic. The Pentagon was about to get unconstitutional. Jane, on an afterthought, read the document while Brad stood by; it was short, simple, direct and urgent. It authorized an official moon trip.

"Senator Branch will have a canary." She handed it back to him with a smile. Brad floated out and shut the door, no doubt on his way to release copies to the press pool. "Call Sanderson, give him a heads up." She yelled at the door. "Got it," the muffled voice of Brad said. At least this order will keep the press busy. It was a nice distraction giving that she didn't have an acceptable speech to share. This will make the news well ahead of her speech copy. No doubt some leaker already passed the military's speech on. Why did the Oval Office have to be a hall of mirrors?

***

Sanderson got two messages while in flight. The first was about the White House issuing an order authorizing an official visit to the moon, against the Pentagon's plan, the second was a notice that the NRO just landed a special ops force in Key West. Clearly the candle was lit on both ends and he was about to add a blowtorch to the middle.

Things were blowing apart. He was happy that he had gone to see Sarah while he had the chance: It didn't look like he'd get another.

SIXTEEN

Mark On The Run

Mark knew instinctively that he didn't have much of a choice, he had to go ASAP. He was ready, he was always ready. Where he'd been and what he had done made it necessary to have such plans. He had contingencies; he had a number of ways to escape trouble but this time he wasn't running away from it, he was running toward it and he didn't have much time.

He drove his pickup truck into town and parked in Key West's police lot. No doubt he was on camera but it wasn't the kind of setup the NSA monitored actively. By the time an APB was released on him, if at all, he'd be long gone. He parked with his license plate facing away from the cameras. Surveying the lot, he saw heat radiating from a couple of different car's motors. New shift was inside. He waited while the last patrol shift clocked out and drove away. Various officers left from the patrol car lot and when things got quiet again he made his move.

Most of the warm-engine cars had keys on the seat or center console, cops don't lock their cars on their own turf. Mark chose the most nondescript car among them and drove off. It would have been fun to take Rickman's Mustang, but that macho-mobile was too easily marked.

He took his time driving, he wasn't going far. He might get out of the Keys before anyone figured it out although it was a long, slow ninety-mile drive. With all its speed restrictions, the Keys were a two-hour bottleneck. Most of the islands were below 45mph. He didn't have that time to kill.

He headed for the little private airfield thirty miles up the road. It was the same place where the local authorities found a security guard murdered. The NRO's people got out of that one unscathed; it was easy to blame aliens these days. Karnack's reprogrammed man was working for the NRO at the time.

Now the place carried an anti-government taint. After the Karnack murder event, Jack Hall kicked out the government's stored aircrafts and hardware and he wouldn't let them back in for no amount of money. Jack only let them in at first out of pressured patriotism which had worn away before it took root. Why would any black man feel beholden to the government? Jack wasn't stupid; he had to play the game for his own protection. Archer did the Hills a favor by giving Jack the out he needed—the hard way.

But still, Mark was careful. He parked across Route One in the convenience store lot and watched a long time, saw regular workers Mark knew moving about, nothing suspicious. Jack even got cameras after Bill was killed but Jack didn't let the NSA tap in, Mark made sure as a favor to him. Jack hated the internet.

Mark backed the car out, drove around the gas pumps, and down the lot's side. He parked well into the brush behind the gas station. Parking in the shade was typical Florida, no one would notice. He crossed the street and walked over to the airfield's main gate. The gas station might pick him up, but it didn't matter, local face-rec wasn't that good. He kept the baseball cap he found in the car and pulled it low just to be sure. Walking up to the gatehouse, he knew the guard, it was Bill's son.

"Pete, sorry about your old man," Mark extended a hand as he approached, Pete took it. "I can't believe someone would do that. Sorry I didn't make the funeral."

"Thanks Mark, you're a good man. Mom got your card; ya shouldn't have sent so much money."

Mark and Pete chatted a little while. It was long enough for Mark to check out the surroundings. He didn't see any unmarked cars; there wasn't any reason why they would watch this place, the Feds stopped parking here, but then again, there was a lot of security state habit spending to burn on pointless exercises. Departments needed to keep up spending so their budgets continued to grow year to year. The new government cameras set around the outside perimeter of the air strip weren't pointed at Jack's hangar; they were directed at the runways. Mark caught up with Jack inside the main hangar's office cubical.

Jack was a man from another time. He was tall and straight and had too much height for a man that flew open cockpit biplanes. Mark imagined bugs stuck in Jack's big white teeth and chuckled inwardly. Jack looked his seventy-four, but he had the fire of a younger man: He acted and thought like a throwback to the barn-storming era.

Too bad Jack was reduced by aviation law to flying sky divers out to the drop zone or crop dusting lemon trees. Jack liked his freedom, that's why he flew. The old flyer would take off and barnstorm across the world given half the chance. Mark trusted the man's courage.

"Mark, my main man, what can we do you out of?"

"You got that fresh dolphin I sent you? How was it?"

"Nothing's better than fresh caught mahi-mahi. What brings you to me?"

"I need a ride out, below radar, how far will this get me? Mark handed Jack a roll with ten K in it. Jack liked to haggle, but Mark didn't have time to play. The big roll meant big trouble, no questions, and Jack knew the drill, they had that talk long before now.

"I filed a flight plan for today; nothing says I have to stay on it." Jack stuffed the roll into his shirt pocket. "If we fly rout twenty-seven, right up the middle, I should get you up to Ocala before needing fuel."

"How about you take me to Rusty's place and then turn out into the Gulf, what if you got lost? Had to ping your way back here, say off the coast of Marathon, nobody would know where you had been."

"I like the way you think, cover thy ass, I'll get Betty ready." Jack put his roll of bills into his desk safe and locked it. "Give me ten, see ya at the small hangar."

Mark figured he'd see the President's speech at Rusty's place, there was time enough to get there by then, but even without her speaking the code word, he was on his way. Jen was right, Jane Albright needed protection and nobody inside the beltway was trustworthy. If nothing else, he'd quell Jen's worries.

Jack took his best biplane, Mark hid in the forward cockpit so the off-site cameras didn't see a passenger.

Rusty's airfield, his destination, was a crop duster's field in orange grove country about 300 miles north, lots of small plans were buzzing around that airspace and air traffic control there was loose with flight plans. Crop dusters didn't fly with the regular traffic; they flew lower, much lower, and with fewer eyes on them.

One of the privateers waiting for work at Rusty's didn't mind a side job. The girl in Ocala always wanted to fly into Georgia, she had family there and Mark had the gas money. Onward into the night Mark bounced his way north three to five hundred miles at a clip, some detours, but he still made fair time and it only cost half the $100K he brought along to buy his way north. His travel pack was losing weight. Getting to D.C. secretly wasn't a problem, getting out again, that would be tough.

He hoped like hell the info Nostrum gave him would get him inside. He fingered the badge she gave him, took it out and read it just before touchdown; it said special access security in big red letters under the blue and white Presidential seal. He could just walk in. Giving his presence away was a bad idea. Breaking into the White House was required for cover. Nostrum hadn't used the former underground railway in a long time. Lately, the White House's front door was open to Nostrum, but she and he knew that door was closing fast and was never safe to begin with—too many eyes on it. Hopefully the blind door was still there.

SEVENTEEN
NRO Busts Aggie

Basically, nobody would give her a break. The Man added more guards and nobody was nice. She wanted to go hit the bag at Mark's but he wasn't home and she wasn't about to get all sweaty in front of these hard guy GI Joe's. She could ask one of the regular MPs to spar, but then again, she'd damage government property. She needed some stress relief, but they won't let her go off the avenue. Her Vespa even had a wheel lock on it. She'd take dad's boat out but she didn't have the key for the gas pumps. Moon Dodger was parked at Sea-Tow but how was she going to get there without the Man right behind her? Spill her emergency escape boat's location, no way.

So, Aggie went at it again. She did a bunch of blogs, not nice at all, basically she ranted and nobody wants to hear that crap so she deleted them. She wasn't sure if Buddy was around, she told him to lay low, so maybe he picked up the blogs or maybe he didn't. She was so bent out of shape, she didn't care. She decided she needed to chill before her gray matter vaporized out of frustration.

OK, the meditation thing was a ploy, but now she wanted to do it for real. *How the hell am I going to get out of this crap pile?* She thought as she waded into the water. A girl MP was close behind. No way would she call Buddy down with Miss Eagle Eye back there. Besides, the sun was low in the west and would cast Buddy's shadow giving him away.

She tried to get into it but all she could do was think about how to get out of there and if she really wanted to do that at all anyway. The idea was scary. Hooky was one thing, but they might arrest her for real. She said to herself just yesterday that she'd take off, but that was wishful thinking, childish. She really didn't want to go to that extreme. She had offers for college that she didn't want to blow. Jen was right; there's always next semester. You can't go sailing off to school with an army in your wake.

"I give up, akkk!"

"Are you OK miss?" Eagle Eye said as Aggie marched out of the water.

"Just leave me alone."

Aggie pushed leaves out of her face as she walked the path, it was filling in like crazy, it needed trimming but they won't even let her have a pair of scissors. Mom kept everything nice, but Mom was gone so the place was more like a jungle than a squatter's paradise.

Aggie got to the head of the path and the guard lady was well back. Aggie pushed a giant frond aside to find a big guy in a black special-ops uniform staring at her with dead eyes.

"Come this way miss," the guy put his gun up to her face.

"What now." Aggie pushed his gun aside and looked past him, there were a dozen men milling around, all in black uniforms. "Get off my land, I'll call the President."

Two more guys moved in fast. One on either side grabbed her arms. The first guy that confronted her was still standing in range. He smirked at her, so she kicked him in the nuts. He went down and flopped away.

"Hey where's your cup, you're out of uniform." She said. The other two didn't laugh; they just drug her into the house.

Mr. Black was sitting in her computer chair. He didn't look much better than when she saw him last on the deck of Grandpa's ship. She heard he didn't die, but he looked like a zombie so maybe he was dead. Mr. Black was pasty waxy white and had bloodshot eyes, he'd pass for a corpse no problem.

The two men lead her right up to Black while gripping her harder. She had a way to break them off, but she wasn't about to do that, not yet. She was too pissed off to do that move anyway.

"Get off me, get the hell out of here, let go…you, you, you smelly butt-holes."

"Release her. It's nice to see you again Miss Piper."

"Jane told you guys to back off what are you doing, this is treason!"

"Sorry to inform you, madam President doesn't call the shots. She hasn't the power." Archer took off his hat and dropped it on the desk. His hair was slick and greasy. "But the people that do, well they need information. Of course, we want your ship, and you won't sell, so I've been sent to persuade you to cooperate, or, well, Gitmo has plenty of accommodations available."

"You fucking butt-munch."

Aggie was working out a way to launch, OK the big guys would get her, but that dick-head in her chair wasn't leaving with all his teeth. She took a little step closer, measured him and put on the humble face. But then there was a commotion outside, somebody with a big voice was yelling.

"Stay where you are!" Archer snapped as his guys backed up to the door.

"I'm a goddamn admiral, stand down. Kowalski code red, code red, we're under attack. Where is he?" came from outside. There were boots crunching gravel. More orders were shouted.

A monument later Sanderson blew into Aggie's little house like a thunderhead. The two black uniformed guys shrunk away. Sanderson suddenly filled the room, maybe his uniform scared them. He didn't look sick like last time she saw him; his face was Rudolf the reindeer red, his eyes were budging. He scared Aggie; she felt a little pee escape down her leg.

"Black, you horse's ass, what are you…don't tell me, I know. Get off my project now!" Sanderson was a pack of pissed off lions. "You men, out, all of you, out, right now goddamn it."

In the background sirens were screaming down Geiger Ave. Aggie felt like she knew what punching a bear in the nose must be like. Black AKA Archer stood up. He and Sanderson stood nose to nose. Archer was taller than she remembered. Aggie thought that bear could just reach out and crush Archer between its paws.

Before she could blink, the men in black had guns pointing at Sanderson, but two of Sanderson's MP's crashed the doorway and instantly had guns on the men in black. *Where's Mark!*

"I have orders." Black said stammering. Even he was unnerved by Sanderson's show of force.

"I'm not out of it yet Archer. You and your crew back up, or Navy comes in shooting."

"Have it your way. This isn't over Sanderson."

Archer made for the door; the MPs parted but held their guns on the other two. Everybody went outside and Aggie came out last. Up and down the lane were a crap load of regular soldiers, had to be forty guys. Archer and his dozen made a fast exit. The regular military guys parted as they passed but they kept their guns aimed. Sanderson followed, shouting orders.

"Any man in a black uniform shows up here again, shoot to kill, goddamn it, shoot to kill!"

In the distance, she saw Sanderson had caught up to Archer at the gate. He took Archer's elbow and guided him into an SUV. Maybe they were talking. Maybe this was a big stupid game to intimidate her.

Before Aggie could wrap her head around it, everything was normal. Everybody had gone except for the regular guards. She had stood there in the middle of the lane for so long she had bugs nesting inside her open mouth. It was about that time she realized there was more than pee running down her leg.

That's it. I'm getting out of here. I'm done thinking about it. Aggie took a shower and had time to eat a stupid microwave frozen diner before it was time for the President's speech. She fell into the new soft, deep couch to watch, feeling uneasy. It had been a really weird day. Maybe the strangest thing was Sanderson coming to the rescue; maybe that guy wasn't such a big butt-hole anyway. Jon never really put the guy down, but then again, Sanderson did put Jon in jail. She didn't know what to make of that guy any more. And Archer, *holy cow didn't I save his life? What's up with that guy?*

EIGHTEEN

State of the Union

President Jane Albright was never nervous; she had made so many speeches she could not count them all. As a local politician, before that, teaching law, and even before teaching she did two years of post-grad civil rights work. She had never once wavered, never misspoke, never had anything but confidence in what she wrote to speak publicly. She proclaimed truth. *Let them scream, facts are facts.* The press used to say of her, when she was a rising star that she was always on the nose: that's why she was elected. Since Aggie Piper showed up with an alien ship the press was happy to flatten Albright's nose. Waiting to go on she squeezed her legs together tight or she'd piss herself.

"Five minutes, Madam President."

No one had dirt on her. There was nothing for the parties to dig out. That an independent won the presidency made them all her enemies. She could not stand aside while oligarch networks further propagandize against the people's good. The corporations, banks and media worked in unison calling their lies ad campaigns or news but she knew better, it was all designed to manipulate the people. It was nothing if it wasn't candy-coated indoctrination. *Wait until they get a taste of this sour pop.*

Checking the backstage monitor, she watched the seconds tick away, minutes felt like days. Her traveling logistics man Jim Butcher slid up next to her. The CIA guys all around were locked on. They didn't like Jim. Jim was too loyal to the Constitution. That's why sis suggested Albright hire him. Congress squashed him as a cabinet pick; they wouldn't allow a disgruntled ex-CIA analyst to have a power position. Thus, she hired him out of her own pocket—another political shot across the bow.

Jim leaned in and cupped his mouth so they could not hear or read his lips. *They do read lips; that's how insidiously they operate.*

"Remember, start slow, go about a minute or two hemming and hawing, it's got to sound like you'll rattle on for a while with the submitted teleprompter speech. The watchers won't start really paying attention until you're running. You'll have a little time before they pull it." Jim's eyes darted around like the bag man in a gangster movie.

She nodded but still found it hard to accept that anyone could or would stop her. She never saw Jim so jittery. She was the President, but she was finding out that didn't mean anything to the bureaucracy. Who knows what they can do? Two years in office and nothing was getting done, stone walls lay in every direction. It was time for this wrecking ball.

A stagehand came over. "Two minutes, Madam President."

She moved over to the edge of the stage and watched senior Senator Guy Smiley take the podium to introduce her. Of course, he had to ramble on a while first pumping his party up while beating down the other party. It was like one twin socking the other.

"Please welcome our first independent President, Madam Jane Albright."

Mr. Upbeat didn't sound enthusiastic. The press did nothing but trash her day to day, Wolf News leading the pack. Hen House news was having a field day with conspiracy nut jobs that were claiming she had made secret deals with the aliens. It was just more planted intelligence propaganda. If it wasn't for Aggie Piper, she would never have known aliens existed; actually no one here would be alive to crucify her.

Jane walked briskly, confidently to the podium. Forward motion always helped her nerves. The audience clapped or booed while the press corps cameras snapped away.

Once it was quiet, she began with the script, one that both parties and the press had a hand in. It was more boring than a sleeping rock. Two minutes into it, she picked up the papers she had read from and the rest of the stack and dumped them on the floor. The room clamored then hushed.

"I am honored to be America's first Independent President. You the people have decided that truth is more important than politics or party, by electing me you have expressed your feeling that your elected and non-elected representatives have abandoned you and I am here to say in this State of the Union address that you are right, the feeling is fact, you have been deceived and abused indeed, and it is time that changed."

She paused. The people in the auditorium stood and applauded while the representatives of both parties on the floor below the stage remained seated, some clapped, most did not. No one up in the very front where important people sat applauded. Some looked pale, others frightened, many were angry. Good.

"Since Aggie Piper brought us this astounding news, that we are not alone, everything is changing and a new world order is necessary. I am not speaking of enhancing the Bush-Obama-Trump doctrines. The order that exists now is not, I repeat, is not what we need; it is a corrupted, greedy power structure and it will not allow humanity to grow and prosper. Defense always knew about the aliens, they have known since 1945. You are not alone in being left in the dark. They never briefed me either. Your government lies to you all the time about everything even when the truth serves better. Lying is all the security state knows."

The crowd reacted, some jeering, some with gasps of disbelief. Journalists scribbled frantically.

"The corrupting powers of this world must end. What this means specifically is an end to the Federal Reserve Bank, an end to the World Bank and World Trade Organization and more importantly, an end to the people behind them. An end to money in politics, an end of corruption; it is time to end America's hegemony."

Jane paused and looked into the camera. She saw him zoom in on her desk monitor. The CIA was fidgeting behind her; men had hands cupped over ear pieces. "What you see is not your government, a shadow government rules you and they are a tempest against human survival, a storm of oligarch taking that provides no rainbow is our collective detriment for human survival. We must stop them."

Jane waited as the audience went wild, people were yelling approval or cheering, others shouting insults. The CIA men on the floor had their hands full. The news media directly in from of her in the press pit stopped taking notes; they too were standing and cheering. She saw a CIA man heading toward her in the monitor screen. Reporters were blocking his way; they won't let him pass easily. Time was running out. Over the noise and clamor she pressed on.

"The oligarchs that control this Earth cannot lead us into this widening universe, they must be stopped. All loyal people, people loyal to the human race must understand that the aliens are not our enemies, the enemy is within. The military industrial complex is our common enemy. All you that serve, police, military, government officials remember you swore an oath to the Constitution and not to protect your banker's fidelity."

A couple of CIA men were now punching and strong arming anyone in their way. Reporters were dropping like flies. TV cameras' green go-lights blinked yellow or went red. Surrounded by media people, the main camera was still working.

"Turn the camera," She pointed at the AV man. "See what the police are doing, beating up reporters, this is not democracy, the CIA is trying to stop this broadcast..."

Two security men charged the podium and grabbed her arms one man on either side. One said, "This is for your own protection, you must leave." Her microphone was still broadcasting; she heard it in her ear bud. The cameras still blinking green went off one after the other as she struggled to stay on stage.

"That's bullshit; you're shutting me up, get away from me. Nice rainbow pin."

The security men ignored the President's orders and literally dragged her off stage. One man had the balls to grab the microphone off of her breast. The last camera was cut before that, but the sound wasn't and police-generated bedlam was heard live around the world. Cellphones recorded all.

Many online videos showing the CIA men mistreating the President appeared immediately. The internet was surly catching fire. Outrage and applause videos flooded Createface, Faceplant and all the pirate internet sites.

As the CIA ushered her back to the White House she had visions of her security adviser's body being pulled out of the Potomac and that horror splashed all over media. She imagined headline accusations, 'President shoots CIA chief.' Other ploys raced by inside her imagination—they were capable of anything.

Jane had a new war to fight. She prayed to God that Jennifer would get there fast. She prayed that there were still Americans in power that would protect her for the sake of the Constitution. She tried to list inside her mind patriots she could count on and the list was short. Only scum floated to the top of government and industry. Most that rode the high plains of power, like Sanderson, were blindly patriotic and that worked against the spirit of the Constitution. Such men were bound by implanted honors and duties taking precedent above the law. What binds the heart more, the letter of the law or blind obedience to false ideals?

The men that showed her to her room and closed the door, who did they work for? How much did their loyalties cost? She picked up her in-house hard-wired phone to call Brad, but the line was dead, just as dead as this democracy.

NINETEEN
Mark in the Dark

Mark arrived early morning in D.C. on a bus. From Vicksburg he boarded a local and jumped from town to town bus by bus. Things were slowing down on the road in the last hours and he was tired, so he slept on the ride. When the greyhound arrived in D.C.'s main terminal he woke with a start. This was going to be tricky, Homeland had cameras everywhere.

He disembarked and saw a crowd gathered around a TV screen, TVs were everywhere, and he knew not to look too interested. Smart TV's recorded watchers and in this place, they had to be wired directly into NSA operations with face-rec. Transportation hubs are how they caught many wanted marks. He didn't think he was listed yet, but that may have changed. It depended on how long it took Sanderson's men to figure out he was gone. It was twelve hours since the President did her State of the Union, so security would be tight, but not wide. He ducked into a rest room and pulled a different hat out of his bag, reflective shades and a Hawaiian shirt. His long short pants would have to do. Lucky the sneakers he found on the bus were his size, people hiding out never changed shoes, it was a tell-tale not publicly recognized. His sandals were a dead give-away. He looked as touristy as he could get. But before he sailed, he reversed his travel pack, the inside was light blue while the outside was black.

Mark side stepped close to the nearest TV. He leaned on the TV's mounting wall below the camera's view and put yesterday's newspaper up to his face and pushed his dark glasses onto his head. He folded the paper so the sports section showed; anyone watching would think he read the horse race results. A gambling man would spend time with that small print section calculating odds so an operative might look past the man with a paper. Once an operative figured out that the paper reading man was a horse fan, he'd move on.

Maybe the algorithm's changed since Mark was active, but human nature never changed. Confirm what you think you know and move on, that's how they programmed it. Mark used that human loophole to his advantage. The programmers would have put their humanity and biases into the search program.

On the TV was Wolf News, pure right-wing propaganda but inside those CIA generated sound bites were scraps of reality.

"For the second time in a week, Aggie Piper's house was raided, Men in black in and out within an hour, false alarm? What do you make of that Marv?" The TV woman said.

Good Aggie got the message.

"I'll tell you Jessica, I don't like it. What is that girl doing with aliens anyway? Is she making arrangements with them? Is she dealing herself into things that aren't good for our country? Why hasn't she given up her spaceship, America needs that hardware."

"All good questions Marv. Her actions don't seem like what a patriot would do and no wonder, her mother, slash lawyer, is a nut job cultist, some kind of pagan pot head and that brings us to the next report, we have Paul Haysacker down in Haiti standing by."

"I'm here Jessica."

Mark ventured a glance at the TV across the lounge; they all played the same channel. The spaceship Mother was in the distance. The damn thing was huge, had to be several football fields in length, but it was the same color and shape as a nondescript gutter cigar. The Army had setup a perimeter, that's not good. Of course, the news didn't point that out. Disturbingly, there was nothing about the speech. Wolf routinely picked her apart anyway they could, and they weren't on that rail. That's not good.

"...The locals and Piper's legal team are still on site, but American security forces are now saying they will have to leave as a matter of public safety. There are unconfirmed reports that the ship has lured residents inside to extract their souls—."

Mark tucked the paper under his arm and moved off. The President's speech was scheduled for a replay in fifteen minutes. The President had told the military 'hands off the Pipers' but they weren't respecting orders. They never respect Presidents. That's how they did everything; claim security issues regarding public protection then move in. It's the same old ploy used for the President's 'protection'. All the while they do what they do. Keep the enemy close. Most of the elected just went along, they didn't know any better, but Albright knows better. Mark picked up his pace.

It didn't matter that Haiti wasn't U.S. territory, the news skipped over that, of course. It's classic propaganda by omission. How long before they tried to crack that ship open? The Powers were moving, hedging little test steps before the boot comes crashing down. In the distance beyond the spaceship was the silhouette of a boat on the horizon. Mark was trained to know what he was looking at and that was a gun boat, a stealth torpedo and rocket carry system. They aren't stupid enough to try blowing it up, what's going on here?

He'd have to trust Sky Flower would keep them off, he had more pressing business. He'd have to get Jane Albright out of D.C. before the hammer came down. Outside he hailed a cab; it took him only a few blocks to the storage unit facility he had maintained for years since retirement. Mark paid the taxi driver cash and the tip wasn't oversized.

In his lock-up was a collection of suits and other clothing, a motorcycle, and many other tools of his trade. He changed into a high cost CIA style suit complete with government issued sunglasses. *When in Rome do as Romans do.*

He selected a plastic gun from his gun cabinet. The only metal on it was a firing pin. The bullets and casings were hard plastic, good at a short distance but otherwise useless. This gun might fire seven rounds before it failed. He hoped it would be enough as he tucked it into his custom armpit holster.

He rode his motorcycle up to the storage office. With helmet on he went inside because a TV was playing. Jane Albright was giving the alien speech, but it was just a clip. The talking heads were saying how a computer failure cut the speech short. Nothing about what she had said. Mark approached the man behind the counter.

"Hey," Mark said pushing the helmet back, "Can ya check 719 for me? I don't know if I'm caught up on the rent, I think I'm OK but still, can you check it. I don't recall sending payment."

While the clerk messed around in his files Mark watched the TV intently. She spoke in the background on stage with no sound while the pundits blathered. He read her lips. Jane Albright was flat out punching the deep state in the nose and you don't punch a bear in the nose. Mark was running out of time.

"You're good," the man said, "Just got the check for another year."

Mark looked back over his shoulder as he made for the door, the TV screen blinked out above the clerk's head and an ad came on. "Thanks man, who can keep up these days?"

Mark kicked over the motorcycle. It was a 1969 Triumph Bonneville. Mark had a former Seal come and go over it on a regular schedule. Carlos made sure it ran and ran right. It was worth the hundred bucks a week to make sure his back up ride was ready. Mark was glad to help a disabled vet, one that was trustworthy. The bike didn't have a computer or electronic ignition, nothing for them to trace or disarm remotely or otherwise mark. He checked the bike over carefully while it warmed up anyway, just in case.

Once the motor was hot he made his way toward the capital building methodically, making sure he wasn't followed. The place would be empty now, Congress always turned out for big Presidential speeches and those bastards weren't going back to work after that. Mark felt for Nostrums' badge and it was safe in his breast pocket, he'd make it OK to the sub-basement, but after that, there was no telling.

He parked in the security lot by flashing the badge. The guard didn't blink. HLS hired cheap. A real player would have given Mark the once over. At the main entry, as expected, the guard spent a little more time. The young jar head patted Mark down, rolled the badge around with his fingers over and over but didn't look at it too closely.

"It checks out," he said and tossed the badge at Mark. "For now, anyway."

Mark went directly to the off-limits elevator and used the key Nostrum had provided. He knew what was downstairs. He otherwise heard rumors about secret meetings, hidden interrogation rooms, stores of weapons but none of that mattered until Jen confirmed it.

He got off into a dark hallway. The man he expected was there. The guard pulled a gun. Mark kept cool.

"Say, you haven't been here before."

Mark remained calm; there was a protocol, a pass key. He showed open hands and reached into his breast pocket and pulled out two new one hundred-dollar bills. "I'm new. I was told room three."

"Three hum? Your friend just went that way. I was told to expect one." His knuckles on the Glock turned white as his grip tightened.

Mark wasn't sure how to respond. Nostrum didn't give him a response for this, was it code?

Mark hated to kill the man, it wasn't his fault he wasn't smart. He was just a man good with a gun and easy to control. They wouldn't have programmed this man for multi-tier code response; they don't waste training money on disposable people.

"I'm the one; the man ahead is mine."

The man lowered the gun, but not far enough. "I guess that makes sense."

Mark inserted the rest of the protocol. "You're a good man, Bill."

The security man turned and marched off. Mark accessed his own gun and palmed it. The guard never looked back. He brought Mark to an unmarked door. Bill opened it and stepped back. Mark walked toward the entry on daggers ready to fight. Shooting scenarios hatched in his mind on the threshold but the place was empty. The hall monitor wasn't allowed to know what was inside. He shut the door once Mark was in. They picked a good rube. The room was empty except for a conference table and chairs, that wasn't good.

The assassin was well ahead of him.

When Nostrum told him about this, he half didn't believe at first but quickly changed his tune. Sure thing, secret basement meetings and why not; that's standard stuff, but tunnels into the White House? She said it was dug in the Underground Railroad days, but he guessed it was done after Truman. They were both half right.

The secret panel was exactly where it was supposed to be. The button worked. A panel of oak wainscot retracted on tracks. Rolling back, the smell of dust and mildew assailed him. There was a hint of fresh blood on that stale air. He cocked an ear. In the distance was gunfire, or maybe not, it was hard to know. He entered the tunnel, just room enough to stand and it was cave-dark when he closed the door. He didn't use his multi-tool's pen light; Nostrum said it would set off alarms. He had to count steps, ignore the side tunnels and feel his way until he reached the correct right-side tunnel he wanted.

He checked the entry in the dark by his senses. The arch was lined with crumbling brick. He stepped in; the tunnel was barrel vaulted like the catacombs and sewers of Rome. The main tunnel had been poured cement and big enough for three to walk side by side, but this was different, it was much older. His extended arms reached either side. There wasn't much room to spare, bad place for a fire fight. The ceiling was just above his head. It was dry so far, but the smell of putrid water wafted out of the blackness. He had his doubts if this was the right way but at least it was old enough to be the right one.

Another shot. This time he was sure it was gunfire. His doubts about the way were set aside. He wanted to run toward that barking gun but he knew better. Rather, he plumbed his resolve and proceeded slowly, very slowly ready to strike down any tunnel rat he found. The way was long, he had five hundred more strides yet to count but he did not hurry. Every step was silent, careful, on high alert. There was no light at the end of this tunnel, of that he was sure.

TWENTY

Aggie's Dead Man Blog

Yesterday sucked. Last night sucked more. They shut Jane down like it was noth-ing. Aggie wanted to fight the Man even more after that. She called Mel and said it's time to blog some serious crap. She held back a little before but now. Screw that. Millions of people followed her on social media; it was time to rattle cages.

Aggie had to get this stuff down first, just in case, before anything happened to her. Mark, her Jedi kick-boxing instructor, was all about just-in-case contingen-cies. She wasn't dumb. She took his lesions to heart. The guy had serious chops.

She sat down at her computer desk to do her next Faceplant blog. She felt an urgent need. Mom and dad weren't around, so she had lots of time to post without Sky or Po-boy yelling in the background about what to say or what not to say. It sucks when your mom's a lawyer. Well, not a real lawyer. OK she has a degree, but she never used it until now. Aggie liked her better when Sky was a full time found-art hippie Earth priestess. Too bad mom's pot plants were all dying.

She felt a little self-conscious about the ratty look of the house. She wanted to clean the place up first, but who really gives a crap? Everybody's poor in most of the country anyway. Everybody knows the Pipers live in an old bait shack outside of Key West and that's high living for an almost-no-income family. Aggie still couldn't wrap her head around the idea that she had a crap load of real money and space bucks...it just didn't feel real. Aggie booted up. The new computer fired fast, but next to the custom job Mel had made for her, this thing was crap.

Of course, the Feds took her computer after the big event—that's what the press called her landing a spaceship on Sunset Pier. That was the start of her problems with the Man. No doubt they'd be watching her now, even before she turned the web-cam on, if Mel hadn't messed with the hardware they'd never get anything out. People liked her live blogs. Her page was bringing in mad cash.

Mel popped up on her screen in a postage stamp window. "You have me?" Mel asked.

"I'm good, you're on, and you see me, right?" Aggie said. "Boy they'll be pissed when they see this."

"Houston, we are ready for liftoff," Melissa said, "We're live in, 1, 2, go."

Aggie's camera's eye lit green. She wanted to go off on the President's speech, but she had a series to pull together, and this live chat was scheduled for the topic at hand.

"Hey, people what's going on?" The live chat started scrolling which distracted her. Aggie had a hard time not reading when something to read was available.

Mel cut in, "Helloooooo Aggie say something."

"Oops, sorry, OK, I'm not like an entertainer, I'm just a nerd. So, a lot's been going on. OK you guys saw my interviews and junk, that's old news. A lot of you want to know what else is going on so I made a deal with Faceplant. Createface might sign on too. All the cash my page makes goes to homeless relief. Mom is big into that and I dig it too so that's that. One reason why I landed my ship, her name is Mother by the way; down in Haiti isn't just to piss off the Feds, and OK that's fun, right, but Haiti needs help and all the government does is crap on them. Just look at how the Feds treat PR all the time. Ten times worse in Haiti. Everything Empire does is a crime, it sucks."

Mel cut in, "I'll post links below on the history of Haiti and Puerto Rico, brace yourself, it's not pretty."

"Yeah so, I want to help them directly. Fund raising and all that crap they do for disaster relief always goes into the pockets of the organizers. I read a study about how that works, all these foundations are scams. Eighty percent goes back into the organization, they all do it. Mel, link that one, too. Haiti and PR are victims of vulture capitalism, look that up too."

"Good idea," Mel said.

"So, you can get this junk out soon, right?"

"I'll have to dig. I'll link below." Mel said. "History and economics dudes already know all these big foundations are just cover for rich bastards who hurt a lot of people. They're trying to leave a positive legacy. Just look at Paul Cartage Foundation, same dope. It's not out of guilt, sociopaths don't feel anything like love; they do it for their egos and tax break money."

"They do it for power and control. If you want all the eggs dress like roosters and control the hens."

"Let's not go off on that." Mel said, "We'll be here all day."

"Yeah, so here's the big scoop, what the Feds don't know yet. Faceplant is the first to hear it. I'm setting up Earth's first space port on Haiti, the rumors are true. If all the governments in the world won't help them, I will. If the Feds take restrictions off PR and let it become a state, I'll setup a space port there too. Screw the Man."

"Aggie, check the comments, lots of questions."

"What am I wearing? You're kidding. OK, mom made me this sundress, yellow's my fav, and I don't do underwear. Next!"

It was scrolling too fast and Aggie couldn't read the questions before they flashed by.

"OK so I'm going to screen shot random questions so I can read them, I can't get to you all. I'll skip anything that the press already asked."

Aggie sorted through a few questions and came to one she liked. She put her screen shot up over the chat window so viewers saw which one she was addressing.

"OK so what's my favorite subject? Oh, hey Kyle, he's from my high school. I like them all. OK I'm not too much on math, but history and anthropology's bitch-en. I'm into untangling the lies they sell us with so-called education. History is the most politicized and screwed with of all the subjects, the real factual junk is pure fascination. Of course, how the establishment infuses propaganda into history text books is fascinating and that's an interesting topic too. I can cite examples…"

"Aggie, move on."

Aggie screened another question and put it up. "How do I think this will affect the government? Oh, you mean like the aliens, that they are here and we know it now. The Man is not happy. Like Jane Albright said, they knew about the aliens for a really long time."

On the small screen Mel held up a card that said, 'redundant.'

"My dad says lots of UFO people like NUFO guessed right. I don't know that much about that, my dad is into it, but yeah, the Man's been sucking up all that good alien tech stuff like deranged hoarders and not sharing. I bet they're pissed, I screwed up their entire evil plan."

Aggie pretended she was twisting a long mustache and she did a fake maniacal laugh.

"Whatever, the cat's out of the bag now so all those industrial complex buttholes lording over us better make sure they stay clear of guillotines. Hint: read the history of the French Revolution. But anyway, in the long run, we'll get a better world out of alien technologies, that's how I think it will fall out."

"Aggie, the clock is running out, we better go."

"Make it so number one…That's it for now folks. We'll see you tomorrow, if there is one."

Mel killed the feed before the shutdown trace hit. There was no way the Feds would let Aggie do a subversive blog, but Faceplant wasn't controlled by big media and Mel found a way to rout the blog around the NSA's interception protocols through Buddy. Of course, it helped that Mel's dad is the guy that invented intercept software and sold it to the spy industry. How long before that rug got pulled, Mel said she didn't know. They decided to record a bunch after the live one. Aggie didn't have much else going on anyway. Mel had saved tons of questions and emails on her server, as yet it wasn't hacked.

Mel had this cool idea, it was a thing called a dead man switch. Aggie asked Mel to make it happen. Aggie never imagined she'd actually need one, but last night, and after tonight...If Mel didn't get to her gear to reset it, everything would spill into the internet all over the world in three days. It was setup to splash the media randomly. They already had a dozen in the can. The longer they were MIA, the more blogs would go out and each one meaner than the previous one.

If the Feds hacked it, same result. That trick Mel pulled back on Sal Bank, using military defense communication satellites was genius. But the Man was on to it.

All Aggie and Mel's junk was being stored on Karnack's cloud, and that cloud was inside NASA satellites and NASA had no clue. Karnack's old system, now hers, was an open, hidden back door.

The only way the authorities could disarm it was first to figure it out, then decommission the Fed's orbiting hardware and that'd be a huge waste. Aggie's blog data would just jump into the next satellite in the string. Mel figured out that's how Karnack got so much info. The Feds could never catch him because he hacked government communications. The alien pirate had his own orbital platforms, too, but he used all the others as well, and all that junk was Aggie's now. That was a little fact the Feds would love to know. She'd never tell them.

"Hello, Earth to Aggie, dude you're vegging out big time."

"OK, OK, what do we want to do next?"

"How about we attack the deep state, use that Chris Hedges quote."

"Did our stuff go?" Aggie wasn't sure if the transfer was working. Buddy out in the yard was how they did the relay. That little robot wasn't real smart, but he did what she asked. As long as he stayed cloaked they'd never figure it out. Karnack must have used him the same way, as a relay. What a waste of a cool semi-intelligent robot.

"Yupper, signal's clear, we're on Createface and Faceplant."

"OK, this one's for the dead man archives, let's roll."

No doubt the NSA was recording, the homestead was wired, but they didn't know where Mel and Aggie's blog was stored in real-time hardware. They had to figure it was local, like on their computers and maybe one of the hubs that the NSA had already tapped.

Mel had opened up Aggie's new government donated computer and plucked out a few things and put some of her dad's stuff back in—it all looked the same. Unless they sent a guy to look at the machine real close, they'd never know. Mel's tools split micro hairs, the government IT guy only had butter knives.

As far as the Man knew, Aggie's subversive words and observations couldn't make it out into the net if they didn't want it to. They were about to find out that wasn't true anymore. The very act of attacking Aggie's stuff insured everybody would know and know who was behind it. Spies hate when you out them.

"Three, two, one, you're on."

"Thanks Mel. I was thinking, there isn't much out there about how things really work. After they killed net neutrality, things have been sketchy. School, forget it, it's all propaganda. Here's some truth. I'll read you a quote from Chris Hedges; he was a news guy, a top *New York Times* journalist fired for telling the truth..."

Aggie brought up the quote and put it on the split screen. "OK so consider this," Aggie read. "'Inverted totalitarianism, unlike classical totalitarianism, does not revolve around a demagogue or charismatic leader. It finds expression in the anonymity of the Corporate State. It purports to cherish democracy, patriotism, and the Constitution while manipulating internal levers.' That's from Chris Hedges' book, *Empire of Illusion*."

Aggie eased back in her new chair. It didn't even squeak. "OK, so, yeah, let's talk about it…"

Aggie explained the man's life, what he had done, what he stood for, his books, where to get them and why nothing about Hedges was ever in the mainstream media. This was exactly the kind of info the Feds didn't want people to think about. But, it wasn't the junk they were trying to hide, either.

Mom warned that the Man wanted to use Aggie as yet another distraction. That's why Aggie stopped talking to the press in frustration over their leading softball questions that were no doubt products of state interests' manipulation. The press called her a truth finder for showing the world aliens, so why stop there? Why not roll with it? Aggie set her mind to fulfilling that handle. After she was done recording a few more episodes, she and Mel decided the Hedges blog would go out tonight. Why screw around?

Aggie needed a distraction of her own. She needed some ploy to deflect the goon's priorities so using the Man's crap against him was pretty cool. They didn't play fair, why should she?

Buddy rolled into the house and did that little spin dance, he completed the data transfer. It was weird how she could read the little robot, or maybe it was just wishful thinking. She projected a thought.

Tonight's the big night.

The little guy did his yes dance. How the hell did it know what was inside her head? Aggie slapped herself in the forehead. She was trying to keep him under cover and he goes and turns off the cloaking. Maybe he can't transmit and cloak, who knows?

"Buddy, go get charged and I don't want to see you come back, got it?" But she thought, 'come back at meditation, but stay invisible.'

Buddy did his yes dance, rolled out the door and flew off. Aggie felt like Buddy got the message, or maybe it was his idea anyway and he put it inside her head? She didn't want to think about it.

Aggie brought up the next cheat sheet. She and Mel had a good one lined up next. She was going to talk about how the government lets the GTO aliens' milk people. She didn't know if it was true, but she'd lay out a good case.

TWENTY-ONE

Sanderson and Archer Deal

Sanderson was expecting a regular NRO man, but he didn't know what to expect from Archer. The NRO was closer to MJ-12 than he was lately—over time Majestic pushed the NRO up and him out to the ragged edges. That much he only figured out recently, but what was the deeper game? Why push him out? MJ and whoever was with them were not to be trusted. Where have all the patriots gone? After they pulled the plug on the President last night, it hit him hard. Men not of the government were calling the shots and ramping up for something big. How much balls does it takes to shut down a sitting President? *Twelve sets of big ones, Goddamn MJ.* Worse, she hasn't been heard from since last night, no press conference, no nothing, media blackout, what in the hell was going on?

He picked up his copy of the new executive order. Even if Albright was dead in a ditch someplace, he still had a green light on the Piper moon trip, his last chance to get that heart. Even if Albright was gone, it took time to resend an executive order, hell or high water, Sanderson was going back to the moon.

The intercom chimed. "Sir, Mr. Black is here." This time Sanderson got a big ugly sailor for a secretary, batting eyes and pretty lips weren't going to distract him again.

He glanced at his new Branford watch; he still hadn't given the girl hers. Archer was late.

"Send him in."

The shadow of a man who used to be Archer drifted in like a corpse on roller skates. What was left of Archer took a seat. Either that control bracelet or the extraction chamber did it, Sanderson couldn't tell, but Archer wasn't who he used to be. *Careful old man, the NRO is not your friend.*

"Admiral, it is nice to see you again."

"Don't butter me up Archer, I asked you here for a reason."

"I came for a reason, too; maybe we can help each other."

"You have my ear."

Archer removed his black fedora and placed it gingerly on Sanderson's nice, neat desk.

"Last we worked together, I was under Karnack's influence. I apologize for that. In good faith, I'll tip you off on this, Brinks is involved with a Special Operations contractor, and they developed a weapon the aliens cannot deflect, no defense. If Piper doesn't give up that ship, they will destroy it. They are fabricating a reason to test their new toy as we speak."

Sanderson eased back into his chair. He had to digest that before he piped in. It was pretty much as he suspected. Yes, he saw what the press was doing, Branford already mentioned the new weapon, but now he got the full story. That mothership was a thorn in the side of MJ. But, something else was brewing; Branford didn't mention his Space Fleet getting refitted. Sanderson put two and two together and it added up to an attack on the moon. It made military sense. Like a lot of solid military concepts, this one will also cost the people dearly. The new device had to be tested.

"What about Albright?"

"From what I could gather, she is being handled."

They both knew what that meant in company terms and it wasn't a day at the park. *That's what I'm afraid of. Time's short.* Archer was always cryptic. He never said anything directly. Sanderson just heard an exception.

"What's the deal, how can we help each other?" Sanderson said.

"I want Karnack. I know he's alive. Every alien has a distress call implant and medical bots are everywhere. The girl dumped him from twenty thousand feet. His home planet is lower gravity, but he can fly, or at least glide in Earth conditions. He is alive. I know it and I want him. Aliens don't kill each other; that's what they want from us, if we survive our childhood, they'll contract use of our warring race."

Sanderson leaned toward Archer. That little speech was considerably more intelligence about aliens than Archer should know. It showed MJ's hand: Warring race, the GTO wants to hire police but what they'll get is a knife in the back. No point in asking how Archer knows such details. Some of it was extrapolation, nobody really knows what MJ wants, or will get in exchange for defense services. No wonder Brinks was in on the R&D. There was a lot of money to be had for Pentagon insiders.

"That's all well and good, but how do I get to him? The Chiefs have tied my hands. They want me to stand down. Your boss is pushing me out."

"You still have access to the tunnel system; you can go to the moon. First, confirm Karnack is there for me; second, convince the GTO to give me access. MJ informs me I'll replace you as liaison, but the GTO won't accept it, and you know why. Make the GTO open up, clear the way for me. We've tried to access the shuttle system. The robots won't fly me. If Karnack is on the moon, I'll strangle the life out of him myself. I'll give back what he tried on me, no machines this time."

Sanderson put his hand on his packet of orders. He had his excuse to go, with or without the Chief's approval. He worked for the Commander and Chief, the President, her orders take precedent. It was a standing order. They'd object, if he told them he intended to fulfill it. He'd go and take the beating when he got back.

"I'll do it, but my way. I have orders to take the Piper girl up for a public relations spin. I'll leave her with the Bug man and work out a deal with the GTO in private. You keep your men off Piper, she's too important right now."

"MJ wants her scalped."

"They want her ship; tell them I intend to hand it over. Convince them to back up and let me work."

"What about the Ram-Education trick, you told the Chiefs, it's been passed onto the GTO. They want a piece of what she has, too. I've been told they already have chambers tuned for her and that Van Ness girl, another sore spot." Black wiped a bead of sweat off his forehead.

"I know how to get around that and you'll help me."

That meeting was passed onto MJ, no doubt Brinks is in up to his eyeballs. Sanderson didn't have the heart to sacrifice the girl, it wasn't necessary. If the military complex was a hammer, MJ was a twelve-ton weight. No wonder nothing came of negotiations. Maybe MJ and the GTO were doing deals and the Joint Chiefs were all patsies. MJ people were capable of anything.

Sanderson and Archer worked out the protocols. If the President turned up dead, he'd go anyway. Archer keeping the CIA and the NRO off his back would make it easier—nobody will shoot his transport out of the sky just yet. If Sanderson had any luck, he'd return to Earth a new man. Let Archer think he's inside this loop. Yes, Sanderson would love to strangle Karnack himself, but if he did, that new heart would surely never come. He had given up on the idea, he just wanted to go out the way he started, a patriot. But now he had a glimmer of hope, if anything, he'd see to it that Piper didn't come back in a box. He and Archer worked out the details. Sanderson would scoop Piper and Van Ness up and shove off tomorrow afternoon. She wasn't going anywhere until then.

"I'll go and alert Van Ness, give her a heads up. I'll make sure she doesn't spill it." Archer said. "She'll record, take a cam, make it look good, a real PR trip for the net."

"Make sure you give Van Ness the info, the girls can't separate until I give the go. The GTO will double cross us given the chance. I want to make sure they put the right ideas into Piper's head."

"I'll handle it." Archer put his dark glasses and hat back on.

Archer departed but something didn't feel right. What was really up Archer's sleeves? He didn't like it but Sanderson would have to trust the man in black for now. Sanderson kicked back in his chair thinking about that pain in his chest, was it real or just his nerves?

TWENTY-TWO

Mr. Black Meets Mel

Mel and Aggie had been working on the dead man switch all morning and she decided to add one of her own. If anything happened, she'd leave a big bread crumb so people would know. Her nerves were raw from Archer's visit, which drove her forward. She had to do something. She turned on the camera, set the software to shoot it up to the cloud on key command, made sure there weren't any intercepts tagged onto her. Satisfied, she began.

"OK so I'm telling you dudes this, if anything happens you'll know." She adjusted the cam's angel and saw herself in the postage stamp view. "I was in my lab. It isn't really a lab, lab: It's the pool house. It's my space now. The main house takes up a whole block. Screw that, inside's like a ghost town. What good is it without ghosts? Why'd my folks build it? What else were mom and dad going to do with their loot? Van Ness Industries rakes in mad cash making high-tech security junk for the government and that's why I'm on the shit list now."

Mel stopped the recording and tried to think of how to say what. She started again.

"It went down like this. I checked my security screens; saw another government guy at the front gate. The house guard pointed the way toward my place. I was thinking he looks familiar. So, I booted my face-rec program and blanked that screen. On one of the other screens I started my recording app and hid the surveillance program window. I let it run in the background the whole time, you'll see."

She put up a screen shot of Archer. "That's the Mr. Black guy Aggie told you all about."

OK so I let Aggie use dad's top-secret phone…illegally. That's why I'm in deep do-do. It was so worth it. It isn't fair how they make us look like a-holes. Stick to the blog.

"The door was open and the guy walked right in and he goes, 'Miss Van Ness?' Like he didn't know me? That's a pile of poop. Hello, everybody knows me."

Mel clicked and the window split. "Here, check out the tape. I'll let it run." The side window showed six different cam views, all too small to make out but anyone could capture one or all and blow them up. On the recording, Mel was saying 'No, I'm the Locke Ness Monster. Whatever you want, see my daddy's lawyer OK, I don't have to talk to you. Read the transcripts. You guys must be perverts, hello it was a sleepover not an interplanetary adventure, god!'

She paused the recording to gather her next words.

OK I stole Dad's spy network password. I didn't know it was all that. If I didn't help save the planet, we'd be in jail now.

"As you can see, the dude just stood there, staring a full minute, he was really creepy, not in a fun way. But he looked OK, sort of. When Karnack had him on control bracelet he was almost dead. Like a wax corpse. I was cool until he lowered his sunglasses. He's got deep, dark dead-pool eyes like an EBU. I almost pissed myself when he looked at me."

She restarted the recording. '...Like it or not miss, Admiral Sanderson is in charge of alien-human relations including security. I'm here on his behalf.'

She stopped the play back recording again for more commentary.

"Let's back up a little. Sanderson was the main guy and my dad's stuff didn't go anywhere without big shot approval. If this Black guy was just another hard-ass CIA man picking scabs, I'd hit the panic button—had my hand on it the whole time. Let dad's security guys handle him. But I wanted to hear him out, ya know?"

"'So, what's to me?' I asked him. Yeah loaded question, I know."

She let the Black recording roll on.

'...Sanderson is putting together an official trip to the moon. It's for public relations, but the primary objective is to allow Miss Piper and yourself to see the moon university. Americans on the moon is good for us. However, we need to know more about it. If it works out, the U.S. Government will allow you and Miss Piper to attend college on the moon.'

She stopped the play back again.

"My finger was twitched over the button the whole time. I knew I had to clam up, not say what I was thinking. Thing is, I don't trust any of them, but I had to know, yeah. There was junk going on he wasn't saying and if I asked he'd just lie anyway. That's how these people are. But his attitude pissed me off. I'll hit play."

'...You'll let us, really? In case you didn't notice this is America. You know freedom of choice and stuff. If Aggie wants to go to the moon she'll go; no passport required, dude.'

'I will lay it out for you; Miss Piper is going to the moon. You are going with her. Your role is to make sure the aliens don't use their mind controls on her until Sanderson gives word. They'll do this subversively if they can. Don't leave Piper alone. Forced general infusion won't take if another human is near. Mixed brain waves, interfere, data can't upload right. How and why is classified.'

'Dude you can't make me, Aggie and I will decide what we're doing, not you.'
She stopped the recording.

"Yeah that was balls. I meant it, too. But I was also excited about the idea. We didn't see much on the first trip, OK nobody knows we went already, but if I'm dead, you guys will know it now, anyway but it was amazing. I can't believe the goon squad didn't figure it out. We must have snuck out like five times before we got caught. Anyway..."

She started playing but talked over the scene.

"Look at that, the man in black set himself down in my gamer chair like he owned the place. What a butt-face. God, I hate government guys, think they can do anything, hey this is my space. He told me here not to tell Aggie, or he'd mess over my dad really bad."

Mel stopped the blog recording again but didn't send it. The entire tape of that guy was already in the cloud, but this was meant to release on auto. The man in black had just left and Mel was still pretty creeped out. She stopped to work it out inside her head.

College on the moon was way cool, Aggie didn't like the idea, but she did. If the aliens could do tricks on us, maybe we shouldn't go. Nice heads up. Nobody really knows how it all works up there and Praytis talks a lot but he doesn't say anything he's not permitted to say. *So yeah, I see what they're up too, they want more info.* It all made sense from government's perspective. Still, she didn't like it, something wasn't right. Maybe it was better to bail.

Mel started the play back again; it was all going on her current recording with the split window. The other window showed her in real time as she watched it with the audience. It began were she left it.

'...No way dude, I'm not letting anyone fry my brains. I'm, I'm not going. I need to think.'

'No need to think, here is why you will go. Your father committed treason. We have evidence to convict him, but as you know, the system and he are well associated, we rather not part with him, but this is a national security matter. Such sacrifices will be made willingly.'

He lowered his glasses again, yuck.

'You'll go and watch Piper's back or your father goes to jail. It's that simple. If you tell Piper, you go to jail. You'll report to me and tell me everything you see. Do not talk to Sanderson. You work for me now, understand?'

Mel leaned into the screen and shut off the playback recording of her meeting with Black. She pushed her chair back and looked at the cam that was recording her at the moment.

"I had a million questions. But that dude wasn't going to answer any. He was serious, they don't jerk around. Folks, these are the freaks that killed millions in the Middle East for oil. What can I do? I have to go if they call me. So, if you see this, that means it didn't go well. Maybe it means the government has me locked up, or I'm on the moon and didn't get back in time, or maybe I'm dead. So, internet nerds if you see this, shit is messed up. Peace out!"

Mel leaned in and hit send. She waited for confirmation and shut down once she was satisfied it went into the cloud. She had set the switch for 24 hours, so if they did go, she doubted it, she had it covered. It was pretty morbid, she always liked that kind of stuff, creepy movies and junk, but she didn't feel OK about living it. She didn't feel OK about not telling Aggie either, but her dad's ass was on the line, and really what was so bad about watching Aggie's back, she did that every day anyhow.

TWENTY-THREE

Bloody Escape

Mark made it to the intersection tunnel without mishap. He counted his steps and turned when necessary. He had walked a long way; it was hard to know how far. This side tunnel was also long. But he knew when he had arrived in the vicinity—his step count was correct. There was noise above, feet, talking, but no alarms. Then feet were running above by way of military double time toward the exit. That was strange. He was under the White House's main entry; he had eighty paces yet to go. He didn't hear any movement after that, just muffled TVs.

The oak panel door he was told to locate was ajar. But, this wasn't the same way others used; only Nostrum ever came this way. He opened it further and the hinges squeaked loud. He stepped in and closed the door before using his pen light. The door's 19th century stained finish had turned black with mold, there wasn't much left of the door styles. Near the floor everything wood was rotten. It was definitely 19th century. *How did Jen figure this one out?*

He found an old knob-and-tube light switch mounted to a board that was cut-nailed to a solid rock wall, meaning to him, that someone around 1910 had wired it. He tried the switch and an Edison light bulb lit above. Was this escape route passed down, others might also know about it? The wiring was over a hundred years old. He needed time to adjust his eyes. The ladder there wasn't too bad, made of rusty steel but passable. He shaded his eyes and saw the hatch above. It was locked from his side with heavy iron slide bolts. Nobody up there could open it without a fireman's ax. This was the right place. Above was the President's make-shift office, a little law library that was setup around 1900, nobody ever used it. It was kept as a historic example until Nostrum made Albright move into it.

Nostrum said it wasn't rigged; he'd have to trust her on that. He opened the hatch and it was under the President's desk. No alarms. He listened, no sound of human activity, but TV's were blaring loudly. They had cleared the building, otherwise he'd hear people, activity, but there was nothing. This wasn't good.

He checked the desk, Jane had a gun, and it wasn't there. He checked his little plastic auto. Mark had an idea why her gun was MIA, and he didn't like it. He went over the layout in his head; Nostrum had drawn a map for him before he left which he memorized and destroyed. The President's residence wasn't far, after the speech that's where she would have gone first.

He brushed the dust off, hung the badge on the jacket's breast pocket and proceeded into to the unknown. The place was quiet. The smell of gunpowder was faint, at first, but the closer he got to the residence the stronger the sulfur smell. Was she dead? Was it a fake suicide like the usual? They'd clear the building for that. The first TV he came across told the story. On it played a clip, the same clip the others played from what he heard, it was a loop, bad footage, the President had a gun on the VP and fired, the man dropped like a sack of lead shit. The tape repeated. So that's the game, ruin her, neutralize her and the VP, and put their boy in. Smart. The footage wasn't HD, on purpose—more intentional confusion.

He put an ear to her suite's door. She was sobbing. No doubt he was on the house security cameras; he had to act fast before they sent in Special-Ops.

He rushed in, something swung but he deflected the blow. It was an umbrella.

"Mark, Mark! I didn't do this."

The VP was on her floor, his blood wasn't coagulated yet. The wound was recent. Mark's warning bells rang. He needed cover.

He bent to the VP. The man was dead. Someone was coming; he pulled his gun and held it under his armpit and pointed it at the door behind him. He stayed in position over the body. When security opened the door, Mark fired. The man's body tumbled down and a nickel plated 38-Special slid across the floor. The CIA had issued Jane that gun. Mark snapped it up. It was a lucky shot and he didn't expect a kill—too bad, he had questions. He'd need a lot more luck. Jane Albright was hyperventilating enough for both of them.

"Jane, you were setup."

"What are we going to do!?"

"We're getting out of here."

"But I need to defend myself, I need to—."

Mark grabbed both her upper arms and faced her to him. "You need to stay alive."

He took her by the hand and they shoved off. No doubt security cameras rolled for most of it. But private areas weren't supposed to be in the loop. He avoided most of the cameras that way. The tape on the TV was intimidation, it was a CGI job, but it would take time and experts to figure that out and all the experts were on the company's payroll. They'd use that fake video to control her, make her do what they wanted. That was their plan, control or discredit. The guy he just shot was a fixer. The last thing they needed was a runner. They emptied the place for this operation; skeleton crew work. There was a chance they'd get away.

"Who was that guy, the one I shot." Mark said as they slipped into the library.

"New Chief of Staff." Jane fell into her desk chair. "Hold up here? If we give up they'll let me live, they won't release it, my reputation…I didn't shoot him."

"I know. Jane, don't be a fool, there's only one way out." Mark wiped the 38 clean, put it back in the drawer and rolled her and her chair back. He got down on the floor, pushed back the carpet, and opened the hatch with a fingernail file he swiped off her desk. From the top it was hard to see the trap door. Some long dead carpenter did a good job. "Down you go."

"What? I can't I'm—."

"Dead if you don't move, we don't have time."

Once they were in the little room below, he latched the dead bolts and prayed they'd have enough time to get clear. Mark whispered, "Make no sound, no talking." They stayed there while feet above ran back and forth, people were shouting, but it was only a handful, like he thought. Once the sound abated, "OK, we're going."

The tunnel below her room went two ways; one way goes to the river, the other back the way he had come. He wasn't sure which way was right, he had got turned around. He took his best guess and started out for the river holding Jane's hand. Her grip was hard but her skin was soft.

The air was fresher, smelled like flowers a short way down the passage. Maybe it was Jane's perfume. In the distance there was a little crack of light. He put thoughts of Jane's lovely scent out of his head. They weren't out of trouble yet, not by a long shot. The faint sound of sirens also came from that direction, had to be bouncing off the river. He heard Jane was an excellent swimmer: If Nostrums' directions held true, he would soon find out.

TWENTY-FOUR

Aggie Escapes

Dave Anderson joined the Marines to get an education. He didn't mind the special duty attachment to the Navy. It was all the same to him. He didn't ever think he would become an MP Sergeant when he enlisted. He told his friends, "I'm going for the GI Bill, man; I want to go to college." He had that in-kind with Aggie Piper. He heard her talk about school enough to know that even if he wasn't allowed to talk to her.

He didn't mean to stay in long enough to become a Sergeant. The military kept changing the rules, you had to stay in longer to get the schooling and by the time you had enough time in you also had a military career on your hands. If they knew he was a hippie at heart they would never have let him get this far. He had no regrets yet, but he saw them on the horizon. He wouldn't have seen the world had he not joined up. He wouldn't have gotten a bunk in Key West; he wouldn't be in charge of guarding the most famous teen girl in the world. He didn't like how she was treated. If Dave knew anything about the military it was keep your mouth shut and do what you are told—that's the price he was recently willing to pay for an education and it pissed him off no end when the government made that goal improbable.

I got the time in, what do I do, hang on another ten years and retire just to start over at what 40 years old?

Maybe it was time to get out before everything caved in. He felt his youth melting away same as the democracy. Back in Maine spring started with a few drips falling from the ice curtains that hung off the house gutters and then the drips accelerated and before you knew it, it all crashed down at once, just like that.

Now 0600 and Aggie was out in the yard in shorts and bathing suit top. He stood there half watching her, she wasn't going anywhere. He had no intention of looking when she stripped. A new guy came up to him as Aggie was heading toward the Gulf side peeling off her clothes as usual for morning mumbo-jumbo.

"Where the hell is she going?" His private asked. "They told us to stop her if she goes out of the zone."

The new man pulled back his carbine's bolt. *Trigger happy asshole.* The media and everyone else was piling on Aggie, but they didn't know her. Even this lump of rock they gave him for house guard was falling for the media's propaganda.

"Stand down Throckmortin." Dave said. "There's a little beach behind the shack, mangroves all around, no boats get in, water's too shallow. She is not going anywhere, it's her daily religion shit."

"But Command said stand on her, I'm going over there."

"If you want to get busted as a pervert, go ahead man. Maybe you're into shit like statutory rape."

Dave thought he'd get a good story out of Aggie twisting Throckmortin's balls into a knot. Nobody took the briefing seriously about her martial arts skills; she's just a scrawny bubble-headed kid. You look at her and your think, naw she's harmless.

"What the fuck?"

"She's back there naked, she goes out into the water knee deep to pray or some shit, does it every morning. There's no way out, no channel, its chest high mud just past the beach. I know, I tried it. You can't swim or walk it."

Aggie was out of sight now. There was a break in the foliage at the path and the beach was beyond. The dense growth gave her privacy. Dave preferred to let her have it. This was still fucking America wasn't it? What about religious freedom? He swore an oath to the Constitution and not some general's brownie point fund.

"I don't give a rat's ass, I was told to watch her. I'm going." Throckmortin said.

"Hold up, I'm going with you. Don't be a fucking pervert. Eyes down."

The two Marines pushed through the undergrowth together making a racket. There wasn't enough of a path for two to walk side by side. Packing AKs and 45s and done up in Kevlar in this heat made it harder, but this duty was worth it. Key West was beautiful. Dave didn't want to see Aggie naked, that wasn't the point; he had his honor to uphold. He just wanted to make sure this idiot didn't do anything stupid. He didn't have standing to override Sanderson's orders. He didn't see shit while busting through the overgrowth. There was nothing worth seeing until his boots hit white sand.

The air was fuzzy and felt charged with static. The hair on his arms rose. Two of Aggie's legs dangled in space about twenty feet off shore and twenty feet above the water. The legs wiggled and kicked upward and disappeared.

"Buddy, get us out of here, go boy!" Aggie said.

Dave laughed like hell. Throckmortin pulled up his AK-47 and waved it around trying to find a target. Dave saw the disturbed air running away and Throckmortin wasn't aiming anywhere near it.

"Stand down, stand down," Dave barked.

"We were told, drastic measures, I'm engaging."

The kid waved his gun's barrel in a big circle. Dave had the feeling Throck-mortin couldn't hit the broad-side of a bull moose at ten paces. The Ak-47's scope wasn't worth a shit for this—all the filters made it impossible to see that air distortion.

"Go ahead; shoot if you want jail time." Dave said. Throckmortin was still aiming in the wrong direction.

Throckmortin lowered his gun. "What do you mean, orders, Sanderson, Captain Sully—."

"Sully? He's an idiot, his dad got him duty here, dad's a full bird commander or some shit. What if some general has other ideas? You know she's the most important person in the world right now and you want to shoot her. Don't be a moron, stupid."

"That's why you're the Sergeant. You'll take responsibility, right?"

"Damn right, but it's better for you if we didn't see nothing, you're not going to tell Sanderson you saw legs just floating off. I'm not collaborating that, not me, I didn't see nothing…fact is we didn't see nothing at all. Copy that?"

"Sergeants know best."

The two walked single file back to the compound. Dave took the rear and stopped to look back. He didn't see any sign of that rippled air. Aggie Piper was away and maybe he didn't want to report her missing just yet. Maybe next shift should do that. When base called for a check at 0900 he took his time. Knocked on the door and waited fifteen minutes then he reported she was gone…again. The search call went out. The place was swarming with agents in no time. Sully showed up and Dave was relieved of duty.

Captain Sully's daddy was a Division Commander and one of the Joint Chefs' ass-kiss boys. So, Sully would wiggle off the hook and that meant shit was about to roll downhill. The usual pitch would be thrown at the usual shit-catcher. When bigwigs want somebody to pay, they always hand some peon the check. He decided he wasn't going to re-up next month when his hitch timed out. That might be why they gave him this fat duty station to begin with. This duty was a reenlistment carrot on a stick and he was tired of shitting orange.

He pulled Throckmortin aside when no one was near and said, "Make sure you tell them I told you not to disturb her, put it all on me, I'll back you. Just don't tell them what you saw or you'll get busted down, too."

The debriefing team picked him up and headed them back to base for a little talking to. On the ride Dave thought about a new direction. They'd need deck-hands on that charter boat he liked. The Captain of the Wave Runner said they always needed help when things got busy: Cash money, too. His unemployment would last the winter on top of it. Tourist season was just around the corner. He was sure he'd make out-processing last that long—sergeants stick together.

Sgt. Knolls over in Special-Ops personnel was an old fishing buddy who had a knack for losing paper work. It seemed that all of Sanderson's admin men had that same talent.

TWENTY-FIVE

Tunnel of Love

Mark was in flight mode. He didn't stop; he plowed on more than a mile down that dark, wet, muddy tunnel before he noticed Jane's hand was ice cold. He never took his eyes off that glimmer of light ahead. That feeling of a dead-cold hand jolted him out of his flight mind. He slowed down and looked back, no flashlights in the distance. He had gone the right way. They would have crossed the intersection by now. Mark stopped.

"What are you doing?" Jane's voice was pitched; she was still running on adrenalin.

Mark was on high alert as they escaped but he wasn't pumped on adrenalin, that's counterproductive, he was simply focused. Feeling and thinking didn't matter, only running mattered but now it was time to take stock. He looked back, still no flashlight in the distance. Jane's outburst didn't set off any alarm. He used his multi tool's pen light and gave her a quick look over. Her pant suit was covered in blood and mud.

"Where's your shoes, "Mark whispered. The tunnel floor wasn't user friendly, it was covered in crudely cut cobble stones, the only saving grace; much of it was coated in muck. "Your feet are cut."

"Cut's better than dead." Jane was breathing hard; she bent at the waist and inhaled deeply. "I left them in the hall, a few doors from...my library...I was trailing...bloody footprints."

"Footprints, shit." The tunnel's mud made it easy to track them. "We better keep moving,"

Mark scooped Jane up off her feet and carried her. She didn't protest. Thank god she wasn't heavy; Mark wasn't in the shape he had been in as an active Seal.

She was built like her sister Jennifer, athletic with not many pounds to spare. Something that didn't show through her daily low-key Presidential wardrobe was that she was in top physical condition. He felt back muscles flexing under her clothes. She had a swimmer's back. She didn't smell bad either.

Mark calculated in his mind what was going on topside. It took time to clear the White House, they would need time to bring people back in. The guy he killed was supposed to find the VP's body and the President covered in blood and his job was to convince her to play ball, or else.

The tape was pre-made. The Company had it ready before they pulled the trigger, it was all meant to intimidate her, control her, now, it would be used openly. The President was known to be a target shooter—that's good for elections. The target range was where they got footage of her shooting that same 38: Political backfire. No doubt, this was all part of the setup.

That man he shot was their shoo-in now they needed a new shoe. Maybe they weren't in a rush to find her, maybe they weren't onto Nostrum's tunnel. Maybe they went to where the main tunnel started. He guessed it was near the Presidential bunker. They would search the house first, might not get to the security cameras right away, they had them looped for the operation so there might not be any footage of the escape. Mark and Jane had a little time before the real manhunt started in earnest. He explained all this but kept walking as they talked. She was upset and it wasn't sinking in.

"Mark, the people will never believe me, I didn't shoot him."

"I know you were setup. We'll worry about the public later. Who shot the VP?"

"I'm not sure; I heard the shot, found him in my foyer. A CIA man came in with the gun right behind me and tossed it to me, I fumbled with it. I didn't know what to do. He snatched it out of my hands and backed out. It was my gun! You came in not a minute after. I just started CPR when you found me…You must believe me Mark. My prints are on that gun!"

"I wiped it clean, remember?" Mark stopped and put her down. He took each of her shoulders in hand and faced her. He saw the whites of her eyes but not much else. "Jane, your mind is racing, you aren't pulling it together. Relax. I need you sharp. Work on your breathing. Focus on that, can you do that for me?" Mark moved to pick her up.

"I'm fine, I'll walk." She said.

A few hundred feet further things got wet. They marched in water ankle deep. Mark slowed down. That slit of light ahead was much closer. Mark saw her face now. Tears had streamed, striping her face with makeup and dirt. She was still pretty anyway.

"I don't understand any of this."

"It was a textbook operation; you did nothing wrong. We'll convince the public."

"What, how, how do I do that?"

"For now, it doesn't matter. First we don't get caught; we'll deal with it when we can."

Mark and Jane proceeded forward. The water got deeper, the tunnel was descending. They waded into the water until it was waist deep. There was a drop-off about fifty feet from the light source. Mark had stepped off unawares and went down over his head. He popped back up unscathed. He tried the penlight. The tunnel's roof dove down sharper until the water level was at the ceiling and there was that crack of light. He felt like they were traveling downhill and this proved it. Before warming and sea level rise, this sewer outlet was above the riverbank, but now it was almost completely underwater.

"This is an old storm drain system. They used to dump waste water into the rivers." Mark said. "That drop is a sludge pit. The light stuff flowed out above it, the pit's how they trapped heavy refuge. There must be a manhole."

They searched. Mark swam out to check the ceiling. He found it, but it was filled with cement. They must have capped it a hundred years ago.

Mark swam back and together they watched the light fade at the ceiling's intersection between the water line. The tide was coming in. No that's not it, this part of the river was too far north, must be the wake of passing ships.

"That light's coming from an old outlet grate, it would have bars, but it's old. Bars must be gone. I'll check it out, stay here."

Mark stripped down to his black Speedo underwear, put his little backpack on and walked in. The water was murky and full of debris. Once away and under water he saw the light ahead but not much else. He kicked toward the light but his foot snagged something, he thought it was weeds. He tried to kick out, but he got stuck. He was tangled. Mark calmed his mind, he knew how long he could hold his breath, but he didn't keep a count. He worked on the tangle; it was an old net, the worst thing a swimmer could encounter. Two minutes plus, his lungs were starving. He thrust upward. Lucky, in the ceiling was an air pocket, but another wake was coming on. He took a breath and went back to work. It was no good; there was no end to that fucking net. The last time he surfaced there wasn't much of an air pocket. He heard the familiar thumping of a huge ship's engines, it was a big one, maybe a laden tanker and its wake would not let up any time soon. The air pocket disappeared just as Mark needed a breath.

***

Jane knew something was wrong. He was gone too long. Did he make it out, did he drown? Mark left her the penlight and she needed it. That little bit of light was gone. She rolled the little device around in her hand. It had a nail clipper and knife blade, clever little thing, she thought, and waterproof, too. Why would he dive without a blade? That was an essential tool for divers. She never dives without one even when snorkeling. She turned it off and it became pitch black. That's when she noticed the lights in the distance behind her. That's when it hit her, Mark needs help. She just felt it. It was time to go, like it or not.

She stripped down to her bra and panties and quickly moved into the water. The little penlight showed her the way and she almost lost her air when she found him. He was out, maybe dead. Without thinking, she attacked the net, freed him and swam them both for the light. She barely made it to the surface before her lungs kicked her in the spine. Mark was pale, not breathing.

They were adjacent to a little sandy beach. She hauled him up there, rolled him over onto his stomach and worked his lungs with her palms on his back while waves from a big ship washed over his legs. Mark finally spilled the water and chocked for air. He puked out a lot of water before rolling over on to his back.

"Damn that was close."

Jane was exhausted and dazed but she got up on her knees, balled her fists and pounded on his chest. "You, you, goddamn it Mark. You can't leave me now! You can't!"

He suddenly reached up, pulled her down, and lip locked her like he meant it. She didn't know what to do; she didn't know if she liked it or not, so full of relief and adrenalin, she could do little but let it happen. Once she came to herself, she pulled away.

"Why'd you do that? I'm the President, you, you…"

"Helicopter," Mark pointed up. "To them we're just a couple of beached lovers."

Jane checked herself, "We're in our underwear for God's sake." She suddenly felt extremely self-conscious. Thank God she matched; bra and panties were black so maybe from a distance it did look like swimwear. What if the press got pictures of this, she'd be ruined. She tried to cover herself as the helicopter banked to fly over them again.

"Don't," Mark said, "we need to play the part. They think we're from that boat moored over there." He grabbed her fists, she forgot to release them, and he pulled her down again. "After they pass we'll swim out and borrow that boat, prove their suspicions." He said into her ear.

She wrapped her arms around him; maybe they would get away after all. This time when he drew her in for a kiss she played her part better. Her acting skills were better than he expected, she thought, but was this really acting? More like reacting. Her part in the play was not a Hollywood kiss. She finally understood what Jennifer saw in him. The man was a catch.

TWENTY-SIX

Buddy in Flight

Her plan worked. Keeping Buddy cloaked really was the shit. They didn't have a clue he was around. It was nice of Buddy to pop out some handles so she could hang on, but she was still naked and had no place to go. Forget Mel's, they watched Mel and everyone else Aggie knew. The lower Keys were swimming with cops so driving out, forget it, sailing? They were on to that.

Aggie needed to get in touch with Praytis and she had no idea how. Nothing that came out of Sanderson was straight. For all she knew they put a bug in her corn flakes and they were tracking her now. Conversations with Buddy were one way, but just like a dog, he understood fetch. How to get a message out was the big question. If they found her fast she'd know they had some way to trace her.

"Only time can tell." Aggie laughed. The sensation of flying was so cool.

Buddy did that little rolling thing that meant yes on the ground but they were in the air floating over Geiger bay's mud flats. She looked down, falling would suck, the water was way too shallow to break her fall and, of course, she saw sharks.

"Why sharks, it's always sharks! I can't hang on much longer we got to land someplace, any ideas Buddy?"

Buddy took off toward the far shore. Aggie felt emotional warmth radiating from inside the little probe; it was like that love glow thing Sky Flower always talked about when Sky and Po-boy tripped on peyote. 'Everything is connected, everything is love,' they said of the experience.

"Whatever."

Aggie was pretty well convinced Buddy loved her, but she didn't expect proof. She thought it was just her wishful thinking. Still, it was weird, feeling what it felt. It freaked her out a little.

What am I getting into? Maybe telepathy is real? Maybe it was just her. Aggie shook off the thought; it was ridiculous to think that.

Buddy descended into Bixby Marina's boat storage lot. Homeless people got kicked out of there once in a while but the place was empty now, or so Buddy projected into her. Maybe Buddy was linked to Mother, but Mother was in passive mode on auto defense, at least that's what Praytis said. Good, after Aggie got past all this crap, once she was done with school, she'd start Mother up and learn how that works. But right now, Mother wasn't on her plate. College came first. *Yeah, I'm stubborn.*

There were about eight rows of dry-docked boats lined up and crammed together pretty tight, maybe twenty boats to a row, if you could call it a row. The place was pretty haphazard. A lot of the boats were old wooden jobs and half collapsed and rotting away in their dry docks. She smelled mold as they flew lower. Buddy set her down near the back fence between hulks.

"Buddy, go find some clothes for me, go fetch!"

The probe blinked in and out of her visual range and jetted off. Aggie searched the back row; behind it was a high privacy fence with swampy marshes beyond. Most of the dry-docked boats were waste cases. A lot of them were once beautiful yachts but long abandoned. "What a waste!"

She got close to one that looked good, a fiberglass cabin cruiser; she climbed up on its deck and opened the cabin's door. But the smell of the former resident drove her back. Obviously, a homeless guy lived in it and it wasn't somebody that took a regular bath. On impulse she sniffed her pits. "Aaakkk!"

Aggie moved on and found a smaller vessel, a fiberglass sailboat; the canvas cover was good and it made a good tent over the main arm. The cover was tied tight to the gunwales. The boat didn't smell, and it was close to the fence for a fast getaway. She untied a couple of eyelets at the stern, parted the canvas like a split door and climbed over the transom.

"Home sweet home, at least until I figure out how to get out of here."

She rummaged around, found a few useful things, like oversized sweatpants, a t-shirt, knives and tools, but no food. That's when her stomach didn't just growl, it barked. She forgot to eat this morning and didn't bring anything.

"OK, so now I'm a hunter-gatherer. Mom will be so proud."

There was no one to laugh at her joke and it wasn't funny anyway. Aggie decided to lie up there, if they had the ability to track her, she'll be eating breakfast in the next ten minutes. She checked the boat's clock but it wasn't running. She heard sirens on Geiger Avenue; helicopters flew over, beyond the mudflats, a Coast Guard fast-boat was racing through the channel. Nope, she wasn't going anywhere for a while.

Hours later, the searchers were still at it and Buddy didn't return either; maybe the little guy knew it wasn't safe. How much did it know anyway? When nothing was in the air above, she went out in her ragamuffin outfit in search of food and managed to make it to the back of the restaurant. Bixby's was a full-service marina, food, drinks, mechanical service, fishing charters, boat slips, it had the works; ten times bigger than Mark's little marina. Behind the main building were some dumpsters but she wasn't that hungry.

Just inside the kitchen's open back door was a utility room with a radio playing hip-hop, mops and junk were hung on the walls, other junk stuffed the room. But it had a small area for employees; just a card table and a couple of chairs next to a nasty-dirty mini refrigerator.

She grabbed some donuts and a can of soda from the break room and split thinking if this is all I'm getting to eat, I'll starve to death. Jail food had to be better. Aggie darted between boats and made it back to the one she settled on, climbed in and ate her stolen meal in the dark thinking, what in the hell am I doing, this is ridiculous.

TWENTY-SEVEN

Pirates on the Potomac

Mark wanted to rest longer, he hadn't slept much in the last few days and his empty gut was crying for mercy. But, now was not the time. He had to find a place to hole up and recover. He had an idea but first he had to get himself and the President off the Potomac. He had glimpsed a boat moored on a stationary float just around the bend and he had an idea of how or more so who, that could be. That boat was trouble. Thompson's Boat Rental was a few hundred yards up river and too far to walk without being seen.

After the chopper changed spiral pattern Jane stood and stretched her legs. The little beach they were on was surrounded by brush; the bank above his head was steep and overgrown with briers. Mark figured it was either Federal Reserve grounds above or one of the many parks and either way not his best choice for an escape route. They could make their way along the shore but it was too exposed, too risky.

"Stay low," Mark told Jane, "I'm going on recon."

"What's that mean in English?" Jane said as she ducked below the brush line.

"It means that boat up river isn't supposed to be moored like that and I need to confirm why before we move. Stay low."

Mark crawled under the nearest tall brush and shimmied his way along the gravel and mud until he rounded the bend and had a good view of the boat. His cuts and scrapes would keep. He watched for a three count, that is three thousand, and then he saw movement. Just like he suspected, it was a security boat. Probably a contractor hired to watch the outside approach. Mark wasn't as far from the White House as he'd like.

He waited long enough to assess what the man had. Judging by the slime matted along the hull's water line that boat hadn't moved in a long time. Agents must be dropped and picked up for each shift. It was a standard perimeter post setup. Mark backed out and made it back to the President.

"What'd you see?" Jane said.

"I see our ride out, how do you feel about another swim?"

Mark rooted around and found an old piece of the iron bars that had once covered the culvert, tested its weight and feel and was satisfied. Jane didn't ask so he explained the plan. She'd swim out to the boat from there, play like she was in distress and make a lot of noise. First Mark would go up river, take to the water and come down and board form the man's blind side. He told her make a lot of noise, keep him occupied, and tell him anything to keep him at the shore facing gunwales. He didn't mention the man had a radio, wore a SecureCo uniform and packed a shitload of hardware. If Mark was with perimeter security, he'd shoot first and ask later. They'd have to risk that the government spook's old adage about security for hire was true: security contractors were cheap, and that means stupid. Money talked, SecureCo only hired wannabes and dishonorably discharged hard-asses. He hoped the man on lookout was of that low quality. Such would give Mark a greater advantage.

Mark made it to his launch point up shore and wasn't seen, but Jane went in too soon, she didn't count right. He had to wait until the man's attention was with Jane before getting wet. The swim was downhill. Forty yards out and forty away and would have been easy when he was younger, but times have changed.

He traveled under water halfway twenty yards; he used to go forty no problem. When he came up for air he heard Jane.

"Can't you help! Please, I don't swim so good."

"Sorry lady..."

Mark made it to the starboard side and surfaced at the hull.

"Hey, you're, no can't be, I was ordered to shoot Albright on sight."

"Who's Albright?"

Mark popped up onto the rail, the man spun. Mark didn't have time to board. The man shouldered his AK-47 while Mark let that iron bar fly. It hit point end first on the man's forehead and knocked him back, the rifle flew overboard, but his man wasn't down.

All the while Jane was yelling, "I'm the President, stop, stop, stand away!"

Shut up Jane, shut up.

Mark rolled over the gunwale as the man charged cross deck trying to pull his pistol. Mark swept his legs and the man came down hard bashing his head on the rail. Mark checked, the man was out cold. Mark took his sidearm and went to the opposite rail.

"Come on Jane, give me your hand." He hauled her up over the side with one mighty pull.

"Oh my God, you killed him, you killed him." She staggered and melted down to the deck. "So much blood, all that blood."

Mark checked him. "No, he's alive, but he hit hard, he'll need medical. Find some rope, tie him, I'll get this junker started."

Mark found the key in the ignition, turned it and quickly discovered the battery was near dead, not enough to fire the engine. He went through the boat. It was a twenty-four foot boat with a cuddy cabin, so it didn't take long to figure out there wasn't a spare battery, or oars. There was a small solar charger on the cabin's roof used to charge the guard's radio and that was no help. Mark wondered when the next shift started.

Jane came up from below. "I found rope. It was in that little space up front."

"Forward compartment. We need to get out of here." Mark said. "Help me get this man below."

"The cabin has water and a first aid kit. I'll make him comfortable."

It wasn't easy. The man Mark had disarmed was a big boy, well over six foot and two hundred pounds. Mark was only five-eight. The kid looked about twenty-five, had a Marine Corp tattoo on his trigger hand, so he was a vet: Mark hated to do damage to one of his kind. He still had that kindred feeling with all his military brothers and sisters although the men behind the veil pulling war strings didn't deserve such respect. It wasn't this man's fault, or any young one's fault, getting snowed into serving a deeply corrupted system wasn't on this kid. Patriotism and propaganda was how the Powers corrupted people.

"I'm cutting us loose." *If I can't get her running, we'll drift to a landing.*

Mark went up onto the bow's deck and cut the tether. He heard his young buck moaning, that was a good sign. He secured the rope and tied down the anchor, some moron had let the anchor get loose. The boat floated down river backwards, he'd have to trim course. She was heading to the Washington side pushed by wakes, he wanted the opposite shore.

"Mark, I need you."

Mark swung the cabin door open to find Jane in the arms of the wounded man. He was on the forward wraparound couch and had pulled Jane on top of him: Held a clam knife at Jane's neck.

Mark stopped cold. The man's blue eyes were blinking fast, blood was still on his face and his vision was impeded by blood flow. *Dilated eyes, he's in shock.* The confiscated handgun was just outside on the pilot's seat. Jane would be dead before Mark could pull it. The last thing Mark needed was a standoff with a man he didn't want to kill, a man who didn't know where he was or what he was doing. *I'm getting soft.*

TWENTY-EIGHT

The GTO

Pharaoh waited in her office, a room of white on white, the desk, chairs even her door styles. It was her respite from the dull grays of the moon, most depressing, and as many other beings worked on Moon Base, the neutral and natural local color was chosen. Did Karnack also make his ship homey? She would ask him once he emerged from Ram-Education. How nice would it be to have an entire ship made to please her eye? Pharaoh would find out when she tricked that Earth girl out of her holdings. It is good they rescued Karnack, he will have ideas about how to proceed with…what was it the Earth ones called it?

"High stick, no that is not right, highjack, yes that is it."

She liked the way that word rolled over her thin lips.

"Define highjack? I'm waiting." The AI asked.

"No thank you. Tell me, where is Praytis?"

"Approaching, ETA ten seconds."

"Open the door." She said.

A more intelligent AI would not ask, it would anticipate, even read your mind if very well advanced, but that is exactly what Pharaoh didn't want in her personal space. Sentient AIs have minds of their own and they talk to each other, they have life-right, and sometimes they go their own way like Karnack's former ship did with that Earth girl.

Smart AIs can't be trusted. Mother's holds contain a fortune in LF and other commodities, getting her to give them up will be interesting, fun and profitable, but not easy. The riches Mother held made Pharaoh's wings quiver. Karnack had the right idea but his methods were a mistake. It was the wrong approach.

Praytis walked up to her quietly, none of his four bare feet slapped the floor.

He knows that disturbs her, it was perhaps the only thing she had in common with Earth people. She did not stand up at her desk when he approached. He wore a ship communication belt. Why would he off ship?

"I see it is confirmed?" she asked. "That Earth girl gave you First Mate status?" *He wears the belt to display his position. He is foolish.*

"Yes, yes she did, it's recorded." The insect-like man said. "I picked her up with one of Mother's shuttles. Mother said Aggie is cool with it, as they say Earth side."

"Where is your control belt?"

"How interesting that you should ask: I did not get one, just this com belt. It seems when Aggie cut Karnack's belt she destroyed the system's control function wire. I had the ship control belt on briefly. Mother is a free agent again. Aggie is Mother's and the other way too."

"This will make things difficult."

"Things, what things?" Praytis stood tall on his rear legs.

He must feel challenged and anger is obvious. I must go carefully.

"I will remind you that you are still under contract with the GTO, you may have a ship second status but you still belong to the GTO. You must not tell that Earth girl, she may not buy your contract. Karnack acquired that material while under the GTO's patronage, those stores belongs to us."

"You can think so if you care to, Praytis said," But Mother disagrees. What's the expression Aggie likes, 'good luck with that Skippy?' I have another Earth saying, 'finders keepers.'"

"I do not know this Skippy, luck is not required, and we have, as an Earth person might say, 'the upper hand.' Be that as it may, we have work to do."

"What will you do?" Praytis lowed himself to his normal height but his usual continence of dejection was not evident. "What game are we playing?"

We, there is no we. Pharaoh was perturbed at Praytis's forwardness. Give a peon contract worker ship-status and they become undeservedly bold. Such behavior will not do, nor would it benefit her to have this underling know the GTO's deeper business. This Earth security concept of need-to-know seemed right to apply. Even primitives can teach one a few tricks, so it seemed. Sanderson has said, keep one's friends close and enemies closer, and that too has merits. Praytis would likely forever be an indentured employee and as such little better than a biological robot, but Pharaoh would not take any risk. Praytis was now suspect but still usable.

"This Earth person, this female, we will have her come here. Perhaps we can work trade terms. I would like to speak with her. Sanderson will make arrangements. She has need of basic communication implants, is that not so? She can afford it. Sanderson would agree. He will help us. Will you do the same?"

"Do I have a choice?"

"At the appointed time, you will meet. Go and get her Earth side, as the case may be, and bring her to Ram-Ed. After which time, bring this Piper person directly to me."

"What about the protocols, where are the rules?"

"The rules are in suspension; our contract has run out just as we were revealed, in no small part because of you. Thus, we have special circumstances and will proceed under emergency protocol. You may go, thank you."

Praytis visibly straightened on the idea of that Earth girl coming. He removed himself with an air of pride. He let his bizarre feet make that horrid sound, a minor infraction, but still it was a show of disrespect.

He likes this primitive Earth being. That idea proved a good distraction from the larger topic of which Praytis missed completely. The last seven thousand years of waiting was not in vain after all, the big payoff was not far ahead. Her wings quivered. Earth's habit of fighting each other was sure to escalate, in fact it was already, this cake was baked and ready for the taking, now all Pharaoh needed was Mother as icing.

"I'll eat my cake and have it too, what a marvelous idea."

"But your brother took it too far, no?"

With that the white wall behind her dissolved. A Tall Gray and a Lepron stepped forward. They were each tri-rulers of the GTO's section of Moon City. Moon City was never considered in the GTO's reckoning thus she was not represented.

"No" Pharaoh said. "It is not that he went too far, but that he acted too soon."

The Tall Gray's little mouth turned up at the corners and the Lepron rubbed his hands together.

"He should have waited like us," the Gray said. "With recent events, our waiting proves well. Surely the Earth's civilizations will soon collapse and all its resources will be ours, and without our instigating mass destruction. We will milk this cow a few more years at best before they finally kill themselves off, leaving us the spoils."

"Our satellites are ready for the inevitable chain death event: Untold LF will we acquire." The Lepron said.

"Nothing can stop us," Pharaoh said. "The social AI predicts correctly. Earthlings are about to fail. And even if they don't blow themselves up, the environment will collapse. It is inevitable. Earth doesn't have time or the will to take corrective measures. You are aware that Space Port AI has confirmed this. Wait just a little longer and we cannot lose."

"Yes, but if that Earth woman discovers her legal status and with it, Earth people's rights, mass death will delay further. If Praytis talks? What of his loyalties?"

"I am taking measures," Pharaoh said. "Praytis is nothing if not predictable."

"What of Praytis?" Asked the Lepron, his kind were always logical and cautious and rightfully so. Should Earth realize its' universal citizenship was at hand, the GTO would be obligated to help them. But as the situation was, the GTO had loopholes in plenty to claim the Earth independently advanced, thus the GTO's obligations were less: at least one Earth person had access to star drive. Such was the evidence and so Pharaoh legally removed the GTO's anti-nuclear war protocol. None of this Praytis could know.

"The GTO will no longer disarm the planet's nuclear weapons as they are deployed." Pharaoh said. "Rather the disarmament probes surrounding Earth are being withdrawn a few at a time and refitted for LF extraction."

The others telegraphed their approval and understanding telepathically. The GTO's long slow habit of mining static LF was over. Soon their coffers would boil over with bursts of Earth human extinction. The best part was that the Earthlings were doing it to themselves, all perfectly legal.

All she had to do was do nothing. Earth's ending was unavoidable. Still, she could not resist helping the process along. Even MJ-12 was blind to this inevitability. The Earth's Shadow Government's greed was easily manipulated. It was too simple: ignorance or lack of acceptance of their realities made it so.

Pharaoh laughed and she had not done so in a very long time. Even so she was careful not to drop a feather. She and her brother for all their similarities were not exactly alike. He was sloppy in hygiene and Earth side operations, she would not be.

The Lepron looked hard at her with his green liquid eyes and said, "What about Praytis?"

Lepron's kind was what Earth people might mistake for one of their legendary magical creatures. Leprons should never have landed in Ireland. But their greed and lust for wealth such as Celtic gold was sure and true. In every legend there are truths.

"Praytis's race are socially honor bound, they do not break contracts. Have you ever heard of a Mantis who wasn't tied tightly by the knots of his honor?" Of course, that aspect of him was previously reinforced in Ram-Ed.

"Still, he is a danger; we should put him back in Ram-Education." The Lepron said.

"He is not stupid, should we force RE upon him against established regulations, he will suspect and I am sure he has fail-safes inside our education AI to prevent...certain influences. As they say on Earth, that will blow our cover. We must still obey the contract conditions the GTO set forth or we won't profit and Praytis will surly suspect illegalities. We must not give him the opportunity to register a legal protest."

Pharaoh wasn't worried and she didn't believe in Mantis rebellions. She flexed her wings which ruffled her long golden hair. She took a few moments to preen. The others waited. They understood her fastidiousness.

"We are willing to push forward." The Tall Gray injected telepathically changing the topic.

But the Lepron wasn't satisfied. He spread his feet and crossed his arms over his chest.

"Praytis will be more useful without us giving him cause to rebel." Pharaoh said.

"He has a big mouth; he blathers all over Moon City." The Lepron said.

"We have waited long to reap what the Earth has on offer, a little while longer won't matter." Pharaoh was growing tired of his repeated questions. She changed topics. "Moon City AI confirms Earth's social structure will collapse quite soon, it has already begun, and our long planted social controls minimize the likelihood of Earth saving itself even if they understand the danger. Praytis can't save Earth, much less himself."

They were all anthropologists. It was well known in human societies that social patterns repeat, every emergent human race fails when thrust into a higher technological age unprepared and unearned by their own means. That is the bases of the non-interference rule, a rule she and her brother broke long ago and now here at the end she would not chance exposing past questionable activity... this is the time to adhere, now that the universe was paying close attention. She must protect the GTO's claim. On the thought, she telepathically told GTO's AI to withdraw her Earth government approved LF raiders.

"Your points are well made," The Gray said in voice. "Pushing our agenda forward may well create suspicions, I concede your logic."

It was settled. The others departed. They would wait and it would not be long. Without her probes disarming nuclear missiles as before, the first one launched will enact auto-harvesters and Earth's LF will be the GTO's. Her wings fluttered, feathers fell and for once she let them fall where they may. She would soon have enough LF credits to regenerate herself another thousand times.

She pulled up Sanderson's control module code. The idea placed inside his head was active. Sanderson will indeed bring the Piper girl in. Good fortune that the American President ordered him to do so as well.

TWENTY-NINE

Aggie in Hiding

Aggie's first night hiding in Bixby's boat storage lot had its up and downs. Being free was the up part, the rest was all down. From the deck of the sailboat she picked to sleep in, Aggie saw craziness from her location a mile plus across the shallows. Helicopters above and cars in and out all night long made her keep her head down and her eyes open. She hardly slept. She saw distant flashlights all night as searchers slogged around in the mangroves. She felt bad for those guys. Whenever a helicopter flew directly overhead she almost had a panic attack. *What's next, drones?*

Aggie tried to settle in about midnight, she had made a decent bed up in the sailboat's small cabin, but she laid there worrying, her mind in knots of fears. What if I'm caught, jail this time? Why shouldn't I go as I want, I'm free right, I'm not a prisoner, why is The Man putting the screws to me? How am I going to get out of this pile of crap? She almost jumped out of her skin when someone tripped and crashed into her hull.

Without thinking, Aggie yelled, "Who's there, who's there ?!"

Crap, crap, crap, I just gave myself away.

"It's me Joe, that you Nina? Heard you took off north."

There was a stream of liquid hitting the ground, water off another hull; the guy was taking a leak. It must be the homeless guy living a few boats down stumbling through. The smell of pee and hot food mixed together, the pee smell was ignored because her stomach had control. Her empty belly decided to do the talking and the rest of her went along, what choices did she have?

Aggie popped her head out from the cockpit cover. "Sorry, I'm not Nina, just passing through, I hope you don't mind."

"That's too bad, I bought extras for her, one time, one time, could have used her tonight. Man, the dishes never stopped coming." It was hard to see in the dark, but the old man turned away and hobbled toward his crib. He looked harmless enough, he sure wasn't an agent.

"Hey you got food," Aggie asked, "I could use a bite."

"It's for her, one time, she earned it, and nobody gets Nina's food."

Aggie climbed out of the boat and caught up to the old man. There wasn't much light, but he had long, gray hair and a beard, and he didn't smell as bad as that drydocked boat he lived in. Maybe it was somebody Sky had helped before, he looked familiar, but Aggie couldn't drop Mom's name and give herself away.

"What I got to do to get some food?" *Crap that might be the wrong question.*

"You got to work if you want to eat, one time, got to work, got to do something one time. One time, just one time, one time."

"That sounds like something the beach lady says." Aggie said. That's what they called her mom when she'd go around giving food out. Sky Flower got vagabonds to help her with finding beach junk for art projects in exchange for food. Aggie pulled her borrowed hooded sweatshirt closed to hide her face. She helped mom enough that some of the homeless would know her.

"I knew the beach lady one time, one time."

"I'll help, I'll wash dishes, please give me some food. I'll earn it, I promise."

The old man burped. The alcohol on the air was mixed with spaghetti. "Kitchen's closed; I'll bring ya to work seeming Nina ain't coming no more."

He ripped open the plastic bag and pulled a paper plate out that was covered with aluminum foil. Aggie thought how wasteful aluminum foil is but she didn't say anything. "Here ya go, what's your name?" The old man parked his ass on an old laid down telephone pole with an alcohol-laden huff. He handed Aggie a plastic fork and dug into the other plate. The phone pole was laid over in a past storm; plenty of room so Aggie took a seat upwind from him.

"I'm Ag...Angel Perry," Thinking fast Aggie had shot out the name of a paranormal author she liked.

"Hmm, whatever you say missy, I'll call you missy, you don't want a fake name too close to your own, everybody does it. I see you're new to this, one time...one time."

"You don't know, I'm——."

"I don't want to know, that's how it works, see. Get it, get it, you'll get it, one time, just one time." He resumed shoveling food into his face and muttering. He suddenly started laughing and yelling aggressively. "One time hear me one time!"

Joe yelling, out of nowhere, made Aggie jump. She almost spilled her much needed plate of soggy spaghetti. She was feeling pissed about it. There was no reason for him to be so grumpy! Aggie took a few deep breaths. Sky always said there isn't any reason in mental illnesses, just accept it. Aggie stiffened but didn't react; if it was Billy mouthing off snappishly she might have socked him. But Aggie felt bad for Joe: many broken people wind up homeless. The government gives little or no help other than to arrest uppity homeless people and stick them in profit-making jails. Joe was safer hiding out here out of the public's sight than in some jail or mental institution. OK he was crazy but at least he was free. She felt a little pang of jealousy.

When Joe was done eating, he became friendly and chatty. He rocked back and forth and told the stories of his life always prefaced with "One time…One time I was a doctor in Iraq…one time when I was in a movie…one time I saw flying saucers…"

Aggie humored him. She asked small questions. It was better to just let him talk and that's how she pieced together his situation.

In drips and drabs Aggie learned Joe was Bixby's dishwasher and they let him sleep in an abandoned boat. He got to use the outdoor shower behind the kitchen. So, he basically worked for meals and some cash. Joe spent his pay on cheap-o wine. He was a vet with shellshock, as he called it. Why the owner let Joe stay was never made clear. Aggie guessed it was due to the shortage of low paid workers in the Keys. Rich kids didn't take kitchen jobs; somebody had to do that work. That explained all the young people living in vans or crammed by the dozen into studio apartments. Kids came down to the Key seeking adventures and wound up wage slaves. They never stayed long.

***

It was late in the morning when Joe came around to Aggie's hideout. She was up early and spent a few hours searching derelict boats looking for clothes and some way to hide her face. She found some big round sunglasses and found a clean do-rag for her head. Joe led her to the back door and past the little break room into the rear of the kitchen. The dishwashing station was separated from the kitchen proper and wasn't in bad order so Aggie started by cleaning the sinks. A big guy in a suit came in. He looked like ex-military, crew cut hair, straight back and attitude.

"What's this, where's Nina?"

Aggie cringed inside but didn't look up. Rather she hunched even lower holding her breath.

"You chased her off, shouldn't have insulted her, one time." Joe said.

Aggie bent lower into the sink with a steel wool pad and scrubbed at the sink's drain ring.

"Good riddance, Nina smelled like piss. I can't have that, she should have used the goddamn shower more, that's what it's for."

The man walked out. That last remark, she felt, was directed at her— Aggie was getting ripe but she breathed easier with him gone. So far, she wasn't recognized. Thank the Goddess.

The Mexican cooks on the other side of the dish deposit counter wall were getting orders and didn't pay the dishwashers any mind. So, Aggie and Joe worked all day until ten p.m., eating a bit when there was time. It was a long day. Joe wasn't much help after drinking all the half-filled glasses of booze that came back after dinner. Soon after dinner hour began Joe was pretty well tanked. Aggie thought this was the usual routine here.

The cooks were illegal, so they weren't going to rat on her but she wasn't taking any chances. Aggie tried avoiding the cooks when they were in the break room but they were too friendly. She went back to turn up the radio and the cooks didn't complain—they were nice to her instead. The wait staff, on the other hand, was stuck up and they didn't ever bother to look at who was washing dishes, so they were easy to avoid. Kitchen work had its big clique like high school. The cool kids vs. the rest. She never did see the chef but she heard him yelling at the cooks. Like school, she was on the low end of the social scale—of course.

There was nothing on the radio news about her and Aggie didn't know if that was good or bad. But there was an awful lot of junk about the President murdering the VP. Crap was flying, Aggie wished the Goddess she could get online somehow. She didn't know what was happening in the world but one thing she did know for sure, she wasn't getting any more help from the President.

THIRTY

Belly of the Beast

Archer had been there once before. When he was first enlisted by MJ, he didn't know who they were, but he knew they were the secret force behind the military, which means the men behind everything. He felt honor then, to be an insider, to be trusted to recover alien artifacts, things no one was allowed to see he saw. He was trustworthy. They must have thought him a good tool and he was until Karnack opened his eyes. Archer would rather have not known how he was used, how expendable he is to Majestic Twelve. But in a way that information was good, he didn't feel like he owed MJ or America anything, they owed him.

Archer should have been grateful that Karnack showed him the deep truths of state. Karnack, however, tried to kill him. Karnack left Archer for dead and only Archer's need of revenge saved him, forced him to crawl after what was left of his life force and now that force had one purpose: Kill Karnack.

Archer entered the conference room deep under the Capital Building. There was a lackey there and several computer screens. Archer was no dummy; he knew who they were behind pixilated computer images and voice distortion. After Karnack, he'd take them out one at a time, and Brinks, too; take what they took from him…his life, but first things first.

"Mr. Black, thank you for coming," One computer said as the secretary, or whoever he was, left the room.

"You have heard that the focuses of the NRO are changing. We are no longer in the business of shooting down alien craft."

"I received the cease order."

"Sanderson appears to be nearing his…end, when his heath fails; he will die soon. We want you to take over. You will be Earth's representative to negotiate with the GTO."

Archer had been maneuvering for years to get this high-powered spot, and he knew it was inevitable but now his reason for wanting the job had changed. Still, he'd play it humble. Keep up the game. Let them outsmart themselves. He was already moving past them.

"It's not my cup of tea; I'm a direct-action man." He lied.

Archer thought about the many aircraft the NRO shot down and recovered. The occupants weren't useful. Branford got all he could out of the wreckage. MJ was after something else and he didn't care what they wanted. With Sanderson out or in, he'd get his ride to the moon. This offer was just another inroad. Karnack must have been picked up and was no doubt a prisoner on the moon: An easy kill. Things were looking up. MJ just opened wide another angle to work.

"That is why we chose you. We need a more direct approach."

"What is it you want me to do?" Archer said. He'd play their game for now and play Sanderson as well. Let them think he's their man. He'd flow with it until the river forked.

"We need you to persuade the Piper girl, once she is picked up again, to share information on her fleet with us. We want the star drive. Anti-gravity we have, but artificial gravity is another matter. No more kid gloves, understand?"

Archer already knew how star drive worked, Karnack had loose lips. Archer wasn't a tech but the concept of what star drive is, he understood the concept, what actually made it work was far beyond any Earth tech's wildest imagination. More paranormal than science but he wasn't going to show his trump card.

Going after Piper was a waste of time, but they didn't know that. Even if they got her ship and she gave it willingly, it won't pan out. That ship didn't need Piper—it had a mind of its own.

"I'll put the screws to Piper, she'll talk. She'll give us access or suffer." *They really think I'll fuck-up the girl that saved my life? I'm not the robot I used to be.*

"That's what we need to hear. When you find Piper, she goes to Gitmo for safe keeping. Keep it quiet, we'll deal with Branford. Leave Sanderson out. He is still useful, so don't tip him off. Consider that his slot is yours. Nothing said leaves this room."

The screens went blank. Archer sat in the dark. Yes, Sanderson was useful, but not in the way Majestic would know. Why do they want Sanderson out? Branford and Sanderson were too chummy. Branford worked out the MAC drive and controls, but the fleet was still a long way from attaining alien flight capabilities. What would they do with star drive if they had it? AI's weren't stupid. The Navy's Space Fleet was a three-legged dog without teeth snapping at greyhounds.

The secretary opened the door and the light from the hall beamed in but the light didn't bother him. MJ was much like Karnack Archer thought as he stood to leave; both were blind to everything that wasn't what they wanted, such as the fact that Archer was good at working blind spots.

***

After Archer left the men sitting at table in the room a few doors down the hall wrapped it up.

"Does he suspect we have the LF bomb?"

"We don't have anything yet, we don't know if it works."

"If he doesn't get Piper to cooperate, we'll find out soon enough."

"Blowing Haiti up seems a bit extreme."

"If we can't take that mother ship...we'll do what we must. We'll blame it on the aliens, the public will buy it."

"More cause to deploy Space Fleet."

The men departed not worried one bit. Archer was the perfect tool. When it came time to take him down he won't see it coming. Majestic controlled the military, the media, the politicians; they will fall into line like they always do. Branford and Sanderson might become problems if the Joint Chiefs cave in, but they had contingency plans for that as well. The President recently learned of such a contingency plan first hand. MJ-12 knew they were unstoppable—they held every card. Each man of the group had his own ideas, his own part in the effort's details but they all agreed on one central point, why control just one planet when you can have a galaxy?

THIRTY-ONE

Aggie Bussing Tables

Aggie had the dishwashing area in fine shape and she wasn't bored, and weirdly, she didn't mind doing dishes either. She hated dishes at home and made Jon do the dishes back at Mark's place before this all started. Washing dishes made her think of Jon. She missed that stupid cowboy. At least the radio played while she worked to take her mind off a lot of crap.

Another siren went off outside somewhere on Route One. Helicopters were all over the Key this morning. They weren't giving up, she was trapped. Buddy hadn't been back since she told him to go and get her some clothes. Maybe they had a way to track him and find her through him? Was Buddy smart enough to know when to stay away? From the little she saw and heard the Keys were crawling with cops. Nothing much on the radio about all the cop activity, for sure, but that didn't mean anything.

"I'm never getting out of here," Aggie pined over a sink full of pots.

"Don't fret missy, Mr. Big will have you bus when we're busy one time, big tips, big." Joe said, it wasn't a good mid-morning for Joe, he wasn't drunk yet. The orders were coming in slow and not many people were drinking. "Sure thing, he'll make me wash all this by myself, one time, one time, that's bullshit."

"Don't, worry, I'll help. Besides, he won't put me out there," Aggie pointed toward dining with her chin. Her hands were full of suds. "Look at me, I don't have clothes, I don't even have underwear."

"Aren't nothing wrong with that." Joe reached under the sink, took out his emergency bottle of Dragon-Breath and took a deep pull. Aggie smelled that cheapo wine from across the room.

The boss came into the back; he hardly ever did that. Boss looked around.

Aggie tried to keep her face in the sink. Her do-rag was wet from steam so she had taken it off; she must have looked like a wet rat. That food dye in her hair had bled and blended into mud color.

"You girl, I need you up front at lunch. Adrian popped, she's in labor. I got a big party coming."

"Sure, I don't knows hows ta weeiter," Aggie said it with dad's Creole accent. Everybody had heard her speak on TV. She knew how to do dad's voice perfectly; Mark said changing your voice was useful for hiding in plain sight.

"That's fine, you bus. I'll put Heather on tables. We got a big group for lunch, bunch of government brass people." He turned and marched out but stopped at the dish pass-through window. "For God's sake take a shower, there's uniforms in the uniform locker, do something with that hair." He turned and was gone.

"Crap, crap, crap!"

"You don't want-ta be found out, one time," Joe said. "I don't want-ta know why, come on."

Joe led her back to the employee changing room where the uniform locker was. It was a little room with a metal door near the showers. The shower was outside. There was already soap and junk there, she really didn't need anything. White sneakers came with the stupid white and black uniforms the place provided. He opened the men's locker just inside the little room and took out brown shoe polish and handed it to her.

"What's this for?" Aggie said examining the shoe polish.

"Your hair, you're blond, that blue and red dye job was good but getting washed makes your hair a lit candle, that's all I'm saying." Joe went back to work and left her standing there.

Aggie slapped herself in the head. It doesn't take much to get caught—any little clue can set off a landslide.

It looked like the President was in deep crap so she couldn't rely on Albright. Everybody was piling on mom, the President, and herself, so they were all on the shit-list. No way would she expose herself, this wasn't a game of hide and seek anymore. She had to stay lost, at least until she figured out what to do. Walking around in a dining room full of government people didn't seem like the way to go, but Mark was big on stealth, she saw his point, right in front of them is the last place they'd look.

Aggie cleaned up, washed the food dye out and flattened down the spiky parts. All dry, she applied the liquid shoe polish carefully; not letting it get on her face was a challenge. Jimmy would have got it done in no time. The dress was too big, her black apron too small, so her boyish hips stuck out more. She was sure she still looked like herself. But Mark's wisdom surfaced inside her. 'Act like you belong: People will assume you do.' If she had a bra she would have stuffed it.

She picked up the bussing tables thing pretty quick, a few pointers from the others was all it took. She always learned fast, but she didn't want to tip her hand. She played dumb, put on dad's accent, and asked dumb questions.

"So, I don't git de money from de table, dats four-shore, gar-un-teeeted?"

"Bitch, you touch my money I'll break your fingers, you get me." The head waitress said. She took off and blew past the boss saying, "Why you got to hire vagrants."

The first half hour was OK, a few people, fishing guys she didn't know, thank Goddess, were in and out. But when military started filing in, guys with fancy uniforms full of breast ribbons she almost freaked out. She saw that one creepy officer guy on TV with Sanderson. She almost pissed herself when he passed by her on his way to the bathroom. She had to press her legs together as he walked past her. After he was gone she took off with the dishes and dumped the load with a crash. She plastered herself against a kitchen wall and tried to breath.

"Crap, crap, crap."

One of the Mexican cooks laughed. "Senorita, ICE doesn't check here, they must eat, too. Big boss's a veteran, si, si."

He waved a spatula at the door into the dining room. Aggie blew out her air and marched forward. She still had a table to clear. How do they do it, she thought, they live under the Man's thumb all the time, at any moment they could raid this place and take all the illegals out, of course if they did that, Key West would empty out, nobody would have staff for menial tasks, every restaurant would have to close, nobody's house would get cleaned.

Go with the flow, go with the flow, Mark's worlds rang inside her head, but she wasn't trained for this crap. She didn't have time to stop and meditate and calm her mind.

"Holy cow, how am I going to get through this day?"

"One time, just one time."

She took a deep breath, pushed open the double door and headed out into the dining room with her tray under an arm and her chin tilted toward her bony chest. The carpet was full of stains.

THIRTY-TWO

Mother's Auto Defense System

Sky Flower was back in Haiti when Aggie went missing a few days ago. The public didn't know. The press didn't report it. While standing on the beach next to Mother it was easier not to worry. The ship comforted her and she didn't know why. Sky wasn't supposed to know that Aggie took off again. If Sky's father hadn't called she would not have known. Sky hated the idea that her father was an important defense contractor, but even so, he was a decent man and he helped his family…when he could. Sky told herself not to worry about Aggie, Aggie has things under control, at least that's what she was trying to convince herself of. *She's almost an adult, I must respect her independence.*

The military was thickly spread around the ship site this morning. Over the last few days more and more military moved in, such as odd-looking boats off shore and she had gotten word that U.S. Government lobby-men dripping with cash were swamping Haiti's corrupt capital. The Army had chased the last of her human shield away just this morning. Everything was changing and Sky didn't know what to do about it other than call in the press…the corrupted press.

The Army had chased the press out at first light and even before the protesters, and the news people were happy to comply. Sky put on a Brook Bother's business suit and put on makeup for the press, a big show down was her plan, but there wasn't anyone left to record the military's abuse. Sky would have done the recording herself but she didn't know how to use the dang I-know phone's video and nothing electronic worked under Mother's shadow besides. The press had telephoto. I-know phones sucked at fifty yards.

It was too hot for a press conference anyway. Climate change was hammering Haiti hard. She resisted the urge to rip her suit off and confront the military in the buff. *Maybe they'd pay attention then?*

Her attempts to fend off the U.S. Government weren't working anymore. They got to Haiti's officials. The only thing left of the local protesters were posters littering the beach and a few tent poles standing off kilter in the sand.

Sky moved into the tree line to get out of the sun. From there she saw yet another probe come down and enter Mother's interior by way of a top hatch. That had been going on since Mother was parked here, everyone was used to it. The Army Corps of Engineers' men hauling cutting torches on balloon tire dollies up the beach toward Mother didn't even stop to gawk. When Mother shut the main hatch the Army-Navy people moved out but they soon poured back in with greater numbers. Sky felt like a tidal wave was coming.

Her phone rang. She was far enough away from Mother to get reception. Po-boy was on the line. She put it to her mouth. She told him the situation.

"Honey Peach you best be gitten up here," her husband said. "You-r old man's right, them GI's want to crack Mother like de oysters."

"I see them now, a team of men are here, they just lit a torch...they have a flame against Mother's side."

"If that don't beat the dog, them are fools. Mother won't take that long guarantee."

Po-boy described what was happening in Washington, congress just voted to annex Haiti and the bill was expected to pass the Senate. But impeachment proceedings debates were slowing action on Haiti and everything else down. The Speaker was getting fast tracked into the oval office. The President was still missing and the news was more speculation than facts.

Wolf News, the right's bully force, led the President bashing pack with no evidence other than grainy film that a child could make on a PC. It was all nothing but a big distraction; poorly made motion pictures aren't evidence. It would never stand up in court. Nothing about Haiti was in the mainstream news and she, the island's biggest proponent, was persona non grata.

Sky lost track of the conversation when streams of a foamy jelly-like material started oozing out of Mother's skin from top down and all over the ship. Above the men with torches there was a blob forming on the hull directly over the workmen's heads. It was fascinating. It reminded her of that 1950s Japanese monster movie where a giant caterpillar encased itself in silk. If a flying insect hadn't gone into her open mouth waking her up, she would have drooled on her silk blouse.

The foam reached out over the workmen like a porch roof and the men stationed around with guns were facing outward as if to prevent interference and, as such, they didn't see it either.

"Amazing, just incredible." *Now it's more like that blob movie.*

"Honey pie, what's doing? You aren't listening."

The blob suddenly whooshed down over the men. The men with guns reacted and fell back. There was a lot of yelling. Sky dropped her phone in the sand and ran to the cries, intent on helping anyone injured. In the time it took her to trot to Mother, less than one hundred feet, the entire hull was coated with that strange material. The men inside the gel were frozen as if held by suspended animation. Sky put her hand on the surface; it was like nothing she had ever seen or felt before. Translucent but many colored like Tiffany art glass but clearer, smooth and cold yet spongy. It was at least five yards thick, but the hull was still visible.

"Lady, get away, get back, get back!"

Sky ignored the soldiers. She didn't feel that she was in any danger. Sky was there to protect Mother and she had an idea Mother understood that. "Mother, if you can hear me, release these men, if they are harmed the military will cause you further grief."

Somewhere in the back of Sky's awareness a little warning light flashed yellow. Sky slowly backed away and joined the Army men. The military's leader was on the radio, men were barking like angry dogs at each other up and down the beach as they took positions. None of them were paying close attention to Mother.

A hull panel slid open inside the gel as Sky watched. Two little gray men came out and moved about inside the material as if it wasn't there. The aliens were moving the men. It looked like that party game where a person pretends to be immobile and you move that person into compromising positions for fun while acting out a scene. The aliens were manipulating living puppets.

Once the robot grays had the frozen men upright and pointed toward the water—the men had been bent to their work—the robots gave each man a little push. The frozen men glided past the edge of the gel like mannequins on ice skates. When they cleared the gel all three men fell onto the sand like cut timber.

Some of the Army men rushed to recover the fallen, but the fallen got up and walked away from Mother without issues. Mother did no harm but by the way the Army was acting, one would think the Army was deeply insulted in some way. Very curious how such men behave, Sky thought as she walked back to the trees for her phone.

Po-boy is right, she thought, there was nothing more she could do here and she did in fact need to get back to Washington. She cut through a stand of palms. Branford Industries' Lear jet had remained there at her disposal. When Sky reached the road, she flagged down a kid on a moped, pulled a change purse out of her bra, unfolded a crumpled bill and handed the child a sweaty hundred-dollar bill.

She tore her skirt up the leg and got on the back of the little motorcycle. She didn't know the local language but Po-boy had taught her the French word for airport.

***

Later that day, an explosives team was sent in. They ran a mole pipe packed with nano-thermite demo charges under the sand and up to the hull. The idea was to blow the foam away. The area under their control was cleared and the charge was remotely fired from off shore. There was no sound. The foam bubbled out and retracted like a piece of chewing gum blown from a child's lips. On examination, there wasn't any damage done except where the bubble had pushed out over the sand. In that area the sand was made into a sheet of volcanic glass ten inches thick.

No harm was done to Mother or the Army, but that didn't stop the Army from claiming that Mother had attacked the United States of America and that news landed stateside well ahead of Sky Flower's arrival in Washington.

THIRTY-THREE

From the President's Diary: Under the Knife

When the CIA man (Name redacted) entered my bedroom without asking and shot my VP, from then onward it all became surreal. My reality went on hold. Everything was muffled; I understand the reason as gunshots are earsplitting, but I didn't think of it then. Was I in shock or simply stunned into a stone pillar? Gunfire in the White House and no one responded. The TV was on, they are always on, one must stay up to date, but on the screen was me and I was the assassin. Shock, I suppose, set in.

When (name redacted) waltzed through my open door with my gun balanced on his finger, (The gun was upside down and his gloved finger was inside the trigger guard) my mind flashed danger, I saw my light fading. In my mind I became a bulb's filament receding like dying embers and I could not move. He said something I was unable to hear so befuddled was I, or I heard it and it didn't register just then or something to that effect, however, he impressed upon me that if I heeled to and accepted controls this event would never be known. Maybe they had a way to hide the body? After his speech he simply tossed my gun to me and I caught it on reflex. There I regained a bit of sense but not enough to turn the gun on him. Rather, I dropped the thing. I fell onto the floor and started CPR, all in a daze, just going on instinct. The man on the floor was dying.

How one keeps his or her sanity in such situations is beyond me. I wasn't educated for this, but I was trained in first aid—useless though it was. And to think I vetoed a bill for more military training due to me seriously considering such outrageous costs. Of course, then again, whatever money the military got they wasted copiously. Or so I thought at the time. I didn't know about the secret space program.

Mark appeared like Sir Lancelot, Jen said he was on the way, didn't she? I was in a movie that moved too fast, so fast that one dared not take a breath. We ran. I was in survival mode. You just do, you don't think. But until Mark came, I didn't think. He did the thinking. I've gained a new appreciation for training.

My life became different on that little boat. Everything was in slow motion. Before I could react, I was a prisoner. I recall thinking, 'I'm in my underwear with someone else's blood running down my face.' While this young, crazed man held a knife to my throat a million thoughts and ideas came together and blew apart inside my mind. Little memories, missed opportunities, regrets on parade. One's life does pass before your eyes on death's doorsill.

Oh, there is Mark. He's back. I thought. He doesn't look happy. He was quite attractive in his underwear, he is well muscled, after all. How long has it been since I've had a man? If only I wasn't about to die. All that flashed within me as the young man's grip tightened. He had one of my arms painfully twisted behind me. I hadn't notice at first. I felt the blade press on my neck, I remember that very clearly. Everything was slow, slow, and slow. Mark seemed to increase, fill up.

"Stand down, stand down, Marine! Are you thickheaded?" Mark ordered.

Mark was every drill sergeant I ever saw all rolled and pressed together into one chunk of a man.

I felt the knife cut me; the young man pressed it harder, a reaction, or jolt of reflex. Blood, my blood ran down between my breasts. It felt like a wet snake seeking shelter.

"Sir, no Sir!"

"Don't be stupid soldier, stand down! At ease, at ease."

"Yes Sir, yes Sir."

Where's the gun, Mark had a gun? Why doesn't he shoot?

The knife slipped and fell, jabbing me in the leg, it was pointed but the cut wasn't bad. I didn't feel it at the time.

"Look son, you're injured, who's your commander?"

The boy let go of my arm, he was a very strong young man. I should have gotten up but I was petrified.

"Bobbitt, Sir."

"That's fine, that's fine, a good commander."

"Sir, yes Sir!"

"Nurse, help this solider into a bunk. I'll report to Bobbitt, son you're on R and R."

"Yes, Sir." The boy said as he slumped.

I woke then, time became real once more. I untangled myself form the young man and helped him lay back. I had forgotten about the rope, there it was on the floor. Was I supposed to tie him? No, not now. Mark came inside and he and I worked together to get the boy situated. His head injury was very bad.

Mark talked him down saying things like, "Soldier, your mission is to get well, no revelry, understand? This nurse here, respect her, for God and country, she will care for you."

Once the young man relaxed and closed his eyes, I used the jug of water there and cleaned his head and face. I washed the blood off him and myself with a fish stained rag.

Mark stayed there with us awhile. I held the boy's hand. Mark lent comfort with soothing words as if Mark were the boy's father. I wasn't aware, but the boat was drifting and we were in dangerous shipping lanes. The young man's radio sounded and Mark faked a radio check.

Once Mark felt sure the injured party was sleeping, he went top-side, as he called it, and found a way to start the motor. He had removed the engine's cover and used the rope I had found to pull over the motor. Once we were underway, yes, I was learning sea jargon, Mark 'reversed course' and we went up river and into the heart of Washington. I thought it was the last place we should have gone. I was on high alert, awash with raw nerves, however, conversely, the drone of the motor lulled the unconscious man into a peaceful state or that's what I assumed. As such, the sound and vibrations comforted me as well after a time. In this way, we made for port. A safe house Mark knew of along one of the joining rivers. Not fast, not in a tizzy. Mark said that's what the regulars expected however much the professional company men, as he called CIA men, would expect otherwise. The CIA was sneaky and they think everyone else is as well.

The regular police expected us to run, but not carefully, as Mark explained. Upriver travel in a boat would not be on either faction's radar...at first. Soon someone would know the security outpost boat was gone, but not why, not right away. SecureCo was a boondoggle outfit. The corrupt owners weren't paying attention. It took time for their command structure to contact the decision makers. That was an eye-opener. Industry rails against government calling us inefficient when it is they who are that. Bully's always accuse the victim of what they do themselves. We had a little time and it proved just enough to escape the dragnet, but of course the long pursuit continued relentlessly.

THIRTY-FOUR

Aggie Escapes

That big general or admiral guy Aggie had seen on TV with Sanderson was a real pig. Once Aggie understood nobody in the room had spotted her, she relaxed. She had to remember to keep up the fake accent, but it was cool, nobody talked to her. Fact was, the big brass military guys treated her like dirt, paid her no mind at all. Mark never said much about it, but he didn't need to. Military was one tracked, whatever the meeting was about was the only thing on their minds, except for general grab ass.

The party had two sets of long tables pushed together with a space in-between. She heard plenty as she filled their glasses or cleared dishes. Drinks were flying and Aggie made sure to pull half glasses, the boss said to do that, why, to sell more drinks, that way she was able to give old Joe lots of drinks. He worked better when he was tanked. She was clearing dishes with her back to the General when she overheard.

"Piper, I don't give a shit, she's dead meat."

"We'll get that ship whether she likes it or not."

"With Albright out of the way, what's stopping us?"

Aggie slowed down and hung out there too long, it was her own fault. Things got quiet behind her. *Crap, they know who I am.* She gathered up her tray and got ready to smash the first face that stood between her and the nearest door. Just as she lifted her tray, a big fat hand shot up her skirt from behind. Her tray went flying, a bunch of men roared with laughter. Aggie spun around ready to kill but she didn't strike.

Not hitting that fat moron was the hardest thing she ever did. That would give her away. Thinking fast, she ran for the kitchen instead while those pigs cat-called after her. General pervert had already touched her butt twice with a glancing feel but that full on grab was over the top. For the second time in an hour Aggie was totally freaked out.

The boss came back right behind her. "They don't mean nothing, get back out there, get that mess cleaned up pronto."

"Are you crazy? They should be arrested. That's sexual harassment!" She didn't use the accent.

"Look you little whore, you've done worse, who're you kidding."

Aggie stormed off into the break room with the boss on her heels. He grabbed her and spun her around. Everything slowed inside her head. She measured him. He was 6-2, over 300 pounds and way out of shape. She knew just how to handle such an opponent.

"Look here—."

Aggie's knee came up hard making his balls into pea soup. As he started to go down she spun out of his grip and arm locked him. Careful to not pull his arm out of the socket, she maneuvered him still gasping for air. Grounding him, she changed her hold.

"Guess what dick brain, I'm a virgin. Nobody calls me a whore."

She choked him out. He lay there like a traumatized tuna. She checked, he was still breathing. *So much for my cover. Now what?*

For some reason the boss reminded her of Sanderson, everything was pointed at Sanderson. The a-hole that just grabbed her ass worked for Sanderson. That gave her the idea. Mark went after him and didn't die. Sanderson would never expect her to show up. A vague plan started percolating inside her head.

She didn't bother to ditch the uniform; rather she quickly made her way around the building and moved from car to car staying low until she made it near to an officer's staff car. The limo had to be his car, had flags on it, antennae, government plates. The car's plate identified the owner—Pig-Man was the Base Commander. The same place where Sanderson had his office and Jon told her exactly where that was. That's just one of the reasons why Jon was in jail now; he wasn't supposed to tell military secrets.

She hung out a few minutes scoping out the situation. A grunt in a formal uniform was over by the door smoking. *I can't believe people still smoke.* That had to be the driver. She made her way to the rear of the car. It wasn't occupied. She cracked open the driver's door, found the trunk latch and pulled. The damn thing sprung up too fast, she barely got back there in time to lower it without the driver seeing.

She quickly lowered the hatch. The trunk was technically still open because she put her hand under the jarred lid keeping it that way. Heat poured out from the compartment. No way was she going back to the job, boss man would make her into crispy toast, but if she got into the trunk too soon she'd be baked bread instead. Aggie hesitated crouching at the rear of the car.

"All this crap just to get roasted, no way."

Aggie hung there watching through the car's back and front windscreens. She had a clear view of the inside of the place. Ex-boss was in front cleaning up, bussing tables but limping as he went. He recovered OK, sort of.

Why didn't he call the cops? Ego, some girl trashed him, or more logically, he had a crap load of illegal aliens on the job. *Whatever.* When the driver waiting near the restaurant's entry snapped to attention, she slipped inside the trunk. It was still hot, but the base wasn't that far and like the boss said, she'd done worse.

The ride sucked. She had to keep a finger on the trunk sensor switch or the dash would light up and tell the driver the latch wasn't secured. A couple of times they hit a bump and the lid squished her hand. With the other hand she had to keep the trunk almost closed without latching it.

She peeked as they slowed and got flagged through at the main gate. The gate's jar heads were busy with the next car; they never gave the big shot's car a glance. OK the a-hole wasn't a general, she wasn't sure what his rank was, all she knew for sure was this guy was a big shot and she got past the Navy base's gate. But did the guy go right to a parking spot so she could get out? Nope, he had to ride around for half an hour like he owned the place. Aggie got a little tour of the base. She was able to see where the flight lines were, there was that.

By the time they parked she was ready to scream. And, they were nowhere near where she had to go. On top of everything she had to pee. When she felt them leaving, she waited a long thirty count and rolled out of the trunk. She lit off across the parking lot and made for a side road, but she didn't go twenty yards down the walk path when some squid stopped her.

"Sorry, I'm new here, you know where admin is? I'm in-processing."

"It's back that way." Aggie pointed. The big shot parked there. She felt so stupid wearing that white and black uniform maybe it showed. The squid stared at her, and it wasn't that-chick-is-hot stare. "I'm new too; I'm supposed to work in the officer's kitchen, any idea where that is?"

"Officer's mess is that way," He pointed, "Over by the single officer's quarters."

He was nice as squids go. His small talk was OK. Maybe he tried to pick her up, but he wasn't crude about it. Aggie took off before he put too many moves on her. He could tell she had to go, everyone on Earth knows that I-got-to-pee dance. Once out of sight, Aggie ducked into the bushes, squatted and let it rip. She left the bushes with wet sneakers.

"OK universe, I'm made to suffer, but can't you give me a break?"

She continued down the walking path and after the path turned it went right past the ball field which had a portable toilet. "Yeah the universe hates me." She said as she looked at her sneakers. They were white but now spotted with yellow dots.

The exercise path circled the currently unused airfield Jon spoke of it and how he liked that spot—it was where he flew RC planes. Having a clue about the layout, she made her way to within a hundred feet of the brick building where Sanderson's office was. That's when the shit hit the fan. She was almost there when sirens went off. That's been going on a lot the last few days. She prayed the Goddess it wasn't about her.

In no time choppers were in the air, they acted like they were chasing a ghost. She felt like she didn't have a chance, but nobody running out of Sanderson's place paid her any mind, people were running around everywhere. Across the airfield men with guns were gathered and pointing at the sky. It was so weird, what was going on? Why were people pointing up at nothing?

Someone shouted, "UFO, UFO," in the distance.

Aggie shaded her eyes. It was Buddy! He was buzzing the base. All she had to do was call and he'd hear her, he had sensors, he'd pick her up a mile away, he was tuned for that. No doubt he was looking for her. Two jets took off from a runway far behind her but it still sounded like a volcano going off. She held her hands over her ears as they shot up and made steep turns.

All she had to do was call Buddy and the crazy would end, but then, she'd be found. Aggie felt like crap, Buddy needed her and she couldn't do poop about it. Some military guy on Wolf Radio yesterday said 'aliens aren't a real threat; we have the means to shoot them down.' Buddy was too stupid to run. He had to sense she was around. Aggie ran for the brick building hoping he'd leave. She felt like crusty poop, she should run to him, not away from him, he was her responsibility.

"Why's everything's got to be so hard!"

She pushed inside and slammed the door. She rested and caught her breath and pressed her ear to the door. Maybe it worked. The jets were further in the distance. She didn't hear the helicopters at all. The sirens stopped. Aggie dragged herself through the foyer and flopped down into a waiting room chair glad nobody was in the building. *Think Aggie, where'd Jon say the elevator was?* She started to work it out but she didn't have to come up with the answer.

She heard someone coming down the hall. She jumped out of her seat and pressed herself flat against the intersection's side wall ready to punch somebody's lights out. The footsteps stopped short as she bounded out of cover.

"Hello Agatha, well, well, well, I've been looking for you." Sanderson said. "You and I need to have a little talk, come on." He turned and took a few steps down the hall, the guy had long legs. Aggie didn't know if she should jump on his back, choke him, or kiss him.

He hesitated and said over his shoulder, "We had better get to my office before they come back."

Aggie didn't have any options. She was revved up, ready for a fight, but the old guy looked beat, he was pale and tired and walked like the grim reaper.

Sanderson wasn't the man she confronted on Sunset Pier the day she landed Mother. She wasn't a bully; she would not attack him from behind like a coward. She took a deep breath, stayed her mind and followed after him. She felt like a deep river, calm on the top but crazy dangerous underneath. It won't take much to break her dam, she thought, but at least she'd hear what he had to say before she clocked him and took his GTO spaceship.

THIRTY-FIVE

Sanderson and Aggie Deal

Sanderson had to chuckle when he saw her. Piper gave him a feeling of hope. He bushed that thought aside. There wasn't much that amused him these days. The Joint Chiefs were on his ass and his own goal, that alien heart he needed, was slipping further into the mists. He didn't have much time left and he wanted to go out well. Serve his country to the last if only he could figure out what that meant in these strange days of empire.

That orb was around; it had to be trying to get to the girl. She had to be somewhere local, that's why the orb kept buzzing the Piper home. Logical deduction aside, he knew she was close by feel, but he didn't expect her to show up in his waiting room. Nobody outside knew she was gone, not the President, not the press, all the clowns in his circus ring thought she left town. He aimed to keep it that way. *Focus Ben, focus.*

"Young lady," He said to the monitor screen. She was breathing heavy, no doubt gathering her wits for an attack. "You are something special, but Al Branford is wrong to think I should trust you."

Sanderson picked up his vintage World War II rotary phone and dialed a number. He wouldn't say it on his cell phone. The NSA can hack any cell phone anytime so it was better to memorize important contacts. The NSA didn't track many land lines, it was too cumbersome. Each tentacle didn't know what the others did and maybe that was the way it should be or one player would gain too much power.

He heard the other party pick up and the other didn't say anything. "I have her, we're moving." He hung up. Maybe they'd get his voice but not the other. It was time to toss caution to the wind.

Before him was a bank of screens and hardware on the opposite wall from where he sat. With his lap top, he activated a call. Brinks' face appeared on the center screen. *I can't trust him either.*

"I'm going to the moon; tell the NRO, I don't want to get shot out of the sky."

"What have you got in mind?" Brinks said.

"The GTO will work with us, they don't have a choice. Piper is MIA, but she'll show up there and I want to setup our little surprise before she arrives."

"What about that damn orb?"

"It's a distraction; she sent it to keep us busy. That's how she'll break the block-ade. Mark Levine must be waiting for her someplace up the line. He's MIA, too."

"You better be right." Brinks leaned into the screen and the feed went out.

Sanderson checked screen five once more. Piper was alert. He pressed a hidden button and the bank of screens before him moved forward, spun around and recessed into the wall. His command hardware became an oak and teak bookshelf stocked with rare books and old Navy manuals.

He walked the short hall mindful to stop short of the intersection and it was good he did. Piper jumped out like a pissed off tiger. He surrendered and invited her into this office. She accepted and followed. He led her in, pulled out a chair for her and poured her a glass of water before he took his seat. He poured one for himself; lately he couldn't get enough water. Her glass was empty before he finished pouring his.

"Miss Piper, I'm glad you came," He wasn't sure exactly how to put it, maybe blunt was best. State secrets and all. What did it matter? "You and I need to work together."

"Are you out of your mind, hello, you're the enemy, the whole government's a big giant turd and you're the biggest shit. I don't think so Skipper."

"That may be so, but I have a proposition for you."

"Why should I make any deals with you?"

"Doesn't matter how you look at it. You're screwed no matter what. Every al-phabet soup security system wants your hardware, that big ship you parked down south is fast becoming priority one. Once they shake things out and figure out who gets what slice of pie between them, they'll take everything you got. I'm not allowed to tell you this; your life isn't worth a plugged nickel. Do you understand?"

"I'm in deep crap, I know that. That's why I came here. You know I know how to kill, I killed Karnack and you'll be next. Help me get out of here or else."

"That's what I had in mind. We are on the same page. As soon as Van Ness gets here the three of us are going to the moon."

"What!"

"I've convinced the Joint Chiefs that sugar will get more than vinegar. With you under our thumb, the GTO will deal, we get the deal we want and you get a chance to see the moon, decide if you want to stay, maybe go to college up there. It'll be great for America, for Earth. Open the door to normalize relations. What do you say, give it a whirl?"

Aggie pushed back her chair like she was going to bolt, but then her shoulders slumped and she sank lower into the leather. Sanderson felt her wheels turning.

"Why would you do that for real?"

Sanderson had a lie already to go. He anticipated her question. He'd get the GTO to milk her mind, they wanted her ships as well and they'll cooperate for a cut, and his cut was medical care. They aren't stupid. He had the executive order to cover his ass. Brinks approved the flight. Piper won't buy half-truth. The girl was sharp.

"Leverage, Earth wants alien technologies, you and your buddy Praytis up there's great for PR, and PR's good for trade. Opening up like this is the ticket. Nixon and China all over again, it started with cultural and educational exchanges. Now China and us, we're tangled like a plate of happy spaghetti. In this deal everybody wins, but the US. wins the most. Help us get what we want and we'll leave you alone, savvy?"

"What if I refuse, what if I just break your neck and walk out?"

"I'm sure Mr. Branford will afford you the very best funeral services available."

Piper leaned back, no doubt calculating. He wouldn't bet against her. If she did take him down, she'd find some way out. The kid was resilient, but the shadow government had long arms and no morality. They get what they want always. The Chiefs approved his idea of a moon visit, but they didn't know it was happening now or that she was in tow.

It was supposed to be public, a giant PR distraction. He wasn't tipping his hand yet. Call this a test run. He didn't trust his superiors. *I'll see what I can see then decide what's next.* It wasn't the first time Sanderson played that dangerous game of walk the razor wire but deep down he felt it was the last time. *Don't let any harm come to her.* It was funny how his mortality kept nipping at his heels. He shook off the feeling.

He still had a job to do, one that would secure his good reputation post mortem if things didn't work out for him and he didn't think it would. Get the star drive for the U.S. of A. at least. He toyed with the idea to deliver it to the public and not the men behind the curtain. He wasn't getting his new heart, but if he had it his way, the shadow state wasn't getting what they want most either; absolute power.

This was a goddamn democracy, wasn't it? It used to be, might be again.

That Van Ness girl has the ability to splash technical info all over the net. Her old man was under the thumb, but not her, still blood is blood. Melissa Van Ness was pretty sharp, too, like her old man. He knew she'd play.

When Melissa Van Ness was brought in she and Piper had a little love fest. Van Ness had a video camera, she'd film the trip. He'd let them put it out on the internet if things worked out. Piper didn't know it, but she was walking into a mind trap. We'll see about that. He was sure MJ-12 had been talking with the GTO all along behind the Chief's back. He planted that seed where it would take root. Sanderson had his counter measures and sources. As much as he liked Piper, he'd sacrifice her for America, or what was left of it. He knew it was wrong, but once he had his new heart he'd fight the good fight again like he used to, at least that's what he had been telling himself in recent years. Piper made him think of his old self, the man that was accountable who honored his high calling and took care of his family. Damn if Piper didn't remind him of Sarah.

His green dial phone rang again. He saw that Archer was in the lobby on his lap-top so it wasn't him on the phone. Nobody had the number. He picked up the phone and covered the mouth piece. "Yes, I see, keep her on life support, don't pull it, I want to be there...yes a few days...I'll hurry."

Sanderson got up, disconnected the phone's wire and placed his old green phone very carefully into the trash bin.

THIRTY-SIX
Official Moon Flight

This time it was supposed to be official he said. She wasn't buying it. Aggie found her way in and Mel was on her way to the Navy base, like it or not they were going. This wasn't her idea of opportunity. Sanderson was going anyway. Why else was he all dressed up in a formal uniform with medallions and ribbons and junk stuck all over him like a Christmas tree? No way he figured she'd show up?

"You know," the Admiral was saying, "This is a grand opportunity, and truth be told, if anything, I'll learn more about the aliens for America. All the years I've dealt with them, I never knew there was a school up there. That might well account for so many small ships as you suggested."

Aggie wasn't sure what to make of him. He was acting too nice. It was obvious he'd been hanging with aliens. She didn't doubt what he said about that. Yeah, she told him about the alien kids just to jar his guilt, but she never thought he'd take that info and run with it. The idea that anything can and will be used against you by the government rang true inside her head. Mom and dad drilled it into her, all her life she heard those two detailing how corrupt and ruthless the powerful were but Sanderson didn't seem like he was that big of a jerk. She never seriously thought deceit applied to everything the Man did, but more and more it looked that way, so she wasn't going to give Sanderson any trust. *I wish I paid more attention.* She had read that sociopaths fake sincerity really well, really good liars. Maybe this guy was like that?

"…You mustn't tell anyone what we're about to do, this is top secret, that is, until it is released and as you may know…well you don't want a target on your back."

He's kidding right? She already had a big fat bull's-eye on her back. Was he threatening her?

Her first idea was right; get away. But, she needed him for that. She'd have to ditch him at some point and she had no idea how to do that. This moon trip thing felt like a big stupid game just to keep her away from her own ship. Why would he just go on like nothing happened? Yeah, he's some kind of psychopath.

That Archer guy brought Mel in then split right away. Aggie was so relieved the walking dead-man didn't stay that she just about tongue-kissed Mel. Aggie jumped up and they hugged like crazy, two butterflies reunited inside the spider's web. Aggie got close to Mel's ear to whisper a few words. Mel smelled like herbs and spice.

"Don't know how, but we got to lose this dork." Aggie breathed into Mel's ear.

Mel backed up with a pained look on her face and shook her head a little. She held Aggies hands, "I missed you too." Mel dove in for another embrace. Close to Aggie she whispered, "Dude, I'm so fucked."

Mel pushed closer, breast to breast; Aggie felt some kind of device on Mel's bra. Did they have a wire on her? I can't even trust Mel, what is this crap?

"All right, all right that's enough. We have a flight to catch." Sanderson said. His face was blushing red.

Sanderson called in his pet MP. It was really stupid; the security guy blindfolded her and Mel. Jon had already said where the access was, but Aggie wasn't going to rat on Jon, bad enough he was already in jail which bummed her out big time. If it were not for her, Jon might be free right now. She was the one that let him come along on Moon Dodger and that made him AWOL. The guy was a hero, but like Snowden, and Manning, Jon got trashed for doing what's right. You do it their way or no way. What a bunch of crap.

She and Mel were spun around before Mr. MP walked them around the little building a few times and through some doors. When told she pulled off the blindfold, she knew exactly where she was. Aggie was facing a big built-in shower. She lifted up her arm and sniffed.

"I don't need one see," She showed the MP an armpit. The buss-girl uniform she had on was really loose so she yanked one short sleeve wide open. "Take a whiff; really, it's not that bad."

"Less stinky if you'd shave those pits once in a while." Mel said. She leaned in wrinkling her nose, as the MP backed up. "I suggest hedge clippers."

"No, I like em this way, keeps the hot boys off me."

"You know that's a lesbian magnet." Mel batted her eyes and pretended to swoon.

"I'll shave everything when I get to college."

"Very funny," beet red Sanderson said. He dismissed the sentry with a wave. "It's an elevator, get in."

He opened the shower curtain; nobody used curtains and pushed in a tile. The whole back wall slid sideways: Of course, it was an elevator and she had to act surprised. The ride down was creepy, the elevator was crude, the walls were streaked rusty and it didn't have any controls. It took forever to reach wherever it was going. When it stopped, the door slid open and it was total black outside. Aggie pressed herself against the opposite wall.

"This is crap; I'm not going out there."

Sanderson stepped outside and lights came on. It was a big cavern, from there she saw tunnels radiating out. The one nearest her side had a little enclosed tram car parked just outside the tunnel's entrance; it was way surreal, like a bad Batman movie. Aggie moved out of the lift cab and squinted. It was a monorail, like what they have in Japan and Disney World but the car was rusty and beat up. Sanderson marched toward the car, but Aggie stood there scoping it all out. She didn't see any where to run to. She turned and the elevator door was already closed.

"Ladies, this way to the moon," Sanderson said.

"Crap."

The tunnel ride was just like the elevator ride, blind and silent but she felt them moving. It took at least fifteen minutes and she totally lost track of directions. The tram brought them to an even larger cavern, it was like an old-fashion train roundhouse but the trains didn't turn on a central wheel, rather, each perimeter train had its own platform. Aggie didn't have much time to orient herself.

Sanderson marched them right up to and into a space shuttle that was parked just off the middle. It wasn't like her ships, more V-shaped than saucer, but it was the same inside. She and Mel grabbed two spots on the round bench seat at amidships. Mel reached under her shirt and whipped out her phone and started messing with it. As usual Mel wore an oversized, black, heavy metal T-shirt and black stove-pipe leg jeans. She could smuggle refugees in there.

"Van Ness, it won't work down here." Sanderson said sort of snappishly. "Say, you don't seem too perturbed by the presence of the pilots. People that encounter them for the first time are usually sickened or scared shitless, literally."

"Dude, I'm New Goth OK, this is nothing. Creepy is my middle name. Besides I've seen them on the computer, you know I recorded it, yeah? I'm the one that had Ernie go back to the compound and cam the wreckage, remember? I got close up pictures in HD of dead grays and Moby hanging on my bedroom walls."

"I'm sure that's it," Sanderson said.

***

Sanderson suspected that Van Ness had previous contact but he brushed it off. Aliens abducted people. Maybe millions had been exposed.

The girls proceeded to do what teen girls do and that was jabber on and on about a whole lot of nothing while the ship warmed up for flight. Sanderson wasn't paying attention to the chatter.

Still, it was odd that Van Ness didn't react to the grays. It bothered him. The NRO had previously concluded that androids emitted a brain wave sedative to prevent victims from suffering out-of-control panic. The sedative made folks physically ill at first. Uncontrollable fear was the natural human response to high strangeness, but it took a few minutes to work on a person during first contact. Van Ness was the exception to the rule. Maybe she had been abducted; she had to have had close contact to acquire the immunity response.

Maybe Van Ness Industries was deeper into alien tech than anyone knew. Too many agencies were keeping too many secrets; he'd never get to the bottom of it. Maybe if he had more time.

Sanderson had Archer work Van Ness over, but that can't prepare anyone for meeting an alien android. Something else was going on here. He felt it in his guts. It didn't matter, the GTO and he had passed info, it was all setup, these girls were about to get mind controlled. He remembered Branford's watch and pulled out the little flat box. He handed it to Aggie.

"It's from your grandfather. Before you bust my ass, he and I are friends strange as that may be. I've known him since before you were born. I checked it out, there aren't any tricks loaded into it…here, enjoy. Al said to tell you it's for your birthday."

Aggie took the watch and looked it over. "Cool a phone watch, always wanted one. I hate smart phones." She put it on her wrist and left the box on the bench.

"Dick Tracy would kill for one of these." Van Ness said.

***

Inside was just like her shuttles, basically round with two gray bio-bots at the controls. The center had a round sofa thing, room for a dozen seated around it facing out. She and Mel sat as far from Sanderson as they could. There was a little bump, the ship was finally moving.

"We'll be landing in 31 minutes, it's always the same," Sanderson checked his watch. "I don't know how they do it."

"Computer, outside view," Aggie said. She heard it inside her head like some kind of mechanical voice but it came out of her mouth. Holographic screens materialized in front of each of them.

"Say, you can't tell it…," Sanderson chuckled in kind of a slow-motion way. "This old sea-dog's learning new tricks already."

"Oops," Mel rolled her eyes and pushed her bottom lip into her mouth. Aggie got the message, bite your tongue bitch.

Aggie knew from past experience on her ship, once she had command, it did what she asked. But before that it didn't do anything she asked. This one wasn't hers so why did it obey? It wasn't supposed to do that. This was weird. More and more she confirmed that Mother had planted something inside her head, but how, why? Whatever it was, she didn't want it. Her brain was her own, right? What about privacy? Aggie was really bumming out.

If having a bunch of spaceships meant becoming a machine, she'd deal herself out fast. Maybe Praytis would show her how to get her head back on right. Then maybe she could just go to college like any normal girl, but to do that she suddenly understood she'd have to give up her fleet. The Man would never leave her alone otherwise.

She could just give up, take the money or whatever. If she did so, Mother won't have anybody decent for her: Giving access to Mother to a bunch of butt-holes like Sanderson wasn't cool. She wasn't ready for that happening but if that was the only way out of this crap pile...her stomach hurt like the first day of 8th grade.

Flying along watching the water, then breaking the surface, then shooting up into space and counting stars as they sailed made her miss flying in Mother really bad. Aggie was feeling way confused. Why can't I just have a normal life? Why's that ship got such a pull on me, it messed with my head, that's why.

"...Any ideas are welcome," Sanderson was saying as the screen blanked out for landing. "America needs all she can get, it's your duty as America's first space students to bring home all you can for our Country."

"For America, what about Earth," Mel said. "What about the mass extinction we're having right now? Don't you think America should clean up the mess we made?"

"Military's full of crap," Aggie said, "America's been messing over the whole world for decades, and you want more, really, how's that going to save the planet?"

"Yeah, good idea dude, let's give America the latest hammer. Let em drive the rest of our collective nails into our dead Earth coffin. We earned the right, yeah? Last sociopath standing wins."

Sanderson's pasty complexion flushed red. He stood too fast and had to reach out to the back of the couch to get steady on his legs. His breathing was deep but ragged, like he was hollow inside. Aggie could almost see flaps of his dead lung tissue shaped like American flags waving inside his chest.

"You don't understand," He said as he lowered himself back into the sofa. "This is war."

"War on the Constitution, ever try reading it? By the way, you kidnapped us, how's that legal? How's that American? Oh yeah, I forgot, only empire matters. We the people are toast."

Aggie was boiling inside but she had to shut up or she'd only get herself in deeper. She spilled one more zinger. "You know right, the police state is acting way above the law so you guys aren't even real Americas. You're the evil empire."

"Navy should look at the internet sometime." Mel added. "Everyone thinks you dudes just want to invade the universe. They're right, it's so obvious. Greed has no boundary."

"From the mouth of babes." Sanderson said.

Sanderson took a few deep breaths; the oxygen on spaceships was pure and well-scrubbed while Moon Base had its unpleasant flavors floating freely on the air. Aggie was never in India, but in her mind the alien's moon air smelled like Calcutta.

THIRTY-SEVEN

Moon Landing

The ship stopped moving. The hull of the little ship split at waist height and vertical cracks four-feet wide appeared in the glossy white walls, one side went up the other down making the lower part a ramp. Aggie had seen this space port before, of course, but she didn't want to let on. Sanderson was a sponge soaking up everything for the bad guys. He was all about whatever grease keeps the wheels of war turning. She'd have to act like this moon landing was all new.

She and Mel put on a good ooh and ahh routine as they descended the plank. She took it all in with lots of "wows," and "cool and far outs." But when Praytis appeared at a hangar door a hundred yards distant, she couldn't help it. She ran to him and wrapped her arms around him. She whispered into his ear.

"Me and Mel are getting out of here without Sanderson."

She already knew the AI respected people's privacy when requested, and that a whisper was off limits. Praytis didn't say it, she got that from Mother, but he did talk with her that quiet way before. He said then that the AI heard everything public. She reminded herself to be careful.

Praytis backed up, nodded and said, "Captain, it is good to see you." Then he leaned in. "I don't know how to proceed with your request without breaking protocol."

"I'll figure it out, K. Trust me?"

"Yes Captain."

***

Sanderson's landing on the moon was the usual. Piper bolted for Praytis as soon as he entered the hangar. She followed him back as he flop footed across the tarmac toward Van Ness at the ship. Sanderson gave them a wide berth on arrival so he could observe.

"Oh my God, it's the Bug man, how cool. Dude, give me some skin bro. Wait till everyone hears about this!" She took a couple of quick selfie pictures and ignored the video camera.

When Van Ness was done snapping, she and the alien fist bumped like old pals. Van Ness overdid it, the first time anyone meets an alien they aren't so chipper. It takes a few minutes of pheromones exchange before one's fear jets cooled. Humans naturally took to each other given time. Contact with robot grays required induced artificial adjustments. But Sanderson felt shaky every time Praytis showed up. He backed up further and checked Van Ness up and down. Did they already meet? Piper didn't know what he knew about aliens and he wasn't saying, so he couldn't ask her a direct question without tipping his cards.

The girls didn't seem amazed enough. Piper had been around the bug man, but why didn't Van Ness have a canary? The size of the hangar and the hundreds of ships parked there didn't faze either one of them. They were putting on an act. Piper was smart and tough, but not an actor. Van Ness and Piper were braver than the situation warranted. Then again, his Sarah, when she was that age, was fearless too, nerves of steel. Piper was made of the same stuff coming out of a hippie squatter family, but Van Ness, the rich girl?

"Oh, it is so good to see Captain Piper and you too, of course Admiral Sanderson." He made a little bow.

Sanderson cringed inside. What did this girl do to deserve a captainship? No training, no experience, just the luck of the draw. Cripes. Piper walked right up to the bug man and wrapped her arms around him. Such action alarmed and sickened Sanderson even at a distance. She liked that damn thing. *Kids today, I can't figure them.*

"Here's my other crew, Mel, meet Praytis." Piper said. Van Ness moved in and she clasped hands with the GTO's man in a formal greeting.

Did Piper just wink at Praytis?

"Crew, have you begun forming a crew already?" Praytis said.

Sanderson shot Bug man a hard-edged look. Bug man isn't supposed to tell them how this works and he knows it. "It's an expression," Sanderson said quickly, "Kids; it means they're in the same social group."

"Oh, I see, yes very good."

Bug man and Piper seemed to have a moment there, they looked at each other a little too long.

Sanderson's mind was running throttle wide open. Clearly there was a lot going on here and he wasn't privy. He shifted into high alert. Van Ness finally tried her video camera, it acted like it was working but it didn't work, nothing worked inside the hangar except the ships. The GTO wasn't about to show Earth its holdings. Sanderson played along. Make them think he was on board. If the

GTO wasn't going to give an inch neither was he. With all of Van Ness's fooling around she had better not miss the ball when the pitch came. Whose side was she on: Principle or practicality? For him the line was fuzzy so he had no way to judge that in others.

***

It was the same dreary tour she had before, a big circle around the space port. Praytis walked everyone around pointing out things like a maintenance shop, a control center, a pilot's locker room, and all were just white doors with stenciled hieroglyphs, doors were on either side of a twenty-foot wide off-white hallway.

From inside the hangar, there were big cubes stuck along the outer walls of the hangar going up twenty stories protruding into the huge dome. *So that must be the rooms behind the doors.* They didn't get to go inside any of the rooms. The markings didn't tell her anything.

They quickly passed through the section that had ugly doors on the outside wall facing the moon's interior. Those doors weren't white, just gray or brown primer, and coated with dirty rust so they weren't GTO property. The GTO would hate her messy bedroom for sure.

Aggie was dying to ask Praytis about the restricted areas, but anything he said would go straight into Sanderson's noggin and maybe get Praytis in hot water with his moon boss as well.

What was weird was what she didn't notice the first time but it was a neon light now. There weren't any people. She didn't see anyone. Where were all the people? There were a few hundred ships parked in the hangar, including a few that dwarfed Mother, so there had to be people someplace. Sanderson was all eyes. She guessed he had done the round before but he was looking for more.

"Oh, here we are," Praytis said. "This is the university, isn't that why you've come?" They stopped at a hall section which had many doors on both sides spaced uniformly about twenty feet apart.

"I don't see a ping-pong table, this can't be a college. Where's the rec-room?" Mel pointed at a cardboard sign taped on the wall over each door. "What's that mean?"

"It's a student's abode, that's his name." Praytis pointed and hurried a few doors down. "See, this is your room, the next is for Aggie."

There was a paper sign attached to the door with duct tape written in English. *Earth duct tape, I guess it is used for everything.* The hand writing was poor, like it was done in a hurry.

"Where are the classrooms?" Aggie asked.

"Oh dear, most of class, as you say, is in your own abode, so to speak." Praytis said.

"Dude, OK so you plug in? That's boring; it's just like home school."

"That terminology isn't quite correct. I'm not allowed to detail the process due to, oh bother, what you call on Earth intellectual property, it's, it's…proprietary."

"It's perfectly safe," Sanderson said. He hadn't opened his mouth the whole time. His sudden participation pushed Aggie's bullshit meter into the red zone.

A buzzer went off, it wasn't loud. One kid, it was a guy like Moby, but much smaller, exited a room. The kid seemed like he was stoned. Aggie waved and said hi and the kid just walked past. One after the other a variety of weird looking people came out and blew past them like they were dirt. They all looked human, some tall, some bright white, some with odd shaped bodies, but they didn't seem overly unearth like. OK the Tall Gray one was out there, too skinny and spindly; it was like the bio-bots but really tall and Aggie could tell she was human and alive. The alien girl moved with ballerina grace which didn't bother Aggie. Mel backed up when that weird kid went by and almost fell over Sanderson.

"Dude, wow I'm so creeped out!"

Sanderson seemed to be having a hard time keeping his lunch down. He was bent over and whiter than before.

"Why didn't I react like them," Aggie pointed at Sanderson. "I haven't seen anyone like that before."

"Conditioning: Your command belt infused…Oh bother, shall we move on to the lecture hall?"

"I have a better idea," Sanderson said. He checked his watch "I need to see the Board, why don't you bring me there and let the ladies spend a little time in their rooms."

"I don't know…there are instructions…well, each chamber must be tuned for the occupant—."

"It's taken care of." Sanderson took Praytis by the arm. "They'll be fine, see, after you drop me off, you can run back pronto. You don't want to disappoint your superiors." He checked his watch. "I should have been there five minutes ago."

Sanderson practically dragged Praytis away. Aggie and Mel were left standing in the hall. Praytis was still in sight but his back was to Aggie when Praytis stopped at an intersection, one of only a few they had seen. It appeared he was giving Sanderson directions.

"Dude, that's so rad, that's the way to do school. But what's a chamber? Check this out." Mel pulled the name tag off her door and switched it with Aggie's.

"What are you doing?"

"Screwing with the system," Mel said. "When have we not?"

"That's a good point." Aggie felt a little like her old self.

They used to have fun so why not have some fun here? This crap was getting too real. Mel and she were always doing junk beyond the call of sarcasm back at Key West High. If she didn't have fun at this school, too, what was the point in attending? Like Sky Flower always said; 'If it's not fun why do it?' Mom was right, but Aggie already knew she wasn't doing school here. Maybe she'd go to Tibet, whatever, but this was her last choice. She had to make it sound good, like she was into it, so the computers would hear it, but in her mind the moon totally sucked. Mel opened the one originally marked for Aggie and ducked her head before going through the mismarked hatch.

"Dude, who cleaned your room, this is the strangest thing I've ever seen."

Praytis was on his way back, she heard his floppy footsteps slapping the floor as she unlatched the other room. He was moving pretty fast. That was weird. Thinking of that, Praytis was acting odd all day, so formal and...controlled. Something was going on and she wasn't allowed to know what that might be.

"Oh, there you are," Praytis said. He wasn't winded at all.

"You're lucky the last bus to Jupiter is late or we'd be gone." Mel said stepping out of the room.

"It's not actually a bus, it is a mining transport." Praytis said.

"Chill P, we're just messing with you." Aggie said.

"Oh, very well Earth humor." Praytis slapped his forehead the way Aggie did. "It has been suggested to me you may like to see your rooms, yours should you decided to stay, that is. The semester is in progress but catching up is not an issue. The GTO anticipated your needs."

"No thanks dude, we're fine, nice hallway you guys have."

Praytis face turned from happy to dog faced. He lowered himself down a little. All four knees bent together. "The GTO will be most disappointed if you fail to visit your assigned space." He said while shaking his head no. "Much effort was spent to accommodate you."

Aggie felt for the guy. No doubt his moon boss was on his ass. She wished she could better read him, she always knew what Mel or Jimmy hand in mind. The guy looked sad; maybe he was in hot water.

"It won't hurt to check it out, right." Aggie said slowly. She looked down at the bus girl uniform she still wore. Maybe they have clothes. "I need to lose this dumb outfit anyway. Tell you what Mel, I'll let you see mine if I get to see yours."

Mel batted her eyelashes, "I thought you'd never ask."

"Oh bother, I don't think, I mean." Praytis grabbed Aggie by the arm and rushed her toward the door marked for her. "You must not change rooms, Sanderson will return soon, and then we must go."

Before she had time to think, Aggie was shoved into the room. It looked exactly like Mel's bedroom at home but clean. How'd they do that? Aggie proceeded to go through Mel's drawers.

"I knew it, cotton skull print boy's underwear. Waist high, must be period panties."

She tossed the underwear on the floor. *That's better, looks more like her room.* While pilfering the dresser for something to wear that wasn't covered in skulls, or black, or had a death metal band on it, Aggie started feeling very drowsy. She almost lay down on the bed, but rather kept rummaging around trying to find something to wear like she was driven, like something inside her wouldn't let her stop moving. Aggie exhausted finally sat on the bed and was about to pass out when Mel screamed. Aggie bolted.

Praytis had dragged Mel out of the room and had laid Mel on the floor. Mel was shaking like a crackhead.

"They were in my head, trying to get into my head." Mel was crying, horror on her face.

"Oh dear, oh my, oh bother…" Praytis was as low as he could get, all four legs splayed out like a spider.

Aggie glanced into the other room; it was her room, just like at home. She noticed the alien script, same as printed on every door in this section. She didn't understand it before, but the room did something to her. The script said 'Ram-Education.'

"I don't understand, I don't…" Praytis said over and over.

Aggie had dropped to her knees and got Mel's head up into her lap. Aggie patted Mel's cheeks. "Come on we're getting out of here. Come on Mel! Wake up, snap out of it."

"But, but, but, Sanderson…" Praytis stammered.

"I don't give a flying poop about Sanderson. Are you with me or not! Come on she's all fucked up."

"Oh dear, oh my…" Praytis helped get Mel onto wobbly legs.

Mel was off balance like an amateur drunk. Aggie steered Mel to the nearest hatch leading into the hangar. She propped Mel up onto Praytis and spun open the air lock handle. Once inside the hangar she looked around, so many ships, nothing was like any of her ships.

One like the transport that brought them there was parked near and its door was open. It had to be the right one. Aggie made for that one half dragging Mel. On that short walk Mel started coming around. The three of them made it up the gangway. Aggie got Mel seated and fell in next to her.

"Dude, what the fuck? Where am I?"

"Praytis get us out of here."

"The Admiral isn't here—."

"I don't give a crap."

"It cannot move until the itinerary is met, I'm sorry, we can't go. It is on auto-flight, only a Captain can override the flight command."

Mel was in a panic, she was starting to hyperventilate. "Just buy it, buy the fucking ship, your fucking rich."

"How much it cost? What am I saying, it doesn't matter, I'm buying it, effective immediately."

"Oh dear, it's processing, title is transferred onto Mother's credit. I must go. I must report."

Praytis started moving to the door but Aggie moved in front of him and stopped him. "This is my ship now, you are my First Mate. You aren't going anywhere. On my ship, I am the law." *How the hell did I know that?*

"Wow, dude you've gone butch. I feel sick, I'm going to barf."

"Shut the door, take off. Get us back to Earth now."

Praytis touched his belt and the two grays came on line. The ship was moving out of the hangar when Aggie told the outside view screens to come on. Sanderson and somebody that looked like Karnack but with tits were inside the hangar near a hatch pointing up at them.

Aggie said, "Put Mel in medical stasis fast." She had no clue where that idea came from.

A thin force-shield dropped out of the ceiling and surround Mel. Mel up-chucked into the bubble and the mess disappeared on impact with the shield. Aggie flopped back into a seat—fighting her own urge to barf.

THIRTY-EIGHT

Sanderson and the GTO

It was a short walk to the conference room. Sanderson had done it countless times before but he never knew exactly where in the space port his hallway was. In the round it all looked the same. That walking tour with Bug man and the kids provided more information than he had obtained in quite some time. Every trip was an educational adventure, but this time he had something substantial to report back to the Pentagon. Sanderson had counted his steps and so had a pretty good idea of how big the space port was and it was much bigger than he thought. That was important information for the Pentagon's contingency planning department where such things as attack plans were worked out.

Sanderson pulled up short of the conference room. *Attack plans, would they attack moon base and cut our own balls off? They can't be that stupid.* Anything was possible where profit motives existed. He had to ask himself was there any money in killing the moon? Sanderson knew of more than a few defense contractors that would think so.

As usual, the door slid open as he approached it. That table Ike had given the GTO back in 1947 was the same but only the winged bitch was in the room this time and she was getting up as he entered. She didn't stand up for anyone. All the chairs were disheveled like the board abruptly got up and left. Wing woman was too neat and orderly to let that stand. Sanderson never could read Pharaoh's face but it was obvious that she was methodical, slow with her words and expressions. There was always a hint of threat just under her well controlled sing-song voice.

She'd make a hell of a poker player, but now the angelic face gave away anger. Her brow was narrowed, her wings twitched and her over-wide open blue eyes were reduced to slits.

"How is this possible, again, how, Praytis. AI ten demerits to Praytis. This is too much!"

"What gives?" Sanderson said. He didn't expect an answer; she never gave him a straight answer.

The AI spoke for the first time in his presence. Sanderson never had direct communication with it before. "No demerits issued. No regulation was broken."

"What, that's...can't you stop it?" Pharaoh screamed like a diving eagle. Sanderson didn't know she was capable of that. He backed up on impulse.

"No: transaction is complete awaiting exit clearance." The computer said.

"Come Admiral, to the hangar, quickly."

The seven-foot-tall winged woman moved fast and tried to push past Sanderson but she bounced off him. She looked big but weighted less than a hundred pounds, more info for the file. He yielded and followed her into the hall. He was surprised at how light she was. How did someone so tall weigh so little? The base was set at Earth normal gravity so it wasn't a low-G reaction. He'd bet his bottom dollar the Navy's biological geeks would love to cut her open like a fish.

Her long-legged stride covered distance quickly and Sanderson had to trot to keep up. This was very bad for his heart. Good, if his heart stopped while here they'd have to fix it.

"What happened," He asked puffing, "What...the mind trick...backfired?"

"You weren't supposed to know about that."

"I set it up. Where'd you think MJ got the idea?"

They were nearing the hall intersection when she slowed. "Hijacking, that filthy Earth girl hijacked a shuttle. She is a poisoning influence. She bought it, never do we sell shuttles!"

That's a shit load of information right there.

They crossed the main hall at a reduced pace and went straight to the nearest hangar hatchway. Pharaoh went in first, Sanderson followed but the bitch didn't go far. She stopped near the hatch and pointed. Sanderson saw his shuttle taking off. He was never allowed to see any craft in flight there before.

He watched with amazement as it soundlessly flew up to the hangar's ceiling, about a thousand feet he guessed, and a section of ceiling became translucent jelly. The craft passed through it like a Frisbee flung at soap suds. Before he could ask she simply said "Quantum foam."

Bunker busters are useless here. Goddamn that matter distortion.

Pharaoh took a few deep breaths and slipped back into her old well-contained self but Sanderson was fit to be tied. He had had about enough bullshit.

"She fucked me," Sanderson said, "MJ fucks me, the Pentagon fucks me, the GTO fucks me, everybody fucks me!"

He turned on Pharaoh who backed up. He pressed in at her until she was cringing against the wall and shriveled to his eye level. He got right in her face. "That's it, I'm done with this shit, you hear me!?" Pharaoh flinched like she was stung by a whip. "I go by the book, do everything by the book, I do my goddamn duty. Try and do it right and everybody fucks me."

Sanderson punched the wall just beside Pharaoh's pretty face. The great and mighty leader of the grand GTO shrunk back and folded into a wad of crumpled paper. Sanderson composed himself, brushed off his uniform and tightened his tie. The alien's wings were vibrating like a tattoo gun as he backed up.

"What, what is, is meant by 'that's it', what are you going to do, I assure you your space fleet…"

Sanderson cut her off with a wave. He laughed like hell. "Oh, you know about our space fleet, of course you do. You know what else? I don't give a shit."

"What do you mean?"

"Let me ask you this," Sanderson said advancing on her again. "I'm not getting my new heart am I, you're stringing me along."

"You have yet to obtain enough LF credits." She said shrinking back as if he was going to hit her.

"I thought so. That's fine, order me a shuttle, the minute I touch down I'm resigning. I'm finished; you are on your own."

Pharaoh started babbling as he walked away. He didn't hear her. He had time before a shuttle was brought up to power so to satisfy his curiosity he walked among the parked spaceships, against all the rules the GTO and Earth had worked out previously. No security people or bots stopped him and that too was curious. He didn't need to respect the alien's privacy or protocols; he considered himself free of it all. Nobody else played by the rules so why should he? He got onto the shuttle only after having a good eye full but he'd keep that to himself. Why give the Pentagon anything when they'll just hand it over to those thieves MJ-12? Need-to-know, he can play that game too.

Rather than work out his report on the way back to Earth as usual, he turned to thoughts of his upcoming and last visit with Sarah. He mulled it over and over in his mind and felt a surge of happiness on the idea that he would see her one more time, and that would be the last time. It was just good luck he woke up from this nightmare of webs in time to see her off. He kicked himself in the ass for not resigning sooner. He wanted to be there when they took her off life support, maybe he'd eat that cyanide capsule at her bedside. Father and daughter going down the river Styx, just two sailors shipping out together, it felt right inside his heart.

He finally realized that the good ship America had sunk a long time ago. He signed on to protect the democracy and he didn't see one worth protecting anywhere. One at a time he plucked the ribbons off his uniform and dropped them on the shuttle's floor. He had no one to pass them down too. He told the shuttle to drop him off on a runway at the Key West Naval Air Station, and much to his surprise, it did.

THIRTY-NINE

Converging Enemy

The little boat Mark had stolen was adequate for the task, if the fuel held up it would have been better. It didn't have the gas, not enough to make it to Bart's place. Mark was forty miles up-river when the tanks ran dry. As the motor started sputtering Mark aimed for a cut in the river bank and gunned it. The last drops of fuel pushed the craft into a make-do landing. The river was still wide here, but the banks were high and the trees overhung their branches low to the water.

When the bow hit gravel and made the boat lurch, Jane reacted. "Hey watch it. I'm trying to clean his wound."

"We're tying up," Marked called, "Stay below."

Mark went over the side into shallow water. A little mud between his toes, but where the boat rested was mostly hard-pack. Lime fossils were eroding out of the bank which climbed maybe ten foot above the water line to what should be farmland above, or more likely now giving the age of the chart, an industrial park. Up and down the shoreline was a thin ribbon of muck laced with shells, some trees jetting out of the bank were at crazy angles although the tree line above wasn't as chaotic. Mark tied the boat to a beached driftwood log. He knew what was downriver, he had watched for landmarks, noted the channel marker numbers and used the old chart on-board to estimate position. He needed to get up river, they could not stay here; there wasn't enough cover.

He started off intending to hike a mile or so upriver and recon their position but Jane came out on deck. She had found a red flannel shirt to put over herself. Mark wore the oversized cut-off jeans that were stowed with Jane's shirt in a forgotten cubby. He didn't carry clothes in his survival pack.

"Where're you going? You're not leaving me alone with this man." Jane said.

"I need, we need a place to stash the boat. We're out of gas."

"I'm going with you."

"In your underwear?"

Jane went back inside. Mark proceeded, but he didn't go far. There was a flooded gully that cut inland just fifty yards ahead of the boat and it looked good. He went back, got Jane and together they pulled the boat up the gully's creek twenty yards. The vegetation over head was thick, so air cover was decent, he thought the spot suitable but the mosquitoes almost changed his mind. With the boat situated, he walked up the creek a few hundred yards and climbed the creek's low bank in a few spots. He had a good idea of where they were. So, he doubled back thinking of how to get a few things they would need. He was pleased to see Jane piling brush up around the stern. She had the old rusted hatchet that hung on a peg, judging by its condition it was used for chopping frozen chum. But something wasn't right; she was frantically swinging that dull blade at the base of a sapling.

"I have a survival knife in my pack," Mark said. "It's sharp."

Jane's hair was short, but her bangs were long and hung wet in her face, what was left of her makeup made her look like a raccoon. "Fine now you tell me, so don't stand there, get the damn knife and help me."

Mark and Jane completed the job in short order. He was impressed that she knew to hide the boat, but it was more just a way to burn tension than forethought in Mark's judgment: She was over-revved. He didn't think her panic was necessary as there was no sign of pursuit. He humored her and silently pitched in. She said she was uneasy, her woman's intuition was screaming, that was her justification for odd behavior. That's how she ran the country so well, she used logic but supplemented it with intuition.

A woman's mind engaged is worthy of respect. Nostrum was as slippery as an eel and uncannily a step ahead of everything. Nostrum saw this danger coming well before he did. He was glad he heeded Nostrum's advice; she had harped on the merits of women's intuition, that's what made her so good she said and he should trust it. The sound of jet drive boats in the distance convinced him of one thing; Jane had more in common with her sister than she knew.

"Get down," Mark said, Jane was near the river's shore, "get down, take cover."

She just got over the gunwale in time. A Navy Swift boat rounded a bend in the river and blasted past them twenty yards off shore. It wasn't a minute later and another jet-drive followed suit along the opposite bank. No doubt, the search was on, but it wasn't public yet, nothing on the AM radio. The guard's radio had a tracker in it so Mark had tossed it into the back of a barge just above Thompson's Boat Rentals as it passed going south. They had no food and the water was gone. There was nothing he could do about it until dark.

"What do we do now?" Jane asked. Her voice was distraught.

"We wait, try and sleep, I'll go out later for food and clothes, there's a strip mall on the other side of this field, used to be a farm just above us."

"So, you are just going too waltz up there in fish-stained rags and buy supplies?"

"No, too many cameras. I'll borrow a few things..."

"Fine, that's just fine. So besides being a murderer, now I'm a petty thief's gun moll receiving stolen property, practicing medicine without a license, how many other broken laws can I be an accessory to? I'm starving, I'm sad, I'm dirty, I hurt all over, I'm, I'm, oh Mark what are we doing? God dang it, God dang mosquitoes, look at me I'm swelling up."

As she spoke tears welled up. Jane Albright the first women to obtain the office, a woman of resiliency, courage and will, was falling apart.

He saw this kind of thing before; after a long adrenalin pumped run, even the best operatives collapse into dismay when it was stop time. It's the down side's reaction to a ripping bi-polar experience.

Mark moved in and held her. Her babbling turned to sobs and she buried her face on his bare chest. She was trying to control herself, she convulsed in the effort to hold back but her tears rolled down his abs. Jane needed release. He took her face in his two hands and lifted her head and got her to lock onto his eyes.

"It's OK we'll be OK, I won't let you down."

"I let myself down, why didn't I see it, why didn't I know, Jen told, me, she told me..."

Now the sobs came fuller. Mark held her tight. There was nothing more he could do, let her get it out—that was the best medicine. The man below deck was moaning again and that seemed to snap Jane out of it. Mark understood. When things are hard, it is good to have a task, a mission; Jane's job was treating the injured man. She broke away and went below. He followed. The boy was in bad shape, something had to be done. Mark made a difficult decision.

"Jane, I have a friend, he's a medic, off the grid. I'm calling him, if we don't get pinged; he'll pick us up here. I'm sure Jen alerted him to keep an ear open for me."

Mark didn't use his own phone. He had a little hacking device with him in his survival pack which he attached to the prisoner's regular I-know phone. Mark had pulled out the battery knowing even off, any phone was traceable. The second he started the phone Mark expected alarms would go off at SecureCo; he'd have to make it brief.

He checked the man one more time. Opened the boy's eye and flashed a light. It was worse than Mark thought. No need to alarm Jane, but this boy was at death's door. He clicked the phone's battery back into place and punched in a number.

"Bart, it's me Mark, I've got a special request, meet me at channel marker 709 R sunrise. Over." Mark hung up and removed the phone's battery.

Bart was a riverboat duty medic in Vietnam. He rode the gun boats and put blown up kids back together for three years. He was more a doctor than most doctors but Bart wasn't qualified, he didn't have a sheepskin hanging on his cabin's wall. Bart had a good memory for medical procedure but he wasn't very good with numbers or book learning. Mark had to trust Bart would remember the code and meet them at channel marker 907 in the predawn morning. At this point, stealing a car would only complicate things.

FORTY

Coming in Hot

This little shuttle she had just acquired was purpose built; Praytis said it was an Earth to Moon shuttle only. It didn't have accommodations for a captain or crew, no command chair, just the round sofa with yellow plastic looking padded seats and the bio-bot's flight station.

"This craft is very crude," Praytis said, "its intelligence is limited. No defense mechanisms to speak of."

"Crap on a cracker." Aggie said.

"Isn't that unsanitary?" Praytis asked.

From inside the medical bubble Mel laughed, "Hey that's my line!"

"She's feeling better, shields down." Aggie said imitating Captain Kirk of the old TV show.

"How do we know your moon guys aren't spying on us? I'm afraid to talk." Aggie said to Praytis.

"It's your ship now, the transfer was confirmed. Base Ship controls communications."

"So…what do you think," Mel said. "School on the moon, how cool is that?"

There was a lot eating Aggie, that Ram-Ed thing and how not-cool the alien kids were. They treated her like dirt. OK they're aliens, different and all that, but that wasn't the social life Aggie had in mind. Her heart sank thinking of how it would be just sitting in a cube all day getting programmed like a robot.

What about ping pong and beer parties? Do these weirdos even know what pot is? And, what about what's behind those doors, storage if that's what it is and it's all off limits, college shouldn't have limits, what's that all about? Too many things didn't add up, too many rules, it all looked so hard-ass stiff.

"Earth to Aggie, hello? Dude, this is the shit, we'll be roommates. I'm all in."

"No way, I'm not doing it. I'll go to school in Alaska if I have to but I'm not going back there."

It didn't feel like opportunity slipping away. First Earth students on the moon, she saw the headlines in her head. Great, more fame and still no friends. She could still go to school on Earth—there had to be a way. Just mothball her fleet and live a normal life for a while. What's wrong with that?

"Forget it. I'm not doing school on the moon."

"Are you out of your mind?" Mel practically screamed it. "Dude, this is history, this is hugely cool, all the kids will crap their panties. Don't you want it?"

"All I want is normal OK? Normal college life, you know, friends, parties, maybe sex. I waited all this time to cut loose. Now I can't, I can't have my dream, what I've worked for my whole life is morphing into crap. It's not fair."

"I'm your friend, what about me? I can't go if you don't."

Aggie's guts came to a boil and she sprung up to her feet. "What about you, what about me!? I'm not doing it. I'm not giving up on school. I got money; nothing's going to stop me."

"Why, why are you're so tight-assed about this, there's a whole universe, fuck collage, fuck all them dumb-ass kids and parties. Grow the hell up!"

"That's what I'm trying to do." Aggie said somberly, she fell back into her seat and put her head down and for the first time in a long time she wished she had her long hair back so she could push it over her face like she used to do and hide from the world. Maybe she wasn't ready to grow up, maybe Mel was right, but it was all coming on too fast. Deep inside she felt like the moon wasn't were she needed to be. Something nagged at her, something Earthbound was pulling her and she couldn't put a finger on it. Before all this, she knew what she wanted, she had a plan. She was focused; now it was all blowing-up.

"I don't get it." Mel said. "Pass on the once in a lifetime thing, you're running like a scared cat."

Aggie spun her ass on the bench seat to face Mel. "I thought you knew me. I'm not running. I had to dodge all the cool kids, now I'm the cool kid. OK the world hates me but I want to be part of it, make my own way, is that so hard?"

"Dude you're not making sense."

"Don't you get it Mel? We were the nerds, pushed out of everything. Look at how pathetic we were. Nobody liked us. Why did we live weirdness, you with your black on black, and me with my kick boxing and hippie dippy bullshit, Jimmy wearing a dress to the winter dance, really, really! We pushed everybody away as hard as they pushed us out. We punked out, we're pathetic. I'm tired of it, I want a normal life, OK. I want people to like me."

"I'm not pathetic." Mel said.

"Running is exactly what you're doing; you dress like a death march. What's that about? What the fuck is wrong with you!?"

"Fuck you Piper." Mel folded her arms over her chest. "Just fuck you, OK."

Mel was stung. Aggie had aimed for the heart, too, and felt worse for hitting it. She couldn't just ignore it. Mom and dad always said they never went to bed angry, that's why they were happy. They always patched up arguments fast. More softly, anger choked down, Aggie reached out and gently put a hand on Mel's arm. Mel shoved Aggie away, but Aggie persisted and shimmied closer to Mel.

"I'm so sorry, I really am." Aggie said fighting back tears. She reached Mel's hands. "Forgive me?"

"Me too."

Mel and Aggie embraced. They stayed that way a little while with Praytis mumbling, "Oh dear, oh my," in the background.

"Did you ever stop to think you're actually pretty?" Aggie said standing. "Under your stovepipe pants and 3X T-shirts you're hot."

"This isn't the body I want, I hate it."

"We don't have to wear nerd uniforms anymore."

Aggie and Mel embraced tightly. Aggie felt tears coming but held them back so Aggie kissed Mel lightly on the lips instead.

"But you said no." Mel said blushing.

"It's still no, for now. I'm not ready." Aggie said moving back a little. "I'm not ready for a lot of things. I like your friends with benefits idea and I'd like to try it sometime, and I'd like to bust Jon out of jail and see what happens, and I'd like to be on the moon for a while, but not yet, not now. I still need to figure things out."

With that Aggie let tears fall. After a few minutes she forced the water off. "I just don't know what to do, what I want, I just feel like I need to stay on Earth." Aggie's tears slowed. "I don't want to live on the moon."

"Oh dear, oh my, this is most disconcerting," Praytis mumbled in the background.

"Look, nothing is over yet." Mel said. "OK the moon sucks. Maybe when you get Mother back we'll go and check it out. Mother will help. I don't trust that Angel chick up there, she's too much like that Angel dude you killed."

"Killed." Aggie said quietly. "I never wanted to kill anyone. It's horrible."

Praytis laughed and that was weird. They never heard him laugh. He sounded like a bunch of people, like a canned laugh track from the old black-and-white TV shows.

"Oh, Karnack is not dead," Praytis said. "He wore a force skin, most spacers do, and I'm sure he was equipped with an auto emergency recall implant. We all have a recall implants. One of our medical probes surely picked him up and even if he was dead, they repaired him, and I'm sure Moon City AI removed the sociopath gene in the process."

"Force skin?" Mel said. "Medical call implant?"

"Moon City, they have a city." Aggie whispered.

"That is correct; all ship crews get them, once the crew member is officially accepted by the Ship's or the satellite City's AI, and there is Space Port AI...Oh dear that is restricted information. Oh bother."

"Sociopath gene, what's that?" Aggie said wiping away her tears.

"I have a better question," Mel said. "What's Ram-Ed and why'd you push that shit on us?"

"It is nothing," the alien said. "One must be adjusted to function within any given environment, for example, the students you saw did not ignore you, they projected greetings but you were unable to hear them. The basic spacer program teaches you the necessary languages and universal space script; it enhances your natural telepathy. It is necessary for space-bound students and spacers alike."

"Let me guess," Aggie said, "But whoever controls the Ram-Ed can tell it what to put in, right, like planting ideas, say, like sell the fleet, right?"

"I am afraid you are quite correct."

Aggie had a strong feeling that Praytis wasn't in on what was programmed. No doubt they didn't tell him much. The boss types always keep their crappy plans to themselves or the worker bees won't go and get the nectar.

"I don't know what you are allowed to say about it, but I don't think Ram-Ed is for me. Actually, I know it's not for me. I'm never doing that." Aggie said.

A chime sounded and Praytis cupped a hand to his ear. "It appears Earth defensive space laser platform is targeting us."

"How do you know?" Mel asked.

"I'm not allowed to say, I'm under contract. This is impossible."

"He means we're screwed." Aggie said. "Let me guess. The Navy has space-ships and orbiting weapons. What else would they do with trillions in black-ops money? I'm right, aren't I? Don't give me any crap, this is my ship, you work for me now."

"I'll never have credit enough to buy out my contract this way; very well, Yes America has a rudimentary MAC fleet, not very maneuverable, armed yes but minimally effective. However, with the new flight control system Branford developed, they will soon have more advanced capabilities, if not already. Earth fleet is being re-fit even now."

"Grandpa built that crap for them, no way." Aggie sat down and covered her head with her hands. She already knew that but it was so hard to accept. "I can't believe he did that, you know these military morons don't use their crap for anything good."

"Fear not, this craft is marked for tracking, thus the military won't shoot it." Praytis said with enthusiasm. "We are registered. So, you see our safety is assured by your government."

"Never trust the government. I see why mom deserted grandpa."

"Tracked! We're being tracked!" Mel shot up off the couch. "Dude, what're we doing?"

"Unless I alter course," Praytis said, "It will take us directly to one of the sub-terranean bases. Of course, I can't change course while Mother is offline. This one is not yet added to fleet ready status, we do not yet have a system's control belt for this craft. Mother is in dormant mode, thus, such processing isn't currently forthcoming."

"This just keeps getting worse!" Mel was practically crying. "Can't you wake her?"

"Oh dear."

Aggie's back straightened. "I'll go to her, she'll wake up if me or Praytis accesses her. She's doing internal refits; she's been getting stuff from Moon Base, Moon Base told me when I was in the...never mind," Aggie shivered all over.

That Ram-Ed thing freaked her out big time. "Praytis, can you get this thing to land in the Caribbean?"

"It always does, Captain." A second chime sounded. "A Navy vessel is closing."

"Make it hurry, evasive action, if it's got any." Aggie said and she felt the craft respond.

Monuments later the ship plunged into the ocean. The craft came to rest in an underground, underwater transportation hub, a larger version of the others they saw. Tunnels radiated in all directions from this massive space. How her ship got inside there, and how it got parked dead center in the hub, were questions she'd ask later...if she ever got the chance.

Several mag-rail line tunnels were lit. Praytis pointed out that one goes to Roswell, or actually White Sands military test range and the other lit rail line one goes to Key West and beyond. The tunnel was expecting Sanderson. Where the rest went, Sanderson was never allowed to know.

"OK, I need a different train that takes me to the surface near Mother, any of them do that?"

Praytis pointed. She could just make out the alien script above the train stop; it was covered with slimy gunk. Aggie didn't know why, but she understood it. It said Puerto Rico. Aggie walked toward it and when her foot hit the raised platform, the station lit up.

"It goes to a cave." Praytis said miserably. "It is an exit under the International Radio Telescope. The exit is hidden among low, steep mountains; its egress is located in a very secluded area."

"Dude, why so glum?"

"I'll be issued demerits when I get back. I've broken too many rules, and they may well fine me into another five hundred years of servitude. I'm so close to buying my freedom, such an irony."

"Dude if you're playing hooky, might as well stretch it, so come with us, yeah."

"Got a better idea," Aggie said. "You're under my command while on ship, so this is what we do. Space port is neutral, take this bucket up, get off this heap and get on one of our smart boats. Pick us up in PR. You have my bio signature in ship's archives."

"Dude how'd you get all that rad info?"

"I wish I knew."

Aggie did know and she didn't like it. Mel was better, whatever that Ram-Ed did, the medical chamber undid. It didn't take right. That bedroom chamber wasn't tuned for Mel. It's weird how Mel's chamber didn't get into Aggie's head; info just sort of bounced around her skull but didn't stick. There were too many questions and no time for answers.

The first thing Aggie was going to do, if she ever got back to Mother, was get deprogramed. Nobody should be allowed inside someone's head. It wasn't right. OK, so her parents were, but that's just upbringing, two-way input, it's something she could control and decide for herself what she'd take from it. You can't escape socialization, but there is no way she'd let a machine do that to her. When she got to college, she'd be her own master of what was added into her awareness.

"Here goes nothing." Aggie said and she lifted the tram's gull-wing door.

Still thinking of college, she had to put such concerns aside but she wasn't giving up. She climbed into the rusty mag-rail car knowing the possibility of going to college was more remote than ever.

If those hammerhead government a-holes don't chill out, nobody will ever get to go to school, not on Earth or the moon. *They have a fucking space fleet. Give a kid a hammer and everything must get nailed.* She saved Earth from Karnack, but who could save Earth from itself? At this moment, all she could do was save her own self, and that looked pretty sketchy. Resurfacing in a PR jungle wearing a waitress uniform, really, how's that going to work out?

FORTY-ONE

Sanderson His Way

Ben Sanderson didn't waste any time. He was no fool. He did not yet turn in his resignation. For once he'd use them rather than the other way around. When the alien shuttle transport dropped him on a Key West runway, he saw no reason to report in to the Pentagon. He just wouldn't call in and open that can of worms. Hell's bells, he wasn't supposed to be on the moon with Piper yet: This was his call. His only permission was the President's last executive order; she was still Commander in Chief. Albright was innocent until proven guilty, that's how the law was supposed to work.

Sanderson flagged down a toad, a small tractor used to jockey aircraft. By the look on his face, the last thing that driver expected to see on the end of a runway's access road was an admiral half out of uniform.

"See anything unusual out here sailor?" Sanderson asked striding up to the truck.

"No Sir, want I should bring you to the maintenance hangar, sir?

"Nothing, no UFO?"

"Not lately, Sir."

"That's fine; take me to officer's base housing."

"In this…Sir?"

The seaman waved his hand to present the short blocky tow truck as if to say, ta-da. Sanderson climbed up and squeezed into the one-man bench seat with the driver and said "Sure why not, drive on."

Once in his quarters, he had the driver wait while he changed into a blue checked flannel shirt and jeans. It was too hot for it, but he liked that shirt. He packed a small bag and loaded a brief case with stacks of hundred-dollar bills. Once outside, the driver eye balled Sanderson suspiciously but Sanderson remounted the toad anyway. Sanderson went into his case and took out three hundred dollars and stuffed it into the man's hand.

"Take me to flight command, I need a ride north...and you didn't see me, understand?"

"Yes Sir! If you ever need anything, I'm your man." the driver said with a shit-eating grin on his face. That sailor must have gotten that lonely toad driver duty for a reason, maybe he wasn't bright, maybe he was less than cooperative and somebody thought it wasn't good to have a muckraker around. Sanderson didn't have to worry about that man spilling his whereabouts.

Air Command was easy to put it over on. Sanderson was a regular visitor. They didn't question him. He had on-demand access to air travel and a lot of that procedure was pre-programmed for fast response. The down side, Air Command would alert Washington and Washington would send a car. The limo driver/agent would call in once Sanderson was picked up. He wasn't going to let that happen.

On the flight, Sanderson had a martini; he never did that on a military craft before. He had set himself above the others in that way. Many of rank had given in to the corruption of power, it was the way, go along to get along. He swore he never would do that, he prided himself on being a straight shooter, responsible with the tax payer's money. But now, as far as he was concerned, he was retired and the Navy owed him.

The car picked him up on the tarmac as usual. The driver wouldn't radio until they were off the flight line, its procedure, if anything one could depend on government rigidity, but the world was inhabited by men and men were for sale. Sanderson had the car stop before they arrived at the regular call zone. He got out, and right back in but Sanderson got in the front seat next to the driver. There, Sanderson opened his case. He pulled a little device out and placed it on the dash. It was an alien jammer that disrupts communication.

"Sir, regulations, you must ride in the back. The cab isn't well armored."

"How's thirty thousand sound to you?"

"Excuse me, Sir?"

"Liston up, I want you to report that I wasn't on the plane, or you didn't see me get off. I changed my mind or something. You'll drive me to where I indicate, I'll get out, you'll get the cash and then you drive away. You never saw me, savvy?"

"I don't understand?"

"You understand freedom, I don't have any and I want some. Take the deal or leave it. You have ten seconds to decide." Sanderson waved the stack at him.

"I'm a freedom loving man, Sir."

Sanderson handed over the bundle and the driver stuffed it into his breast pocket. "Onward my good fellow."

Sanderson had the driver leave him in an industrial park Sanderson knew of, and there he rented a pickup truck. Without delay, he headed out for New Jersey making damn sure his I-know phone was off. Maybe that was his mistake. He should have removed the battery.

He traversed the Pine Barrens as before but while crossing the jet flight test proving grounds that were situated over a desolate scrub-pine forest, a military chopper flew past him and landed on the two-lane road ahead of him. Sanderson had half a mind to ram the damn thing. But he stepped on the brake instead, got out and marched toward the chopper, ready to chew ass and spit nails. He lost his taste for it when Archer jumped out of the Huey's open door.

"Goddamn it, I should have punched it." Sanderson said referring to the truck's gas pedal.

"Admiral we had a deal," Archer said shouting over the sound of the chopper's engines. His open suit jacket was whipping around like a flag in a hurricane. Sanderson could make out Archer's ribs projecting through his white shirt. "I want Karnack."

"I'm retired, bug off."

"I have your daughter; she's being transported to Bethesda."

If he had a gun, he might have shot Archer on the spot. Instead, Sanderson hauled off and punched Archer square in the face. Archer went down like a sack of shit. Sanderson stood over him, waiting for the Man in Black to get up so he could clock him again. He'd never kick a man when he was down, but in this case, it took all his self-control not to do just that. Archer wasn't about to pop up like a cork. He looked small and pathetic. Sanderson unknotted his fists and took half a step back.

If Sarah was in the secured wing at Bethesda, he'd never get access as a civilian. Retirement would have to wait. At least they have the best equipment; they'd keep her alive until he got to her. Fine, get Karnack then I'm free. Sanderson had a few ideas about how to do that. He'd need an alien ship not under the GTO's control. Moon base didn't have shit for security. Sanderson would find Karnack and drag him back to Earth kicking and screaming, whatever it took. He'd need Piper. Where they hell was she? Might be the NRO had a line of Intel on that. *Goddamn the NRO.*

Archer had managed to rise up into a sitting position; his white shirt was soaked with blood. Sanderson kicked Archer in the chest and marched off toward the chopper leaving the truck and a hundred K behind. He planned to give the cash to the nursing home employees. It didn't matter anymore.

Two men went and got Archer and helped him into the chopper. Two big burly regular Marine MPs sat either side of Archer stink-eyeing Sanderson all the way to Fort Dix.

"If you want him, I'll need Piper's shuttle." Sanderson said into his in-flight head set.

"That's easy," Archer said. The handkerchief Archer held over his nose muffled the man's voice, but Sanderson still understood. "Piper will go after her base ship; we'll wait for her there. If she doesn't…Mother is scheduled for…"

He couldn't make out what Archer said, scheduled for what, destruction; fat chance. MJ isn't crazy enough to kill the golden goose. But then again, they've done worse, much worse. They didn't have a problem with dropping the Twin Towers.

Sanderson removed his mouth piece and shouted over the rotors. "Believe it when I see it."

Did the NRO kidnap Piper's parents? Sanderson would not put it past them and with the President gone there was no one left to check the Shadow State's rogue activities. Hell, on one level or the other they were all rogues. He told himself state corruption wasn't his problem anymore; the system was too broken to fix anyway and it didn't deserve fixing. They built their own bed of nails, let them bleed out. He really didn't believe deep down that it was impossible to fix a broken democracy, but within its current state of mismanagement the odds were razor slim. *Not my problem.*

Sanderson eyeballed Archer, a man once a hero now nothing but a walking stiff bent on revenge. That's what happens when pride and duty sucks the humanity out of you. All we need is a complete shift in human nature, sure why not. Sanderson told himself, that'll fix everything.

"I can't even fix myself."

"What's that?" Archer shouted.

Sanderson ignored the question and wondered if he could salvage what was left of his life before the end. He checked his watch. His heart was overdue to fail; his pacemaker needed batteries, alien batteries. No, it was too late for any kind of salvage operation. He couldn't save himself much less his country. He felt like an atheist preaching Christianity.

FORTY-TWO

Run Through the Jungle

Aggie had watched the outside view on screen as they descended into Earth's atmosphere. Nearest she could tell they had splashed down in the Bermuda Triangle, a very long way off the coast of central Florida. PR had to be a few hundred miles away. It would be a long tram ride and she was hot to get going. But Mel wasn't at her elbow when she got to the rail car. Aggie turned around and Mel was half way between the landing hub and the platform fifty yards out, she was just standing there with her eyes fixed on the ceiling. The shuttle was gone. Aggie didn't even notice it had left.

"Mel come on, let's go! Scrape your jaw off the floor."

Mel trotted up to Aggie and jumped up onto the platform. "Dude, wow, didn't you see it? The ceiling turned into mint jelly, the ship went right through it, and now it's rock again, what the heck?"

Aggie felt like she should know the answer, but that wasn't inside her head and it kind of pissed her off a little. Aliens don't tell you everything. All she could say about it was, "That's pretty far out."

They got situated in the tram, no seat belts, and the thing took off the moment the door closed. Like the ship, she couldn't tell how fast it was going. Aggie thought it might be a while. She realized she was starving. It was already late in the day and she hadn't had any food since eating at Bixby's. Mel's belly was making gurgling sounds too and that didn't help.

"I hope they have food," Aggie said.

Mel reached into one of her leg pockets, her stovepipe pants had tons of pockets, and she pulled out a pair of granola bars and handed one to Aggie. Aggie started chewing and it was like munching baked sawdust.

"Got any water in there?"

"Nope, just snack bars and my phone charger. Dude, I forgot to take video footage, I was supposed to shoot all that moon junk…Poop I left his video cam on the shuttle. Wait, I got back up." Mel messed with her phone. "Nothing's on it, it all got wiped, Sanderson bullshitted me."

"Ya think? Screw that guy. I'll never trust him again, not like I trusted him much anyway."

Aggie was surprised when the tram felt like it was slowing, she could just make out the squeak of breaks, maybe nobody goes down here and the rail's rusted? Then like nothing, the thing stopped, it was only a few minutes since they left the landing spot. Maybe it was changing tracks? Panic welled up in her, what if it was stuck, out of power, broken; they'd be stuck in a tunnel under the ocean. Aggie felt her heart racing; she didn't realize she was squeezing Mel's hand too hard. But then, before she could say anything the door popped up and the interior tram lights came on brighter.

"Wow what a freak out." Aggie said climbing out of the car with Mel on her heels. They stood on the platform scoping the small room out, not easy in limited light.

This place wasn't like the others, just one small cavern, the walls were rough, tool marks like an air chisel were there on the walls which were wet and the sound of dripping water came from every direction. Spider webs were strung off whatever wall surface was dry. It didn't seem safe. Aggie smelled mildew and rot. She didn't see a ceiling, just a dark void, no way to know how far it went.

"Creepy, I like it," Mel said. "When I get home, I'm asking Mom for a cave system, plenty of room under the house for it, getting tired of the pool house anyway." Mel moved off the platform and Aggie followed. "Hey, I don't see an elevator."

Ten feet away from the tram and the tram door shut silently, Aggie caught it in the corner of her eye and turned to go back to the car but before she took a step, it shot away down the tunnel leaving them in total darkness.

"Great, just great, Mel you got a flashlight on your phone, right?"

She did but her battery was low so they had to feel around more than look and that wasn't going well.

Aggie put a hand on a giant centipede and almost pooped her pants; she forgot how much she hated bugs. Praytis looked like a bug, but he didn't feel like one. After the third or fourth uninvited creepy crawly she encountered, which fell off the wall and went straight down her loose-fitting uniform's top, she was boiling. She pulled the material as far from her body as it would go and shook it until whatever was inside fell to the floor. Frustrated, she screamed, "Light I want light!"

The elevator slid open right in front of her with a massive screech; clearly it hadn't opened in years. The light inside was too bright, Aggie had to look down and there she saw the thing that she had just shook out of her dress, but it wasn't some slimy bug, it was a scorpion. She screamed again but louder.

"Get it away, get it away!" Aggie jumped over it and into the elevator.

Mel crouched down to the ground and poked at it with her phone. The little creature backed up snapping its claws. "So cool, I used to be so scared of arachnids. You know you can eat these things, in some places like Indonesia, its' a regular snack."

"Shut up and get in here."

"You said you were hungry."

When the elevator reached the top, and it seemed a long slow ride, the door would not slide open all the way. They had to squeeze through the crack and it didn't actually reach the top either so the floor was above waist level. It took some doing to worm out of the car. Aggie made it into the tunnel but she wasn't happy. She was covered in muck and sweat. Wet dirt ran down her face. Mel was tiny compared to Aggie so she had less trouble getting out. This time, leery of losing the light, Aggie quickly jammed a rock between the elevator and floor.

The light it cast was low and pointed like a beam but it was better than nothing. Still, there wasn't much to see, just a short rough cave dead ending at a pile of rubble. At least it was dryer.

"Oh great, I guess aliens don't do planet side housekeeping. Let's see, we dig or we go back, I'm not going back."

Aggie started pulling rocks off the pile. It didn't seem like a cave in, the ceiling above was OK. The aliens had to have blocked it, or maybe the people outside blocked it from their side. Whatever, Aggie was tired of caves, she just wanted out. Mel joined the effort complaining about her fingernails the whole time. She had painted them black and put little skulls on each fingernail for the sleep-in.

Of course, on the other side of the pile was still more cave and this one was full of creepy crawlies. By the time they made it to the cave's entrance it was dark outside. Not much of an escape hatch, it was half the width of a normal door and head-banging low. Thick vines and other plants overhung and covered the exit, she had to push her way praying to the Goddess there weren't any poisonous insects in that mess. Aggie almost walked off the edge. Outside was jungle and it was steep going up or down and she couldn't see how far, but she was still glad to be outside, until the first mosquito bit.

"Great, just great, can this get any worse?"

"Like yeah," Mel said, I don't see any spaceships, do you?"

"Crap."

There wasn't much they could do until morning. Aggie had to trust Praytis knew where the cave was and he'd find them. So, they battled a way back inside and using some big leaves, they covered the hole to keep blood sucking bugs out. There was a little trickle of water running down a crack in a section of cave wall so she and Mel licked rocks to get water. Aggie decided it was best to wait, how long could Praytis be? It turned out to be a really, really creepy long night.

***

Praytis had done as requested, after all he was duty bound to adhere to the Captain's orders. It took a little time. He had to call in one of Mother's shuttles, and since that took time as Mother's auto response wasn't efficient; he arranged to have the latest acquisition upgraded as per his Captain's previous orders. He was told not to leave the spaceport so he did not. Had he, then Pharaoh would have had the option of ordering him to a different duty.

It was a strange thing, to balance between commands. But Captain Piper was explicit, and she gave him direct orders. However, he had a choice; he could have reported to the GTO upon landing but oddly, he felt no compunction to do so. And that was strange for him. He felt the pull of two obligations but for reasons he didn't yet understand, it seemed to him that Earth had stronger gravity, no pun intended, but he recognized there was a pun before him. *How Earth like, I must say.* Perhaps this Earth managed to endear itself to him? This was most unusual. Then again it was a pretty planet.

Praytis had arrived in Preto Rico at a time he thought would be well past Captain Piper's arrival so she should have been there, but she wasn't, or was she?

His sensors weren't picking them up and no wonder, the bio diversity of this jungle was tremendous and the shuttle's on-board memory of Earth fauna was limited and so wasn't very useful. Mother handled more detailed memory archives directly and projected it as required, but Mother was in re-fit and her local AI's weren't very sophisticated.

Praytis floated over the rip between mountains, the Earth based radio telescope was just on the other side of the taller one. He tried to think of what to do. He wasn't used to deciding things for himself without computers or living supervision. Logic dictated that he should return, have this shuttle upgraded with better bio-files, but that would require him leaving the space port and that was against orders, further his additional order was to meet her here. Logically, she would not move about at night. Not wanting to disobey several orders, whereas the GTO only had given one direct order, it was a matter of mathematics.

Praytis landed the ship in a little hidden valley and turned in for the night with a clear head. He would not leave until new orders were sent and whereas in this valley, so close to the radio telescope, and whereas direct communications with Earth humans was not allowed or practiced by the GTO, he did not expect any calls from the GTO, and moreover, new orders could not be received there unless the GTO ignores their own directives—such was unheard of. Communication would require a light beam signal and he was not ordered to activate a laser receiver. Logically he would have to go on with his last order and search for her until he found her or determine she was indeed missing, that is to say, not locate-able. That didn't seem quite logical, to stay here indefinitely while somewhat skirting GTO rules, but for once in his service to the GTO, it was his call to make and he accepted that responsibility. Perhaps ship service was more interesting than anthropology. That would explain why the GTO wasn't forthcoming regarding such comparisons. It appeared his only option was to 'wait it out,' as they say Earth side, for a reasonable length of time and that too was his call.

FORTY-THREE

Mark and Bart

Mark didn't sleep all night. He could not take that chance. He was pleased to note that few boats passed by their position overnight. Perhaps the searchers were focused elsewhere, but he knew better than to let his guard down. Pre-dawn he had made his way south to the bend on the river and waited there in the dark. He covered himself with whatever brush was available and was glad for the bug repellent he found on board. He knew it was Bart long before he saw the old work horse appear out of the mists. The thumping drum of an old low-revving diesel motor that chugged like an early hit-and-miss farm engine, carried far. Bart passed Mark's position and on south two hundred yards before turning to at the channel marker. Lucky the fog was out and off the water but it would soon dissipate. Bart's boat was an old wooden bay boat formally used for crabbing in the Chesapeake's shallows. It didn't look like much and that was the point.

Even in the predawn light Mark noted the crayfish pots piled up on the fantail that were well lashed down. Mark used his pen light and flashed the signal. If Bart wasn't looking in the right direction, according to prearranged coordinates, he and anyone watching would not see the signal. No response. Mark tried again. Bingo, it took. Now things had to move fast.

He ran back to Jane and woke her up. She quickly stripped for swimming, and together they got the wounded man, now semi-conscious, into a life jacket and out of the boat. Together they waded out while Bart chugged up to them. Bart's boom lift, used to drop crab pots, was employed to get the wounded man up and onto the old wooden deck.

Mark didn't see much of her in the dark, but he knew his way around The Nightingale. She was more a barge than a speedboat but sizable at twenty-eight feet.

Bart's work boat sported low gunwales and a ten-foot beam. She had a modified tri-hull but you would not know it from the water. From all sides she appeared as a flat-bottom Garvey which was known by its hull type, designed without bilge compartments. It was a perfect working platform to gather blue claw crabs, or crayfish or smuggle contraband by way of hidden blister compartments between hulls. Mark had helped Bart set it up and he never thought he'd call in that favor. Before the Pipers, he considered unwanted vets his only family.

It took all three of them, but they got the man into the forward cabin and onto the lower cot before he passed out. And just in time, the echo of a jet boat was floating on the air. There was no running for it. It was time for a smuggler's ploy.

Mark lifted one of the deck panels and said "Get in, hurry."

Jane stared into the blackness. He was sure the odor didn't help matters. "What about you? There's no room."

"Don't worry, got it covered, hurry up, if they got infrared we're caught. Underwater is safe."

"Easy for you to say."

Jane slipped down below the deck. He replaced the hatch and slid a tub full of crawdads over the spot. He got on his knees and spoke into a deck crack. "Spin the latch, keep quiet. Here they come."

Mark took a fast survey and slipped over the side. The jet was running alongside a regular police boat and they beelined right for Bart's craft with enough bodies to take the Nightingale apart. Bart was a known conman bullshitter and pain in the state police's ass. Mark hoped they didn't run Bart's info and find his rap sheet.

Mark moved in the water around the Nightingale keeping his head just out of the water enough to breathe. From there he made out the two different boats' motors, they were both coming up on the starboard side.

"You there, this is the police, prepare to be boarded."

The Nightingale's engine was shut down. "Hold your horses, hold your horses, you want me to anchor?"

Mark felt the police boat bump Bart's docking tires which hung off the gunwales' panicles. He felt feet hit the deck an instant later. The jet boat gunned its motors and started around to portside at the same time. Mark ducked under and came up between hulls where he knew there was an air pocket. It wasn't the first time he used that trick.

From there he heard the clamor. The police were tossing the boat, traps went over the side. When they got to the tub of crayfish Bart blew his stack.

"What you doing, can't a man make a living? You know how long it took to get that catch, Jesoos B. Chrips! Leave my catch be!"

Mark could almost see Bart swinging a gaff at them. Then there were footsteps inside the cabin.

"What's this?" An authorities' voice demanded.

"Ain't you ever seen a drunk mate before, or you just pretend to be sailors? Low down amateurs. Leave the boy be, he deserves restin, who'd you think pulled all them traps last night?"

At least one of the boarding officers must have had sea-legs and that's what Bart was likely banking on.

"All right, all right old man. Just relax. Come on men, this old sea dog's got nothing."

Boots on deck said they were leaving.

"Hey what about my traps, isn't you gonna help me, gosh darn police. I never!"

The jet and the police boat clunked into gear and the police cruiser took off south, but the jet drive boat did a once around slow. Mark imagined Bart shaking a fist at them. The jet boat was astern and it was close when she gunned it. Mark heard the roster tail hit the transom and Bart with it by the string of cusswords that followed.

The boats were far enough out but Mark waited. He waited a long time until Bart had the traps back on board. Only after Bart hit the deck three times with the back end of a gaff pole did Mark resurface. Once back topside, Mark quickly signaled Jane to unlock.

He opened the hold. That water the Navy had jetted over the stern half-filled the little bilge void. Jane had six inches of air space. She looked like a wet rat. Mark and Bart each took one of Jane's hands and lifted her out.

"I'm so tired of water." Jane said. "I feel like a prune."

"Come on lady, I'll get you some dry duds."

The cabin at the bow of Bart's Garvey wasn't a typical cutty-cabin, it was tall enough to stand in and square. There was a two-level bunk bed, two chairs and a card table and a couple of old bedroom dressers screwed to sidewalls. The pot belly stove wasn't lit. In the old days boatmen would spend as long on the water as it took to make the catch and that meant sleeping on the bay if necessary. The head was forward but wasn't used for nothing but storage. The door was ajar and the interior's contents that were rifled by the police were tossed everywhere. Mostly boxes of fishing gear and rubber deck suits.

Bart handed Jane an old pair of gray sweat pants and a blue t-shirt and backed up. Mark and she were both in their underwear, barring that Mark had his small survival gear backpack on—he never took it off on a mission unless he had to. Mark turned for the door to give Jane privacy, but Bart remained.

"Come on, give the girl space, she might want out of that wet bathing suit." Mark said it that way not to alert Bart to the fact that the President was only wearing bra and panties.

"That there's what I was waiting for."

Mark clamped a hand on the back of Bart's neck and led him out onto the deck. It was past dawn but a still fog now lay on the waterway. No sign of the police. Mark didn't see far. Infrared didn't care about fog.

Mark sized up Bart. He had changed over the last ten years. He never was tall, but now he was slumped and inch shorter, his thick hair was always gray but now it had gotten thin. The crags in his face were deeper and even his gray-blue eyes looked worn down. Bart was always long haired yet clean shaven but now he sported a scraggly, spotty beard. The moniker old sea dog fit a like glove.

Bart fired the boat and they started chugging up river. The best she could do was four knots. The wheel was on the cabin's wall above a stepped platform. Bart had to mount the bridge platform to see over the cabin to pilot. Mark held the wheel while Bart climbed up on the pilot's chair. There, he lit a joint, took a few deep pulls and handed it to Mark, but Mark waved it off.

"No thanks," Mark said, "I'm on duty."

"I never been on duty straight; to each his own man." Bart took another deep hit, snubbed it out and put it in the top pocket of his bleached-out cowboy shirt. Mark knew Bart had grown it himself. He was self-sufficient and not the type to waste anything he took pains to produce. He grew his food, hunted and worked the water. In Vietnam, Mark was told, they called him backwoods Bart. That's one handy set of skills.

At this speed, it would take a few hours to make it to Bart's place. Mark didn't think the man below would live that long, but there was no rushing Nightingale. Jane stayed inside with the young man on the ride northwest and that was good. Bart didn't need a pretty girl distracting him. And nobody wants to die alone.

Bart had a Marine Band weather receiver and a low-grade CB radio. There wasn't much news to be had by either one. How things were stacking up in the world was important, but for now, only survival mattered.

FORTY-FOUR

Jungle Madness

When Aggie woke it was still dark. A faint yellow glow told her it was sunrise. It felt weird that the roosters didn't wake her. Maybe Dave shot them. It was dead silent, not even passing boats. Aggie rolled over reaching for her pillow but the body next to her wasn't that. She bolted upright.

"Cave, we're in a cave!"

Mel sat up. "Dude, if that what it takes to sleep with you, I'm getting a cave for my b-day."

A big bat winged by, Aggie didn't see it but she heard it squeak and felt the air. She waved her hands around frantically

"Hold still, they don't get tangled in people's hair, that's a misnomer. Bats are mad cool," Mel said as she got up. "Waving your arms like that, you might hurt it. Did I mention I love bats?"

"You would. I'm getting out of here. It smells like pee."

Aggie would have crawled to the exit but the borrowed waitress's uniform she wore was too long and her knees didn't clear the material. Rather than stand, she crouched and duck-walked to the cave exit. She plowed headlong into the foliage and tumbled out of the opening onto the other side almost rolling down the hill. But there were so many plants big and small so she couldn't roll far if she tried. Mel helped her get up. Both of them were covered in black mud, dead vines and bat poop, so that's why the floor was soft, bat poop. Mel didn't look as bad, her clothes were all black, but both of them were a royal mess.

They balanced along the steep hill holding on to saplings and surveyed the place and they didn't see much. Big tress and thick foliage lay in every directions. Yeah, this was an actual jungle, full of bugs and spiders and snakes. The realization sent a shiver down Aggie's back.

The sun was out but with the mountains all around she didn't know what time it could be. It was already hot, worse than the Keys, and dripping humid. Aggie checked her watch. The battery was dead. Mel's I-know phone was also dead. No way to get location or direction.

"Praytis said we were near the radio telescope, we should go there, at least they have food and water, and maybe we can charge our phones and call grandpa. He'll help us." Aggie slapped herself in the forehead. "Yeah right, like the government doesn't have people there, somebody will call the cops, like hi we're just a couple of dirty but formerly famous girls wanted by the Feds by now, just wandering around the jungle and we thought you might want to feed us and junk, yeah right."

"Do you even know his number?"

"Crap, crap, crap!"

Aggie and Mel argued for twenty minutes about which way to go. Praytis said the telescope was below, but below what? The cave or the sky and which way was it anyway? Mel wanted to go up the hill and Aggie wanted to go down, but from what they could see there was nothing in any direction. Both of them were hungry and thirsty and fed up so the path of least resistance was it and that meant downhill into a denser bio-mass.

Aggie removed her black apron and tied it to a tree near the cave so they'd find it again. Twenty yards downhill she turned to look for the marker and there was no sign of it.

***

Paul Henderson was a doc student intern at the Arecibo Observatory and he wasn't happy. He liked the assignment; in fact, he requested it, wrote the grant himself and was grateful to the National Science Foundation for its grant money and the opportunity to work with the telescope. But, things weren't working out at the moment.

His goal was to look at distant and near galaxies with a new focus; he had a few ideas of how to interpret the data that was somewhat unique and original. To get a doctorate one must do the same but different and he was on to something that fit. He had this crazy idea that ships like Mother were out there and he thought he had a way to find out. They must use low frequency waves to communicate over such long distances and that end of the spectrum was largely ignored—pulsars and black-hole radio emissions were far sexier.

But the telescope was in disrepair and never brought up to its full potential since hurricanes, one after the other, wreaked havoc on the equipment every season. Having a bunch of senior scientists floating in and out didn't help and worse, some of them brought their kids. This was supposed to be a quiet concentrated effort and it wasn't. He was disturbed regularly. A telescope that was barely used anymore due to a lack of funding and interest was fast becoming a tool of the U.S. military. A lot of good it did the defense people, aliens didn't use local radio and his equipment liked long distances anyway. Not a peep from the moon.

When the aliens were exposed every observatory was enlisted. Real research stopped. The assumption among scholars was that eventually the aliens would share and many questions would be answered, so there was little point in putting money into telescope time. Paul didn't buy into that theory, but the extra people on station did. He just wanted them all to go away.

Overnight he didn't get much time in and what little he got, he'd process this morning before going to bed. But the three teenaged kids in the listening room were upsetting his concentration. He had his headphones on and discovered that some Earth surface activity got mixed into his observation, maybe kids with a walkie-talkie. Perhaps it was the same kids that were messing around at the facilities' listening stations.

Just to screw with them, Paul took his headphones off and jacked the volume. *I hope I blow their ears out.* Along with the faint sounds of distance galaxies two girls were talking in the background. The local interference was scratchy but discernable.

"Bats, I hate bats, it's light outside but…what's wrong with bats…oh great what'll we do…" came over the wall speaker.

"Hey, that's Aggie and Mel!" One of the kids said.

"No way, can you tune it in." Another kid said. "It's her dead man switch, they tried to snuff it but it keeps coming back on, stupid Feds."

"Yeah, stupid Feds."

Stupid Feds? That sounded exactly like what Piper often said. Paul watched her video blogs like everyone did, they just appeared without permission, but he lost interest, he was busy and there wasn't anything anyone could do about it except turn the knob. The girl was a pariah, she was bashed left and right in the media. Was anything she said actually true, where was the evidence? It wasn't worth his consideration; he had a doctorate to earn.

"No, that's not the blog, but that's her, I'd know her anywhere." One kid said getting up. "Come on you guys, let's go, let's check signal tracking."

The group got up and left and Paul was glad. Now he'd get some work done. Let them bother someone else for a change. Maybe he could salvage some of the recording. It was interesting that at least one of them knew how to run a lot of equipment, but his father was one of the scientists here so it wasn't that strange.

Paul worked on until ten a.m. and then it was off to bed without any usable results. He erased the recording as that Earth-bound signal splash made his recordings unworkable. Yes, it came from Earth; it wasn't from a satellite, just some kind of atmospheric reflection and it wasn't worth his time to separate the mixed data. He put it and himself to bed.

***

Aggie and Mel finally made it to the bottom just to find the ground going steeply up on the opposite side. At least there was a little stream running through.

They got some water hoping no parasite came with the free drink. Water never tasted so good. There were some fruiting trees and brush with berries but neither one knew if it was edible or what it was. Aggie's stomach demanded something to fend off the pain but she wasn't about to try the fruit.

Mel was about to bite into a green pear-shaped thing but Aggie slapped her hand and knocked it away.

"Forget it, it might kill you."

"It's better than starving." Mel was more pale than usual. The only girl in Key West without a tan flopped down onto a fallen tree and crossed her arms. "I'm not going anywhere until I eat."

"How do you feel about sushi," Aggie said eyeing the stream. There were lots of little fish in it, little clams or mussels and fresh water snails clung to the bank's root overgrowth.

"I don't do meat," Mel said. She never sounded more miserable.

"You do now," Aggie said and went to work gathering. " Space girls do what we must." The fish were hard to catch but with Mel's help they formed a little fish weir in the creek with some fallen logs and forest floor muck. They forced a bunch of little fish into a small side pool where Aggie was able to splash them out onto land.

Aggie had been eating all kinds of natural stuff her entire life, dad was a naturalist fisherman so the idea of eating wild stuff wasn't a big deal. Aggie had eaten crawdads and raw oysters and even snake, but Mel, a city girl, wasn't hot on the idea.

Aggie had found an aboriginal spear point in the stream bed so she used it to cut the fish, more like hack it open, and remove the fresh water clams from their shells. Aggie stuffed a dozen into her mouth before noticing that Mel wasn't eating.

Aggie held up a little clam strip. "I thought you like clams. You like girls, right, tastes the same I hear?"

"Funny, very funny, think I'll just die now."

It took some convincing but Mel finally ate a clam, and as she was super hungry, she ate it without vomiting it back. Mel ate more clams and even ate the raw fish and she had to admit it wasn't bad. Raw fish doesn't taste like fish; Aggie had to explain it over and over before she tried it because Mel hated fish, or really the idea of eating fish because of that fishy smell. Refreshed, or at least not so starved, they decided to follow the stream. It was the logical thing to do but after going downstream a little way the caiman that they spooked changed their minds so up the opposite hill they climbed for the next hour.

It was maybe eleven a.m. when they finally made it to the top. Aggie sat down tired and filthy and looked back across the valley at the way they had come and she didn't see the cave at all. But she caught a glint of something shiny over on the opposite peak.

"Something's there on the other side," she said. "It's metal."

"Don't tell me Praytis has landed." Mel said. She had removed her big pants and tied the legs around her shoulders like a cape. Mel's t-shirt was so long it passed for a dress.

"I don't think so," Aggie said. "I need a better look." Aggie found a palm tree that was doable and she climbed it. Once in the fronds she had a better view. "Guess what," Aggie called down. "The telescope is the other way."

Aggie climbed back down scratching herself all over. "Praytis was right; the cave is below the telescope: I saw the tops of the guideline towers. It's on the other side of that ridge."

"Don't bullshit me!"

"I would never shit my favorite turd," Aggie said, without a hint of humor. "We have to go back."

"OK fine, we go back, but I'm resting, I don't care." Wake me up when the cows come home." Mel lowered herself down with a yoga-like scissor leg motion and laid down on the soft forest cover. She didn't even swat the ant that crawled onto her face. Aggie sat down next to her. They were both exhausted.

***

After Paul finally left, Ernie had the listening room to himself. He was able to determine that the signal appeared to be local. It may have been a bounce. The odds of Aggie showing up here were astronomical. But it sure wasn't her blog. He was about to give up when he picked it up again. Mel and Aggie were talking. He dialed in, had the computer triangulate. Yup that's them and they were in trouble.

Ernie wiped the file and ran out to go get his drone. It wasn't really his, it was his dad's and it was a nice one. Dad used it to fly files over to the other work stations or tools to the men doing repairs on the dish. It could carry a lot of stuff. Ernie wrote a little message and taped it to a bottle of water and put some energy bars in the same carry bag. The drone station was just a little room. It's one set of controls was mobile but the fixed controls worked better. Just outside the door was the launch platform protruding off the main deck.

When his dad came in Ernie jumped with surprise.

"What are you up to now," Dad said, "That drone is not a toy."

"Found some hikers, they're lost, I'm giving them some food; I'm showing them how to get here."

Dad looked at the screen that showed location and the little package Ernie put together. "Son, get over to ridge three. Turn the beacon lights on. I'll fly the supplies out. Someone should be there when they break cover, it's bad footing all around. You know the ins and outs."

"OK Dad!" Ernie took off like a shot.

Dad had to deliver the survival package, Ernie knew he would. But Dad wouldn't know who the hikers were. Aggie and Mel were likely covered with grime. Of course, Dad didn't look at blogs, so he didn't know about the dead man blogs either. Ernie loaded a backpack with food and water and headed out. He thought they might not want to come in, maybe they'd take off. Maybe the Feds were after them. He'd be careful not to give them away. He was so excited to finally meet them, he almost forgot the pack.

***

Praytis spent the day tuning his sensors. The bio-diversity of a jungle was quite the challenge, but he was making progress. He caught a few spikes that were not wild pigs and not men of the observatory and so he was convinced that his Captain and company were near and not in the tunnel system. Aggie's bio-specifications were unmistakable albeit hard to isolate in this environment. Praytis was very old and one thing great age taught him was patience. And there was a small side benefit, the longer he stayed Earth side and out of the GTO's control the more flummoxed Pharaoh would be upon his return. Ship duty had its pleasures.

FORTY-FIVE

Aggie's PR Crew

Aggie and Mel were sitting on a log on top of a hill swatting bugs and cursing their luck. Before striking out back the way they had just come, Aggie decided to have a look around—there had to be a road somewhere going to the observatory. So, they topped the hill and scanned the other way. The way down appeared easy. There was a road alright, but with a military check point. They had a gate, two armed men, and a jeep. A military box truck was stopped at the gate. The two MPs were giving the driver a hard time. They were all on the same side, how'd that make any sense? The scene was too far away to see clearly, but by the way the MP was waving his hands around she could tell he was yelling. So, the girls retreated back to the log-seat they had found before. It was the only semi-clear place on this hillcrest.

"Dude, are we fucked or what? If I don't get some real food soon, and a mosquito net, I'll lose my mind." Mel slapped a bug off her arm.

"When'd you get one? I know I'm crazy, but I thought you were only half nuts. I hear buzzing. You hear that?"

"Look at the size of that bug," Mel stood up and pointed out into the air. "No way, it's a drone."

"Yeah we're fucked. It's coming right at us, looks like it's got a bag on a string hanging off it."

"Let's hide!" Mel turned her head this way and that way but there was no way to escapee and no place to hide.

"Just act like we belong, whoever is running it might think we're just part of the local scene. Maybe it's delivering pizza to the butt-head twins at the road-block."

"Yeah, dude you have lost your mind." Mel slowly lowered back onto the log. "We're fucked."

The drone was a big one, better than any kid's toy. It had four rooters and each one had to be like three feet around. It flew right over head and it was too big to get right on top of them as the trees right behind were really tall. That bag it carried was on a tether and it was coming down at them while the thing stayed in place. Aggie had to climb up onto a nearby big rock to reach it. The craft moved closer to her and she unhooked the bag. The thing shot up from weight relief, turned and went back the way it had come.

Aggie climbed off the rock and sat back where she was before. She opened the bag, two bottles of water and a couple of power-bars. Mel tore into the food bar while Aggie sucked half the water down before she noticed a piece of yellow note-book paper wrapped around the bottle and attached with way too much tape. She shoved a chunk of power-bar into her mouth and chewed while she removed the paper. There was a little hand drawn map and it showed where they were and where they needed to go. Yeah, back across the valley but there was a short cut. To the right was a cut in the mountain side, and the note said to go that way and follow it up, it said he would meet them at the top. It was signed Ernie.

"Ernie," Aggie said, "I don't know any Ernie."

"I know one but it can't be him."

"We had food and water; we should run the other way, what if we're recognized?"

"Dude, I don't know about you, but this adventure is over, yeah? I've had enough." Mel got up and started moving downhill. She stopped a few yards down and said, "Hello, it's an observatory, you know nerds, we'll be safe, just got to get past the mall cops." She pointed in the direction of the road block.

Mel had a good point. OK the military sucked, but they don't work for or at the observatory, it's international anyway, it's not America's junk. OK they can block the road but they don't own the place, right?

"Hold on bitch, I'm coming."

"I do have that power over women."

They made it downhill no problem, but they had to move a bit east to get onto the trail that led uphill. To do that they had to walk the stream and that was a freak-out because the caiman was still there. They managed to get around it. She had read that that kind of coccidian didn't attack people but she didn't believe everything she read, so they went wide fighting underbrush. They got back into the water. Aggie picked up another leach on her leg while bushwhacking; she was so tired she didn't care. Taking on a blood-sucking bug for a safer walk was worth it.

The trail was steep and by the time they got to the trailhead, they were both ready to collapse. Aggie expected to see a military guy or some other pissed off adult when they crested the hill, but what she got was a short, chunky kid about age thirteen wearing sneakers, Bermuda shorts, and a Hawaiian shirt.

Aggie stopped in her tracks. "Hey Mel, when did astrophysicists' start hiring midgets."

"You got it half right."

"Aggie, Mel?" the kid said. His voice was too deep, she expected a squeaker.

Mel bolted and almost knocked the kid off his feet with a flying hug.

"Holy crap, it's that Ernie, no freaking way!" Aggie jumped in on the group hug.

***

The ship's rudimentary AI had dialed into a good signal and alerted Praytis.

"Yes, I do believe you are correct, that's her bio, and Melissa as well."

"You want to go?" The computer asked inside his head.

Praytis checked the screens. The girls were on a ridge, one of several that ringed the location above the dish. But there were problems. Guide wires and towers were all around the dish with many coming off the ridges so maneuvering was manageable but risky. More so, there was an unidentified human there as well and GTO rules would be broken. Once more, flying over the dish was not advisable and also non-regulation. At close range the station's Earth humans may detect the shuttle, and it was possible that the telescope may hamper cloaking. It was quite a quandary. The computer recorded Praytis's thoughts and had no comment regarding his assessment and logic thereof, thus he had to decide on his own and if felt good.

"Waiting, where shall we go?" The ship asked.

"Stay well clear of the dish, as before, and continue monitoring their movement. We shall have to remain hidden until we find an opening. Our primary mission is to recover the Captain; however, we mustn't break protocol unless…"

"You are aware, "The ship said, "That Mother's fleet isn't committed to follow Moon City or GTO protocols?"

"Yes, I know but I am so enlisted, of course not while within Mother's realm, but…I need to consider my options."

Praytis leaned back onto his rear legs and scratched his chin. He liked puzzles but this was a tangled one. His first idea was best for now. He would wait. He wasn't one to be rash. He wasn't accustomed to making snap command decisions thus he would think more on how to go about retrieving the Captain.

As an anthropologist he knew well that Earth humans had uncanny abilities for making fast assessments and producing immediate actions or reactions, albeit they were often wrong in either case. Praytis called up the galactic law library. It was ten thousand years out of date, but it was a starting point.

***

The walk around the dish was a long one, but at least they had a trail. Ernie and Mel chatted away the entire time. The place wasn't full of government people. Ernie said the military guys down the hill were Homeland Security and they weren't supposed to come up to the observatory, at least that's what Ernie understood. Car motors caused interference and the place was now international with embassy-like status. Aggie imagined the truck driver didn't give a rat's butt-hole; he just wanted to make his rounds. Maybe they could sneak onto the truck if it ever got up here and slip out.

Aggie stopped on the trail and slapped her head. "Dope, this is a radio telescope, can't we send a signal?"

Ernie was leading the way. He stopped and said, "Not without major effort. Dad might know how, but I don't and I don't think we should tell him who you are. You should see the news. All the TV stations are calling you a traitor; people think you helped the President do the murder. They say, how else could she have gotten away, right?"

"Crap...I guess Oxford is out."

It sank in at that moment; she wasn't going to get to go to college on Earth at all. She just had to accept it, she had to accept a lot more; like Mother was her responsibility and she had to do something about the butt-holes who were after her ship but she didn't have a clue what to do about it. She didn't know what to think about the President but for sure, Jane Albright wasn't going to help her anymore.

Where the hell was Praytis?

The observatory had a bunch of buildings with it, some were residential quarters, others office space or for whatever utilities the telescope required. Ernie had his own room. They climbed up over the back deck, it was all metal, and Ernie's room was on that lower level. He wanted them to avoid his dad and the other scientists that were there so they went over the back fence.

Ernie's room wasn't a mess; Aggie didn't know how anyone could sleep in a bedroom without clothes all over the floor. Aggie didn't want to sit on the nice clean bedspread. She was still filthy dirty. Mel moved right into Ernie's computer desk and started clicking away.

"Nice setup, dude, mad memory. Hey Captain, what'll we do now?"

"Shower, that's what I'm doing then we'll figure something out."

"Low tech, I like it." Mel said.

"Hey stop stealing my thoughts. Can we borrow some clothes, Ernie?"

"Sure, bathroom's there." He pointed out a closed door. "I better go see Dad, let him know you're all right, don't worry, I'm not giving you away. He's so busy trying to pick up alien communications he barely has time to think. Big bonuses for the group that breaks into alien communications."

Ernie left. Aggie stripped and kicked the rags into a corner. Nakedness was no big deal to her, but Mel hedged. Aggie walked into the bathroom, it had a nice big shower. "Come on, let's share, we don't have time to screw around, what if his dad comes?"

"I'm, well, you know I got a pass from gym, it's because..."

"Because your daddy paid the school board," Aggie said. "Yeah, I know you're insecure, that's why you dress like a pot belly stove. Get over the body shame already, will you." Aggie grabbed Mel by the hand and pulled her into the bathroom. "Get naked bitch."

Mel tried to close the door but Aggie didn't let her. Too much steam, the room wasn't that big. They got in and got clean and Aggie barely noticed the situation. It felt so good to get the crud off. They stayed in the hot water a long time and afterwards there were plenty of nice, soft towels at hand.

Aggie got a pair of cut-off denim shorts out of Ernie's dresser and a loose white t-shirt. Mel put on blue walking shorts; the kid probably went to a prep-school, and a man-tailored vertical striped button-down shirt. Mel's combat boots didn't match at all—maybe Mel could get some shoes off Ernie. At least Aggie's borrowed boy's flip flops didn't look that bad. The clothes were loose but fit well enough although the shirt was tight on Mel's boobs. Mel's outfit must have been from when the kid was younger. It wouldn't fit him now.

"Holy moly, look at you." Aggie said, "You do look human, and pretty too. I knew you had a nice body, and your boobs are great, weird how you don't notice bodies when they're naked."

"Speak for yourself. I notice everything. Do you ever shave your pits?"

There was a quick knock and Ernie came in shutting his door behind.

"I told Dad you were lost hikers and you were getting cleaned up. Said he'll have someone drive you to town, but then there's an emergency."

"What, like military or what?" Mel asked while trying on a pair of sneakers. She rejected them and slipped on Ernie's rubber shower flip-flops.

"Nope, there's a UFO buzzing the compound, a little round ball of light. Dad's pretty upset."

Aggie and Mel both said it at once, "Buddy!"

They rushed out of the room and down a short hallway. Aggie found herself on an observation deck. There she called and Buddy raced up from the parking lot below. He did crazy circles in the air before calming down and landing on the deck. He nudged Aggie's leg and did the same for Mel and Ernie, and so occupied they didn't see Ernie's dad come down an outside stairway.

"Aggie Piper, I knew it was you." Dad was a tall, skinny guy with glasses, graying hair and a big smile plastered to his face.

"You won't rat on us! Will you?" Aggie cried.

"Don't be ridiculous, you saved my life. Besides, even if I was so inclined, there's no time to have the police up here. You will be long gone before I could even make the call." He pointed behind the trio. "I do believe your limo has arrived."

Aggie and crew spun around. Aggie's shuttle was suspended in mid-air. Its hatch split open and a gangway had projected away from the ship's hull and onto the aluminum decked drone station that protruded past the railing. Praytis stood in the ship's doorway.

"Captain, I've had trouble locating you. I hope you don't mind, but I took liberties in that I called up your personnel probe. I hope this is acceptable?"

"When I get up there I'm going to kiss you square on the lips," Aggie said opening the drone's landing gate.

"Oh my."

"We are so out of here." Aggie marched up the gangway with Mel on her heels, but Ernie stayed behind. "Come on Ernie, you're crew now."

"Is it dangerous?" His dad asked. Ernie looked a little freaked out. That night on Sal Cay Bank was hard on him, no doubt. And he wasn't used to Praytis yet. Praytis was way stranger than grays or even Moby.

Aggie had to answer honestly. "It might be. Ernie after this is over, I'll come back. I owe you a trip to the moon."

Once Aggie and Mel boarded, they took off for Haiti without delay.

FORTY-SIX

Mark at Bart's Place

Bart's place was up in one of the many small tributaries that flowed into the upper Potomac. Mark had never been there by way of water and he saw the wisdom in it. Bart's cabin and small barn were just off his rickety dock about fifty yards through thick woods but you would never see the house if you didn't know where to look. Land access was the same, he recalled, well hidden. Bart bought a sliver of dry land surrounded by swamp off the back of a farmer's property because the farmer couldn't make use of it. There was no deed transfer and this family farm wasn't corporate controlled, so no one looking for Bart could track him down, even the numbers on the Nightingale's hull were obscured.

To say Bart was paranoid would be a mistake. The man was aware of what he saw around him. When you know the reality of The Powers That Be and they know you, you have a choice, either join them or hide. Bart had had his fill of participating in state hegemony back in Vietnam.

Bart and Jane had the injured man's arms and Mark took his legs and together they moved him into Bart's cabin. The place was on stilts and the ramp up was steep, so they were lucky to make it inside in one piece. The inside was clean and well organized but you'd never think that from outside. The great room wasn't so great, one bedroom and a kitchen with a wood-burning stove. There was a sliding door in the kitchen to the deck on the back of the cabin facing upland. The outside was rustic but the inside was well appointed with antique furnishing and bookshelves stuffed with hard cover medical books. The entire place was less than nine hundred square feet.

They laid the man down on an antique daybed. Bart got on his knees immediately and looked the man over, used a flashlight to check his eyes. The patient hadn't moaned or made a peep in hours; Mark feared they were losing him.

"Boil water," Bart said getting up. "I got to go in."

"What, you must be kidding, can't we call a doctor?" Jane said.

"Sure, if you don't mind showing doc a corpse." Bart motioned Mark to the wood pile, "Stoke it up good—and hot Captain. Look lady, he's got brain swelling; got to get the puss out."

"Puss, what are you talking about! What about X-rays?"

"What'd you know about it!" Bart snapped like a mean dog. "I know what I'm doing. You want X-ray, I got a 19th century foot X-ray gizmo out in the barn, works too, why don't you bring it in and we'll squeeze his head till it fits in the foot slot?"

"Look Mr. I was a nurse before I went on to law school."

"Jane, let it go!" It was Mark's turn to snap. He knew Bart and if Bart said the guy was critical, he was. Mark suddenly remembered why he didn't much like civilians, they were too slow to do what was necessary, just more interference underfoot. Politicians were the worst. They'd debate buying umbrellas in the middle of a hurricane. They always missed the big picture. Mark expected Bart to go off on her but he was standing there scratching his chin.

"Nurse eh, good, I'll need help." Bart handed her an old doctor's surgical kit that was 100 years old, the leather bag had seen better days. "Here sterilize them, autoclaves in the cubby; I'll go fire the generator."

Bart walked out and down the plank. Jane stood looking after him with her legs wide and hands on hips. "I never, that man, I don't…"

"Shut up Jane," Mark said. "Do what he says."

There wasn't much talk after that. Things pulled together. Jane got into the swing of it. There was nothing more Mark could do but stay out of the way.

Mark lowered himself into an old overstuffed chair and watched from a distance. It was better that way, too many cooks stirring the pot and adding his germs was a bad idea. Mark realized how tired he was and on doing so, he closed his eyes and kicked back for a cat-nap. His survival pack was still on his back so for the first time in days he took it off and laid it next to the chair. The straps left deep red marks on his chest; some of his skin was rubbed raw. Let's try this again. Mark leaned back and put his feet on a hassock.

Bart had an old AM radio on. Bart liked music while he worked. Classic rock played softy. Then the news came on. Top story was that the murderer Jane Albright was still at large. Mark dozed off as the news faded into commercials.

Four hours had passed before Mark woke. The kid was bandaged up and sleeping. Bart and Jane were at the kitchen table sipping coffee like old pals. The leftovers of a big breakfast were scattered on the table; the plates were licked clean. Mark poured a cup and grabbed a cold pancake off a paper plate, dumped bacon crumbs over it and rolled it up like a burrito.

"How's he doing," Mark said around a mouthful of cold, fried batter.

"He'll live, don't believe there's no permanent damage but he'll be wiggy for a while: Should be up in a few days."

"That's good; then we'll move on. Can you see him off?"

"Aye, but I rather not, I don't want to be found, too many questions, I don't have a car, they'll have to come here. You should take him, you'll need a hostage. Jane here gave me the story; I don't want that brought down on me. I didn't see you, you didn't see me. You get me?"

Mark got it all right. He had to get down the road before the wounded man learned where he was and the further from here the better.

Mark had a plan. He'd take the johnboat up creek and inland, there was a used car dealer with a scrap yard behind it along the creek with plenty of cars to steal that would not be missed. He could buy one but that might expose them and that reminded him. He picked up his little survival pack and pulled out a stack of bills. He had twenty thousand left. Mark split the pile and handed half to Bart. Bart said there was a good car in the back lot.

"Bart, I don't know how to thank you, you know she was setup."

Bart took the cash. "Don't matter what I know because I don't know any-thing." Bart shuffled the cash like a deck of cards and smelled it. "Had a good fishing season yes sir, sold a lot." He shuffled the cash again. "Yes sir, made good dough."

"If there is anything I can do for you, I will," Jane said, "When this is over...I don't know how to—."

"What's that, some wind blowing, you hear that bird Mark?"

Early next morning Mark proceeded with his vehicle acquisition. Jane met him at a little country road whose bridge was over the creek a little further up the waterway. They were lucky; Bart was right, Mark found a decommissioned police SUV waiting for the crusher and it still had a government plate on it and better still, it ran. It was an older model but passable and there was room in the back to lay the man down. All the cop gear was stripped out but it still looked like a cop car. It was a K-9 unit that smelled like wet dog.

The wounded man looked better, his fever was gone, and he was able to walk a little. The man made it up the bank, climbed into the back and passed out again. With any luck, they'd be on the other side of Pennsylvania before he regained consciousness again. Mark knew a safe house on the Pa./Ohio border.

FORTY-SEVEN

Sanderson Closing

Sanderson was alone in one of the redundant command communications control booths of the USS Raven, a high-tech missile platform ship; one of Branford's designs. The damn thing could probably fly. It was completely enclosed like a Civil War iron clad. He monitored communications between ships in this convoy. Archer was on his way to the Raven. The fleet was closing in on Haiti and the Navy blockade gave this little task force a wide birth. He saw on multiple screens that the last of the population's evacuation ships were steaming away. But the satellite view was disconcerting. Sanderson picked up the com and dialed the bridge.

"Captain, Admiral Sanderson here, my scope has a lot of civilians still on land. There's a new protest camp around that alien vessel. You can't launch."

"This is Captain Stern. Sir I have specific orders from the Joint Chiefs, one of which is to ignore your contrary requests. Orders are stay on schedule whether civilians refuse to leave or not, I'm sorry, they were warned."

"That's goddamn un-American," Sanderson shot back.

"Need I remind you, you are here as an observer. The Joint Chiefs are in session, we are in contact, they are watching our progress in real time; there are no new orders."

"Bastards, this is America, goddamn it. We don't splash civilians."

"I have orders. Keep my com clear. Stern out."

Sanderson pulled up his laptop and set it on a gauge cluster and booted up. He had a link to the session chamber where the Chiefs were gathered; it was time to drill them a new set of assholes. This was bullshit; a public relations nightmare.

What in the hell was going on here? The America he knew appeared to be finished once and for all. He keyed up the com window and pressed go. The Chiefs should stand up with pride for what was right, but to them right and might were the same thing. He tried it again. His laptop's Pentagon communication feed was rejected—they refused to hear him. They won't listen to reason. Sanderson was out of options.

One thing he felt sure of, if that missile launch went off as planned that would be the end of alien-human relations. America's government was about to set the nation back many years…again. If he managed to stop the fleet, he'd be arrested for treason and that would be the ultimate end to his years of service. He didn't want to go out like that but what or who was he serving now? America as a democracy was finished and those pumped-up bastards didn't care. The Joint Chiefs were being played and they had to know it so they had sold out with purpose. Only MJ-12 could do that, twist the Chiefs into a pretzel and get away with it. What were the benefits? Was it world domination, power, greed, control, the usual but bigger? Nothing made sense anymore.

Sanderson had an idea. He was about to send a radio message when the hatch swung out and Archer blew into the small space…gun first.

"Don't get up, Sanderson. Keep your hands where I can see them. You weren't supposed to be on this tub. Observation Corp is behind with fleet support. What are you up to?"

"What the hell, Archer, what's with the gun? Who are you with? I thought…"

"I'm with myself." Archer pushed back his fedora and aimed the gun at Sanderson's head. "I should shoot you now as a stowaway. Majestic won't mind, but we have a deal and I'm holding you to it."

Archer held the gun steady as a rock. Sanderson knew well Archer's service record and psychological profile, the man had served with distinction, and he was a pro. But, Archer wasn't his former self either. Sanderson thought of the video of Archer dying on the deck of The Contention because of that damned alien control bracelet.

That's what changed him, Karnack changed him, and not for the good. It would have been better if he had died. Archer used to be a good man. He was snowed like the rest of security operations people, but like the Admiral's Seals and the other special-ops men, Archer once had a good heart. That's how the man started out. Sanderson had to pluck that string and play it for all it's worth if he wanted to stay in the game. He'd pull that trump as the time came.

Sanderson checked his watch. His heart would give out in a few hours at best and a lot sooner if he got too excited. He wasn't going to let Archer cheat him out of a glorious death.

"I still have my honor," Sanderson said. "I never reverse my word, you know that. You want that ship, that's your ticket to Karnack. Killing me isn't getting you there. Take out Mother and you are done. I'm telling you Piper will show up. I'll make her cooperate. She'll take you up."

"How?"

"My people have her father tied up." Sanderson said, but it was a lie.

"What people, you don't have any people?"

"You don't know everything Mr. Black. I've had over eighty years to create networks." He bluffed.

Archer pushed his fedora back further with the barrel of his Walther auto. "Perhaps, you don't know everything either. I have orders, Piper shows up or not, that ship is a test bed, MJ will test LFB on time."

"What if I convince Piper to surrender her ship?"

"I'd call it a win-win." Black said and left the dark room.

Sanderson went back to the com and dialed into the infrared array's data feed. Piper would show up, she had to or game over…for everyone.

FORTY-EIGHT

Aggie Above

It felt like home although the shuttle Praytis returned with was one of her new ones. The captain's chair came up from the floor without her asking, like it knew what she wanted. The ship had taken off as soon as the door was closed and ran right over to Haiti. She was holding over the island at forty thousand feet trying to decide what to do, or really how to do it.

"Where to, Captain?" Praytis asked. "Shall we attempt a landing?"

"Crap, I wish I could talk to the ship myself," Aggie said. "What are we up against?"

"There is a way to induce telepathic communications, but that would require Mother inserting com implants, very helpful as such devices allow one to interpret various languages internally as well. Quite standard spacer modification, that is."

"Yeah I know, forget it."

"No way dude, I want one!"

"Nobody's putting anything inside my head. It's already too crowded." Aggie said resigning herself to the necessary of an intermediary. "We got to get Mother out of Haiti before those butthead's hurt her. Why else would they send a fleet of warships?"

"I would advise caution as it appears, according to our sky-eye network, that indeed a military force is approaching Mother. Security mode reports that the Navy intends to launch a missile against Mother."

"Crap I don't know…what'll we do? I better call my mom, Mel you charged the phone at Ernie's?"

"No, it's dead as shit. What about your wristwatch phone?"

Aggie had forgotten about it, Sanderson gave it to her from Grandpa, but she didn't trust Admiral A-hole at all. So, she never actually turned it on.

She raised her wrist to look for the on button but she didn't have time to find the switch. The ship made a crazy dip and steep sideways turn; it took a second for anti-gravity to catch up so the sudden G-forces made her insides feel like jelly.

"What was that?!"

"Automatic defenses: Mother is in auto mode and that includes all of her ships and probes," The ship suddenly pitched again." Buddy had been dodging attacks quite a bit of late, it seems the NRO is…" The ship shifted wildly and Aggie had to hang onto her chair arms. Mel fell off the bench. A vision of cheesy movie earthquakes with people flying flashed into her mind. "…NRO's back on the hunt."

"What's after us?"

"A MAC killer, it is an explosive rocket. This one was launched from a water-borne vessel. The explosion isn't a big concern, but such force causes deployment of our quantum jell which actually allows an EMP pulse to penetrate. This projectile must get close, thus evasive action is instigated, unfortunate that the MAC killers are smart and…" Another radical shift. "…they can…"

"Praytis, shut up and dive."

"Sorry, I don't understand."

"Dive down at the Earth, aim for the Navy."

"Which Navy do you prefer? The Brit's are presently steaming toward Bermuda…"

This time the ship rocked violently. There was an explosion on one of the holograms and in the same shot another rocket was banking toward them.

"Jeez, down there, down by Haiti. Fast, now!"

The shuttle dove at more than missile speed and stopped just above the water in between two large military ships. On one tactical holo screen the Navy ships showed up and they were big ones, two destroyers. Another monitor showed relative positions; they weren't near the attack force. So this must be support. Holo screens were lit up all around Aggie now and she didn't even notice them coming online. Each one showed a different picture and Aggie was able to perceive what was on them all, all at once. Aggie was getting the hang of it. A weird calm came over her even though she saw on screen six that a MAC killer was closing from above. Before the ship could react, she gave an order.

"Uncloak and pull up next to the big ship, twenty feet above water, twenty out and stay away from any gun barrels. When that missile gets really close go straight up at speed."

OK she saw that one in a movie. She knew that regular guns can't hurt her shuttle. Bullets and cannon fire just bounces off. She saw everything on the screens, like clockwork the missile raced in, missed them but impacted the hull of the battleship.

"You realize you just attacked America, right?" Mel shouted.

It was like a fog to Aggie. When she was in the chair, as before, she zoned into the ship and everything else was like hearing with clogged up ears. The EMP had gone off and the battle ship was dead in the water. Its diesel engines that drove the electric motors that made the screws go were toast.

"Hey, they hit us first right, I'm only defending myself! OK, let's really dive; this thing goes under water, right?"

"Well, I'm not supposed to…yes, yes it does. However, defense Mode AI says that a launch platform is closing in on Mother and they are scheduled to fire in only five minutes."

"I got to think about it, park us over by that other big ship."

The shuttle cloaked and found a dead spot along the destroyer's hull. One screen indicated that one was a nuke powered ship and they'd be crazy to fire EMP at it. That would cause a core meltdown.

Aggie was in a panic, time was short and she didn't know what to do. Wild ideas flashed in and out of her consideration. She rejected them as fast as they came. There was no safe way to get to Mother without somebody dying. She didn't want anyone down range of any attempt to kill Mother to suffer. And she didn't know if Sky-Flower was still down there. Screen five showed a protest camp in the trees next to Mother. On impulse she looked at grandpa's watch for the third time. "I wish this thing worked!"

"It works," Praytis said. "It came from Mr. Branford, correct; you have to switch it on manually. But it is based on our designs. I programed it myself." Praytis put a hand on his ear like an old radio announcer. "Yes, it is functional. Your bio-functions power it."

She switched it on and Grandpa's voice boomed over the tiny speaker. "Aggie where are you!"

"Grandpa! I'm above Haiti. In my shuttle, they want to blow up Mother!"

"I know, I know, listen, they're pinging, I've got to go, trust Sanderson, he'll…"

"Signal is gone," Praytis said. "Very cleaver, it was three-way. Branford's other watch is on the launch boat."

Together Mel and Aggie said. "Sanderson!"

"I hate that guy, why should I trust him…because Grandpa said he's OK… Crap."

"Dude, we got to do something!" Mel pointed at a screen: Sailors were racing toward them in an armed dingy.

"Praytis make us go underwater and bring us up alongside the rocket launch craft, fast, OK."

The shuttle dove and raced to the spot. The weapon launch boat had just stopped engines to make ready to fire. Aggie was under the water ten feet from their portside when an idea grabbed her. She activated the watch's other channel.

"Sanderson, it's me Aggie, you there?"

"I am. I've been monitoring your shenanigans. I would advise you to surrender. The Navy isn't a one-trick-pony."

"OK I'll do that, but first we talk, on my terms, my house." *Yeah Sanderson is full of tricks, be careful.*

"Are you crazy?" Mel demanded. "You can't give up, not now not after all that shit we been through, they're going to kill Mother!"

Sanderson came over the phone watch. "I can protect her, but we have to make a deal before time runs out, what do you say we parley? The Navy wants that ship, will you negotiate?"

"Yes," Aggie said. "I'm ready to give in. Stand by to be boarded; you come up top side, we'll talk on the deck, just me and you OK. I'm cutting this watch off, Aggie over and out."

Mel was watching Aggie intently the entire time. "You're smiling." Mel said. "You lied, didn't you?"

"Whatever, the government does it all the time, right? Shouldn't I do the same?"

"What are you going to do?" Praytis said.

"Take a hostage, what else? They won't shoot at us with an Admiral onboard right, they can't be that messed up, right? Right?"

Aggie knew the government was more than messed up enough to take out their own guys but what else could she do? One Sanderson had to be worth a crap load of guys. Use their stupid games on them the same way they do it to others. She wasn't a spy, so maybe it was stupid. Aggie imagined the move just like she did for training in martial arts. Mark taught her to visualize it, see it happen inside her mind then execute the move. She was pretty good at opponent control. Sanderson will extend a hand, that's when she'd take him. If he fought and they fell into the water together, they'd be shark bait. This had better work.

***

Sanderson was on the bridge with Archer, Captain Stern and the bridge crew. The entire conversation was heard by all. Archer shifted from foot to foot, he didn't like it. Sanderson knew Archer's tells.

"There you have it," Sanderson said. "Last chance to take that ship in one piece, you can test the LFM on Piper's shuttle after I board Mother, everyone wins. What do you say Captain, be a hero for America or a puppet drone?"

"If you can work it out in two minutes, I'll postpone launch. It takes thirty seconds from command to swing out the launch boom and fire, so that's your warning, that boom moves you have twenty seconds to get below before exhaust fries you, understand?"

"Submarine's breaking water ten yards off port side, Captain." The sonar tech said.

"I need an armed detail." Archer said.

"No time," Sanderson snapped, "you want that ship or not?"

"You go with him" Stern said to Archer, "Move. Clock's ticking. I have orders."

"If I get a clear shot at Piper, I'm taking it," Archer said as he mounted the ladder to go topside. "I have my orders."

Sanderson started up the tunnel way to the deck and stopped half way and said over his shoulder. "Fine, kill a helpless little white girl. If you can live with that Archer so be it, I can't." Sanderson said with dead aim at the man's heart strings while looking down from above. He didn't know if Archer meant it or if that was just for the benefit of off-site watchers, maybe it was just cover for Archer to shoot Sanderson or Praytis. "What's a dead child to you? Just another scalp on your lodge pole."

Sanderson never mentioned it before, but he knew Archer's father was a Native American who fought and died in Vietnam protecting rice farmer civilians. Archer never mentioned it, but Archer's father had faced off with a company of Vietcong who were attacking a friendly village and Archer's father was alone. The rest of Longfoot Archer's recon-unit retreated leaving helpless women to suffer the ravages of the Commies. Sanderson had ways of getting into secure files. Many a South Vietnamese girl was raped and murdered by the Commies; Sanderson saw the top-secret pictures. Archer would have seen them too…if he had the guts to face it. Longfoot faced facts and died a hero to prevent an atrocity.

Sanderson was winded and weak from climbing the tube, he barely had the strength to spin the watertight hatch's lock. As he planted his feet on the iron deck his watch's timer went off.

***

The shuttle was hovering about thirty feet above the water. The alien hull split and a gangway was projected onto the narrow deck of the weapons launch boat as Sanderson arrived topside.

Aggie stood in the open door and watched the dial spin on a deck hatch. The ship wasn't really big, maybe sixty-foot long, but it had almost no deck space. A force-skin would have been handy.

The whole government boat was covered in angled plates like a stealth bomber. She had her craft hover parallel to the top of it so nobody could shoot right over top the military boat and hit them. She'd have to do this fast. The sea craft was really low to the water for a sixty-foot boat; it was nothing like the fancy yachts around Key West.

As Sanderson got to his feet a big rectangular hatch ahead of the deck amidships retracted forward, there was a rocket in a cradle sitting there just below deck but it didn't come up. Sanderson was as white as a sheet. Aggie didn't know how she could think all that in a flash; her brain felt like it was on overdrive.

Aggie took a few steps out onto the plank but at the same time Archer climbed up out of the deck right behind Sanderson. That ass-wipe had a gun out. *If I could communicate with Buddy I'd have him push that butt-munch over the side.*

Sanderson didn't say anything, he just leaned forward and staggered onto Aggie's gangway and moved toward her really fast. Aggie waited for his hand to come up half way across the ten-yard long ramp, but it didn't happen. He cried, "Duck," and charged her. Shots were fired. Sanderson plowed into her and knocked her back inside. "Sanderson yelled evasive action!" But he didn't need to. The ship reacted on its own. By the time Aggie got up off the ground, her ship was out of range with shields up.

Sanderson lay on the deck on his back panting but before she could say anything he had his mouth on the watch phone. "Stern, hold fire, I have Piper. I'm going in, hold fire!"

"Blood, I hate Blood," Mel said, and fainted. Praytis caught her before she hit the deck.

"You're shot!" Aggie cried, "Medical, medical!" Blood was seeping out all around him onto her nice clean deck.

"No time, get over there, wake Mother up, get out before..." Sanderson fainted and his eyes rolled back into his head. Sanderson's I-know phone was in his hand and it was yelling, "Confirm, confirm!"

"Get to Mother, go." Aggie said. Praytis hesitated. "Just go!" Aggie yelled.

A medical shield proceeded to engulf Sanderson but Aggie knew it was too late.

***

Archer threw his Walther auto at the craft as it shot up and out of sight.

"Goddamn Sanderson! He tricked me, goddamn it."

Archer had quickly assessed the situation and decided to shoot Piper and Sanderson and rush the ship. The launch cradle was lifting to fire while he watched the spaceship ascend. He didn't know if he got Piper and there wasn't time to guess. The alarm went off. He quickly remounted the tunnel way ladder. The hatchway closed behind him and spun shut automatically before he had time to lay a hand on it. Where was the blast off, what happened? It was launch time. He was in a hurry and the tunnel way was too slow. He didn't have the skill to slide down like seamen do. The bridge was three or four decks below. Whoever heard of a bridge below decks? There was no com in the tunnel and he didn't have a walkie-talkie. "Stupid, stupid, stupid."

Archer burst onto the bridge. "Fire, why aren't you firing?"

"Sanderson reported he has Piper."

"He's lying, fire, I'm telling you fire. I shot at Piper and hit Sanderson."

"We still have one minute," The Captain snapped back at Archer.

"Sir, we have that alien shuttle approaching the target." The radar man said.

"Start the firing sequence," The Captain said. "In thirty seconds, Archer, it'll all be over, now get off my bridge before I have you keel-hauled."

Archer stormed off to the communications cabin. Sanderson was done. He hit him twice, two in one lung and with any luck he got the heart too. He was pretty sure pass-through bullets didn't hit Piper. Sanderson wasn't going to produce Karnack, he should have known it, but at least he had the satisfaction of knowing Sanderson was finished. The positives began to sink in. Sanderson's job was his now, he'd get to the moon just fine although it would take a little more time. Things were looking up. Maybe the girl survived. Piper was Stern's problem now, let the Captain live with killing a child.

Archer had hesitated back in Pa. thirty years ago, he didn't feel bad about shooting the EBU in retrospect, but in Cryersville that day the alien robot had looked like a child, he swore to his father's sprit he'd never kill a child. He caught hell for waiting that day. He would have refused had it been a human child.

He replayed it in his mind. He didn't shoot a child this time either. He was sure his rounds missed the girl if they passed through Sanderson's body, that's why he aimed as he did. Archer felt like he could take revenge on Karnack with a clean slate. He was satisfied with himself as he watched the LFB launch on screen. That little piece of his humanity which he had tucked away in a wall-safe inside his damaged mind survived intact and Sanderson turned the key that unlocked it. Maybe Sanderson wasn't such a monster after all. But old Ben Sanderson was dead, of that he was certain and he didn't feel bad about it.

FORTY-NINE

Under the Gun. From Jane Albright's Diary

The trip north was uneventful, in hindsight but flying down freeways and back roads alike at breakneck speed wasn't my idea of a relaxing Sunday drive. It was invigorating, to be sure. I must say however, I was impressed with Mark Levine's skills. He drove like a devil and talked like top-shelf salesmen when we were rightfully pulled over. How that Ohio State Trooper didn't recognize me was nothing short of a miracle. Mark flashed him a badge, I only found out later it was a Presidential Security Detail badge. This irony needs no further description.

That evening, having snaked around several little-used country roads without street signs, we arrived at Mark's safe house. It was a simple wood structure, not rustic like Bart's place, more a little shot-gun shack at the end of a dirt road. It was dry but surrounded by swampy cedar tree woodlands. Mark explained that it was situated as an island within swamplands surrounded by three massive corporate farm properties. The house was still privately held, but Mark never did say who owned it. He had a habit of making allies out of forgotten heroes. That owner, I was told, was a secret: just another of the countless secrets Presidents weren't allowed access to. The policy called 'need-to-know,' has long kept Presidents away from many truths, such as the alien presence. One good example, I learned later, is the fact that President Truman had dropped twelve H-bombs on Japan but aliens had intervened and only two succeeded. I digress.

The exterior of the 'shit-box,' as Mark called it was intact, the old siding was by way of faded yellow vinyl, and the roof was shingled but the tab edges were curled upwards with age. The interior was less modern, an old ceramic coated cast iron sink like my great grandmother had on her 1900 farmstead. It was situated with an old-fashioned hand pump for water. The pump worked. There was no power but plenty of candles and I was relegated to using an outhouse—that bought back memories of the family farm.

The place was dusty and Mark and I cleaned as best we could before bringing the young man in. Lucky the beds were covered with plastic so they were dry and clean albeit they smelled earthy.

At that point, we still didn't know his name. He had no identification on him. That was planned; his ID would have been left inside his base locker room before he was transported to his duty station. Mark explained on the ride that subversive operatives, even those working for America as this man's security company did, would not carry true ID as a matter of normal procedure. Mark explained many such things on the road as there were many hours to occupy and I must say it was quite an education.

Presidents are not well informed on the minutia of security operations. My sister, an operative herself, never spoke of such things. As I understand it, she wasn't permitted, but I knew better. Jennifer would surely answer any question I had, but I feel she was more concerned with protecting me from the horrors of what she actually did for a living. To her the little details of spy-craft weren't important; to her it was second nature, even habit. I find it fascinating. If the population had known before now how far afield the deep state had gone, there would have been blood in the streets with bankers, generals, CEO's and CIA directors all together swinging side by side from ropes.

Such skullduggery is still in play even now. I dare say the corrupted deserve hanging, but I am not a proponent of civil unrest or unlawful vigilantes. Earth cannot afford to fall victim to our more primitive response mechanisms on the threshold of wild advancements. As yet our base proclivities linger; that may well be what turned the young man, that is to say he had an animal instinct response to his situation.

He was laid in bed and propped up, still weak but able to communicate. He faked his weakness, it was a ploy to find an opening and I fell for it hook, line and sinker.

Mark was resting and I brought the man a meager plate from the food stuff we acquired on the road. He ate well and we talked. Of course, I am famous for my speeches and when any open ear presents itself to me, I can't help but fill it with salient words. I said too much and in fact I said everything. I confided in him and told him the truth, the why and how he woke up to find himself five hundred miles from where he started a few days prior. I thought we had connected. I should have been suspicious when he would not tell me his name. Mark's internal alarms surely would have gone off.

The man said he would join with Mark and me. He said he understood and would uphold the Constitution. There would be no trial for me I explained. No justice I explained. The forces that controlled us all, the shadow government, would have me killed at first opportunity and he and Mark as well. Of that I was quite certain. The young man agreed.

I exited the little bedroom and told Mark that we have an ally. I was seldom wrong about a person's character. Had I known who the young man was connected to, I certainly would not have trusted my own judgment.

Mark decided to go and speak with the young man as he was awake and out of danger. It wasn't a split second; the moment Mark opened the door and walked in a heavy object came down out of the shadows and struck Mark down. Before I could think to react, the man had Mark's little plastic gun. The adversary stepped over Mark's prone body, raised the gun and pointed it directly at my head.

"What are you doing, he saved your life?" rushed out of my mouth. I was appalled and stunned by such sudden, unexpected, indiscriminate violence and the primal impulse that drove it.

"That's the only reason I don't kill him now." He said. "Albright, you are under arrest."

The man and I exited leaving Mark on the floor bleeding. My captor would not accord Mark the same care he himself had received, was my angry thought as I was forced into the rear of the SUV. I hammered on the tailgate as we bounced down the dirt road. I could not see out as the windows were tinted and the front facing slide door, also tinted, was locked from the other side. My faith in humanity wavered that day.

FIFTY

Aggie in Orbit

Aggie was in her Captain Kirk chair on Mother's bridge trying to wrap her head around what had just happened. The bridge was the same as before, just a big room with off white metal walls and floors with some spaceship looking chairs that might have come off the Flash Gordon movie set, a couple of desks full of dials, and two gray bio-bots forward of her seat who drove the ship. It felt like home, but it would have been more home-like if mom's bongs, and dad's dumb books littered it. She missed the smell of fish that always hung on dad no matter how well he washed.

As her shuttle swooped into Haiti's air space a rocket was launched from that weird ship, at least that's what Mother's security mode said. Her shuttle came in from directly above and Mother opened her top forward shuttle hatch near the crew quarters. Just as the shuttle touched Mother's landing deck, auto clamps grabbed on and Mother shot up at the speed of light. They rode the missile's blast into orbit. They surfed a tidal wave.

The weird part was what it felt like. Aggie and crew were knocked to the floor. Anti-G lagged. Pressed to the floor Aggie's mind exploded with overwhelming joy, acceptance, fear, endless knowledge, and blinding acceleration. In a heart-beat they were in orbit. She saw and felt it all at once then it was gone. It was like dying and getting born at the same time. It shook her up pretty bad, but it also felt right, too.

Aggie was in a daze for about ten minutes and when she got back to normal Praytis was showing Mel the manual communication's station. Aggie described what she felt to them but Praytis didn't say anything and Mel brushed it off. Mel and Praytis were too busy trying to figure out if the military knew they had escaped, so the pair pretty much skated past Aggie's questions.

"So Praytis, so all that was real, I really sensed it, right?"

"Yes Captain," he said turning slightly. "That is Mother's way of telling you she is happy. She very much likes you. It is not every day a Captain gives up a control belt and until our return, she had not the opportunity to mention her thanks and appreciation."

"Oh, OK."

She still didn't understand. But Praytis wasn't allowed to say too much about it. GTO rules suck. She wanted to ask how she felt it, but she already had an idea. Like it or not Mother tuned into her mind based on data the ship acquired when they flew together before; be it a fleet shuttle or Mother herself, the ship's AI network was gathering input right along. Aggie had spent only a little time with Mother since she took the ship off Karnack and landed on Key West, but that didn't stop Mother's learning process. Aggie knew that in her bones.

"So, I guess when I sent Buddy back, he told her junk and woke her up when we were picked up. I wondered why he took off from PR like that." Aggie said, really, she was just talking to herself trying to sort it all out.

"That's right, Captain." Praytis didn't turn away from the control array this time. Mel was deep into something.

"Hey, don't call me Captain! Just Aggie, OK? So where are we now?"

"We're just down range of the International Space Station in a parking orbit pacing it," Mel said. "I think we are out of window view. Earth side won't dare send a missile at us; they'd wipe out the ISS. But, it doesn't look like they know where we are or that we are even here, nothing on scrambled communications. I think they think we blew up."

"What makes you say that?"

"Dude, check this out."

A couple of holo screens popped into existence above and forward of Mel's station. Haiti and surroundings were on view screens from several angles. Where Mother had been parked on the northern tip of the island where she was well away from Dominica but that rocket's effect reached out to everywhere on the whole island. The entire land mass was in fog, but where Mother had sat was a fountain of lights and smoke miles high. It looked like a lawn sprinkler spraying multicolored water and suds. Aggie didn't want to really know more, she was just beating around building the courage to ask that one big question. The answer she was pretty sure would freak her out.

"It acted as a creation bomb. That is how we seed lifeless planets." Praytis said. "One has never been used in this way. Of course, theoretically, LF explosions cannot destroy. Curious that the developers would think Life-Force can cause destruction."

"Earth military people aren't rocket surgeons," Mel said.

Praytis did a double take, "Oh yes, I see Earth humor, very good. It is well, however, that the American's have proven theory. I read a massive influx of life forms: Most interesting, indeed."

Praytis and Mel returned to the desk and Aggie had a million questions more, but she had to get this big one out first.

"So, how do we get rid of the body?" She tried to say it casual, but she was on the edge of tears and it came out stuttering.

"Body, what body, all our bio-units are functional."

"Sanderson, he's dead right? I never had to deal with a dead person; I don't know what to do." Tears welled up. Aggie only let one fall. Instead, she wiped her eyes with the back of her hand and lowered herself into the other com station chair.

"Dear me, I see, yes, well oh dear, I'm not supposed to tell you, but you are the Captain, well..."

"Christ on a cracker spit it out already," Mel said twisting a knob. "Oh, that's the satellite tracker, cool."

"Perhaps in a few days he will become irredeemable...as yet...He is not dead, not exactly—."

"What, what are you talking about!" Aggie jumped up out of the chair. She and Mel both said the same thing. Mel's way of dealing with bad stuff was to go into nerd activity mode. Mel pushed away from the control desk.

"He is in stasis; you did place him in medical shield. It will preserve him temporarily."

"Can we fix him?"

"Well, I mean, I...well...I can't—."

"That's it! What do I have to do to get you to answer a question; you want my first born or what? Anything? What do I have to do to save Sanderson?"

Praytis lowered his body bending all four legs into weird angles and looked at the deck. His hair was thin on top. *Yeah he wasn't allowed to tell GTO secrets. I got that. Too fucking bad.*

"Tell me or get out now, no ship, just get out, OK, just float away in space. I'll fire you."

"Way too butch, dude."

"Under threat of harm I can...You can buy my contract." Praytis let out a lung full of air that rushed out so hard and fast Aggie would have felt that wind from ten feet away. And then he lowered himself almost to the deck in shame. He resembled a squashed spider.

"That's it!" Aggie slapped her forehead. "Why didn't I know that? I did, I just didn't think about it. Stupid, I'm so stupid. Make it so, you hear me Mother! Buy Praytis's contract."

Praytis looked like an anvil was lifted off his shoulder. Bug man sprung up with a big wide smile. "I may now speak freely, I am official Crew. Mother accepts my application. Should you accept her invitation you too will have direct contact with her data...and further benefits."

"I know, I know, I hate to be morbid, but what do we do about Sanderson, he'll die soon, right?"

"I will answer, as Sanderson is incapacitated he doesn't have the ability to negotiate for regeneration, and as it is costly, only the Captain can agree to the price in his stead as he is under your care. However, the cost is one hundred Earth years of service normally, should you repair him, he will be obligated to this ship for that span. Should he refuse after the fact you must buy him out as well, that will cost you two hundred years of service. It is a form of indentured service, such as a military contract a soldier makes on Earth when he…signs up."

"Dude, where do I sign? Can you sign me up, yeah?"

"I don't get it, why, how's that work?"

"It is a symbiotic relationship. Mother needs crew, for purpose and direction of life such as all sentient beings, living or not, require, it is universal. The crew's own life force powers the mechanical aspect of Mother's shell which keeps crew-members alive."

"She's a living being, but she can't live alone." Aggie said. Fireworks were going off inside her head, all kinds of info was exploding.

"Once you are crew, you qualify for regeneration and data access, but as is, your current position is temporary, once you die of old age Mother will ask an-other to become Captain."

"Wow, dude, maybe I don't want to join. You mean re-gen keeps you alive forever, yeah?"

"It is conceivable, but re-gen normally will keep one much longer than con-tract, it does increase one's life span beyond minimal payment. Such is quite necessary for the spacer's life.

"Crap that's a lot to think about. Do I have a choice?"

Aggie retook her Kirk chair. It was a lot to think about but if she didn't do something Sanderson was toast. One thing was certain; she wasn't going back to Earth with every spook in the world out to get her. They were really, really pissed at her. Forget college, it wasn't happening and she was finally ready to accept that fact.

OK, so she didn't really kill Karnack and that was good because she still believed in her hippie ways. She was for peace not war. But Sanderson saved her life, he took her bullets, she owed him. She just could not let the guy die. Doing so flew in the face of everything she believed in. Love was better than anything, it mattered. Material stuff didn't matter and Mother wasn't just stuff, Mother was much more. Aggie had responsibilities and she felt it was time to face up to it and a lot more.

"I'll do it; I'll buy Sanderson in, put him in the regeneration tank or whatever it is."

"You do understand." Praytis said. "You must become permanent crew. You must allow Mother's Ram-Ed. She will not re-gen a visitor on the word of tem-porary crew, there is no binding otherwise, no way for her to trust you. Should Mother re-gen anyone willy-nilly, she would never have peace, people would assault her, chain her down planet side."

"I understand. I know that. Maybe that's why Ram-Ed freaked me out before. I can't let Sanderson die."

"Dude, you're mad butch."

"One condition," Aggie said. "Nobody gets inside my head unless I ask them. Mother can't just steal my thoughts or help herself into my head whenever she feels like it."

"That is the standard rider. You and she will work out such details in conference."

Praytis led Aggie and Mel aft and down a section to the crew quarters—there were rooms for forty crewmen. Mother had already decorated rooms for them both. Aggie's ship room was a duplicate of her room at home. Wood panels made out of old pallets, the same old beat up bed and dressers, the free standing closet. Dad had converted an old sea container into her room and attached it to the converted bait shack they called home. No doubt the design was taken from Aggie's own mind when Mother and she first met. It smelled like her room, too. Maybe she was ready for a new bedroom set. She was really going to miss home and a constant reminder was a bad idea. *Homesick already and I haven't gone anywhere.*

The Ram-Ed procedure was simple. She only needed to lie down and fall asleep. She was told she won't remember what went on while under induction. She would wake up as if from a good sleep and other than her ability to understand space tongues, she won't notice much of a difference: that's what Praytis said. She got naked as usual and got under a thin blanket but not before folding up Ernie's borrowed clothes. She fell asleep thinking of returning his stuff to him. Praytis and Mel left Aggie lying on her bed and dozing off.

Aggie woke to find Mel at her door peeking in. "Dude, I was going to get some sleep myself but they said you were waking up, how you feel?"

"A little lonely, a little washed out. I could use some company."

Aggie sat up and patted her bed. Mel and she spent countless hours sitting on Aggie's bed talking or reading to each other from paper books or looking at Mel's I-know phone or doing class homework projects. OK, for that girl time Aggie had clothes on. Mel had changed her clothes; she lost the stuff she got from Ernie and had put on silky PJ's that Aggie could see right through.

Mel sat on the edge of the bed and said, "What now? You're looking at me funny. I'm tired yeah, I need sleep. Last night sucked eggs, I'm fucking exhausted."

"I think I'm done saving myself for college." Aggie said reaching out to Mel. Aggie pulled Mel down and kissed her. "I think I'm ready."

"I think so too," Mel said. She was trembling a little. "I hope I'm as ready."

It was Aggie's first time but Mel had some experience. They spent the afternoon learning new things together. It was all new, everything was new. So for a few hours the universe turned without worry or care. It was a deep calm before another storm.

***

Captain Bob Stern of the USS Raven had his hands full. His ship was dead in the water and although they were out to sea and well out of range, the LFB took his power out and that didn't make sense. No engines or batteries were operable but all the ship's screens were lit. All screens, be it computer or sonar or radar or his I-know phone and they all showed the same thing. It looped the U.S. Navy attacking an island which had civilians surrounding the good ship Mother.

There was no military force for him to attack as was previously released for consumption. That unstoppable transmission showed the world that the U.S. was capable of mass murder. Right after the LFB stuck, everything mechanical went dead. His satellite links to space borne observation platforms with it. The alien spaceship was gone; there was no sign of it just the loop of the island blowing up—video his ship had taken blended with satellite images and other military observation feeds. The volcano like eruption continued for hours. On the horizon there was nothing but cloud and fire and sideways rainbows. He hoped to God it wasn't broadcast everywhere, but Stern knew in the back of his mind it surely was. Mother's revenge.

Stern had sent men topside with a high powered telescopes. They reported there was nothing more to see. But toward sundown that changed.

"Sir," A man called down from the open hatch. Stern ordered all hatches open, the air conditioning like everything else was out and the Raven was hotter than a tin-can inside a slow cooker.

Stern looked up the tunnel way and the man's sweat falling from above splattered his cheek.

"What is it Spec?"

"You better come see this, Sir."

Stern hadn't left his post since the strike so his hands were wet with perspiration; his uniform was a wet rag. Making the climb was tricky with sweaty hands. When he exited topside a cool sea breeze tickled his face. It was the best thing he felt since shoving off from Florida. Most of his crew was spread out all over the Raven hanging onto the deck's service door handholds; he would not let his men suffer the heat below.

The seas were calm. His men there were safe, tied off with harnesses and all wore life vests as ordered. There wasn't much in the way of deck on his stealthy launch boat. Someone handed him a pair of binoculars.

"I'm not seeing this." Stern said. "A statue, it must be, what thirty feet tall, where did that come from?"

The Raven had been drifting toward Haiti all day and it wasn't far off shore now. The sparkler effect was abating hour by hour and the fog thinned as well. He saw trees and they were not only standing, which was unexpected, they were better than two hundred feet tall. Among the tress stood that statue, but it seemed to be moving.

He looked again. "What is this, what am I seeing here?" He asked no one.

"It's a man, a giant man." The Chief said.

Chief wasn't the kind of man to entertain tall tales. As a boy Stern loved the novel Gulliver's Travel's and it was in part why he first loved the sea and lusted for books of Argonaut adventures yet Stern was always the realist, he never expected his own adventures. He never thought he'd be living Gulliver's life but it seemed to him that that was becoming a distinct possibility. If the winds didn't change, he'd find out firsthand what the Lilliputians would have felt if they were real. But this was real. That was a giant man and he did not look happy. He shifted his view and saw something else.

Stern grabbed Chief Smith by his wet-rag shirt and lowered himself down onto the steel deck. Having his men see him faint would not do. He mounted the binocular and looked again. The Locke Ness Monster was swimming toward his vessel. As such, his skivvies acquired a sudden deposit of brown matter. He never did get the words 'battle stations' out before The Raven was sunk.

FIFTY-ONE

Meeting of the Minds

Aggie was lounging in her command chair. She had Mother make one just like Sky Flower's reclining lounge chair. Aggie had grass put on the deck, flower pots, shrubs in bigger pots and sunlight lamps installed on the bridge. Mel's communication station was the same as before, a metal desk and a PC looking control station but the rest of the bridge was a park. She had the grays' station made into a little grass hut. It was exciting at first, remodeling, setting up quarters, getting to know the ship and Mother better, but now she was bored. Crazy crap was going on back on Earth but what could she do about it? Nothing, of course, but she still wanted in. The news said she was dead so maybe they were safe... for now. Yeah, things were cool, orbiting Mars was OK, and Mother's spy system was still intact...for now. And best yet, it didn't seem like anyone's Earth military knew they survived.

What bothered her was about mom and dad. Watching the world mourn Aggie's loss wasn't fun. Mom cried on the evening news...not cool at all. Not for the first time she looked at Grandpa's watch and wondered if she could contact him from there. She raised it up to press the on button.

"Don't do it," Sanderson said. "Somebody's got to know we survived. They'll be watching Al Branford like a hawk."

Aggie spun her chair around to face him but blinked instead of commenting. It was hard to get used to it. Ben Sanderson was now physically thirty years old and his hair was down to his ass and what was really funny, he liked his hair that way, too. Who would have thought it? The nicely trimmed black beard counterpoint made him look like a hipster hippie. She still didn't know how he got the button-fly jeans and a Grateful Dead T-shirt.

"He's right," Mel said without turning from her com desk. "If people back home knew how many satellites Earth has around Mars and the rest of the solar system they'd shit."

"Billions, the complex took billions of the people's money, they'll riot." Ben said.

"Anyway, some of them are capable of picking us up." Mel said.

Aggie was about to launch an argument but Sarah waltzed in which made Aggie miss Earth and Mom and Dad even more. Because Sarah was near death and so old, Mother had to re-gen her back to about six years old…a six year old with a partial memory of old age but with the maturity of her current age. The kid went straight for Aggie's pet bunny. Miss Bubbles was an oversized, black, flop-eared domestic rabbit. The kid could barely pick it up.

"Sarah, will you please leave Miss Bubbles alone?" Aggie said, "You'll scare the crap out of her."

"I don't have to, right Daddy?"

Ben was in his favorite reclining chair with his head back, feet up and hands behind his head. "Listen to her Sarah, she's the captain."

"I don't want to!" With that Sarah ran off the bridge. It was a big ship she could get lost, hurt or even killed, but Mother had a soft spot for her and kept an eye open for the little girl. All the ship's bots and systems were tuned to keep her safe.

"Nobody else listens to me either." Aggie said miserably.

"That's not true, and you know it." Ben said. "Mother put me in charge of security, but we still went ahead, on your orders. We took a big risk when we went and got all this." he waved his hand referring to the living stores they picked up on an excursion Earth side. They almost got caught. "I was against it, but, there you have it."

"You're full of it." Mel said. "You were just as into it as the rest of us."

Praytis came through the door about then and no one heard him coming. His floppy feet didn't make that sound on grass. Of course, he heard everything that was just said, he's crew and wired in. But even so, his sense of hearing was way better than Earth humans and he had to have overheard them from the gangway.

"Must Earth people bicker so much? I would say we have more pressing business to consider. We can't stay here forever. I suggest Alfa Centuri. There is a good spaceport there and an active trade economy."

"Dude, are we not space bitches? I'm with him, let's get out of dodge."

"I don't have a problem with it," Ben said, "It'd be a hell of a lot safer, you know the GTO, the pentagon, MJ-12 and all the rest are pulling out all the stops, they'd give their eye teeth to keel haul us. If we go back there…forget it, we can't do them any good." Ben was referring to the previous argument about saving the Earth. "We don't have a snowball's chance in hell of saving them."

"But what about the people, the people are…" Aggie stammered.

"…Always too late," Ben said. "Face it Aggie, they'll cook us alive and you can't stop them, you can't stop the Powers That Be."

"If we don't help the Earth is finished" Aggie cried bolting out of her chair.

She was so mad she felt like she'd spit nails. She wasn't a quitter, OK she quit school but that was different. Mother projected that the Earth would last another generation or two. The chances of Earth maturing enough in the short time they had was nil with so many power-hungry factions vying for control, not to mention the GTO pulling strings, and now the military has access to technology that sci-fi nerds couldn't have imagined. Saving the Earth from itself was impossible. She had to admit it. She had to face the facts. Growing up sucks the big one. The environment will collapse and wipe them all out anyway even if the stupid deep state wasn't driving humanity over a cliff. The planet was sick and dying and nothing can stop it.

Aggie released her balled up fists and got her breathing under control. She cleared her mind and eased back into the command chair.

"What if we just go back for our parents?"

"Sky Flower won't go; she's all up in everything, fighting for the president, who by the way is still missing." Mel said. "Forget it. My folks are too rich to leave."

"Mel's right," Sanderson and Praytis said together.

"But it does appear," Praytis added, "according to the social AI, that the public isn't accepting the media's propaganda about the VP's murder. Many have pointed out the flaws in that video. I suppose they were in a hurry to get it out and so they processed it poorly." Praytis pushed up on his rear legs. "I do believe public opinion is swinging in favor of Madam Albright despite America's media efforts. This works in our favor as well, should we venture another foray."

"Fine and dandy, but that's not helping us." Sanderson said. "Albright's still on the meat hook."

"OK fine, fine, I'm out voted, OK we'll go but at least let me say goodbye. I'm using Grandpa's watch. Mother will you patch me?"

One of Mother's sub-computers responded affirmative. Mother herself seldom took an active interest in mundane crew actions. She was too busy and mostly indifferent about small matters.

Aggie activated the watch phone and spoke into it. "Grandpa, it's Aggie, yeah, I'm OK. I'm in space with...I can't tell you, but anyway I'm going to the stars so tell Mom and Dad I'm OK, OK? I love you, tell them I love them." Aggie had to shut the watch down before she started bawling. One baby crying on this ship was enough. The signal had a few minutes delay due to the travel distance but Mother's breadcrumb satellites relayed it perfectly and faster than Earth's systems could.

"Did it go Mel?" Aggie didn't need to ask. A few minutes later, the answer was already inside her head.

"Yeah and wow looks like you got a return call...wait, intercepted, somebody, more than one, heard the reply, what the fuck?" Mel looked at Praytis.

"I'm an anthropologist, don't look at me?"

"That tells me they know we're here," Sanderson said. "We better get going."

"Play the message Mel."

"Aggie, it's grandfather Branford. It's not in the news, Space Fleet knows where you are and they are planning an attack. Because I just told you that, my life isn't worth a hard-times token. I'm leaving here pronto with your father in tow. We must run, Mom's in a safe house. They can't use us to draw you in. Aggie, it's hard, but you must leave. We'll be safer with you gone, if they can't use us to get to you, they'll leave us be. I see they are tracing this. Aggie, we love you, but get the hell out of here. Branford out."

"That tears it," Ben said, "I was right, we got to get lost and fast."

"I get it OK. Fine we'll go." Aggie was almost in tears.

"It's cool dude," Mel said, "we'll come back when things die down, we are not done."

No one had noticed Sarah was back, she came and went a lot. But now she stood in the center of the bridge and a spot light came out of nowhere and lit her. The light focused on her forced everyone's attention. "We aren't going any-where." Sarah said in a voice not her own. It was an ancient voice and somehow distant yet present. "We aren't going anywhere until I have a full crew."

"Shit," Ben Sanderson said.

The light went out and Sarah fell on her butt onto the soft grass. The rabbit immediately jumped into her lap. "Miss Bubbles!"

Aggie laughed. She forgot Mother had a vote, a really big vote. In the back of her mind Aggie knew this was a terrible turn. There was a huge chance of fail-ure, but she was glad. Mother had what she needed to get to the next star system. They could pick up crew there. But Mother had her own ideas and Aggie wasn't going to argue. Finding crew members wasn't going to be easy, it would take time and in between, who knows maybe they'd save the world. Aggie had her doubts, but she'd try. Ideas about who to pick for a crew started filling her mind. They'd have to find Jon.

"OK Mr. Security, get busy and figure out how we're going to do this."

"Hold your goddamn horses, I'm working on it."

"Daddy, you said a bad word!"

Aggie flopped down on the floor, picked up the bunny and offered it a blade of grass. Miss Bubbles took it and chewed, twitching her nose in a comical way. Sarah laughed and rolled on the grass. The rabbit jumped out of Aggie's lap and onto Sarah's belly. Aggie laughed and rolled too. For the moment, all was right in the universe, but it wouldn't last. Suddenly she didn't feel so alone. She'd con-vince her parents to come, and Jon and all she had to do was find another thirty volunteers and survive the mission. Somewhere in the back of her mind Aggie heard Mother say, no problem.

THE END

ACKNOWLEDGMENTS

A lot of people went into making this work of fiction. I'd like to thank my beta readers, Kathy Roscoe, Lisa Cross, Pat Anderson, Dean LeVar and Cecelia Faiga. Thank you Gayle F. Hendricks my book design and formatting guru and Pattie Giordani for proof reading and line editing. Many members of the Lehigh Valley Writers Group (GLVWG.org) have given me supportive encouragement over the years and deserve recognition. Special thanks to my long-time friend and mentor Angel Ackerman for schooling me by editing many of my past projects. My greatest appreciation is for my life-mate Lisa Cross who puts up with me and was instrumental as a story critic, spell checker and test reader; without her support I could not write.

ABOUT THE AUTHOR

Rachel C. Thompson, writing fantasy and sci-fi as R.C. Thom, began her writing career after surviving a devastating motorcycle accident in 2003. She has since published non-fiction pieces in newspapers and magazines and a handful of short stories along with cartoons. *Soul Harvest* is her second novel but first published. Her short story anthology, *Stalking Kilgore Trout*, and fantasy novel *Dragon Fire* are available now in print and e-book. Look for her follow up to *Aggie in Orbit*, *Aggie in Space*, due in 2019. Her novel *Book of Answers* will be released late in 2018. Email her at rc@rcthom.com or visited her web site at rcthom.com.